TWO STEEL BANDS GRIPPED HER ARMS

She screamed, of course, loudly and long, wrenching free of whatever it was that held her.

"Hey, hey it's just me. Mac."

Rose let out a string of swears. "You scared the hell out of me."

She heard him chuckle, the sound as disembodied as it was when it came over the intercom. "No kidding. I thought you'd left. You can't see me, can you." It wasn't a question, but a statement of certainty, as if he knew if she could see him, she would have somehow reacted differently.

The voice was suddenly closer, melting over her, warm chocolate drizzling all over her body. "No. I can't see you." But she could feel him, feel the heat coming from his body, an unnatural heat.

"I have to go now."

"You don't have to run away."

"I'm not running away," she said with forced casualness. And she wasn't; she was standing so still she could hear her own breath.

"This is the closest I've been to another person in more than two years. It's strange."

"*You* think this is strange?"

THE SEXIEST DEAD MAN ALIVE

Jane Blackwood

ZEBRA BOOKS
KENSINGTON PUBLISHING CORP.
http://www.kensingtonbooks.com

ZEBRA BOOKS are published by

Kensington Publishing Corp.
850 Third Avenue
New York, NY 10022

All Kensington titles, imprints and distributed lines are available at special quantity discounts for bulk purchases for sales promotion, premiums, fund-raising, educational or institutional use.

Special book excerpts or customized printings can also be created to fit specific needs. For details, write or phone the office of the Kensington Special Sales Manager: Kensington Publishing Corp., 850 Third Avenue, New York, NY 10022. Attn. Special Sales Department. Phone: 1-800-221-2647.

Zebra and the Z logo Reg. U.S. Pat. & TM Off.

First Printing: March 2004
10 9 8 7 6 5 4 3 2 1

Printed in the United States of America

ACKNOWLEDGMENTS

Special thanks to Chef Loren Falsone, who took time out of her extremely busy schedule to give me a glimpse into the joy and terror of opening up your own restaurant. And thanks to Lucy DiMase for giving me some insight into what it's like to come from a large Italian family. Grazi!

Chapter 1

*Deep Chocolate Pot-de-Crème with whipped cream and
Carmela's torchetta, $8.00*

"So we're sitting there at dinner, and I'm thinking I
could get over his Elmer Fudd voice, when he says, 'I'd
go pay the check, but I have an erection.' "

Jenn nearly choked on her French fry. "He said *what?*"

Deadpan, Rose repeated herself. Then, "That's weird,
isn't it?"

"Oh my God, yes," Jenn said, slapping the table with
the palm of her hand. "On a first date? In my book, you
don't mention your sexual appendages until at least date
five."

Okay, so she'd known the guy was weird—known it
even before he started talking about his dick. But Rose
was somehow hoping that just this once, a guy could
turn out normal. Or even seminormal. "My life sucks. I
knew he was too good to be true."

Jenn leaned forward so the other patrons of the Chili's
Restaurant wouldn't hear her. "Were you, you know, doing anything? Playing footsie or even holding hands?"

"No. Just sitting there. Okay, I was naked, but other

than that, no, nothing." Rose grinned. "Honest to God, Jenn, I was just sitting there. Guys don't get erections that easy, do they? It's not as if I'm some super model." Rose looked down at her decidedly un-super model body. In her opinion, the only thing her petite Italian parents had given her that was remotely modellike was her long, wavy, brown hair. She took a sip of her mineral water wishing the glass contained something a bit stronger— like a Dewers.

"Well, if guys do get 'em at dinner, they don't talk about it. Not on a first date." Jenn gave a little shudder. "That was very weird."

Rose let out a sigh. "I thought so. And he's so perfect otherwise."

"I don't know. That Elmer Fudd thing was hard to take."

Rose pushed a curling strand of hair away from her face and leaned her chin on her hand, the picture of dejection. Elmer Fudd had had potential. He'd come up to her at Monroe's, an East Side bar that attracted the suit and tie crowd, and seemed completely captivated by her. It was nice. Flattering. And if his intensity seemed a bit, well, strange, Rose figured she could get used to a guy who was completely focused on her. But Elmer turned out to be a little too focused. "Why are losers so attracted to me?"

"They weren't all losers."

"Name one who wasn't," Rose challenged.

"Ummm. The lawyer. He wasn't a total loser."

Rose rolled her eyes. "Oh, and living with your mother when you're thirty-five is okay with you?"

"Some women might think it was cute."

"He was too attached to her if you ask me."

"That's gross."

Rose shrugged in agreement. "I don't have anything against a guy loving his mom. In fact, it's kind of nice.

But Steve gave me the creeps after a while. I think he used to slip her the tongue when they kissed good-bye."

"Stop it," Jenn said, purely disgusted even as she laughed.

Rose drummed her fingertips again her mouth. She was thirty-two years old, and the last long-term relationship she'd been in was during her early twenties. It wasn't as if she *needed* a man, though a guy sure came in handy sometimes.

"You'll find someone," Jenn said; then her eyes widened. "Whoa. Lookee there. Cutie at ten o'clock."

Rose squinched up her face in disgust at the look of pure lust on Jenn's face. "Jenn, you're married and pregnant."

Jenn turned back, completely unapologetic. "I'm not dead. I don't know why people think it's easy to turn off the radar as soon as you get married."

"I thought it was an auto shut-off."

Jenn pulled a face. "I'd never act on it, but it doesn't hurt to flirt a little. Sheesh. You sound like Brian."

"Uh-oh. I smell a fight."

"Oh, it's nothing really," Jenn said. "At least I don't think so."

"What did you do," she said, playing the long-suffering friend.

Jenn got that look on her face that told Rose she was guilty as sin and didn't care a bit. "Brian caught me *almost* kissing a guy. Our contractor."

Rose closed her eyes and took a deep breath. "You're kidding, right?"

"It was no big deal. I came to my senses in time. But according to Brian I should be flogging myself daily and kissing his feet begging for forgiveness. Which I did, by the way."

"You kissed his feet?"

"Ha ha. No, I begged forgiveness for *not* kissing the

guy." She shrugged. "Don't worry, everything's all right. Anyway, I was looking at that guy for you."

"Please don't even think about setting me up. It's not like I'm desperate or anything."

"I know," Jenn said quickly.

Rose narrowed her eyes. "You think I *am* desperate."

"No I don't."

"You've turned into one of those women I hate."

Jenn smiled good-naturedly. "I have not."

"You have. Just because you're married . . ."

"And pregnant. Don't forget my biological clock had been put on pause." She smiled.

Rose gave her longtime friend a sneer. Domesticity looked good on her. Her once spiky blond hair was now a sleek bob that looked fantastic with her Nordic features, and the small amount of weight she'd gained since she got married made her face look less angular. "Okay. Pregnant. Just because you're married and two weeks pregnant doesn't mean that I want to be married and pregnant. It doesn't seem all that wonderful to me."

Jenn just tilted her head, a patronizing gesture that said, "You poor disillusioned woman."

In mock misery, Rose covered her face with her hands. "God, I'm thirty-two. Do you realize that means the earliest I could possibly have a baby is thirty-five? I was *fifteen* when my mother was thirty-five."

Jenn burst out laughing. "You could get pregnant tomorrow if you wanted to. And anyway, you don't really want to be like your mother, do you?"

No, Rose did not. She would rather have been like her grandmother, the woman who actually raised her. Mom was not the typical Italian mother with a kitchen in the basement and Saran Wrap covering the good living room furniture. Rose, who to the horror of her attorney mother would rather be in a kitchen than anywhere else, had the misfortune of having a career-driven mother who had set out at an early age to prove she was not typical. Her mother dumped her father when he suggested they have another child, and looked at her daughter as if she'd been spawned by an alien. The fact that Rose was a fantastic cook and pratically running Anthony's Ristorante meant nothing.

"I'm old-fashioned. I'd like to have a husband or at least a boyfriend before I have a baby. And that takes time. First I have to meet him, then date for a while, then fall in love, marry. All that takes *years.*"

"Let me dig your grave now, then."

"You might as well."

Jenn laughed again. "You're being stupid."

Rose sighed, checking her watch. "Maybe. Listen, I have to get going. You remember that personal chef job I applied for?"

"The one that pays 80K?"

"Yeah. I've got an interview in an hour in Kingstown. It's strange, though. I still don't know who I'll be working for and I don't know whether I'll have to prepare anything, so of course I had no idea how to dress," Rose said, looking down at her black capris and sleeveless cream cable-knit sweater. "Do you think this is all right?"

Jenn shrugged. "I have no idea what a personal chef is supposed to wear. One of those white smocks and funny hats?"

"I considered that, so I brought my stuff just in case. I'd think for that money they'd want to know what they were getting. I still can't believe I got an interview. You should have seen how lousy my application was." Rose fished in her purse for money to pay her part of the bill.

"I'll call you later in the week. Maybe you can come over this weekend."

"Okay. Maybe." Rose wouldn't. Couldn't. She liked Jenn, but seeing her in her perfect suburban home was depressing. Jenn had been the wild one, the partier, the one who had a hangover on Saturday mornings. The one who slept around. And now she was Married Woman with a handsome husband, gorgeous house, and a baby on the way. She didn't even work anymore, and for a single woman that was perhaps the oddest creature of all. Jenn was still Jenn, but . . . not. Especially not at home with her husband, Brian. She was like a different woman, Betty Crocker meets Courtney Love.

As soon as Rose reached her car, her mind was on the interview. Clearly, she had little to offer someone who was looking to impress clients or ritzy friends. She could cook the pants off some formally trained chefs, but it meant nothing without a resumé. Working on Federal Hill at Anthony's Ristorante didn't carry much weight, even if Anthony's served the best Italian food on the hill.

On top of her lack of experience, she was cursed with a strong Rhode Island accent, a dismal cross between Boston and New York accents that made anyone who possessed it sound illiterate, and a tendency to be brutally honest. "That mouth of yours, Rosalie, it gonna get you in big trouble someday," her grandmother told her too many times to count—and usually after a fight with her mother.

Rose glanced down at the directions before spotting Marlin Road. Between grand houses and high hedges she saw the intense blue of water, and her stomach clenched a bit nervously. She'd known no one who could offer a personal chef eighty thousand dollars a year would live in a normal house, but these houses were more like mansions than ordinary homes. The road, purposefully rural and narrow to please its well-heeled residents, wound its way along the coast shrouded by towering maple trees planted long ago to give the road a bit of elegance and privacy. This was not the campy, beachy crowd. This was New York and Connecticut money, people who talked in that clenched-teeth, jaw-thrusted manner.

"Jesus," Rose whispered as she stared at one particularly elegant house. "These friggin' people must be loaded." Then she frowned, realizing how brainless she sounded. "My gracious," she said in her most eloquent accent. "How well off these residents must be." She'd tried to lose her cursed accent, even considered going to a voice coach; but that cost money, and extra money was not something she had a lot of. Every extra penny—and there weren't a lot of those—went toward her dream of owning a restaurant. Her mother could have helped, with the reluctance of a pit bull giving up a bone, but Rose hadn't asked her mother for a loan since she'd been sixteen.

Suddenly, the sky brightened, and she found herself staring at a small sandy beach. A discreet sign to the left informed the riffraff that this was a private beach. Somehow she'd missed the turnoff. "Three fifty-seven," she mumbled, and pulled a smart three-point turn to head back the other way. She drove the road again, craning her neck to read the numbers tacked onto strong pillars, wrought-iron fences, and fancy plaques. "Three thirty-three . . . three forty-nine . . . three sixty-one—Shit." She slammed the brake. "Where the heck is this place?" Growling out her frustration, she pulled another three-point turn, this time cursing the idiots who designed such a narrow road. Crawling along so slowly she could hear her tires moving against the smooth, black asphalt, Rose peered for the ghost house. Then she saw a small opening in the dense woods, a dirt road disappearing into the gloom of an overgrown mass of brush and trees that were just beginning to leaf.

Rose turned in, wincing at the screech of branches scraping the paint of her ten-year-old Honda. She was searching for some indication she was on the right drive, looking for a number nailed to a tree, when she saw it: a surveillance camera tacked high on an oak tree, its red light blinking. It looked like the sort of camera outside a bank.

She rolled down her window. "Hi," she said, and waved

to whoever might be watching. If this was the wrong house, she wanted whoever was at the other end of the dirt road to know she was friendly. As she drove, she noticed more cameras, some angled toward the road, some pointing into the woods.

"These people must be totally paranoid." Or part of the witness protection program. Or members of some underground crime family. Maybe that's why she got the interview, because of her Italian last name. Rose grinned, picturing her face plastered on the front of the *Providence Journal* with the caption, CRIME FAMILY COOK.

The road brightened ahead, and Rose saw a glimpse of the house. It stood like a large white box in the middle of a huge clearing, looking like something that belonged in California—big, concrete, modern, and cold. It could have been an office building for all the warmth and character it possessed. Rose, who lived in a city where "modern" meant a house was built in the 1920s, instantly disliked this pretentious square thing. While the lawn was so perfect it didn't look real, not a single flower or bush had been planted to soften the exterior of the home, and Rose wondered if the starkness of the place was mostly functional; an additional precaution against whatever marauders the people in the house were trying to ward off. To one side, though highly visible, was a small guardhouse, the kind she'd seen at military bases.

Rose told herself not to prejudge the occupants of the concrete cube. And what did she care about the people anyway if they were willing to pay her eighty thousand a year to do something she loved?

As she approached the house, a security officer stepped out of the small guard building and waved her to park next to a beat-up old Jeep. Rose smiled, sensing a kindred spirit in the guard, who owned a car even older than hers.

"Rose Pisano?" he asked through her open window. Now this could be an added benefit—the guy was gorgeous, boy-toy material if she'd ever seen it. Boy toy was one of Jenn's favorite expressions and pertained to the kind of guy who looked good on your arm, was probably good in bed, but didn't have the mental staying power to last longer than a month. Boy toys were for recreational purposes only.

"That's me."

"Please follow me."

Rose jumped out of the car, burning with curiosity about the people who lived here. She rubbed her hands over her arms to ward off the chilly air; it was about ten degrees cooler here by the ocean. "Work here long?" The best way to get a guy to talk was to ask him about himself.

"About six months."

"You like it?"

"It's okay." *Me caveman, me not know many words.*

Ah, but he had nice pecs bulging beneath that blue polyester-cotton blend shirt of his. Rose gave herself a mental shake. This guy was probably a depressing ten years younger than she was. "They have a lot of parties? I'm applying for the personal chef position and have no idea what I'm in for. If I get the job."

The guard stopped and quickly eyed the house, as if he were nervous, as if his job depended on him keeping his mouth shut. "I've never seen a soul come in or out of that house."

"Except the owners?"

"No. No one."

It was all so gothic, Rose had to stop herself from giggling. "You mean you've worked here for six months and you haven't seen anyone?"

"A guy comes to mow the lawn in the summer once a month. And Bert's delivers groceries once a week. But no one goes inside. Not even me."

Rose gave the guard a hard stare. He was tall and athletic, maybe twenty-four, and he was distinctly nervous about talking to her. Or was it that he was nervous about being *seen* talking to her?

"How many people live here?" Rose asked, catching the guard's paranoia and looking at the windows to be certain no one was peering out at them. The black squares offered up little information about the interior of the house, and Rose wondered if they were made of special glass like the stuff some people put on their cars. People like bad guys, people with something to hide.

The guard shrugged. "I don't know. Like I said, I've never seen them. A guy talks to me via radio and a phone in the guardhouse."

"Isn't that kind of strange, don't you think?"

The guard shot another nervous look at the house, then eyed Rose for a moment before dipping his head and whispering, "It's fucked up if you ask me."

Rose fought a chill that threatened.

"There's three shifts and a weekend shift, and no one—no one—has ever seen anybody come in or out of that house. There's no car, no boat, no friggin' nothing. One of the guys even went to town hall to check out who owned the place, but it's the same corporation that signs our checks: Clarke Enterprises."

"Maybe it's some old guy in a wheelchair."

"Maybe." But he didn't seem even close to believing that.

The guard clammed up as they approached the front door. He pressed a button for an intercom. "You're interview is here." He turned back to her. "By the way, the name's Paul." The door clicked as it was electronically unlocked, and the guard pushed it open, immediately stepping back.

Rose gave him a look of mock terror. "Well, Paul, if you hear any screams, come running," she said, then laughed. The guard didn't even crack a smile as he stepped up to close the door behind her.

Two things hit Rose when she walked into the entry hall: it was as cold as a tomb and appeared completely abandoned. The huge entry hall opened up into a room that overlooked the Atlantic, and neither area had a stick of furniture that she could see. The marble floor was dusty. Cobwebs hung from the high ceiling and coated the fancy chandelier above her head. A camera, its red light blinking, had been installed near the chandelier. She half expected a bat to come dashing out of some dark corner. "Hello?" she said to the camera. No answer.

Then she saw an arrow written on a piece of paper tacked to one wall. It pointed to a small room off the entry hall, which was also empty, but for a chair and a telephone. And a camera in one corner. As she walked into the room, the phone rang.

Rolling her eyes at the ridiculous drama, Rose picked up the phone nearly ready to tell whoever was on the other end they could shove their job. "Rosie's House of Horrors." If the guy didn't have a sense of humor, she didn't want to work for him anyway.

He laughed, a rumbling sound that was pleasantly normal. "I know this all must seem strange."

His voice, deep and rough, sent a shiver of sensation from her ears to her toes. It was as good as the longest, deepest, wettest kiss Rose had ever had. She jerked the phone away from her head, then cautiously brought it back. "Very strange," she said slowly, looking up at the camera. "Can you see me now?"

"Yes." Again, that long, deep kiss.

Yes, yes, oh my God, yes. She was having phone sex, and that thought was so bizarre, she laughed aloud. He was probably fat and old and very, very pale if what Paul said was true about him never leaving the house. Rose conjured that distasteful image in her head to ward off any more erotic thoughts. "Is there a camera in the kitchen?"

"In every room. Except the bathroom."

Okay. Now that she had the old-fat-pale guy in her head, she could carry on a conversation.

"Are you hiding from the law?"

"No." He still sounded amused.

"Just hiding?"

That was the only way to put what he was doing, Declan realized. Hiding from the world.

"Why don't we talk about the position." He already knew she wouldn't take the job. Too bad, because she was the best-looking of the lot. Two men had answered the downstairs phone only to tell him without preamble they were no longer interested in the position. The woman, a skinny throwback from the sixties wearing a tie-dye T-shirt and a long ugly skirt, had looked as if a lion were about to eat her. This one, this petite woman with the long, wavy hair, looked completely relaxed, amused by his theatrics, and definitely not interested in the job. Perhaps he could convince her.

If he had to hire a cook, he might as well hire one who was nice to look at. He'd tried to find the most desperate from the dozens of applications that came in, and she looked as though she might need a break or money. He was so damned sick of eating frozen dinners, he thought he'd puke if he heard the sound of the microwave dinging out that his dinner was ready one more time. He'd weighed the risk of discovery over the joy of eating something edible, and food won out.

"Okay. Tell me about the job," she said, pulling her legs up to sit cross-legged in the chair. There was something so sexy about a woman sitting cross-legged. Too bad he'd never meet her in person.

"You'll work five days a week, preparing lunch and

dinner. I also expect you to prepare lunch and dinner for Saturday and Sunday before you leave on Friday. I don't pay medical or dental, but you'll get two weeks paid vacation a year, but not consecutive weeks."

She chewed on her thumbnail, the only indication she was a bit uncomfortable. "Are you in the mafia?"

"No. I prefer healthful food. I don't eat much red meat. I'd like for you to prepare a menu monthly so that I can pick what I want from day to day. I have food delivered by Bert's, and you'll have to prepare a shopping list."

"Are the cameras always on? Because I don't think I could cook if I thought you were watching all the time."

He sighed audibly. "I'll turn the camera on in the kitchen only when I need to talk to you."

"So I'm never going to see you. Face-to-face."

"Never." A shame. She was so damned pretty. Another thing he'd never thought about when he'd started all this. No women. No sex. What a stupid plan.

Declan hadn't thought about the complete isolation. Actually, he *had* thought about it, anticipated it even. But he'd never realized he would come to hate being alone, dreading each day knowing the only face he'd see would be his own. He found he missed life far more than he thought he would.

"I don't know . . ."

"Is there a problem with the salary?" he asked, knowing full well he was paying a ridiculous amount of money.

When she rolled her eyes and shot the camera a look of disbelief, he laughed again. God, it felt good to laugh. He had to make her take the job; it had suddenly become a necessary thing to have someone—anyone—to talk to.

She uncurled her legs and stood up facing the camera. "You've got to know this is very weird. I'm extremely uncomfortable with this arrangement."

Okay. At least she was still talking to him. "I understand," he said, deep and low. For some reason she jerked the phone away from her ear. He heard her take a long, shaking breath. Shit, he was scaring her. "Listen, I'm a normal guy in an unusual situation. I just want to eat something that doesn't come in a box."

She scrunched her face up in thought, clearly waging an internal battle between common sense and greed. *Come on, take the job. Take it.*

"I'd like to see the kitchen before I make any decisions."

He smiled. The kitchen was the one thing about this concrete prison that the former owners did right. It was a state-of-the-art, high-end cook's fantasy kind of kitchen, with every gadget and appliance imaginable. And it had an incredible view of the Atlantic. "Go to the end of the hall, take a left, and you'll see it."

He flipped a switch, turning on the two kitchen cameras. In front of him, the monitors blinked on, and he waited patiently for her to come into view. He wanted to see her expression when she saw the place and was not disappointed. It was like showing a starving woman a buffet table loaded with chocolate cake.

She stared up at one of the cameras and pointedly moved a finger over one of the stainless steel countertops. "It's a bit dusty."

"I'll clean it."

Rose stood in the center of paradise and moved in a slow circle, taking in every detail. She didn't want him to see her salivating over the Aga range, the double Subzero refrigerator, or the super-quiet ASKO dishwasher. And—oh my God!—it even had a Miele convection steam oven. She'd asked Tony a hundred times to install one, and he'd complained such a luxury was way beyond his budget.

"What do you think?"

If only he didn't sound so desperately lonely. So incredibly sexy. *He's fat. Pale, old, and fat.*

But that's not how he sounded. He sounded young and gorgeous and hungry.

Rose's dream man.

She looked up at the monitor and gave him a smile. "I'll take the job."

Ellen Lang sat limply staring at the cassette tape in her hand. It had come too late.

When Ellen sent away for it just six weeks ago, it had seemed like something fun to look forward to. Leah had been so excited, her brown eyes lighting up reminding Ellen what her little girl used to be like. But Leah would not hear the song now, would not giggle to hear her own name. Her seven-year-old daughter lay in a coma, waiting to die, not waiting to hear her very own song.

The company, Angel's Songs, wrote songs for terminally ill children and their families. Ellen had filled out a questionnaire and included a video tape of Leah taken before leukemia had hit, before her wispy little girl had turned bloated, before she'd lost her long chestnut hair to the chemotherapy that wouldn't work. In Ellen's mind she always thought of her daughter as Before Leah and After Leah, and she could never decide which image of her daughter hurt more. Her grip on the cassette tightened. Ellen wasn't certain she could listen to the song now.

She let out a long sigh. God, she was tired. Matt and she took four-hour shifts to be with Leah so she wouldn't die alone. It was the one thing Leah had wanted: Mommy and Daddy by her side when she went to heaven. Three times already one of them rushed from the Ronald McDonald House to the hospital, panic gripping their hearts in stark fear that they wouldn't be there when their daughter gave up her fight.

Ellen slipped the cassette into her Walkman, put the earphones on, and pressed the play button. She'd expected a happy tune, full of kid language and goofy sound effects. Instead came a haunting, beautiful tune, a woman's voice, soft and soulful, and words that gripped her heart and didn't let go. It was as if whoever had written this song did so for her and Matt, not for Leah, as if this person knew what was in their souls better than they did. By the time the last note echoed in her head, Ellen was sobbing.

"Honey, what's wrong. Why are you crying?" Matt rushed to her side, his face ravaged by a grief that had stayed with them ever since the doctors told them their three-year-long fight to save Leah was futile.

Ellen shook her head, tears streaming down her face. "It's Leah's song. It came. It . . . it . . . Oh, God, Matt, it's perfect."

Relief swamped his face, and Ellen knew he'd believed that in the ten minutes since he'd left Leah's side, she had died. Alone.

"You scared the hell out of me," he said, smiling gently at his teary-eyed wife. Through all this, Ellen had rarely cried, insisting there was nothing to cry about, that they would beat this thing. Even after the doctors told them hope was lost, she'd refused to give in. Her daughter would live, a miracle would happen. She would not die.

But this song, this beautiful, wonderful song, unleashed the grief she'd hidden deep inside.

"Matt, you've got to listen to this. It's the most beautiful thing I've ever heard." She rewound the tape and handed the Walkman to her husband.

Matt gave her a skeptical look and pressed play. And Ellen watched his face transform as he heard the words, listened to the music that surely was touching his heart the way it had touched hers. By the end of the song,

Ellen could tell Matt was fighting tears, a fight he lost when the last note sounded.

"Jesus Christ, who the hell wrote this thing?" he said roughly, dashing away the wetness on his face and jerking the headphones off.

"I don't know, but I'm going to find out. I want to thank whoever wrote it in person."

"How did they know all this stuff? How did they . . ."

"I filled out a questionnaire, what Leah likes, doesn't like. And I sent a video of her. The one of her playing at the park. I never expected anything like this."

"Does it say who wrote it?"

Ellen looked through the packet that came with the cassette. It included only an invoice and a letter thanking them for their order. "It's a company out of Kansas. I could call them. I'm sure they'd tell us who wrote the song. And if they don't, I'll just tell them the Lieutenant Governor of Tennessee wants to know," she said, smiling at her exhausted husband who'd been trying to carry out his political duties while watching his only child die. "Right now, I'm going to sit with Leah. I'm going to let her listen. You never know, she might hear it."

"You go ahead. Call me if there's a change."

When she reached her daughter's room, Ellen stood at the door looking at Leah, her eyes shifting, as they always did, to the photograph she'd tacked above Leah's head. The Before Leah, not this bloated, hairless little creature who broke her heart to look at.

"Hi, honey. Your song came. Want to give it a listen? I think it's so pretty." Ellen placed the earphones on her daughter, then kissed her forehead, closing her eyes against the agonizing wave of emotion that hit her. Throughout the song, Leah lay unmoving; not even a flickering of her eyes told Ellen whether or not she could hear the music. Ellen chose to believe that somehow Leah heard the song and understood the magic those words contained. She laid her head by her daughter's on the cool, crisp hospital sheet, holding her hand, wishing as she'd wished a thousand times that she'd look up and see her own Leah with her bright brown eyes and wide guileless smile.

"I'll be okay, Leah," she lied in a whisper. "I know you're tired, baby. Go to sleep, go to sleep."

Chapter 2

Double-marinated half chicken with preserved lemons, herbs, crispy potato torta, roasted red onions and broccoli rabe, $21.00

Rose sat cross-legged on her old and comfy sofa, phone tucked in her ear, a big bowl of popcorn on her lap. "I got the job."

"Oh my God, that's fantastic," came Jenn's enthusiastic response.

"I guess." Rose wasn't sure she'd made the right decision and was close to calling The Voice to tell him she'd changed her mind.

"What do you mean, 'I guess.' With that kind of money you'll be able to move out of that dump and into a nice place on the East Side."

"It's not that much of a dump," Rose said, looking around her third-floor apartment. It was a dump. But it was a big dump and it was hers. So what if the appliances were from the sixties. They still worked. Sort of. And she'd installed ceiling fans so it didn't get *that* hot in the summer. She didn't really mind lugging her dirty clothes to the Laundromat. Or lugging groceries up three floors. Besides, the rent was low enough to allow her to save money for her restaurant.

"It's a dump," Jenn said flatly.

"You're just jealous because you don't have your own place anymore," Rose said, clearly not believing a word she said.

Jenn laughed. "So tell me about this job."

"I don't know, it's kind of weird. I'll only be cooking for one guy."

"What's he look like?"

Rose rolled her eyes at Jenn's transparent attempt to find Rose a boyfriend. "I don't know. That's the weird part. I didn't meet the guy in person, just talked to him over the phone. He won't let me see him."

"What do you mean?"

"I mean he's some kind of recluse or freak or something. He lives in this waterfront concrete box in Kingstown all by himself. He's got security cameras all over the place. And the guard I talked to says he's never seen anyone go in or out of the place."

"That is weird. Tell me why you want to take this job?"

"There are about eighty thousand reasons," Rose said dryly.

"Oh, yeah. I guess with the security guard you're safe in case the guy is some sort of psycho."

"That's true. At least my body would be found quickly." Rose popped a bit of popcorn in her mouth, moving the receiver away so Jenn wouldn't have to listen to her chew.

"How did he sound?"

"Normal. Even nice. More than nice." Rose could almost picture Jenn sitting up straighter in rapt attention.

"What does that mean?"

"I mean, he's got the sexiest voice I've ever heard in my life."

"Sexiest *voice?*"

"I can't explain it."

"You've got the hots for your boss." Jenn dissolved into a fit of giggles.

"Let me clarify. I've got the hots for my boss's voice. For all I know he could be some fat old guy. Frankly, I prefer to think of him that way."

"Not knowing what he looked like would drive me crazy," Jenn said. "And it's so romantic. Kind of like Mel Gibson in that movie where he's all scarred and he's too ashamed to show his face."

"Two seconds ago you were convinced he was a psycho. Anyway, I'm pretty sure he doesn't look like Mel Gibson," Rose said.

"But he might. And you'll never know unless you sneak up on him someday."

Rose laughed. "I can't do that. And I'm not sure I want this job. It's too weird. Then again, I did tell him I'd take it. And it is an awful lot of money."

"You could get a real car," Jenn teased.

"You just want to live an exciting life vicariously through me now that you're an old married woman."

"Ha ha. But true. What's this guy's name, anyway? Maybe we could go on-line and find out all about him."

Rose shook her head in disbelief at her own stupidity. "I don't know. I never asked and he never told me. I guess I'll find out on Friday when I bring him his menu. In fact, I've got to get working on it. The next couple of weeks are going to be crazy for me, 'cause I'm doing double duty. The Voice wants to start right away, but I can't leave Tony without a cook."

"So what is it about his voice that turns you on so much?"

Even though they were talking on the phone, Rose could feel herself flush. "He doesn't turn me on, you pig." Only as much as a hot, wet kiss did. A long, slow, hot, wet kiss.

"What happens if he has a face and body to match his voice? What then?"

"I'll jump his bones," Rose said, laughing. "But that's not going to happen."

"Yeah. Probably not. If the guy was that good-looking, he wouldn't be a recluse, right?"

"Right. Anyway, there's this security guard working there that's potential boy-toy material," Rose said, purposefully directing the conversation away from her strange reaction to her client's voice.

"Oh, really?"

"He's probably a good six years younger, though. When did I start getting too old for good-looking guys? Not that I'm looking, mind you."

"There's nothing wrong with looking," Jenn said.

"I'm not looking. I'm perfectly happy."

"I know you are."

If Jenn had been sitting next to her, she would have smacked her one. She sounded like her mother when she'd told her about the job—patronizing. "It may be difficult for you to believe, but not everyone finds happiness with a perfect husband, house, and kids. Some of us like the grittier side of life."

"You are so full of shit."

Rose let out a snorting laugh. "Yeah. I know. Hey, I'll call you later in the week."

Rose hung up the phone and gave her apartment another hard look. She'd lived there for ten years, and she figured she could live there another ten years if it meant getting her restaurant. She knew she was too old to live like this, that she needed real furniture that came from a nice store, not Harry's Bargain House where you could buy a roomful of crap for four hundred bucks. She closed her eyes and imagined herself greeting patrons, making up menus, cooking. She could call it Rosalie's or maybe Pisano's. She wanted a place that was homey and comfortable and had the best Italian food in Providence.

It would be paradise.

Declan watched her talking to no-neck the guard, a severe frown on his face. What the hell could they be talking about? The security guard had an I.Q. of a rodent, and she hadn't struck him as the type of woman who went for the all-muscle, no-brain type. She was wearing jeans that fell low on her hips revealing a small amount of her stomach, just enough to tantalize, just enough to make him wonder if she'd pierced her navel. Man, he loved a woman with a nicely pierced innie. She had a frayed hole in the left knee, which was bent and sexy, and every once in a while, she'd touch her hair—bring it back from her face, throw a long strand over her shoulder. He doubted she was even aware of what she was doing, because it didn't looked staged. She looked natural and interested in every word the moron was saying. Feeling only a little guilty, he grabbed his binoculars and trained them on her midriff. Nothing. Good. Then he wouldn't be haunted by what it would be like to lay his head on her stomach and play with the navel ring with his tongue.

"Look at her," he said aloud and very much to himself. "Tossing hair: one of the ten clear signs a woman is interested in you." He turned away from the pair and looked into the mirror. "Talking to yourself and expecting an answer: one of the ten signs you're going crazy." He laughed.

Not so long ago, he probably wouldn't have even looked at his new cook twice. Well, maybe twice. Two years ago he would have passed her by as he passed by so many women. God, all those women. What he wouldn't give for just one of them. Just one who had looked at him as if he was some sort of god. All he'd had to do was smile and they'd be ready to hop into bed and fuck his brains out. His brother used to joke that he wanted his leftovers, and Declan would say he was welcome to the main course. Because it got old after a while. It got stale and rotten and . . .

Now he was alone staring out a window at a perfectly normal woman who looked hotter to him than any boob-enhanced fake blonde he'd ever slept with. He'd turned into a pig. That's what more than a year without sex will do to a guy.

He looked away from the two talking below, fighting the hot jealousy that burned in his gut that they could have such a conversation in the open, with not a care in the world. They could flirt and go out and maybe have sex while he stayed in his tomb and waited for . . . what? Everyone to forget him? For his brother to resurrect from the dead?

This wasn't a life sentence. It always had been meant to be temporary, until things calmed down, until he was ready to confront the hoards. Meanwhile, he was stuck in his room. Declan looked around at his unmade bed, his baby grand piano piled high with paper, his couch, his cursed microwave placed on what was supposed to be his bedside table. He was a grown man living like a college student. He should be married with two kids, not hiding, not living in fear.

Through his window, he heard her laugh, and he smiled because she had the nicest laugh, rich and colorful and light, like a stained-glass window. He knew in his gut, which twisted with horror at the thought, Rose would somehow be the biggest mistake he'd ever made. He shouldn't have hired her; he should have suffered through this time alone.

The buzzer sounded, and his finger paused, hovering over the button, shaking. He could call this off, go on day by day for another year like he'd planned. He pressed his lips together, a man making a life-changing decision. His stomach growled, and he let her in.

"Hey, I'm here with the menus." She shook them over her head at the camera in the main hall. She was so damned cute. He had to stop thinking that everything she did and said was cute.

"There's a dumbwaiter in the kitchen. Use that to send them up." He flicked on all his cameras so he could watch and listen to her as she made her way to the kitchen. A pig and a voyeur.

"I wonder why they call it a dumb waiter," she said as she walked. "I think they should have come up with another name. Like ele-waiter." She stopped and slapped her knee, the one that poked so sexily out of her jeans, laughing. "Ele-waiter."

It really was funny. She was funny and he was cursed. Funny, cute, and a good cook. God, he felt like the phantom lusting after Christine Daae. "Very funny," he said dryly.

"By the way, what should I call you?"

"Just call me Mac."

"Just Mac. You have one of those names without a last name? Like Madonna and Prince?"

"That's right." He narrowed his eyes when she rolled hers.

As she walked over to the dumbwaiter, he lost sight of her. Then he heard the hum of the motor as it brought the menu up to him, and she stepped into view, a wide smile on her face.

"You know, I could have climbed inside without you knowing. You've got a flaw in your high security."

A wave of sickness hit him, that old horrible fear that used to grip him. His heart pounded, and his palms got sweaty, his breathing shallow. She was right. Anyone could crawl in the dumbwaiter and get to him. Anyone.

"Don't ever try that. I'd fire you on the spot."

The hairs rose on the back of Rose's neck. She'd been

stupid to think there was nothing wrong with this guy. A person didn't lock themselves away unless there was something seriously wrong. The way he'd just sounded, my God, it was scary. That voice she'd thought was so sexy had carried so much menace. And fear.

She took an unconscious step backward, and the smile she'd had slowly disappeared. "I won't," she said, looking directly into the camera.

Silence.

"I promise." She held up her hand like a Boy Scout.

"I'm sorry," he said so softly she had to strain to hear him. "It's just that I've made this decision to live this way, and for now I have to stick to it."

Rose continued to look at the camera as if she were looking right at him, her curiosity increasing tenfold. "Are you in any danger? I want the truth." She was so tense, her back hurt, and she forced herself to relax. Paul, the guard, was right outside, and even though Mac had frightened her, she sensed he wasn't a threat to her. *I hope my instincts are right.*

"No. I'm not in any danger." And then he said in a voice that ran through her like hot, fizzy soda, "And neither are you."

She shook her head. "I didn't think . . ."

"Yes you did. And I'm sorry."

Just then the phone rang, and Rose let out a scream worthy of a horror movie.

"No," he said, chuckling. "I didn't scare you a bit." A pause. "It's my mother. Hang out down there awhile and I'll send you down my selections. Then you can let yourself out. Good-bye."

Good-bye? Just like that? At least the guy had a mother. That proved he wasn't spawned from the devil, she thought, letting out a small laugh. "I crack myself up," she said softly as she looked around the kitchen. A slow smile spread on her face when she realized that some time in the last few days, he'd come down and cleaned it from top to bottom. Just her luck this man of mystery was also thoughtful.

"Hey, Mom. What's up?" Declan settled back in his black leather chair, ready to talk to the only other person in the world to know where he was.

"Hey yourself. I was just listening to the radio here. You're in big trouble, kiddo. I think the game is up."

"Oprah Winfrey's show called," Ellen said into her cell phone. "They want me to be on to talk about Leah."

She sat in her car at a rest stop and watched as a woman and a little girl walked toward a Porto Jon, the girl skipping and tugging, the woman laughing. A white flash of hatred for the happy pair ran through her, and she squeezed her eyes shut.

"Matthew, did you hear me?"

"Yeah. That's great."

Since her daughter's death, Ellen Lang had been on a crusade, using her status as a minor celebrity to raise money for cancer research, while her husband did nothing but work and sit and stare into space. She'd been on several local radio talk shows, as well as the local news in Nashville. She was *doing* something. Oprah's show was huge, and she felt giddy with success.

"You're certain you want to do this?" She heard the hesitation in her husband's voice, and it pissed her off. How could he not know how important this was?

"Yes, I want to do this. We're talking a national show with a huge audience. I've already talked to Angel's Songs, and they've agreed to let me buy the rights to the song as long as most of the profits go to cancer research. Of course I agreed. They do get ten percent of proceeds. This is a terrific opportunity, and I'm not going to pass it up," she said, knowing she sounded confrontational and not caring. It was maddening how damn complacent he'd become.

"I just think you ought to take a break. It's only been a month, Ellen, and you haven't taken a breath."

"And I'm not going to. Leah is more important right now."

"Honey, Leah's . . ."

"Don't say it. I know Leah's gone. You don't have to remind me." She heard his sigh, almost felt it scraping along her raw nerves.

"I never meant to imply that you don't know Leah died. And I know this is how you're choosing to deal with losing her. But you can't fix this one, babe. Not with all the money in the world."

God, she couldn't stand that therapist's tone he took with her when he was trying to calm her down. "Thank you, Doctor. They want to know if you want to appear on the show, as well. I think your participation would be a wonderful benefit." Ellen gritted her teeth at the silence. "They need to know today."

"I can't. It's still too raw for me." She heard his voice close up and felt nothing but anger.

"Are you implying that I don't hurt over her death?"

"Not at all. Christ, Ellen."

"Because I hurt, Matt. Don't you for one minute think I don't hurt." Her grip on the cell phone became painful as the woman and girl, both comically holding their noses, emerged from the Porto Jon. She looked away to the traffic rushing by.

"I know you do."

"I've got to go. I have an interview with *The Tennessean* in about an hour. I'll see you tonight."

"Late. We're working on that budget deal with the Democrats."

"Right. Talk to you later."

And she disconnected.

Chapter 3

Spaghetti carbonara with fried egg, sweet peas and parmigiano, $15.00

Sitting high above Atwells Avenue, the main drag for Providence's Italian Federal Hill section, is a huge pineapple hanging from an arch that crosses the road. To strangers, it is often confused with a pinecone, and more than one tourist has scratched his head wondering why in the world someone would hang a pinecone over a city street. It's a place where shoppers can buy fresh dough for bread or pizza and the rich smells are enough to make a starving man die of happiness.

Along this road were some of the best Italian restaurants this side of the Atlantic, and to many of the people living in this old neighborhood, Anthony's Ristorante was one of them. The locals referred to it as Tony's, and it was mostly the locals who frequented it.

Rose still remembered going into Tony's when she was a kid. She always ordered the same thing: chicken parmesan with a side of ziti. Like nearly every other item, chicken parmesan with a side of ziti was still on the menu. Nothing had changed since Rose went to Tony's with her grandmother and grandfather for a Saturday night meal while her mother studied, and later, worked. Tony had seemed so old then, but he'd only been twenty-five, proud as a man can be to have his own restaurant. When Rose was sixteen, Tony's was like a second home to her, so it was natural that she work for Tony for her first job the summer of her senior year. Her mother had approved, thinking it was a good way for Rose to earn money for college. But that summer it hit Rose that she was doing what she wanted to do for the rest of her life. It took another year before she could garner the courage to tell her mother that she had no intention of going to college to take prelaw. She was making what seemed like a fortune at the time, and after graduation, she moved out as her mother first yelled criticisms, then advice: "Always hold your keys in your hand at night. Get one of those deadbolt locks. And no boys, Rosalie. You're only seventeen." And she'd cried, to Rose's horror.

Rose didn't make a clean break from family, of course. She spent nearly every night at her grandparents' before going home to her tiny, shabby and very cool apartment on the second floor of a four-story tenement. It was the happiest time of her life. She didn't care that she worked six days a week; Tony's was home and she loved being there. Every extra penny went into the bank, into what she'd called her restaurant fund. When she was twenty-five, she invested ten thousand dollars in the stock market, adding to it periodically. She drove a crappy car, bought clothes secondhand, lived in an apartment whose rent for years was below three hundred dollars a month, and saved money like Scrooge.

It was only when she hit the big three-o that a small amount of panic set in. She had no idea how she'd gotten so old and done so little. She had one friend, a slightly bigger apartment, no boyfriend, no kids, no home, but she had a boatload of cash and a dream—a dream that still seemed infinitely far away given the pittance she was earning at Tony's. Hope had renewed itself when she saw that ad for a personal chef, and the dream she'd had for so long suddenly seemed within reach. In five years she'd have enough cash to open a restaurant.

Rose stood outside Tony's and swallowed down her guilt. She'd put it off for as long as she could, but every time she saw Tony she almost burst into tears and slobbered out the truth. She had to tell him now, and she dreaded it.

The faded red awning above her flapped in a late April breeze. It was mildewy, and part of the A had chipped off over the years. Six years ago Tony had thrown a red indoor-outdoor carpet on the ramp leading to the front door, and it lay there still, dirty and shabby, making Rose wonder if Tony didn't like spending money or didn't have the money to spend. For years Rose had been bugging him to update the décor a bit. It looked exactly the way it had when she was ten years old. Dark red floral carpet, paneled walls, bad Italian landscapes, red vinyl-covered booths, and hard uncomfortable chairs.

"People don't come here for the atmosphere; they come here for the food," Tony must have said a hundred times.

And that really worried her because over the years, Rose had almost completely taken over the kitchen while Tony handled the management, staffing, and customers. Tony had gotten into the habit of talking to his regulars, sitting down with them, even eating with them, and hadn't worked in the kitchen in at least four years except on the rare occasion when Rose was too sick to work. Rose loved Tony like an uncle, but he was infuriating. She'd tried to offer some different types of items as specials, and when they didn't sell, he nixed the entire idea. His idea of a "special" was a regular menu item at a slightly lower price. As someone who loved to experiment with food, working for Tony was excruciatingly frustrating.

Yet, she'd miss him and this place.

Rose gritted her teeth and went in, walking directly to Tony's office, a tiny, paper-cluttered closet off the main entrance.

"Hey, Tone. Got a minute?" Rose had known Tony for more than twenty years, and he still looked almost exactly the same as when she'd first met him. He wore his dark hair slicked back, and he had a neatly trimmed mustache. He must have trimmed it every day because it never looked as if it grew. Rose remembered thinking when she was a kid that it must be fake, because it was always so perfect. He wore what he always wore: a white oxford shirt, black tie, and black pants. It never varied, and because he was always clean, Rose figured he must have six of those outfits in his closet. She'd never seen him in anything else. He was a wiry, energetic forty-seven-year-old with an eye for the ladies and a string of almost-wives. He was loud and gruff with a heart that broke much too easily. And Rose knew she was about to break it in about two minutes.

"Shorthanded tonight. I've got to call in Heather again. I'd fire her if she wasn't so willing to come in. What's up?"

"You know I've been planning a restaurant of my own." That got his attention. He slowly lowered the pen he was holding and looked up at her, his dark brown eyes snapping with interest. "I've decided to take another job, Tone. It pays an incredible salary, and I'll be able to get my own place within five years."

"I see."

"I really appreciate everything you taught me, and I'll stay on as long as you need me . . ."

He shrugged. "Go. Go now if you want."

"Tone, stop it. I'll stay two weeks to help out until you find another cook."

He got all indignant, pure Tony. "You think I can't still cook?"

"You know that's not what I'm saying. I know how hard you work, and I also know that you can't possibly do two jobs."

"Let me tell you something, Rose. When I first started this restaurant, I did everything. I greeted the customers, took their orders, cooked their meals, and brought the food out. And I could do it again."

"Don't be an idiot."

"Don't you," he said, pointing a finger at her, "think I need you so much. You go on, take your fancy job."

Rose rolled her eyes. "Will you please cut the crap, Tone?"

"Okay. Two weeks. Fine."

She smiled and kissed his cheek. "Fine. And, Tony, thanks."

"Yeah, yeah." He picked up his pen again. "How much you getting paid?"

"Eighty thousand," Rose said, feeling lousy because she knew what he was thinking, that he would match whatever it was. But Rose knew no small restaurant owner could afford to pay someone that amount and make a profit. He let out a whistle.

"*I* should take that job," he said. "Where is it?"

Rose didn't want to tell him because she knew he'd be suspicious of anyone who would be insane enough to pay that amount of money to cook for one person.

"I'm the personal chef at some fancy house in Kingstown. It's on the water."

"New Yorkers," he muttered, then picked up the phone to ask Heather to come in, dismissing Rose with a grumpy wave of his hand.

"I'm in big trouble, Nonna. I think I'm interested in my boss." It was a perfectly ridiculous thing to say, even more ridiculous to think, but there it was. Rose, despite her Herculean efforts to imagine some old letch, conjured in her brain the image of the perfect male. Like Jenn said, it *was* romantic. She should think the guy was creepy, but instead she found herself intensely curious and more than a little attracted to him. To a voice.

No, it wasn't just that. It was the things he said, the way he said them, with an underlying emotion that was almost tangible.

Angelica Fortino looked up from the ravioli she was stuffing—she made ravioli every Wednesday morning without fail—and said, "What's his last name?"

Rose grinned. "I don't know. He's very mysterious, which is probably why I'm so interested in him. Also he made some nice selections from the menu. You've got to respect a guy who chooses eggplant parmesan over a cheeseburger."

"He's Italian," Angelica said with a sharp nod. "He rich?"

"Scads of money. Oh, by the way, we're getting married tomorrow."

Angelica shook her head. "You make fun with an old lady who only wants to attend her only grandchild's wedding before she dies."

Rose looked at her grandmother fondly, before jumping up from her seat at the food-laden table and kissing her soft cheek. "You're only seventy-two. A spring chicken."

"A spring chicken with creaking bones and gray hair. I look in the mirror and I can't believe that old woman looking back is me. I tell you, Rosalie, it's tough getting old."

Rose just laughed. She refused to think about the reality that someday, and probably far sooner than she feared, her grandmother would die. It was unthinkable to have a world where she couldn't come and sit and watch her Nonna rolling out pasta or making her famous sausage. Famous on Federal Hill, anyway. She'd spent countless hours watching her grandmother cook;

it was where she'd developed her passion for cooking, for making people happy with food. While her mother had been going to law school, she'd been helping her grandmother in the kitchen and cherishing every minute. Angelica was constantly cooking something. And when she wasn't cooking, she was delivering it to neighbors. It was Angelica's one sadness that her son hadn't lived long enough to give her a dozen grandchildren to feed. Of course, she had a daughter—a daughter who couldn't cook a decent sauce, who wouldn't eat half the food Angelica made because it might put a little padding on her skeletal figure.

Rose wanted to shake her mother when she thought about how much she was hurting her grandmother with her rejection of her Italian roots. Rose knew it must have been difficult growing up with parents who spoke in heavily accented English, who still acted and dressed as though they lived in Italy. Even after twenty years a widow, her grandmother still dressed in black. She wore a handkerchief on her head unless they were visiting. Everything her own mother rejected, Rose embraced with a ferocity that an armchair psychiatrist could have figured out. She was rebelling against her mother just as her own mother had rebelled against Angelica.

"You're not that old," Rose insisted. "And you will be at my wedding even if it's ten years from now."

Angelica looked horrified. "Ten years? You gonna wait until you're forty-two to get married? What about children, Rosalie. You can't have children when you're forty-two."

"Lots of women do nowadays. Besides, I didn't say I was going to wait until I was forty-two; I just said it might be that long, and if it is, you'll be there."

"I'll be eighty-two by then." She shook her head that such a tragedy might occur. "So, this new boss. What's he look like?"

Rose filled her in on the entire story, embellishing

here and there, and leaving out certain interesting information about her granddaughter's odd reaction to a certain sexy voice.

"Sound like a crazy man to me," Angelica said.

Rose stood up and gave her grandmother a hug. "I think this one's okay. And he sure won't have a temper like Tony."

"Tony gonna burst someday he get so mad," she said, chuckling. Tony and her grandmother were old and good friends. "You tell him about the new job yet?"

"I did. He acted like he didn't care, but I know he does."

"He understands." She turned to her and patted her cheeks none too gently. "You have a dream, Rosalie. You make your dream come true, right?"

"Right."

Rose kissed her grandmother's cheek. "I have to go work for my mystery man, Nonna. I'll see you tonight, okay?"

"Mystery man," she said. "Crazy man you ask me."

Chapter 4

Pappardelle with beef rib ragu and parmigiano, $16.50

Linguini pescatore. Mussels, clams, squid, scallops. White wine, olive oil, garlic. And of course, linguini. Rose arranged the mussels artistically around the plate and planted a sprig of fresh parsley in the middle. Behind her, the camera light flashed on—she saw the reflection in the gleaming stovetop hood—and she waited for the telltale click that told her he'd turned on the intercom. And waited. Smiling to herself, she reached behind her and scratched her behind vigorously, then pretended to clean out one of her ears with her index finger. Still silence. *I hope he's enjoying himself.*

Narrowing her eyes, she let go a massive sneeze directly on top of his meal. *Click.*

"Umm, Miss Pisano?"

She pretended to be startled as she spun around and looked innocently up to the camera. "Yes?"

"I've decided to go with something else for lunch. Something lighter."

"Can't you eat this?" she asked, looking at her beautifully prepared meal. "I just put on the finishing touches.

And linguini pescatore is not very good warmed over."
She tried very, very hard not to laugh. Because she
knew he was up there wondering if he should admit to
seeing her sneeze into his meal and knowing that if he
did, she'd know he'd been spying on her.

"Ummm."

The sound of those m's melted her resolve. They
made her think of sex. *Old, pale, and fat. Old, pale,
and fat.*

She heard a small puff of air as he made up his
mind. "I saw you sneeze."

"Ah ha!" she shouted, pointing an accusing finger at
the camera. "You were spying. And you promised not
to. I ought to throw this perfectly unsneezed-on meal
right in the garbage."

A long silence. He was embarrassed. Good.

"Sorry." He sounded like a ten-year-old—not sorry
at all but knowing if he didn't apologize he might not
get what he wanted. "It's just strange to have someone
here, knowing that I'm not alone."

Great. Now he sounded like a gorgeous guy pleading for clemency. A gorgeous and very lonely guy, and
she wondered, just fleetingly, whether he was manipu-
lating her.

Rose turned back to the plate. "Just don't do it again.
Okay?"

"I'll try." She could almost hear the smile in his voice.

"Try really hard."

"Last night's supper was fantastic, by the way. You're
really good." He'd had roasted salmon and homemade
gnocchi.

"Thanks." It came out terse, and she really didn't mean
it. Rose didn't believe Mac would harm her or was watching her for some kinky sexual reason. In her chef's uniform she wasn't any man's fantasy—more like a little
Q-tip.

She heard the intercom click off and relaxed, then

noticed the reflection of the camera's red light in the hood again. She turned around and gave him her fiercest look, fully expecting him to immediately turn off the camera. She stared and stared, exaggerating her impatient stance, letting out a visible sigh of irritation, a rise and fall of her shoulders. Then she picked up his plate and held it hostage over the garbage disposal. The light immediately flicked off. She tried to be pissed off, but she couldn't do it. He was having fun with her. The poor guy hadn't had contact with another human for a long time and was probably just bored.

Rose scribbled a note and sent it with the meal up the dumbwaiter. *How old are you?*

Later, after she'd cleaned up, she heard the buzz of the dumbwaiter returning the dirty dishes. Among the dishes she found a note. *Thirty-five.*

Something dropped hard into Rose's stomach. He was young. Why did she have to write that note? She'd been much better off thinking he was some old guy up there, even though she'd known in her heart he wasn't. He was thirty-five with a voice that made her do embarrassing things to her panties. It was positively mortifying.

"Okay," she said softly to herself. "So he's young. So what?" He could still be pale as the underbelly of a fish and fat as a well-fed pig. It didn't matter. He'd told her himself she'd never see him. That curiosity came raging back, a prickling along her spine.

Who *was* this guy?

It was six o'clock and nearly dark out by the time she finished cleaning up. She surveyed the kitchen, then went about shutting off lights before going over to the intercom and pressing the button.

"Yes?"

"I'm going home. Good night."

Then she walked out of the kitchen and was nearly to the front door when she realized she'd left one of her soiled chef's uniforms in the utility closet. She walked back, her eyes automatically going to the camera in the corner to see if he had it on. It was dark, like everything else in the house. Dark and cold. How did the guy live like this? She'd watched that old werewolf movie with Jack Nicholson and Michele Pfeiffer the other night, and it fueled her imagination. Of course, she knew vampires and werewolves didn't exist, but when it was pitch black inside and empty and cold and, well, spooky as heck, she couldn't stop herself from thinking that maybe, just maybe, Mac was some sort of monster. She felt like she did when she was a kid in her grandmother's dark cellar, telling herself no monster lived here but having the distinct and blood-chilling feeling that something awful lurked in the dark. Something that at any minute was going to leap out of the darkness, spring at her like some silent menace, teeth bared, long strands of gooey saliva dripping down. . . .

"Stop it, idiot," she whispered.

Rose walked to the closet, her sneakers silent on the tile floor, and grabbed her dirty uniform. She forced herself to walk normally out of the kitchen, feeling ridiculous for letting her imagination run wild. She opened the kitchen door to the utter blackness of the long hall that ran between all those empty, cavernous rooms, and paused. Clutching her uniform, she walked quickly down the hall, turned the corner to the front door, and slammed into something tall and hard and very alive.

Two steel bands gripped her arms. She screamed, of course, loudly and long, wrenching free of whatever it was that held her.

"Hey, hey it's just me. Mac."

Rose let out a string of swears. Then: "You scared the hell out of me."

She heard him chuckle, the sound as disembodied as

it was when it came over the intercom. "No kidding. I thought you'd left."

"I forgot one of my dirty uniforms," she said, her eyes straining so hard to see, they hurt. It was no good. The best she could do was make out a very faint outline of a person, a tall person. If she wasn't staring right at him, she wouldn't have known he was there at all.

"You can't see me, can you." It wasn't a question, but a statement of certainty, as if he knew if she could see him, she would have somehow reacted differently.

The voice was suddenly closer, melting over her, warm chocolate drizzling all over her body. "No. I can't see you." But she could feel him, feel the heat coming from his body, an unnatural heat.

"Are you sick?"

"No. Why?"

"Because I can feel you. Like you're steaming or something."

He laughed again, deep and rich. "I was just working out." He shifted, she could hear him move.

"I have to go now." Even though she told herself Mac was just a normal guy, she couldn't stop the fear from curling her stomach, from sending a hot frisson of terror to the base of her skull.

"You don't have to run away."

"I'm not running away," she said with forced casualness. And she wasn't; she was standing so still she could hear her own breath. She could hear his, slow, measured. He smelled an odd combination of clean and sweaty, as if he'd showered right before working out, and for some reason her fear vanished. She breathed in deeply, telling herself she was trying to figure out which soap he'd used. Dial. Or Irish Spring.

"This is the closest I've been to another person in more than two years. It's strange."

"You think this is strange?"

He let out a soft laugh. Her entire body tingled, tiny

heat prickles moving from her spine to the top of her head, down her arms to the tips of her fingers. It wasn't fear, but something else. It was the same tingle she'd get when someone told her a moving story, or when she looked up into the sky and saw something unexpectedly beautiful.

"Am I scaring you? I don't mean to."

"Well, I am in the dark with a complete stranger."

"Not complete. Here, let me introduce myself." He waited. "I'm holding out my hand," he said, a smile in his voice.

"Oh." Rose groped for his hand and hit his forearm, immediately jerking her hand away. The darkness must have made her sense of touch more powerful, because in that instant she felt the fine hair on his arms. Then he captured her hand, his grip gentle but strong.

"I'm Mac. Pleased to meet you."

Holding hands was never meant to be as darkly erotic as this. Rose let out a nervous laugh, feeling depraved and embarrassed, and eternally thankful it was too dark for him to see her mouth open, her eyes glaze, her cheeks flush. She tried to pull her hand away.

"No," he whispered. He held her hand, a solid pressure, his fingers wrapped around hers, unmoving and unrelenting. Rose closed her eyes, silently begging him to let her go. Not because she was frightened, though the logical part of her reminded her that she should be, but because she wanted to lean toward him, against him. Slowly she became aware of something tugging at her brain.

"You play the piano," she said suddenly and with certainty. He immediately dropped her hand, leaving it cold and holding nothing but air. "You do, don't you? I had a boyfriend who played keyboard in this awful wedding band. His hands were like yours."

"How so?" He'd moved away, far enough so that even if she'd wanted to, she couldn't have touched him.

"Strong. Your fingers have this equal energy. It's hard to explain. I'm right, aren't I?"

"I play."

"Ooo. A secret revealed. You better watch it, Mac, I'm going to guess your identity any day now."

"Good night, Rose," he said from the kitchen door, his escape complete.

"Good night. Piano man."

At night, when Rose was walking toward the front door, the house felt particularly cold and cavernous, her footsteps sounding unnaturally loud on the hard, marble floor. She was fairly certain Mac wouldn't venture out again until he was absolutely sure she was gone. But, still, her heart kicked up a beat as she walked down the darkened hallway, her eyes straining for the entry hall. She stopped, her ears straining for the slightest noise. There, a teasing bit of sound that could exist only in her mind. When she got closer to the staircase, she realized she heard music, light and lilting, echoing through the tomblike house. Rose caught her breath audibly as she tiptoed to the base of the stairs and looked up. The stairway was black as pitch at the top and lit slightly by the transom windows above the front door three-quarters of the way up. Rose tilted her ear to hear better, ready to flee at any unexpected noise. But all she heard was a beautiful, lilting tune she didn't recognize. The music was too far from her to determine whether it was a recording or Mac, with those strong fingers pressing down lightly on the keyboard. The music stopped suddenly. Then she heard a series of chords. Mac.

Great, she thought. Sexy voice, strong hands, and played the piano. That was all she needed to push her already embarrassing imagination into overdrive. Rose walked up the first step, than the second and third, and up again, stopping to sit at the sharp edge of light from the windows, frozen to the spot, rigid with excitement and fear. He began playing again, the music soft, melting over her.

"Who are you?" she whispered, lost in the music and the darkness and the impenetrable loneliness she suddenly felt. She shook her head and stood, stepping quickly down the stairs as silently as possible, knowing she was running away from a man who hadn't the foggiest idea he was slowly, and tortuously, seducing her.

The next night, she fought the urge to light her way to the front door. She'd a feeling Mac would make darn certain she was gone before venturing downstairs. He wasn't playing tonight, and she shook away the feeling of disappointment. Rose was at the front door when she heard, "Good night."

She didn't scream this time, just turned slowly around. There near the top of the stairs, two bare male feet were visible in the light shining through the transom windows above the front door.

"I see your feet," she called out. He wiggled his toes. "Pretty soon I'm going to put all these clues together, Mac, and your hiding days will be over."

She stood there waiting for some sort of response. "I have an idea. Move down a step every day until you're entirely revealed."

Declan smiled, knowing she couldn't see it. "I don't think so."

"Come on. Personally, I think someone would have to be awful full of themselves to hide out like this."

"I so value your opinion," he said dryly, watching a flash of irritation cross her face.

"I probably wouldn't even recognize you, you know. You're probably some famous classical pianist that no one knows unless they pay attention to that stuff. Which I don't, by the way."

"Nice try."

She put her hands on her hips and peered up the stairs,

her eyes narrowed. "You ever see that movie with Mel Gibson. *The Man Without a Face?*"

"Who's Mel Gibson?"

She looked completely stunned, and he found he enjoyed saying outrageous things just to see what her expression would be. "You're joking, right?"

"Right." She took a step toward him, and he withdrew. He didn't trust her suddenly. "Stop there."

"Oh, Mac," she said, her voice tinged with disappointment. "I'd never hurt you."

You already have. Looking at you hurts me.

"Good night, Rose," he said, standing and moving up the stairs, his bare feet silent on the cold, cold marble.

"You know," she shouted up the stairs, "you've got to trust someone someday."

He kept going, smiling at her words that were so wrong. He couldn't trust anyone. Not even himself.

He found that out the next night when he stood at the top of the stairs wondering what the hell he was doing there. He'd thought about her all day, the way she'd looked peering up the stairs, daring him to reveal himself, sounding and looking so tough when he knew all he needed to say was "boo" and she'd scream in terror. She'd been scared to death the night they'd bumped into each other; he'd heard it in her voice. God, she'd been so soft in that instant of contact. He missed the feel of a woman in his arms, the smooth skin, the sexy curves, the intoxicating scent. What a jerk to offer his hand knowing what it would do to him. Christ, he was a masochist.

Now he thought, what the hell, play a little game that would go nowhere. Flirt with her. Nothing could happen. Ever. And so, when he heard her moving toward the front door, he stepped down, revealing feet and shins.

"Are you naked up there?"

He laughed. He hadn't smiled so much in years. Rose stood at the bottom of the stairs, her long hair pulled loosely back, a riot of curls struggling to be free of her inadequate hair clip. He could see her face in the glow of the security lights that made it as bright as daylight outside his house. She stared up at him, looking irritated and curious and beautiful. What the hell was he doing sitting on this step? What happened to his resolve? One pretty, funny girl and he was going to throw everything away?

"I'm not naked."

"Let's see a little knee."

"I don't think so."

She sighed in mock disappointment and went to the door. "Nice legs," she said, and let herself out.

For four nights he played the game, telling himself he was insane. He moved down another step and another, until nearly his entire body was revealed. He couldn't have said what, other than boredom, made him play the game. All he knew was that he couldn't wait until the moment she walked by the stairs and looked up, an expression of pleasant surprise on her face when she'd see he'd moved lower.

"You're getting mighty brave, Mac."

"I'd say you're the brave one. You don't know what you'll see when you look up here. You don't know who—or what—I am."

She pretended to shiver. "You're not fat and not old. I'm pretty certain you are fully human. Your legs are hairy, but not too hairy. You're probably ordinary and I'll be disappointed. This will only be fun if you're hideous or gorgeous. So," she said, cocking her head to one side, "which is it."

"I'm the scariest thing you've ever seen."

Her eyes flashed. "Gorgeous. Nothing is scarier than a gorgeous guy who knows it." With that, she left.

* * *

Rose hadn't looked forward to work like this since her first days at Anthony's. It had nothing to do with cooking and everything to do with her secretive client. This little game they were playing, this flirting, was only increasing her curiosity about him. From the chest down, at least fully dressed, he was way more than ordinary. So far he'd dressed in sweat shorts and a T-shirt—without shoes or socks. He had nice legs; she hadn't been kidding about that. Fascinating legs, strong and hairy and long. And he was blond, another clue. Rich, young, tall, blond, played the piano. If Mac wasn't careful, she'd figure it out. Just for fun she'd gone on-line and done a search on concert pianists. The only blond one she found was Russian, and Mac was about as Russian as she was.

Tonight's step would reveal his face, and she wondered if he had the courage to make it. Probably not. The day dragged by. It was Friday, and she had to make his meals for Saturday and Sunday. The cooking part of this job was a bit boring, and she had to admit she missed the craziness of Anthony's. A Friday night there was wonderful chaos, with Anthony running in and out of the kitchen about a hundred times to make certain everything was going smoothly. She missed her assistants, kids still in college or high school with enough energy to make it through a Friday night then go out partying. She missed her customers who would insist she come out and say hello. But all that paled when she thought of her restaurant and the money she was making every week cooking for Mac. She now figured that in one year, not five, she'd have enough money to buy a restaurant of her own financed mostly by herself.

While she was here, she planned to try different recipes, use Mac as a guinea pig. He'd complained only once, and Rose couldn't say that she blamed him.

She'd read about salmon recipes in Sardinia with a light white sauce over penne. It sounded wonderful, but her version stopped way short of wonderful. He hadn't really complained, just written a note on his dirty-dishes tray: "Take that off the menu, please." Polite, young, rich, and probably good-looking. With that voice. And a face she just might see tonight. No one that incredible from the neck down could be ugly on top. Could they?

Rose placed the last of the meals in containers and put them in the fridge, then looked around the kitchen to make sure all was in order.

"Ro-ose."

He called to her from the dark, a voice shadowed with mystery.

"Oh, I'm so scared," she said to herself, fighting a little tingle that tried to make its way up her spine. It was silly, really. He was just a guy afraid to show his face. But why? Because he was hideously deformed? Because she'd recognize him? Again she heard him call out.

"I'm coming," she said. "Ready or not."

She walked down the hall silly with anticipation even as she told herself he wouldn't dare reveal himself, not after taking such ridiculous precautions to prevent her from ever seeing him. When she got to the stairs, she looked up.

"Ha! I knew you were too chicken."

And then he ran down the stairs toward her, a flash of a man, a horrible, disfigured man. Gruesomely horrific features, mashed and indistinct, a head without hair . . . a head in a nylon stocking. Of course, by the time her mind had registered all that, she'd run back toward the kitchen screaming at the top of her lungs, screaming way too loud to hear him laughing behind her.

She turned, mad as hell, to see only his dim outline in the darkness. "Very funny, jerk."

"Aw, come on, Rose. You only got what you deserve." He was laughing at her through the stocking, his voice sounding slightly muffled. "Kiss me," he said in a deep, frightening voice. "Don't you think I'm handsome?"

"You're probably wearing that stocking to hide something really awful."

"I am." He'd taken the mask off; she could tell by the way he sounded. And he was closer, in her space. She could feel him and hear him, and she knew if she reached up just a few inches, she'd touch his face. And so she did, just to scare him for once.

He jerked away, then stilled. Then leaned forward, allowing the contact.

"No scars," Rose said, her fingertips moving over his forehead, fingertips somehow alive with sensitivity. "You need a shave. You have a cleft chin, and a big mouth." Because he was smiling. "Whoa. That's some honker you've got there," she said as her index finger traveled the length of his nicely shaped nose.

"You think so?" he asked, sounding slightly wounded.

"No. Actually, you feel pretty much"—*Gorgeous*— "normal." Rose dropped her hand because she was feeling anything but normal at the moment. There's something that always happened to Rose's blood the instant she became aroused; it would thicken and slow and pool. It was delicious and warm and could scare the hell out of her when it happened unexpectedly. He must have sensed it, because in the pitch black of the hall he sure couldn't have seen it, but somehow he knew he could lean forward and kiss her and she would let him. And he did and she did. It was short, no tongue, just his lips slowly mouthing hers, his face nudging a little closer, his nose lightly brushing her cheek, his breath puffing her face.

She moved back, just enough to break contact. "I could sue you for sexual harassment," she said.

"Am I harassing you?"

She stared at his black outline and knew she was the biggest idiot on earth because if he said in that moment he wanted to make love, she would have. She didn't know his name, didn't know what he looked like, but no man—ever—had made her as hot as she was right now. It was his voice, his kiss, his laugh. Man oh man. She was a nice girl, the type who would almost always love someone before she jumped into bed with him. And here she was, horny as heck, from a kiss. A voice. A man in the dark.

She answered him by grabbing the side of his head and drawing him to her and kissing him silly. With tongues and groans and hands that started to wander. Her hands. He was just standing there, she realized after about thirty seconds. That stopped her cold.

"Now *that* was sexual harassment," she joked, laughing as if she hadn't lost control with a complete stranger.

"That was something all right."

Oh, God. Could he have said anything worse?

She laughed, a nervous little sound, and brushed her hair back with a shaking hand. "What that was, was a mistake. Even if it was just a joke, I shouldn't have done that. You're my boss, after all."

"Yeah. Right." He'd backed up a step.

"Okay, then. I've got to go. Have a good weekend." She scuttled around him, heading for the door. When she closed it, she leaned against it, pushing her head back hard. "Shit. Shit shit shit."

"Shit!"

"I know, I know. I can't believe I did that. Can you?" Rose said into the phone. Thank God for Jenn.

"I could believe *I* would do that, but not you. And all he could say was 'that was something all right'? What a jerk."

"No. He wasn't a jerk, I was."

"Rose, honey, don't forget who kissed who first."

"True, but I didn't have to attack him after. I'm so embarrassed. I don't know how the heck I'm going to be able to show my face there on Monday. I can't quit. I need the money."

"This is the strangest relationship I've ever heard of. I'm so jealous."

Rose laughed. "For all I know I was kissing some ugly guy. The funny thing is, it wouldn't matter. I've heard of people falling in love over letters. I always thought it was a bunch of bunk, that once they saw each other they'd realize they'd made a terrible mistake. But I really don't think it would matter what Mac looked like. I think I would still have kissed him."

"Let's not get crazy, here. You can say that because you can imagine some gorgeous guy in your head. But if he was a real creep, you wouldn't feel the way you do."

"Jenn, you are so shallow."

"And so are you."

Jenn was right. Until now, Rose had followed certain standards. Seeing a man before kissing him was usually one of them. If she found out he was butt-ugly, would she feel the same?

"You're probably right. But I may never know. I really think he means it when he says I'll never see him."

"Listen, Rose, this guy is a weirdo. Class A psycho man. Nobody hides out like that. Nobody kisses women in the dark after scaring them with some creepy mask. What the heck is wrong with you? If I were you, I'd quit, beg Tony for my job back and go on with my life."

"Gee, when you say it like that it sounds downright sick."

"Well?"

Rose let out a sigh. "I know what it sounds like. I know. But Mac's not weird. He's . . . nice."

"Oh my God."

"It's hard to understand."

Rose could almost see Jenn biting her lip. "Just be careful, okay?"

"Okay." Rose pressed the phone off and laid it on the couch. Was Mac some psycho? She'd thought wearing the stocking was actually funny, in hindsight. But now, with Jenn fueling her doubts, it *was* awfully . . . creepy. She shook her head. If Mac had been some deranged murderer, he would have offed her before now. Unless he was playing some sort of sicko cat-and-mouse game, gaining her confidence, making her like him, before locking her in the basement and torturing her.

Maybe she *should* quit.

The phone rang, and her heart sped up tenfold. Probably Jenn.

"Hello."

"Hey, it's me, Mac."

"Oh. Hi." Rose squeezed her eyes shut as the memory of her kissing him flooded her.

"I was wondering, if you're not busy tomorrow night, if you could . . ." She heard him swear, but at a distance, as if he'd taken the phone away from his mouth. "I go for walks on the beach. At night. I thought I could use some company."

"Ummm."

"Yeah. Forget it."

"No, it's not that. I have plans, that's all."

"Sure. Okay. See you Monday." He hung up, and Rose smiled. Mac wasn't a crazy killer; he was just a lonely guy who was maybe a little bit weird. Maybe a lot weird.

But Rose was starting to think she liked her guys a little strange.

Chapter 5

*Seared scallop gratin surprise with caramelized onions,
carrot puree, wild mushrooms and roasted asparagus,
$29.00*

Rose couldn't stop crying. She just couldn't. It was
the saddest song she'd ever heard. And that little girl was
so adorable, so alive, and now she was dead. She wished
she'd never turned on the television, never watched stupid Oprah Winfrey and her stupid sad show.

"Why are you crying?"

Rose jerked and wiped her face, whipping around to
stare at the camera. "How long have you been watching?"
she asked, narrowing her red-rimmed, watery eyes.

"I just turned it on and heard you crying. What's
happened?" The concern in his voice was really very
sweet.

Rose started laughing. "I was just watching television and it was so sad. I cry at Hallmark card commer-
cials, too, so don't worry about me." Rose had been
working for Mac for two weeks, and he rarely turned
on the kitchen camera. Just her luck he wanted to say
something right when she was in the middle of a good

cry. "Oprah had on a mother whose daughter died of cancer, and they played a song. It was the saddest most beautiful song I ever heard, and it got to me."

"A song?"

She thought she heard disbelief in his voice. "The song was about the girl. There's this company that writes songs for terminally ill children, and it was one of those songs. It really was incredible," she said, wiping her nose with a paper towel.

"Do you remember the girl's name?"

"Laura, Leah, something like that. Why?"

The camera shut off.

Shit.

Declan picked up the phone and hit speed dial.

"Angel's Songs," came the cheerful voice.

"I need to talk to Sylvia Wright."

"And who may I ask is calling?"

"Just tell her it's one of her writers."

He heard a click that told him he'd been put on hold. And then he heard his song, "Leah's Song," being played as the hold music.

Shit.

"Sylvia Wright."

"What the hell is going on, Sylvia?"

"Is this Mac?"

"Hell yes, it's Mac. Why am I hearing my song everywhere?"

"Correction, Angel's Songs' song. You know that. Actually, the rights are now owned by Ellen Lang."

Declan slumped back in his chair, the air knocked from him. "You're kidding."

"This is going to be one of the largest funding campaigns we've ever had. All profits go to cancer research after we get our ten percent. It's a fabulous opportunity."

He could tell she was nervous by how fast she was talking, but it didn't matter how nervous she was; the deed was done.

"You didn't think to let me know?"

"Well . . ."

"Damn it all, Sylvia."

"I'm sorry, Mac. I knew you'd be angry. You know we're within our legal rights to do anything we want with the song as long as it doesn't affect our nonprofit status."

"This was not part of our agreement," he said, his voice edged with steel.

"Mac." She let out a sigh. "I couldn't pass this up, and I was afraid if you knew, you would object . . ."

"You're damned right I'd object."

"Mac, listen, the *Today* show called this morning and wants to do a piece on us. You can't buy this kind of publicity. For the record, it wasn't an easy decision. I know how much you value your privacy."

Declan sat up straight. "I wouldn't want that privacy breached in any way. Is that clear?"

"Since I don't know who you are, I doubt that's a problem."

Declan didn't like her affronted tone. He knew better than anyone that if someone wanted information, they could get it. He'd hidden his trail well, but it wasn't an infallible plan. Someone curious enough could discover who wrote "Leah's Song." He let out a shaking breath.

"Do you know what the Langs' plans are for the song?"

"I do know they are in discussions with several labels," she said reluctantly.

"What?" Oh, God, this was turning into a nightmare.

"Apparently there are some pirated versions out there and . . ."

"You're kidding."

"The Langs want to make it available for wider distribution."

Declan dropped his head into his hand and started laughing.

"This is a tremendous opportunity for us. I promise you I will do everything in my power to protect your privacy."

"All right. You do that. By the way, consider our relationship terminated." He heard her try to say something before he angrily cut her off and threw his phone hard into the couch across from him.

Maybe nothing would happen. Maybe it would all end and no one would get curious about who wrote the song for Leah. He remembered that song so well, remembered the little girl he wrote it for. She'd reminded him of his brother for some reason, and he'd written that song, more than all the others, from his heart. He'd sent it out knowing he'd written something special, gratified that it would ease her parents' pain. Never had he thought it would go further than that.

And perhaps it wouldn't.

From somewhere below, he heard a loud bang. Quickly, he turned on the monitor, relief flooding him when he saw Rose still in the kitchen working on his dinner. He liked having her here, despite the danger. He'd been trying like hell not to talk to her too much, but when he saw her crying, he couldn't ignore that. Man, when she cried, she *cried.* She moved out of range, and he flicked off the monitor. He refused to turn completely into some voyeuristic creep. He had to hand it to her; she'd been a good sport about everything. Sometimes, he'd turn on the camera just to see how long it would take before she noticed. She'd turn, fire in her eyes, and start yammering away and threatening to quit. And then she'd crack a smile and laugh. Thank God he'd never met her before, because he would have fallen in love and ruined her life.

Declan swore beneath his breath, not liking where his thoughts were going. That was one thing about being alone; he had entirely too much time to think about how soft her lips were against his, about how she tasted, about how hard he'd gotten when she'd kissed him. A tidal wave of lust that nearly knocked him to his knees.

He stripped down to his skivvies, ready to work out until he dropped from exhaustion. He didn't want to think about "Leah's Song," and he sure as hell didn't want to sit around lusting after his cook. He put in his old Nirvana CD, cranked up the volume, then jerked on his lifting belts, grabbed up a set of weights, and started working out as he stood in front of his window overlooking the ocean. His mind went blessedly blank, just as he'd intended.

Rose walked around the deserted house, looking for the source of that bang, but each room she entered was completely empty and couldn't possibly have been the source of such a loud noise. She decided to go outside and talk to Paul to find out if he'd heard it. She opened the front door and looked down, horrified.

"Oh, my God." Paul was lying on the ground, his head completely bloody, and next to him was a large light fixture that used to hang above the door.

"Paul? Can you hear me?" Not even a moan escaped the prone guard. "Oh, this is bad. You're really hurt." She grabbed his radio, her hand shaking as she quickly figured out how to work the thing. "Mac? Mac? This is Rose. Mac?" All she heard was a light hissing noise. She tried again with the same result. "Stupid recluse." She dropped the radio. "I'll be right back, Paul. I'm going to get help." She ran into the room where she'd conducted her phone interview with Mac, grabbed the phone, and dialed 911.

"911. What is your emergency?"

"I'm at 357 Marlin Road, and a security guard has been badly injured. A light fixture fell on him."

"Is he conscious, ma'am?"

"No. It looks pretty bad. There's lots of blood."

"I'm sending out a rescue now." Rose could hear her telling the rescue personnel the information, so she hung up and ran to the foyer.

"Mac! Mac!" Rose jumped up and down in front of the camera before noticing it wasn't on. Rose wanted to throw a brick at the camera, and then throw one at Mac. Paul was dying out there, and he was locked up by himself somewhere on the second floor. Rose eyed the staircase, gripped with indecision.

"Oh, hell." If she lost her job, then fine. She had to tell Mac that his security guard might be lying dead or dying on his front steps. Besides, she needed to get poor Paul a blanket or something. She knew better than to move him, but at least she could cover him up. Wasn't that what you did to prevent shock? Without another thought, she raced up the stairs, yelling for Mac the entire way. When she reached the top of the landing, she heard the low thumping bass of a stereo and followed it down a long hall. As she passed the rooms, she couldn't help but notice that they were as empty as the rest of the house. What kind of freak was this guy, anyway?

Finally, she reached the last door in the hall. No wonder he couldn't hear her. He was playing Nirvana so loud it was almost painful. She banged on the door anyway, not wanting to barge in on him. Afraid to, really, because despite everything, she didn't want to lose her job and maybe if he heard her, she could avoid seeing him. He'd lower the music, and they could talk through the door.

But no. He didn't hear her even when she hurt her hand for all her banging. "Okay. Here goes nothing."

She opened the door.

"Oh my God." It came out like a whisper. After all, it wasn't every day a person saw perfection in the male form. *Yummy.* His back, thick with muscle and shining from sweat, was to her as he did a series of pull-ups in time to the music. He was long and lean and had enough muscles to share with a few of her old boyfriends, and they were all exposed to her nicely shocked eyes. His hair was a wavy reddish blond and pulled back into a neat ponytail. Rose blinked and shook her head, mortified that she'd taken time to stare at him—lust after him, really—when Paul was downstairs bleeding to death. Eying the stereo, she walked over and turned down the volume.

Mac immediately spun around.

Her heart beat a million times in that split second when her eyes told her brain something that simply couldn't be. "Oh. Oh, oh, oh. It's you. But it can't be you." Her mouth opened and closed a few times before Rose could finally say, "You're supposed to be dead."

"You're fired," he said, glaring at her before jerking up a towel and drying himself off with angry movements.

"Why aren't you dead? You're dead." Even as she spoke, Rose on some level knew how ridiculous she sounded. Clearly, Declan McDonald was not dead. It was like finding Elvis or Princess Diana or John-John Kennedy standing here. It was *that* big. Declan Mc-Donald was alive. *Declan McDonald.* Then: *Oh my God, I kissed Declan McDonald!* Not that she'd ever been such a big fan, but everyone knew who he was: *People* magazine's Sexiest Man Alive two years in a row, one of the most talented songwriters, with the voice that ran through you like . . .

Hot fizzy soda.

Now it all made sense, she thought, relieved she hadn't been reacting sexually to an eighty-year-old man. Any woman with a pulse got hot and bothered over Declan McDonald. Right now her pulse was beating a fast staccato: *Take me, take me now.*

He just stood there, this Adonis out of every woman's fantasy, looking majorly pissed.

"Hey! Why *aren't* you dead?" When he'd disappeared in the Colorado mountains it had caused a major uproar. Search parties spent weeks looking for him, then looking for his body. Finally, his teary-eyed mother— his *lying* teary-eyed mother it turns out—pronounced him dead. For weeks, television had been deluged with biographies, interviews, and specials about the multi-Grammy-award-winning songwriter/singer. The major networks covered his funeral live, and even Rose had shed a couple of tears over it all. Now here he was, alive and well, looking mad at her just because she'd discovered he *was* a creep.

"Sorry to disappoint you." He stared at her as if she were somehow to blame for his lying to the world. "Christ. This day couldn't get worse. I am so *fucked.*"

Rose cringed at the venom in his tone. "I won't tell anyone."

He laughed. "Yeah. Right."

"I mean it. I don't reveal secrets," Rose said with total honesty.

"What are you doing up here anyway? I thought I made it pretty clear that you weren't to see me."

Rose's jaw dropped in horror. "Oh my God, I forgot. Paul!" She began running in place, looking around for the blanket she'd come up for, her ponytail whipping around. Spying one folded at the end of the bed, she rushed over, grabbed it, and began running from the room.

"Paul the security guard?" she heard him call.

"He's lying bleeding to death in front of your house." She could hear him following her, bare feet on the hardwood floor. "The light fell on him. The one above your door. The ambulance will be here any minute."

Behind her, his footsteps stopped abruptly, and she turned to look back at him. "Aren't you coming down?" She watched a dozen emotions cross his face before he shook his head.

"I can't."

Declan McDonald was a coward. Behind that beautiful male body and that equally beautiful face was a coward. "Fine," she said, rushing down the stairs. "I'm not fired, by the way."

"You are," she heard him call out, but she just smiled. He couldn't fire her for fear she'd reveal he was alive. She would never do it, not if he asked her not to, but he didn't know that. Her job just got infinitely more secure.

Declan peered out the window making certain he wasn't seen as he watched the ambulance roll down his long driveway. He felt about as low a being as the scumbags who had forced this lifestyle on him. It didn't help that Rose had looked at him the way his mother used to when he was kid and up to no good. Disappointed. God! He couldn't stand that look. He could hear her coming up the stairs, making no attempt to be quiet. She was stomping her pint-sized feet up his marble staircase, fury in every step. It should have been refreshing to have a woman look at him with something other than feral lust, but for some reason he found Rose's disappointment maddening.

"He's alive. Not that you care." She stood there at the threshold of his prison, arms crossed and mad as hell, one leg extended with foot tapping out a nice little beat. Tap-tap, tap-tap. She wore her chef's outfit, which made her look about five-foot-nothing and about as shapeless as a roll of paper towels.

"Of course I care. And what are you still doing here? I fired you." Somehow, in the minutes between his first angry dismissal and now, his words had lost their potency. He realized he wouldn't fire her. Couldn't.

She lifted her chin and stared into his eyes. "If you fire me, I'll stop at the first phone I see and call the *National Enquirer.*"

She was a lousy liar. "No you won't."

That threw her. She shifted, and her brows came together in a funny little frown.

"Yes I will."

He walked toward her until she was forced to lift her face to keep eye contact with him and peered into her eyes. He stared and stared until she faltered, until those dark brown eyes flickered and her mouth quivered as she fought not to smile. He could have stared at her forever, capturing every detail that he'd seen only as a fuzzy picture in his TV monitor. She wasn't beautiful, but Rose had something else—a face that was nice to look at and skin so smooth it didn't look real. She wore no makeup that he could see, and yet each feature was sharply defined, including that mouth he'd kissed and now found he couldn't take his eyes off.

"Okay. You win," she said with a grin he found incredibly appealing. "I won't tell, but you still can't fire me. And don't think you can use your celebrity charm to get your way all the time because it won't work. Frankly," she said, looking down at her finely pared fingernails, "I never was much of a fan."

"Oh, really?" He raised an eyebrow and crossed his arms to accent his biceps, a gesture he'd used in the past that drove women crazy.

"And I think you look goofy like that," she shot back as she plopped herself onto his couch. Settling in for a long visit, so it seemed. "So, what's your story? Why are you doing this?"

"I'm just a guy who wants a little privacy." He looked pointedly at the door.

"Yeah, well, we all want a lot of things." She was ignoring him. One thing he wasn't used to was being ignored. "Maybe it's none of my business, but I think what you're doing is pretty rotten."

He could feel his anger growing. She didn't know anything about his life, about what could force a man to hide away from the world, to live a life so desolate he thought he might go crazy from it. "You're right, it's none of your business, and I really don't give a flying—"

"You swear too much."

"—flying *fuck* what you think." She cringed. Good. Except he really didn't want to fire her or have her quit. What he really wanted was to pretend she'd never wandered up here and seen him.

"Declan McDonald," she said slowly, as if tasting his name, her eyes scanning his face. "What are you doing living like this?"

He shrugged, acting casual, as if he liked this hell he'd created for himself. "It's temporary."

"Hiding out? You mean someday you're going to announce to the world, 'Hey, I'm not dead. Sorry, everyone, for causing so much trouble.' "

Man, she was busting his chops. "Yeah, whatever you say. I planned two maybe three years. I don't know what I planned, but I'm not ready yet to go public. No way in hell."

"Do you even have a clue what happened after you supposedly died? All the people who were crushed because they thought you were dead?"

"I know exactly what happened. A bunch of people who never met me claimed to mourn my passing. And another bunch of people who couldn't stand me claimed they loved me. It was all bullshit."

No wonder they couldn't stand him, Rose thought; the guy's a jerk. She stood, walked to the door, then turned, arms folded belligerently over her chest. She liked him better when she could use her imagination about him. "Well. Am I fired or not?"

"Not."

"Should I bring dinner up in person or do you want me to use the dumbwaiter?"

"The dumbwaiter is fine."

Rose had to stop herself from rolling her eyes. "So we're supposed to pretend this never happened? That I didn't see you, is that it?"

"That's it."

"What are you so afraid of? I already know who you are."

He looked down at the floor, hands on hips. The backs of his hands still glistened with sweat from his work-out, and the waistband of his shorts was stained dark. His shorts were loose and a ratty maroon, all faded with a logo she could hardly read: Westfield High. She smiled a little to think that this icon still wore old shorts from high school. She didn't want to notice things like that, little details that made him more human.

"I've got enough going on right now," he said finally. "I don't need any more complications."

"What, you're concerned I might interrupt your workout sessions?"

He tilted his head and gave her a look. "I work on my music all day, sometimes all night. One of the reasons I hired you was because I wasn't eating right, sometimes not at all."

"You mean you're writing? What are you doing with all the songs?"

He looked over his shoulder at a thick pile of paper stacked up on the baby grand piano. "Two years' worth right there." He sounded sad, and Rose fought an inner battle to keep thinking of him as a self-centered jerk.

The things this guy could do with his voice should be criminal. "I need to work, and I don't need interruptions from anyone."

"God forbid anyone interrupt the great Declan McDonald."

He took a couple of steps toward her, jutting out his perfectly clefted chin, then pointed a finger, jabbing the air like some sort of marine drill sergeant. "That's what I don't need. I don't need attitude or sarcasm or some adoring fan hovering over me."

"I don't even like you," Rose shot back, meaning every syllable. "Personally, I think your songs are sappy, commercial crap."

His nostrils flared, and his eyes narrowed, right before he placed his very large hands near her neck. Rose, for just a fraction of a second, was truly terrified. Not even Paul was here to save her from a man who could have gone off the deep end for all she knew. Then he started laughing, and he gave her a little shake, as if completely overcome with the hilarity of someone not liking his work.

"You are one hot ticket," he said, dropping his arms even as he continued to laugh. He stared at her, his eyes crinkled and lit with humor, and Rose felt herself being drawn in, sucked in hard. If he'd bent his head and kissed her, she would have wrapped her arms around his neck and her legs around his torso and mauled him silly. She realized he'd stopped smiling, realized his eyes were dropping to her mouth, which was open and panting and probably drooling.

He stepped back, suddenly finding her shoulder interesting. "I think it's a very bad idea for you to come up here."

Rose composed herself as well as she could, praying he didn't see, but knowing he had, how easy she would have hopped into bed with him. Her grandmother would have been horrified. *That's it, girl, think of Nonna.*

"Rosalie, you be a good girl, now." She hadn't always been good, but she'd never slept with someone she didn't know.

"I don't want to be your girlfriend. Heck, I don't even want to be your friend. I'm your chef. But I think now that I know your big secret we can have a more normal working relationship. Frankly, the cameras give me the creeps."

He stepped back even farther, spinning around to search for something, then grabbed up his shirt and put it on. *Probably the last time you'll see that chest live and in person. Pity.*

"Let me be frank," he said, buttoning up his loose white cotton oxford. "I don't think we could continue a casual working relationship if you came up here every day to chat."

Rose agreed wholeheartedly, but refused to let him know she lusted after him. He was arrogant enough by far. "Believe me, I think I could restrain myself from—" And then she remembered her conversation with Jenn: *"What happens if he has a face and body to match his voice. What then?" "I'll jump his bones."*

Rose cleared her throat. "I could restrain myself," she repeated hesitantly.

"Well," he said. "Maybe I couldn't."

Chapter 6

"Basically, Ms. Orucci is going to talk about your efforts to raise money and awareness for leukemia, and then we're going to play about thirty seconds of the video."

Ellen nodded at the assistant and took another sip of coffee, outwardly composed. It was getting so the more she talked about her daughter, the less it hurt, almost as if she were talking about something that hadn't torn her heart apart. She wore a navy blue business suit she believed was the perfect blend of severity and femininity. She felt in control, by now an old hand at interviews and dealing with the press. "How long will the segment last?"

"We've scheduled four minutes. I know that sounds like a short time, but in TV time it's a fairly long piece. We have some flexibility, and it could be longer. It's amazing what we can fit into four minutes." The young woman darted a look to the clock. "Why don't we get set. We're going to sit you in a chair, promo the spot. You'll see the camera light go on. Just smile and look pleasant. Then we go to commercial, and after that you're on. Any questions?"

"None."

Ellen followed the woman, fighting a feeling of euphoria. She couldn't have asked for anything better than a four-minute spot on the *Today* show. It was even better than *Oprah*, because it added a real legitimacy to her campaign, and it was a great place to debut the video for "Leah's Song." Since the song's release on Merit Records two weeks ago, it had made a steady rise up the music charts and now sat at number twenty-one. Millions were being raised for the cause. Matthew's apathy was the only thing that dampened her pleasure. He'd refused to participate in anything related to "Leah's Song." Ellen could only hope he'd come around once the state legislature broke for the summer.

Kate Orucci walked over to her, hand extended. "I'm so pleased you could come in today," she said warmly before sitting down and adjusting her earpiece. "I'm going to start with an introduction, facts and figures about leukemia, before we get to the questions." She looked up to the camera where a man in headphones was giving her a countdown. "Here we go."

"We're back and here with Ellen Lang whose daughter Leah died just a little over a month ago of leukemia. Though mortality rates for leukemia have decreased dramatically in recent years, more than two thousand children die each year of this disease, and the medical community agrees more has to be done. Since her daughter's death, Mrs. Lang has turned tragedy into triumph by single-handedly raising more than three million dollars for cancer research, mostly thanks to 'Leah's Song,' a song written for her daughter. Why don't you tell me about the song?"

Ellen smiled. "The song was written for Leah by a company called Angel's Songs, who writes songs for terminally ill children. But the song far exceeded our expectations."

"I'd like to add that your husband is Matthew Lang,

Tennessee's lieutenant governor, and who some tap as the next governor of that state."

Ellen fought not to frown. What did her husband's political aspirations have to do with her campaign to raise money for leukemia? "Yes. He also was amazed by the power of 'Leah's Song.'"

Kate leaned forward. "There's actually quite a mystery surrounding this song. No one knows who wrote it, do they?"

"That's right. We've tried to find out, to thank the person, but not even Angel's Songs knows who the author is. Apparently it was part of this person's contract to remain anonymous."

"And no one has come forward? This song is generating an enormous amount of money. Do you expect someone to come out of the woodwork and try to claim some of the booty?"

Ellen smiled. "Of course, we considered that possibility, which is why we bought the rights to the song. Part of the proceeds does go to Angel's Songs. And the woman who actually sings the song is receiving a small royalty as well."

"Why don't we watch the video. I have to admit, the first time I saw this, I cried like a baby. I think anyone with children would be affected the same way."

Ellen relaxed as the video was played. It was a mix of shots of her daughter playing and the singer, who turned out to be an ethereally beautiful young woman with waist-length, brilliant blond hair. Interspersed with those images were still shots of her daughter as she declined. As always when she heard the song, Ellen had to fight the tears that threatened.

"That is incredibly moving," Kate said. "The person who wrote that song must have lost a child, don't you think?"

"All I know is I'd like to thank whoever it is in person. It's been a real godsend. The Leukemia Society informed me yesterday that this is the single largest fund-raising campaign in the history of its existence."

"And I imagine it will only get bigger. I want to thank you for speaking with us. By the way," Kate said, turning toward a camera, "if you want to contribute to cancer research, a phone number, web site, and address are on the screen now. Next up, summer cooking . . ."

Ellen let out a long breath. It had gone perfectly.

Rose looked over at Declan, trying to figure him out. He sat on a barstool by the kitchen's island wearing shorts and a baggy T-shirt. He was barefoot and looked tired, as if he'd been up all night. His jaw was covered with golden beard growth, his hair tied loosely with what looked like a piece of string. He sure didn't look like some big star at the moment. He looked—besides incredibly sexy—like a regular down-on-his-luck male model. Rose grinned, then looked away so he wouldn't see her smiling. After a week, she still couldn't believe she worked for Declan McDonald. The worst part was not telling anyone. God, how she wanted to tell Jenn, tell anyone. She was bursting at the seams with wanting to spill her guts. But she'd promised not to, so she wouldn't. *Cursed promise.*

The first day after discovering him, Rose didn't care that she hadn't heard a peep out of him. It felt so strange knowing he was up there, probably half naked and sweaty, working out his frustrations by pumping iron. Pumping, pumping. The sight of him doing those pull-ups was seared into her brain, which refused to listen to her when she told it again and again that he was definitely off limits. Out of her league. Carried too much baggage—God, did this guy carry a load of problems. He'd never know that the night she'd discovered him, she'd pulled out her old Declan McDonald CD and listened to it. Twice.

By the third day, she was beginning to get irritated. He hadn't even turned on the camera to try to sneak a peek at her. What did he think, she was going to turn into one of those rabid fans that used to follow him around all the time? That she'd become obsessed with him? She *had* gone to the library and looked up *People* magazine's biography printed after his supposed death, but that was simple curiosity, not obsession. Rose completely discarded the idea that he was lusting after her. Yeah, *right*. The man who had dated Julia Roberts and Nicole Kidman, among a long string of super models and other gorgeous creatures, would not be interested in Rosalie Pisano. *People* described him as, of course, sexy, but also as aloof and private. *More than you know,* she thought as she'd read that part. She wanted to add arrogant and antisocial to the magazine's list of attributes. Over the past few days his silence had become difficult to take.

On day three, he symbolically broke the silence by sending down a note via the dumbwaiter: Turkey Club instead of pita. Thanks.

She stared at the note, then glanced up at the camera almost hoping it would be on. The light was off. More cursive notes followed: Good salad. Liked the bread.

Each one she stared at, then crumpled up. For some crazy reason, she felt as though she'd lost a friend. She missed catching him with the camera on, missed their little conversations.

When he requested less salt in his gazpacho soup, she wrote back: Write better songs.

And so it went for five days until the phone rang, and then less than a minute later, he called down to ask if he could join her in the kitchen to watch the *Today* show.

"Thanks for letting me join you," he said with a voice that sounded as if he'd just woken up, and settled himself into the chair.

Rose just turned up the volume. Most times, the TV was a drone in the background unless something caught her eye. Working completely alone was more difficult than she'd anticipated. She was used to the loud bustling of Anthony's, not this tomblike atmosphere. Every chop, every scrape of a pan, every breath she took seemed amplified in this cavernous kitchen. So she'd bought a little portable television to keep her company.

It took maybe a minute for Rose to figure out that Declan was the one who wrote the mysterious "Leah's Song." She looked at him, but his head was down studying the kitchen's spotless black and white tiles. He didn't even look up when the video was played. Rose wouldn't even have thought he was listening, until she noticed his white-knuckled grip on the stool's edge and the way he kept flexing his jaw. By the time the piece was over, his face glistened with sweat, and he looked so damned vulnerable Rose felt her heart turn to mush.

"They won't find you," she said softly.

He looked up, something deep and painful in his eyes. "I've told myself that, but I'm just kidding myself. It's only a matter of time. I should just get it over with. But the thought . . ."

"It would be crazy, wouldn't it?"

"Insane."

Rose shut the TV off and sat across from him, elbows on the island, hands fisted under her chin. "Didn't you think of that?"

"I fucked up so bad, I can't believe I did it." He looked up to the ceiling and let out a long, half-hearted scream.

"Why did you do it? You had to know you couldn't hide forever." Rose half expected him to get up and leave without answering her. Instead he gave her a long look, then finally smiled.

"You ever have anyone take a picture of you going to the bathroom?"

Rose laughed. "Actually, yes. A boyfriend thought it was hilarious. Ha ha."

"How about a stranger in a public rest room looking over the stall?"

"No, of course not. I hate to say this because I'm sure you've heard it a hundred times, but what did you expect? You're an entertainer, a celebrity. Doesn't it come with the territory? And it's not as if you're the only one the paparazzi followed around. You're not unique."

He looked disgusted with her assessment. "You think I wanted that kind of life? I just wanted to write music. I really thought I was doing something special, making people happy. Hell, making good money. But then it turned, got all screwed up. I don't know when it changed, when the paparazzi started targeting me, but they did. Every date, every walk, every time I ate in a restaurant. Every time I wiped my nose or took a piss was documented."

"So you ran away?"

He shook his head, and she got distracted by the way his ponytail flopped behind him. He just wasn't the ponytail hippy kind of guy. In every picture she'd seen him in, his hair had been cut short, though in every photo he managed to look as if he needed a shave. In fact, at this moment he had about two-days' beard growth sprinkling his face, which did nothing to soften that granite jaw of his. It came to her then that with short hair he looked like one of those forties recruiting posters of a cleft-chinned, hard-faced marine. He didn't have pretty-boy good looks; he was handsome in the classic shaving-guy way. Lips that were full but not creepy, lashes long and straight shadowing those mysterious dark blue eyes. He gave her a half grin with those lips, and she suddenly found she wanted to take a nibble. Bite. Lick. Suck. Rose cleared her throat. "You know, you really need a haircut."

He laughed, deep from his belly. "Where were you two years ago, hmmm? I could have really used a good laugh then. I know I need a haircut, but that's the least of my worries."

"Good, because I thought you liked it that way, and to be honest, it doesn't flatter you." *What a liar. Everything flatters him.* "So, what made you do it?"

"When you're dead, you don't typically go to the barber."

"Ha ha. I meant, why did you run away? Was fame and fortune too much for you?" She said it a bit sarcastically, because, really, a person could have only so much sympathy for someone who was rich and famous. Sure, there could be a downside, but it sure beat living on the third floor of a hot tenement in Providence scraping together every nickel and dime to pay for a restaurant that might fail the first year.

"I already told you why I did it." He pushed away from the island, shutting down, shutting her out.

"You mean that's it? Someone takes a picture of you in the john and you just say, 'Well, I'd rather the world think I'm dead than take any more of this.' That can't be it."

She could tell he was getting mad, which made her think maybe she was right, even if it made no sense. Sure, life could be tough for celebrities, but you didn't pretend you were dead.

"That's it, darlin'." He pushed away from the table angrily, almost toppling over the barstool before he righted himself. He hopped off the stool and started stalking out of the kitchen. *Nice ass.* They came to her, these inappropriate observations, even when she was thinking he was a jerk, even when she wasn't even aware she was looking at him.

"Hey, you don't have to get all mad. I'm just curious."

"Just curious. I'm sure you are. Everyone's curious.

What does Declan McDonald eat? Where does he sleep. Who does he sleep with? Where does he take a piss? You know something? *I* don't even care about those things. Why the hell should you or anyone else?" He jabbed a finger in her direction, a hard, violent gesture that she supposed was meant to make her be quiet.

Rose just let him go on, calmly listening as he vented. "Are you finished?"

He was breathing hard, like a person unused to running who had to catch a bus. Closing his eyes, he took a long, deep breath. "Yeah. I'm finished."

"Good," she said, feeling her hot Italian temper start to rise. "Because I want you to know that I don't care about any of those things. I really don't. But a person would have to be pretty callous not to watch you for the past few minutes and not know that something is eating you alive. And I think it's more than someone taking a picture of you when you didn't want them to."

He looked down to the floor, a habit she already was beginning to recognize.

"You keep looking down. What's down there that's so interesting."

As she'd hoped, he let out a chuckle. "The blood flows better to my brain when I look down. You want to know why I'm here?" He looked at her, and darn it if Rose didn't feel the air whoosh right out of her lungs. "Blame it on *It's a Wonderful Life*. It was on the day before I ran away. I thought, yeah, I'll disappear and everything I hate will just go away. I called Mom and she told me to do it. Escape. Disappear. Even after that, I wasn't sure. I was skiing and about to go down, and I saw them, about ten photographers waiting at the bottom, waiting for me to fall on my ass or kill myself against a tree just so they could get a shot of it. Something came over me. I thought if I didn't run away, I might kill one of them. I mean it, I felt this rage, this, this searing hatred." He held out his shaking hands in front of him as if he were picturing them around a photographer's throat. "It was the scariest thing I've ever felt because it was the most alive I'd felt in years."

Rose felt her skin prickle. "And here you are."

"Here I am."

Chapter 7

Nonna's apple pie—caramelized apples layered with flaky tart crust and whipped cream, $8.00

She marched into his room, Little Miss Mary Sunshine, without even knocking. She was wearing those jeans with the torn knee, the ones that hung low enough to show her perfect navel. Crazy thoughts entered his head, thoughts about her standing there naked. Thoughts of her sweaty and laughing and naked on top of him.

"We're going out tonight."

"I'm working." He was working, but it wasn't going well. He just couldn't get the refrain right; it sounded too much like everything else he'd ever written. And suddenly everything he wrote sounded like sentimental crap. Thanks to his chef. "And what the hell are you doing up here?" He wasn't mad, didn't even sound angry. In fact, he was glad to see her, even if seeing her drove him a little crazy. He liked her. A lot. And, of course, he wanted to sleep with her and wouldn't. Because this was one girl, one life, he didn't want to ruin.

She clapped a hand over her mouth. "Oh my God. Declan McDonald," she shrieked, doing a fair imitation of the women who used to spot him in an airport or restaurant. "Can I have your autograph? Can I touch you?" He was laughing by now as she ran in place and giggled, a fan overcome with seeing her fantasy in real life. "Oh, can I have a kiss?" With that, she fainted dead away, falling comically onto his floor.

Declan walked over to her prone figure, watching as she feigned being unconscious. Then he hunkered down and put his face down close to hers—so close he could see the tiny sparkly things in the small amount of eye shadow she'd put on. "I think I can accommodate that kiss," he said, knowing her eyes would immediately open. He wasn't disappointed. "You have nice eyes."

"They're brown."

"A nice brown. You've got a dark brown border, but inside it's golden brown. Like a watered-down Pepsi." He watched those eyes narrow, apparently disliking his fine poetry.

"You should put that line in one of your songs," she said dryly.

"You still want that kiss, lady?" What the hell was he doing?

Ruining a life.

Her lips parted, and she let out a little gasp, the barest hint of sound reaching him but enough to give him a hard-on and make his own breath a bit labored. He wasn't certain if that gasp meant she was turned on by the suggestion or just shocked.

"I think I just might faint again if you do."

He knew she was trying to be funny, but the breathy way it came out felt like a hard blow to his stomach. He was horny, and good God above, it felt good. "I think I just might take that chance. I always aim to please my fans."

"Oh."

He kissed her. He pressed his lips against hers, keeping his eyes open to gauge her reaction, and was surprised to see that she kept her eyes open too to gauge his. He smiled, and so did she, their lips still touching.

"Can I still get that autograph?" she asked.

He shoved away good-naturedly because he sure couldn't let her know he'd been about a millisecond away from losing control. Here he'd been having a very nice fantasy of what her gasp would sound like right before she came, and she was probably thinking he was just going along with the gag.

Rose sat up, her legs outstretched, her arms straight back supporting herself, and looked up at him. "I thought you could use a night out."

"Very funny."

"No, I mean it. We could visit my grandmother. I can guarantee you she's never heard of you. She doesn't have a television and wouldn't know you from Adam. Honest."

Declan went to his piano, running his hands over the keys, listening to the thump-thump-thump as he lightly pressed down on them. She wanted him to go out, to ride in a car, to walk into someone's home. She hadn't a clue what she was asking.

"No way. Can't take the chance."

"It's perfectly safe. I even asked her if she knew who you were, and she said, 'Declan who? McDonald? Now don't tell me that you gonna date some Irish boy.' I swear to God," Rose said, laughing at her imitation of her grandmother. "The only star she'd recognize is Frank Sinatra, and I'm pretty sure he's really dead."

He pressed middle C over and over, loud then soft, a mirror of the silent argument going on in his brain. "What if the car breaks down?"

She pursed her lips. "Now that could be a real possibility," she admitted. "My grandmother could give you a haircut."

He brought his hand to the ponytail he wore. He really hated his hair long, but didn't want to cut it himself. "*You* could cut it."

"Oh sure, if you want to look like a freak. I wouldn't dare. But Nonna used to work as a barber with my grandfather. They had their own shop for years."

He turned and stared at her. She still sat, her head tilted, her long curling hair hanging down and nearly brushing the floor, asking him to go back to his old life. He'd come to accept that if he were to take a chance by going out to a restaurant or taking a walk on a beach in the daytime, he must be prepared to face the consequences of discovery. And he just couldn't do it.

But the idea of walking out of here, of having a normal evening, was almost as tempting as Rose was this very instant, looking up at him with those huge eyes.

"Stop looking at me like that."

She jerked her head back a bit. "Like what?"

"Like you really expect me to go with you to your grandmother's. I can't."

She pressed her lips together in disappointment. "It's no big deal," she said, standing up. "I thought maybe you'd like to get out of here for a few hours."

"I get out all the time. I run on the beach every night."

"Like a vampire. No, you're worse than a vampire because even a vampire pretends to be a normal person at night before he kills his victim. Aren't you going crazy cooped up in here? I couldn't stand it. I need the sun, the rain. Have you ever gone out in a real downpour and lifted your head to the sky?"

"Sounds like a good way to drown."

"Ha ha. Honestly, I don't know how you've done this so long. I'd have lasted about two days before I fessed up."

Any thoughts he'd had—and he'd had a bunch—of her and him getting together were dashed. He couldn't expect someone as full of life as Rose to stay secluded with him. And even if he ended his isolation, what woman could stand staying in a hotel room for days at a time in an effort to avoid the press? Who could take sneaking out the back way of every house, hotel, restaurant, and theme park they visited? If it had been just him, he could have handled it. But his career had never been just about him. It had killed his brother and nearly destroyed his mother. He would never impose that life on someone he loved. Ever.

Not that he loved Rose.

"You get used to it. When you're a celebrity, you deal." He shrugged.

Rose shook her head in disgust. "You know, you need to get over yourself. I'm getting sick of this whiny woe-is-me crap. And if this is what you call dealing," she said, waving a hand around his room, "then you're a pretty sad case."

His expression went from indifferent to fierce. "You don't know shit, lady. So why don't you just mind your own business and leave me the hell alone."

"Fine. I'll do that."

Rose spun around, more angry with herself than with Declan. What had she expected, that he'd find her so irresistible he'd put his seclusion in jeopardy? That stupid kiss meant nothing; he'd just been playing around, and she'd got lost in some ridiculous fantasy. She was just one of a million women who found themselves infatuated with Declan McDonald. Besides, did she really want to be with a guy who was so screwed up about his own celebrity? Stars had their pictures taken. It happened all the time. They didn't all like it, some even sucker-punched the photographers, but they didn't fake their own deaths and hide away from the world for years. Declan's reaction was so far over the top it was difficult to believe.

"Where are you going?"

She wanted to keep going, but something in his voice made her stop. Already her anger was sliding away. It could burn so hot so fast. Then just as suddenly, it was gone, and she could laugh at herself. She'd driven many boyfriends crazy with it.

"Home." She turned to look at him, trying to steel herself from feeling sorry for him, from feeling anything for him.

"I thought you were going to visit your grandmother."

"That is home. I have my own place, but that's home."

"Must be nice." She heard the bitterness but fought the sympathy she wanted to feel.

"It is nice. And you could come with me. No one would know."

That head of his slumped down again; apparently that meant his brain was weighing his options. "I know you think I'm crazy."

"Yup."

He put his hands on each side of his head and looked up to the ceiling, letting out one of his primal screams. "Why did you have to come up here?"

"You mean now or the first time?"

"The first time. It's my own fault. I had to know you'd figure out who I was."

She annoyed him. "Do you really want me to leave?"

He stared at her, and she felt her entire body grow warm. No, not just warm, hot and prickly. This was so bad, this hot, prickly feeling that came over her when she looked at him.

"No. I don't." It came out reluctantly, like a woman on a diet refusing a piece of chocolate cake. "Are you sure your grandmother doesn't know who I am."

Rose flashed him a huge smile. "I'm sure. Anyway, even if she did know who you are—which she doesn't," she added quickly when she saw a bit of panic in his eyes, "she wouldn't tell a soul. She's even better at keeping secrets than I am. By the way, this was not easy, you know, keeping my mouth shut."

"I bet."

"I know to you you're just you, but to the rest of the world you're huge."

He tilted his head and looked at her in that intense way of his, as if he were trying to see something beyond what she said. "What about you, Rose?"

"Me?" she asked, jabbing her thumb against her chest. "To me you're a self-centered jerk who is way too full of himself." When he laughed, Rose felt something swell inside her, something euphoric, something scary. He laughed when most guys would have been insulted, when most wouldn't have known she was trying to be funny. Rose couldn't count the number of times she'd had to explain to someone that she didn't really mean what she'd just said, that she was trying to make fun. It was so damned tiring. Declan got it; he got *her.*

He flopped down on the couch and put his hands behind his head. She wished he would stop doing things that made him look so gorgeous, but she supposed it wasn't his fault. "So, if I go with you—*if*—would this be a date or something?" he asked.

"I suppose you might consider it a mercy date."

He raised his eyebrows in confused surprise, as if the thought were beyond belief. "You think I'm a charity case?"

"Actually, yes. Look at you, stuck here all the time, totally alone without a soul in the world to talk to except your cook. It's pathetic."

He sat up with that, completely flabbergasted, and Rose pressed her lips together so she wouldn't laugh. And then he got down on one knee and flung his arms out to the side. "Marry me."

Rose laughed. "Okay." Then dissolved into some full-fledged snorting guffaws. "You know," she managed between laughs, "you really are full of yourself. Not that I blame you. I guess it must be pretty heady to have all those women throwing themselves at you."

He got up off his knee and sat back on the couch. "It is."

Rose frowned, not liking his answer and not liking

that she didn't like his answer. She was totally, completely, ridiculously infatuated with him. It wasn't that he was who he was, though if she were completely honest, his celebrity was a bit of his appeal. It was the entire package: The tortured man hiding from society. The hot, muscled, intelligent, talented, tortured man. Plus he got her odd sense of humor. And he liked her cooking.

"You wouldn't believe the women I've had throwing themselves at me. At first it was kind of fun. And then it was annoying. I just wanted to tell them to get a life."

Rose's face flushed, seeing some of herself in those women. She'd had the hots for him when she'd only heard his voice. Was she so different from those groupies who were willing to sleep with him just to say they had? "It's just that you're so irresistible," she said lightly.

He wiggled his eyebrows suggestively. "Do you find me irresistible."

"I've resisted so far."

"So far," he said thoughtfully, but he was clearly teasing. "That means I still have a chance."

"Like a snowball's chance in hell," she replied, crossing her arms over her chest in an attempt to look tough.

He narrowed his eyes, a jaded hunter whose interest had been piqued by a new and interesting prey.

Rose backed up a step, letting out a nervous laugh. "That was not a challenge."

"Wasn't it?"

"No. It wasn't. I'm good for one mercy date and that's it."

"Just one, hmmm? How about a mercy kiss?" he said so low her chest felt an odd vibration. Or maybe that was just lust surging through her body. *Danger, girl.*

"I don't give mercy kisses to jaded celebrities. There's something so sad about it," she said with nonchalance.

He laughed and stood. "You're a pistol," he said. "Okay. Where does this grandmother of yours live?"

"Providence."

He took a deep breath, and in that moment Rose got a glimpse of just how difficult leaving this house, this safety, was for him. "Okay. Let's go."

Even though it was going on dusk, Rose decided to take the scenic route, a winding road that hugged the coast. Declan sat next to her, a big ball of tension, and Rose thought the drive might relax him.

"You'll see. Everything will be fine."

Then she looked in her rearview mirror and saw the flashing blue and red of a police cruiser.

"Oh God oh God oh God."

Now, if they'd been in bed together, Declan would have been pretty happy hearing those words come out of Rose's mouth. But then he saw the police lights and felt Rose slow down and pull over and thought he just might puke right there.

"I must have been speeding. Shit. I'm so sorry. It'll be okay. I'll just give them my license and registration, he'll give me a ticket, and then that's it. Oh, God."

Declan closed his eyes, mentally preparing himself, feeling a calmness steal over him. *So, this is it. Two years of hiding is over.* He opened his eyes, ready to be recognized. He forced himself to relax the death grip he had on the vinyl seat.

"They never bug the passenger," Rose said. She was shaking so hard, she had a tough time rolling down the window so she could talk to the approaching officer.

"Do you know what the speed limit is here?" The cop was a woman.

"I think it's thirty-five?"

"I clocked you at fifty."

"Fifty? I don't think I was going that fast." She talked as fast as she was driving—Rose after fifteen cups of black coffee. Declan reached over and squeezed her thigh. *Shut up.*

"Have you been drinking tonight?"

"Drinking alcohol?" She was being too friendly, Declan thought, too loud, too chirpy. She was going to blow it. "No. I don't drink. Except at weddings and things like that. Or New Years."

"Please step out of the car."

"Why?"

The officer repeated her instructions, and Rose, with a worried look in his direction, got out of the car and shut the door. The officer leaned in and shined her flashlight in his direction. "Sir." Declan had been staring out the windshield at the black ribbon of road in front of them, offering only his profile. With a feeling of inevitability, he turned his head.

"Yes, Officer?"

She blinked. And stared. "Wow." The cop smiled, and it transformed her face, turned her from a bull-dike cop to a pretty woman. Declan tried to take a deep breath, but he couldn't get air into his lungs. *Here it goes.*

"You look just like that dead guy, that Declan McDonald."

"Yeah. I get that a lot." He flashed her a grin, the kind he'd used a hundred times on women he thought he might want to sleep with. He didn't want to sleep with this one; he just wanted her to cut them a break.

"Your girlfriend been drinking?"

"No, ma'am." And he gave her that aw-shucks look again, that lopsided grin guaranteed to work on every female—except perhaps Rose.

The cop straightened away from the car. "Miss Pisano," she said, looking down at Rose's license. "Please slow it down and have a nice evening."

Rose blinked. "Thank you, Officer," she said slowly, glancing at the grinning passenger in her car. She threw herself into the driver's seat and glared at him. "What did you do?"

He shrugged, all innocence with a dose of masculine smugness. "I just smiled at her. Like this." And he mugged for her.

"You smiled like that and she let you go? You look goofy. Ugh. What is it with women?" He didn't look goofy. He looked gorgeous, as usual, but Rose would be damned if she'd let him know that. He was far too confident about his ability to seduce women. Like a woman would throw herself at him just because he grinned at her. *Please.*

"I can tell you're turned on," he said with a straight face, though Rose didn't know how he managed it.

Rose laughed. "You're something else, you know that?"

"Are you gay?"

She knew he was joking but pretended to be mad. "If you're implying that just because I haven't slept with you yet I must be a lesbian . . ."

His laugh was enough of an answer.

"You are the most arrogant man I've ever met."

"I bet I could give you one kiss—a real kiss, not like that one before—and you'd be begging for me."

Rose stared at him, felt a slow heat burn from her toes to her breasts, and lied with a straight face. "You are so wrong."

Behind them, the cop put on her lights and drove off, apparently in pursuit of some bad guy. In her wake, the night was eerily quiet except for the persistent chirping of nearby crickets. On a summer's night, this road was a busy strip, connecting touristy towns all along the scenic waterfront route. But it was still May, and all the tourists were still in their winter homes, leaving Declan and Rose very alone. Somehow more alone than they'd been in that cube of a house Declan called home.

"I don't want to be another notch in your piano," she

said, finally saying out loud what she'd thought about a hundred times. He'd slept with God knew how many women, many who were super-model material, and Rose sure didn't want to follow that kind of act. Actually, she did—and she didn't. Okay, she really, really did. But she wouldn't. She knew herself well enough to know that if she slept with Declan, her heart would be involved big time, and she just couldn't allow herself to be that ridiculous. For one thing, she never allowed herself to sleep with someone she didn't think might be long term. After her breakup with Gary Fortuna, the one man she thought she actually could marry, she tried getting over him by sleeping with a few guys only to realize there were worse things than having a broken heart—like waking up naked next to someone you realize you don't even like.

"My piano is notchless."

She gave him a look. "I just thought it would be good for you to get out of your house. Before you get too weird."

"Am I weird?"

She looked at him as if he were insane. "Declan," she said, with infinite patience, "you live in a sugar cube protected by guards and cameras, you don't leave and no one comes in, and you're pretending to be dead. What do you think?"

"When you put it that way it sounds like I should be committed. So this really is a mercy date?"

Rose tried to stop her smile, but couldn't. "I wouldn't really even call it a date."

He grasped his shirt over his heart. "You are the cruelest woman I've met." Then he turned to her, those blue eyes of his making her warm and self-conscious. "I've already decided we can never get together, so you can relax."

"Oh. Great." She felt disappointment drain through her like thick oatmeal.

"Rose. Look at me."

She let out a puff of air. "You don't have to explain. In fact, please don't."

"You idiot, look at me."

She did, with belligerent indulgence.

"I like you, Rose."

Yeah, like a sister.

"And I don't want to hurt you." *Great, the it's not you, it's me bit.* Rose couldn't believe how much it hurt, but it did. "You wouldn't believe the women I've had throwing themselves at me. At first it was kind of fun. And then it was annoying. I just wanted to tell them to get a life."

Declan wanted nothing more than to reach out and stroke her hair, to bury his face against her neck, to bury himself inside her. He hadn't had to deny himself what he wanted in a long time. He was being heroic, for God's sake, and all she could do was give him a look like he was some kind of asshole.

"You have the biggest ego I have ever had the displeasure of experiencing," she said as she pulled back onto the road.

"What?"

"You think I want to sleep with you? Is that it?"

He blinked. "Well, yeah."

Rose laughed. She laughed at him, at his heroic denial. He was sitting there half aroused, and she thought it was funny. He didn't know how he'd read her so wrong, but he had. If he was perfectly honest with himself— something he hadn't thought about doing—he'd admit he hadn't tried to read her. He'd just assumed that Rose, like all women he'd met, wanted to sleep with him. Man, he *was* an ass.

She flicked on the radio, a clear sign she did not want to talk, and changed to another station when "Leah's Song" came on. "They play it all the time, you know," she said. "It's a huge hit."

He'd known it was from his discussions with his mother. She hadn't heard a record get so much play time since his first and biggest hit, "Memories of You." That particular song skyrocketed to number one and stayed there for weeks. A string of hits followed, but nothing ever surpassed that first big song. Except this.

"This song is going to end up exposing me. I just know there are about a hundred reporters out there looking for the mysterious songwriter. It's only a matter of time before they find me."

"Won't you be just a little relieved that all this is over? No more hiding?"

"No," he said flatly. "And if I do decide to end this, I want it to be on my terms, not some slimy reporter jumping out at me with a camera."

She let out a throaty little laugh. "I wouldn't want to be you when that day comes."

"Me neither. I have nightmares about it."

"Really? What are they like?"

"I never remember the details," he lied. He didn't want to tell her that in his dreams, it was his mother, not him, who was surrounded by reporters. Her face contorted with fear, the cameras flashing at her while she screamed and tried to escape. In the dream he tried to get through to her, throwing off person after person, only to have his mother get pulled deeper into the throng of photographers. He knew where the dream came from: his brother's funeral. But every time he had it, he woke up drenched in sweat, his heart beating hard in his chest.

Declan pushed the nightmare from his mind and watched as Providence came into view. It was a pretty little city at night, a charming mix of old and new, a few high-rises surrounded by solid, old buildings. From the highway, the entire city was visible, from the old three-story tenements to the state capitol's white dome.

"Just like that TV show," he said.

Rose let out a snort. "Hardly. Providence is a little

grittier than that. But it sure films nicely. My grandmother lives on Federal Hill, which is a bit like Little
Italy in New York. Some of the best food in New England
is made right here, and my grandmother's cooking ranks
right up there at the top."

Rose pulled off the highway and made her way down
a maze of streets that all looked identical to Declan.
Row after row of three- and four-story tenement houses
flew by as she navigated around her home territory. She
stopped her car in front of one of the few single-family
houses on the street. A set of four steps led up to a tiny
yard, surrounded by a short chain-link fence. Declan
stared at the neat 1920s bungalow, struck by how homey
it seemed, how unlike the huge house he lived in. Lights
glowed softly from within the house, whose windows
were covered by shades pulled down low.

"We're here." She let out a puff of air, and Declan
realized she was nervous.

"Nice house," he said, meaning it.

"You should see my mother's. She's got one of those
huge East Side mansions. I love the outside, but inside
she completely ruined it. It looks like your house."
Rose cringed, realizing what she'd just said. "Sorry."

"Don't be," Declan said, laughing. "I hate the place,
but it suited my needs. This place has character."

"Yeah, it does, doesn't it," she said, her voice softening in that sexy way that made him wish for things that
could never be.

Rose opened her car door and did a quick scan of
the quiet neighborhood before ducking her head back
in. "The coast is clear," she said, all drama. It was windy,
and her curling hair lifted all around her making it look
as if she just might fly away.

Declan heaved himself out of the car and stretched
casually, all the while his eyes scanned the surrounding
houses and yards for a sign of a photographer lurking
behind a car or bush. It wasn't that he didn't trust Rose—

he did—but he'd been caught before when he'd thought he'd finally thwarted the press, and he didn't want it to happen tonight. Not with Rose. It could scare the hell out of someone who wasn't expecting it. It could make them drive too fast and careen off the road. It could kill them like it killed his brother.

"You coming?" she called.

The neighborhood was almost eerily quiet, and he relaxed, taking one last quick look around before following Rose to the back of the house. He watched as her long hair bounced back and forth, drawing his eyes to her round butt. Nice.

"Nonna, we're here," she called as she walked into the room.

Even before he stepped into the large old-fashioned kitchen, he was overwhelmed by aromas that immediately transported him back to a little Italian restaurant he used to go to whenever he was in New York. It was one of the few places untarnished by memories of stalking paparazzi or frothing fans. The creator of those tantalizing scents stood at a large stove, a tiny woman with iron-gray hair bundled up in a loose bun at the back of her head. She looked up with a huge smile as her granddaughter entered the room, then peeked around to greet Declan. Her smile froze, and Declan in that instant knew that she knew.

"So nice to meet my granddaughter's boss," she said, hardly missing a beat, making him think that perhaps he was paranoid.

Maybe she didn't know.

"She's a terrific cook. And from these wonderful smells, I know where she learned her stuff."

Angelica beamed as she took off her apron, throwing it casually onto the kitchen table and in that moment transporting Declan to his childhood and his own long-dead grandmother who used to wear aprons just like that faded flowered one. He hadn't thought of his grandmother in years, hadn't even realized he held that memory. But there it was, reminding him with painful clarity of a world he'd lost and could never get back, a world of family and dinners filled with noisy kids and harassed but loving parents.

"You two come sit in the parlor while I finish dinner. It's almost done. You sit and relax now." She waved them down a small hall and into a parlor that looked surprisingly contemporary with its cream-colored carpet and pinstriped cream and blue sofa. It was a long, rectangular room with a fireplace at one end and the home's front door at the other. A picture window, a large shade pulled down, dominated the room.

"You two sit," Angelica said, a big smile plastered on her face. Declan narrowed his eyes. Something wasn't quite right. She knew, of course she knew. "Oh, Rosalie, I forgot. I need your help in the kitchen."

Rose looked taken aback. "You need my help?"

"Yes. In the kitchen." And she waved her down the hall.

It was all Declan could do not to laugh aloud when he heard Angelica's furious whispering.

"Do you know who that is?"

Rose feigned ignorance. "Who?"

"It's Declan McDonald."

Rose's stomach dropped to somewhere near her knees. "You know who he is?" she said with disbelieving dread.

"Rosalie, I might be old but I'm not stupid."

Rose darted a look down the hall to make certain Declan couldn't hear them, then ushered her grandmother deeper into the kitchen. "I told you my client's name. You never said a word," Rose accused.

"I didn't think you'd be bringing a dead man to dinner," her grandmother said, hands on hips. She pointed a finger toward the parlor but kept her snapping brown eyes on her granddaughter. "Do you know who you have in there?"

"I think she does."

Rose stifled a groan when she heard Declan's deep voice. She turned to see him leaning up against the doorway, arms folded over his chest, eyes crinkling with good humor tinged with the smallest bit of worry. "Sorry."

"Is this going to be a problem?" he asked, his gaze drifting to her grandmother.

"No. No, it's not. I'm so sorry. I didn't think she'd know who you are." She turned to her grandmother, who was staring at Declan. "How do you know who he is? You don't even have a TV."

Her grandmother disappeared into what used to be the home's small den, but what was now her grandmother's bedroom. She came out with a stack of *National Enquirer*s. "There was a story just the other week about someone who saw your Mr. McDonald in a hotel in Utah." She flipped through the stack until she found it, then placed it on the Formica-topped kitchen table. On the cover was a fuzzy picture of someone who was about the same size as Declan but whom even Rose could tell wasn't him.

"My mother told me about that one," he said with a small shrug. "Elvis all over again." He sounded purely disgusted by it all.

"Except," Angelica said with censure, "you are alive. And hiding away. What kind of life is that?"

Rose grimaced, fearing her grandmother's bluntness might anger Declan.

"It's better than the alternative, I assure you," he said evenly, but the way he pushed off the doorway told Rose he wasn't prepared to defend his decision.

"Look, Rosalie, he's getting mad at me. At an old lady. That one has the Irish temper."

Rose knew her grandmother was teasing, even, perhaps, flirting. Still, she felt the need to protect Declan.

"No he's not."

Declan surprised her by saying, "Yes, actually, I am."

She pointed a finger at him. "You are not allowed to get angry at my grandmother. She's a saint." Rose walked over to her grandmother and threw her arm around the older woman's shoulders in an overt show of solidarity.

"That's right," Angelica said, wagging a finger at Declan, "I'm a saint."

Rose watched as Declan held a small internal battle, then smiled broadly. "You two are something else," he said, chuckling. "And neither is a saint."

"Now, young man, you tell me. How long you gonna hide out?"

"Nonna, I really don't think Declan wants to talk about this tonight. I promised him a night out where no one knew who he was, not a night being interrogated by a little Italian pit bull." Rose kissed her grandmother's cheek.

Angelica would have none of it. "You bring Declan McDonald into my house and I'm not allowed to talk to him?"

"It's all right, Rose, really. But I reserve the right not to answer. And I'll have to insist you promise not to tell anyone I was here tonight."

Angelica appeared to weigh whether or not to be insulted by Declan's request, but ended up promising. Rose had never seen her grandmother act quite this way. Throughout the night—especially while she was giving Declan a haircut—she flirted and teased, and Declan flirted and teased right back.

After a dinner of pasta, Italian sausage, and a salad, they went into the parlor for dessert. She watched him as he ate his panettone with relaxed relish and realized she'd never seen him this way—at ease, comfortable.

"You know, Rose, this is something you might want to add to your menus," he said, putting a forkful of the stuff in his mouth. She didn't mean to do it, but when his lips closed over his fork, her eyes followed and stayed cemented, watching as he wiped a bit of sugar off with his index finger. And licked.

Her eyes darted up to see if he was just teasing her, but he was looking at her grandmother—and her grandmother was looking at her. Rose flushed, then looked down to her own nearly untouched plate, mortified that she'd been so transparent. She could hear her grandmother now: *Rosalie, you gotta stay away from that Irish boy. He's no good for you. You're gonna get hurt.*

Yep. She probably would. Because even she knew she was getting a crush—a big-time, heart-throbbing, lust-producing crush. And Declan, well, he was just going along for the ride. A man like him had seen it all—had probably done it all. And with the most beautiful women in the world. Rose pushed her fork into her dessert and stared at a raisin at the end of her fork, sharply aware that if she wasn't careful, she would embarrass herself and Declan by doing something stupid and letting him know how she felt.

Declan laughed at something her grandmother said, and she looked up and smiled, too, even though she hadn't the faintest idea what they were laughing about. Somewhere outside a car door slammed. It took a few seconds before the alarm in her brain went off.

"A car," she said, leaping out of her chair.

"I didn't hear anything," Declan called to her as she hurried to the window.

Rose pushed the curtain aside, fully expecting the car she'd heard to be the neighbor's. "Oh my God, it's my mother." A quick look told her she'd already gotten out of the car and any second would be walking in.

"Oh, goodness, I forgot, your mother said she was going to stop by tonight to pick up that old clock." The offending clock, its pendulum frozen to the left, sat on the mantel.

Frantically Rose looked around for a place to hide, finding only a small coat closet. They didn't have time to escape into the kitchen and out the back door.

"Rose."

Declan's deep voice penetrated her panic. They were trapped.

Like some bad movie, Rose watched as the doorknob slowly turned. Then she grabbed Declan's arm and pulled him into the closet with her just as the door opened. They stood face-to-face surrounded by coats that smelled like her grandmother's perfume, a slice of light coming into the closet from the top of the ill-fitting door. She slowly took a deep and shaking breath and heard Declan do the same.

"Lucia, I forgot you were coming over for the clock. Here you go. Good night now." Rose smiled at her grandmother's attempt to get rid of her mother.

"Isn't Rose here? Her car's outside." As Rose's mother spoke, it was obvious she was walking farther into the room.

Something squeezed her arm. "Ow."

Declan moved his lips close to her ear. "Sorry," he whispered, lightening his steellike grip on her upper arms but not letting go. Her eyes adjusted to the dark closet, and she could see his face, the whites of his eyes and a vague idea of an expression. He looked pensive, as still and rock-solid as a statue. Declan leaned into her again, so close she could feel his warm breath against her cheek.

"How long do you think we'll be in here?"

Rose shook her head: *I don't know.* She waited for him to move back, but for some reason he stayed there, his cheek even with hers, his breath bathing her skin. She realized her breasts were pressing lightly against his shirt and for the first time understood what all those novels meant by "heavy, aching breasts." She would have laughed aloud if her throat weren't so clogged with lust. *Suddenly, his lips swooped down upon hers* (she'd actually read that once, though she didn't know what swooping lips looked like. She'd pictured lips disembodying themselves, sprouting wings, and attaching themselves to the poor woman) *and she tilted her head back. Yes yes, she uttered, succumbing to the raging . . .*

Her grandmother said something, but Rose couldn't hear because suddenly all she heard was her breathing and his and a strange soft roaring in her ears. They were talking, her mother and grandmother, about her, and she really should pay attention; but all she could think of was that she had to stop her knees from shaking and her arms from flinging themselves around his neck and her mouth from . . .

From kissing him like she was right now. *Oh God.*

He moved his mouth over hers softly, as if aware of how insane it was, as if he were asking her permission, which was very sweet and very sexy. The tiniest of sounds escaped her throat as he thrust his warm tongue against hers. His hands flexed on her arms, squeezing and releasing in time with the motion of his mouth and tongue. He dragged his mouth to her cheek, then to her neck, and she let her head flop back. God she loved it when a man kissed her neck, and this particular man knew what he was doing. Man oh man.

"I'm sorry. I'm sorry," he whispered so softly she didn't worry about anyone hearing them. "I just can't stop myself." His mouth moved to her collarbone, and she had the nearly overpowering urge to push his head down to her breasts, perhaps the dumbest thing to do considering her mother and grandmother were about ten feet away chatting about something. He moved his hands to her waist, his thumbs to just below her breasts, and he stopped kissing her and pulled back. Rose strained her eyes to see his face, his expression, and she pulled him close for another kiss. When he moved one hand up to her breast she just about collapsed right then and there. She gripped a belt loop on each side of his hips and drew him closer, until she felt his erection hard against her. Deep, deep inside, he let out a sound that made her want to strip him naked.

"Let's not talk about Rose tonight."

That stopped her lips in their tracks. They both froze as they realized Rose's grandmother was right outside the door.

"Why do you always defend her. She's *my* daughter."

"And she's my granddaughter, and I don't want to discuss her tonight. That's it, Lucia. *Il fine.*"

Rose pulled away, embarrassed that she'd lost control in a closet, as well as distinctly uncomfortable about the discussion. She tilted her head downward to listen, but Declan lifted her face upward with a hand to each side of her jaw. He kissed her softly, then withdrew, and she could see the white of his teeth as he smiled.

Tap, tap, tap.

"The coast is clear," Angelica called.

Rose immediately opened the door, not wanting her grandmother to guess that any hanky-panky had gone on in the closet. "Thanks, Nonna."

She looked at Rose then Declan, then narrowed her eyes. "My Rose is a good girl," she said, pointing a bony finger at Declan. "An' she need somebody that's gonna be around."

"Nonna!"

"I've said it and that's it. I don't care. I'm old and I can say what I want."

"You've always said what you want."

Her grandmother chuckled. "You're right. But you listen to me this time. Now. You two go home. *Mi sono stancato.* I'm tired." She waved an irritated hand at Rose's worried expression. "I'm just getting old."

Declan kissed Angelica good-bye and whispered something into her ear, and the old lady gave him a brisk nod.

When they got back into the car, they took one look at each other and started laughing, big snorting guffaws out of Rose and deep rumbling laughter from Declan.

"I bet you never had a night like that one," she said, still laughing.

"What were you thinking coming in the closet with me?" He'd said it lightly, but Rose thought she sensed a bit of accusation there, as if she'd planned everything that happened in that tight little space.

"I argued with my mother today, and I just didn't want to deal with her again. I never thought you'd molest me the second we were alone together," she said, clearly baiting him.

Either he didn't get the joke or preferred not to carry on with the gag. "It was a mistake," he said flatly.

Heat flooded Rose's cheeks. "You've already stated your unequivocal desire not to get involved with me. Don't worry."

He let out a puff of impatience. "Don't be an ass."

"Oh, now I'm an ass."

"I didn't say that. I said don't be one."

"Clearly implying that I am one."

He threw up his hands in defeat. "Okay. You're an ass."

In a small voice Rose asked, "Do you really think so?"

"No, you idiot, I don't. What I think of you is . . ." He clamped his mouth shut leaving Rose to fill in the blank.

"I didn't plan the whole closet thing, you know."

"I know," he said, irritation and impatience obvious in those two syllables.

"And *you* kissed me. You leaned toward me."

"I know," he said between clenched teeth.

"I just wanted to set the record straight. I'm not one of those women you talked about before."

Declan squeezed his eyes closed. "Please be quiet."

Rose gave him a look, then started the car, pulling out onto the deserted city street a bit faster than she should have.

"I'd like to make it home without being stopped by the police again," he said dryly.

Rose let out a humorless laugh. "Sorry. That's how I drive when I'm angry."

For a long time, the two were silent. They were just hitting the country roads of Kingstown when Declan spoke. "Don't be angry."

"You haven't been around many Italian women, have you? I stopped being mad about ten miles ago." Rose gave him a quick look and saw the hint of a smile on his gorgeous lips. "By the way, what did you say to my grandmother right before we left?"

"I told her she didn't have to worry about you. That's all."

"Oh." But Rose had no idea what that meant. Did it mean Rose's grandmother didn't have to worry because there was no chance of them becoming a couple? Or because he didn't plan to leave?

They were silent again until she pulled up to the guard gate just to let Tom, the night-shift guard, know who it was. Tom was a widower and a retiree who discovered working at night was better than being home alone in the evening.

"Hey, Tom," Rose said.

"Hello, Rose. Hello, um, sir." Tom bent down and peered into the car, frowning when he saw only the back of Declan's head. He looked from Rose to Declan as if he were bursting at the seams to ask her what the heck was going on.

"He's Elvis," she whispered, then pressed on the gas. Tom looked befuddled for a moment, then smiled when he finally got the joke. "He's a good guy, but a bit short on brain fuel if you know what I mean."

"He was smart enough to go to town hall and try to

find out who owned the house," Declan said, sounding grumpy.

"Paul told me that before my interview. Who is Carol Clarke anyway?" she asked, referring to the CEO of Clarke Enterprises.

"My mother. It's her legal name, but everyone thinks she's Carol McDonald. We set up a corporation; she signs the checks."

"You thought of everything."

He stared out the window at his house, and Rose had the distinct impression he was trying to avoid looking at her. "Almost everything." When he finally did look her way, she was struck by how angry he looked, though she instinctively knew he wasn't angry with her.

"What's wrong?"

He just kept looking at her as if he was majorly teed off. And then in a movement she didn't have time to react to, he put a hand behind her neck and dragged her to him, kissing her with near violence. She pulled back defensively. "Hey!"

He didn't say a word, just moved his eyes over her features before pulling her again toward him, this time slowly, gently. "I'm sorry," he whispered. He kissed her lips, brushing so lightly it was hardly a kiss, but boy did it feel good and she forgave him his rough kiss just like that. The kiss deepened, their bodies shifted, and he fumbled with the seat belt, letting out a deep sound of satisfaction when he finally got it undone and could move closer.

Rose's hand just happened to be resting against his rock-solid thigh, a nice place to be and very convenient. She moved her hand just a bit and happened to brush a telling bulge in his pants. He moved his hips toward her, and she spread out her hand, touching his penis through his jeans. "Oh my," she breathed, exploring his length and finally finding the tip that hovered near the waistband. His breathing was jagged, his body solid and taut, his heartbeat fast and hard against her. He pushed himself against her hand—hard—and she smiled when he let out a deep, deep moan.

"Jesus, Rose."

And then he pulled back to his seat, his eyes squeezed shut, his face tilted toward the car's ceiling.

"You're a virgin," Rose said, and he laughed.

"I feel like one," he said finally, then shook his head. "I'm not going to fuck this up. I'm not going to, Rose."

Rose studied his profile, the deep lines of strain near his eyes and mouth. "You're really worried about me, aren't you?"

"Hell yes. Do you know how many lives I've ruined? You are not going to be one of them."

"You think having sex with me will ruin me? I happen to think more of you than that. You can't be that bad."

Again, he laughed, and Rose smiled, glad he liked her sense of humor. Then he turned his head and looked at her, serious down to his toes. "I will end up hurting you. I can't get involved with anyone right now, or ever. This is not going to happen."

"Don't I have a say in all this?"

"No."

Rose let out a sound of exasperation. "Why not?"

"Because you don't know what can happen. Someday I'm going to have to end this, I know that. And it's not going to be pretty."

"I could handle it."

"You can't say you can handle something that you've never experienced. And besides, I don't want you to have to handle it. It would kill me to see your picture in some tabloid, your life ruined because of me."

"I've said this before, but I'll say it again: you sure do have a high opinion of yourself. We're talking sex here, right? Not love. Not marriage. Sex." *You, Rose Pisano, are a big, fat liar.*

Some emotion she couldn't read flickered in his eyes. "I haven't met a woman yet who could have sex and not become emotionally involved."

"Sure. You're right." He was right. Rose knew she was already half in love with him. "We'll take the high road. We'll be friends."

"Right. Friends."

"Friends who don't kiss," Rose said firmly.

"Friends who try really hard not to kiss."

Rose's eyes drifted down to his wonderful mouth.

"Rose, if you do that, I don't know how long I can keep this promise."

"What," she said, "I can't even look? That's not fair."

"Please, Rose." He'd gone all serious on her again, making Rose feel guilty.

"Okay. Friends." She held out her hand, and he shook it. And she tried not to think about how warm that hand was, how strong, how good it had felt on her breasts.

Friends. Right.

"You slept with him, didn't you!"

No, she hadn't, but Rose flushed anyway.

"Oh, my God, you did," Jenn said, clearly delighted with the idea of Rose sleeping with her boss.

"No, I didn't sleep with him. Honest."

Jenn pushed back into the cushions of her floral couch, a movement that made her already-large stomach even bigger. The two friends hadn't seen each other in weeks, and Rose was shocked by how pregnant Jenn looked. It was startling to see someone she'd known nearly her entire life look so different, foreign. Jenn was the girl who jumped up on stage, beer bottle in hand, and sang along with the band. She wasn't this soft, feminine girly-girl with a gentle hand resting on her unborn child.

Even though they hadn't talked in weeks, Jenn had

known the minute Rose agreed to come over that something was up. She hadn't been able to keep it out of her voice, apparently, when they talked on the phone, and when Rose arrived at her doorstep, Jenn had dragged her to her living room, forced her to sit, then pronounced Rose was sleeping with her employer.

"But you've seen him and you didn't even tell me," Jenn complained, and Rose felt a twinge of guilt. "He's gorgeous, isn't he?"

"He's . . . pretty much perfect," Rose said, a big grin on her face.

"I *knew* it. Didn't I tell you?" Jenn turned toward her, one knee tucked up onto the couch. She was two months away from giving birth and was all belly. Rose was certain that if she ever got pregnant, she would be one of those women who got all puffy and bloated and fat. "So, what's his story, then."

"He's an artist and likes his solitude. He's very normal. Well, pretty normal."

Jenn frowned. "What do you mean, 'pretty normal'? Who is he? What's his name?"

She shouldn't have said anything. She shouldn't have even called Jenn. But here she was, practically in love, and she had no one to talk to about it. "I can't tell you."

"Why?"

"He's a real private guy, and I promised not to reveal his identity to anyone." She knew everything she said would only pique Jenn's interest. Already Rose felt as if she were betraying Declan just by admitting to Jenn that she'd seen him.

"You mean I know him?"

"Sort of." Rose let out a groan. "Listen, Jenn, you've got to trust me. I know it sounds strange, but he's really a nice guy."

"Sounds like a weirdo to me. Okay. Tell me all about Mr. Seclusion."

"He's very good looking, brilliant, and—"

"Oh, my God, you're in love with him," Jenn said in a rush.

"No, no."

She pointed a finger, her eyes getting narrow. "You can't fool me, Rose."

"I'm not in love," Rose said forcefully. *I'm in love. I'm in love.* "I'm in lust with a bit of like thrown in. A lot of lust and a lot of like."

"And you haven't slept with him?"

"No."

Jenn was truly confused, poor thing. "Why not?"

"It's very complicated."

"How complicated can it be?" Then she let out a long *ooohhh.* "He can't get it up, can he?"

Rose buried her head in her hands. "I cannot believe I am having this conversation with you." She peeked through her fingers. "Yes, he can get it up." *Big time.*

"Then what's the problem? He's married."

"No."

"He's gay?" she asked tentatively.

Rose laughed, a real guffaw. "No. God no. It's all very sweet, really. He doesn't want to hurt me. And he would, I know he would, but I'm starting to not care. A very dangerous thing. Jenn, *he's* the one stopping things."

Rose had just rocked Jenn's world; she could see it in her face as she tried to process such improbable information.

"There's only one thing to do with this guy," Jenn said, acting the authority on all relationships. She could, Rose figured, she'd had enough of them.

"What's that?"

"Marry him."

Chapter 8

For a long time, Ellen sat in her car in the driveway of her home. No, her house. It was just a house, a lovely one, a stately brick home built amongst other stately brick homes. It was dark, the night quiet. No light shone from the house. No one was home.

She closed her eyes a brief moment to steel herself before getting out of the car and going into the house. There were times when she'd wished she hadn't removed every little sign of her daughter from their home. Those dolls and drawings, pound puppies, and glittering pink fingernail polish. Leah's room had been converted into a guest room, all her things put in boxes and sent to the Salvation Army. She refused to make Leah's room a shrine, thought other parents who did so were refusing to accept their child's death. Of course Matthew had been livid, claimed she was refusing to accept Leah's existence. She'd never seen him so angry as the night he went into their daughter's room and saw it stripped bare. Angry and sad. He'd cried, standing on that bare wood floor looking at her as if she'd done something horrible, while Ellen had watched, oddly unmoved. He didn't understand that Leah's room was a perversion now. They didn't have a daughter. She was gone and nothing—not frilly curtains or a well-worn stuffed animal—would bring her back.

But sometimes, like now, she wished she hadn't taken everything away. Because she wanted to curl up in Leah's bed and hug her little teddy bear to her heart and pretend Leah hadn't died. She wanted to bring out her little jammies, the ones with the hearts sprinkled on them, and see if she could still breathe in her daughter's just-bathed scent. Ellen shook her head, angry that she'd allowed herself to even think such a thing. It wouldn't help anyone to dissolve into despair; it wouldn't bring Leah back; it wouldn't make her feel better.

She opened the front door and flipped on the foyer light. High above her, the chandelier became brilliant. Already she felt better. As she went farther into her house, she flipped on lights until it was bright and cheerful. The moment she entered the kitchen, she threw off her heels and took off her tailored suit jacket, letting out a sigh of relief. This crusade she'd taken on was tiring. She'd spent the day with record executives talking about why distribution was so slow. The song was climbing the charts despite the problems, reaching number fourteen just last Monday. Merit Records' best guess was that it would be in the top ten next week and maybe even come close to number one. They were as surprised as she was that the songwriter hadn't come forward to try to grab a piece of the enormous financial pie being generated by the song.

Ellen went about making coffee, scooping the rich dark crystals from a bag of Starbuck's house blend into the basket. She went to the dishwasher to retrieve the pot. "Shit." She stared at the plastic handle in her hand, then down at what was left of the pot. This was the second pot the cleaning crew had broken by placing it improperly into the dishwasher. This time, though, she was ready, for she'd purchased a backup just in case.

She walked downstairs and was about to open the storage closet when she stopped, her heart pounding hard in her chest. It was a closet, but it also had been a "secret" playroom for Leah when she'd been well enough to play. Ellen had forgotten.

Pressing her lips together, she fought for the courage to open the door. This was just the sort of thing she'd been trying to avoid, stumbling upon little reminders that would cut into her heart like thorns. With a little shake of her head, she opened the closet and flipped on the light.

Everything of Leah's was gone. What she'd forgotten, her cleaning crew had apparently remembered.

"Thank God," she whispered, her voice shaking slightly.

At the far end of the closet, Matthew had tacked up a full-length mirror so Leah could see herself when she played dress-up. Ellen gazed at her reflection, taking in her pale face, her wide eyes, the dark circles beneath them. Then she saw it. In the corner of the mirror, down low enough for a child to touch, was a little handprint.

Ellen's eyes flooded with tears as she walked over to the mirror, seeing only five fingers and a palm left there by her daughter's sticky little hand. "Oh, baby," she whispered, kneeling down. With a hand that shook, Ellen placed her palm over her daughter's, gently so she wouldn't smear it, gently so she could imagine it was flesh and blood and not simply cold glass. And she began to sob, tears that hurt, that came from a soul far more battered than even she realized. She crumpled up into a ball and wept, saying her daughter's name again and again.

She didn't hear him come in, but when her husband held her to him, she let him. For the first time since their daughter died, she allowed Matthew to touch her.

Finally, she looked up at his pain-ravaged face. "She's really gone, isn't she?"

"Yes."

She cried anew, and he held her, his gaze drifting over his wife's head and settling on the mirror, in the corner, where his daughter had once rested her sticky little hand.

"Hey, buddy, what's shaking?"

Declan smiled, even though his gut hurt like hell. The last time he'd felt this way was in the weeks before he'd decided to disappear. Anxiety or dread or premonition made him feel this way. Or maybe it was just that he wanted to make love to a woman he was beginning to think he could possibly, maybe, someday love, and he couldn't. She was taking this friend thing like a joke. The past two days since they'd had dinner at her grandmother's she'd been calling him buddy, pal, sport—generally driving him crazy with it. He knew her enough to know she was one of those people who joked when they were nervous or scared or mad.

She sure was going to be mad when he told her she was fired. But he couldn't take it anymore, and he was convinced that once she was out of his life, she'd be out of his thoughts.

He flicked on the intercom. "Good morning."

She looked up at the camera, and his chest hurt, reaffirming his need to fire her. "You sound like hell. Need some company?"

"Not a good idea."

"Oh," she said, and then did a little dance. "I'm too irresistible, hmmm? Too sexy in my chef's uniform?" She grinned up at him.

"Something like that."

"What a grump. If you're going to be a grump, turn off the camera so I can work. Fish today. Some poached salmon in a light lemon wine sauce should cheer you up."

"Sounds good."

With that monotone answer, she threw a dish towel at the camera, yelling out *ha!* when it stuck. Just as well. Seeing her, even that grainy black-and-white image of her dancing in his cold, cavernous kitchen, was a kind of torture. He flicked off the intercom and stared at his piano, trying to ignore the pain in his stomach. He hadn't been able to do much more than stare at his piano for a long time. He was in a major funk, and when that happened his piano became an enemy, an object that mocked him. *You can't write music anymore. You never could. It was just studio magic, a hot body, and a handsome mug. Face it, loser, you never would have made it if it weren't for MTV and VH-1.*

He'd actually gotten a letter once that said just about that; he might have written it himself.

"Christ, stop feeling sorry for yourself," he shouted, strangely despondent when he realized no one would hear. He grabbed up the phone and jabbed the number to his mother, forgetting that it was only six in the morning in Arizona.

"Hello?" came her froggy voice.

"Mom. It's me."

"What's wrong? What's happened?"

"Nothing. Hell, I forgot the time."

"What's wrong." This time the panic was gone from her voice, replaced by motherly indulgence.

"Nothing. Everything." The two listened to the soft hiss of the line for a while as his mother waited patiently. "I just called to see how you were doing."

"At six o'clock in the morning? How do you think I'm doing. I'm sleepy."

"Yeah. I'll call later." But Declan didn't make a move to press the off button on the phone.

"I should be up anyway. Now. What's wrong?"

I'm horny as hell and I want to make love to my cook but I've decided to be noble and live like a monk. And

*for some strange reason my heart hurts as much as my
dick.*

"I think I'm going to fire that cook I hired."

"Rose? Why?"

"Because she . . . Because I . . ."

"Oh boy."

"I don't know what to do with her."

"Oh boy oh boy."

"Mom," Declan said, letting out an exasperated burst
of air. "You're not helping."

"Do you love her?"

"No," he said quickly. "No. Definitely not love. Probably not."

"But?"

"But nothing."

"But you might be falling in love?"

Declan flexed his hand on the receiver and squeezed
his eyes shut. "Yeah."

"Oh boy."

"Would you stop it with the oh boys?"

His mother let out a chuckle. "So this is the terrible
news you've called me about?"

"There's no way I'm going to bring down another
person. It's not going to happen."

"Honey, take it from me, you can't stop love from
happening if it's meant to be."

"Oh, yes I can."

"It's not like turning off a faucet."

"Sure it is." He could do it, stop this thing in its tracks
before it turned into something he couldn't control. He'd
done it before, felt the beginnings of something stronger
than like and lust and broken it off. It was remarkably
easy.

At precisely noon, Rose tapped on Declan's door while
balancing his lunch tray in the other hand. "Lunchtime,

Sport," she called, feeling happy despite Declan's sour moods lately.

"Come on in. I need to talk to you."

Rose's stomach did a little sick flip-flop, but she put on a dazzling smile anyway. "Sure. What's up?"

Declan sat at his piano bench, his back to the piano, hands resting on his thighs, as if he were about to bolt. He looked as if he'd just gotten out of bed, as if he hadn't combed his hair. He wore baggy sweats and a well-worn blue T-shirt; his feet were bare. Rose had never seen a man, not even Declan, look as impossibly sexy as he did right now. *Man oh man oh man.*

He looked at the tray, at the ceiling, at the rug—anywhere but in her eyes—and Rose knew whatever it was he was going to tell her she wasn't going to like.

"I'll put the tray on your table here," she said, shoving aside several balled-up composition sheets. Maybe that was why he was so ornery; he was having trouble writing. But she looked up at him and caught him staring at her like a kid stares at a pet dog he's about to bring to the vet to be euthanized. She bit her lip and wiped her hands on her white smock. "Well?"

He surged up, as though he'd sat on a tack, startling Rose. Then he stood there glaring at her. Dipping her head a bit, she looked up at him. "Declan?"

In two steps, he was in front of her, his breath coming out harshly. "I want to fire you. I'm going to fire you."

Rose was as surprised by her response as she'd ever been. She would have thought she'd be angry, that she would stalk from the room and say good riddance. Instead, to her complete shock, her eyes welled up, and her throat closed so tightly that even if she'd wanted to yell at him for being such a jerk, she couldn't have.

"What are you doing?" he asked, his panicked eyes taking in her watery ones.

Rose could only shake her head. She couldn't even

swallow down the big clot of grief in her throat, so she backed away, bumping into the table before turning to run from the room. It was just like her, she thought with disgust, to not even know how much she loved him until he threw her out of the house. Now she was acting like a fool, shedding tears over him, like a hundred other women probably had.

She hadn't gone halfway to the door before he caught her and turned her around to face him. Stupidly, she just kept shaking her head and desperately trying to swallow, knowing on some level she must resemble a fish gasping for air on a riverbank.

He gripped her upper arms, firmly holding her in place. "Rose, you have to understand. I can't do this. I can't have you here. I don't want to . . ." He let out a curse that made Rose flinch. "Don't you understand?"

Rose finally found her voice. "Let go."

He blinked as if furious. "I can't," he bit out, then brought her so close their lips were nearly touching, and their entire bodies were pressed together. "This is such a big mistake," he said softly.

"What is?"

He kissed her, and if there was one thing Declan McDonald could do better than write songs, it was kiss. Rose had been kissed by a dozen or more men, had enjoyed most of it, but this transcended every other experience she'd had. No one had made her feel so hot, think so much about sex. No one had made her want to strip naked and devour a man the way she wanted to devour this one. He thrust his tongue into her mouth, and it was delicious. Not sloppy. Wonderful. *Tasty.*

She moved her hands to the waist of his loose-fitting sweats and pushed down. The pants fell to the floor, just like that, and she let out a laugh. "You're not wearing underpants," she said, moving her hands over his hard, smooth buttocks. He let out a deep groan and shoved his hands beneath her smock.

"How do I get this thing off?"

Rose backed away, a grin on her face. "I'll do it."

And with one fluid motion, she pulled and unsnapped, revealing her peach-colored lacy bra that made her small breasts look bigger. Miracle indeed.

"Is that what you've been hiding under there this whole time?" he asked, his eyes growing hot as he looked at her.

"Yup."

"Now the pants."

Rose looked at him standing there, his penis making a tent with his long and loose T-shirt, his sweats down around his ankles, and did a running leap into his arms, wrapping her legs around his waist. He caught her, letting out a rich laugh. She could feel his erection on her bum and squirmed.

His breath caught in his throat, and his eyes closed as Rose nuzzled his neck. He walked over to his unmade bed, kissing her deep and hard, and flopped down on top of her, letting out a grunt as they landed. Then he stood, pulled off her shoes, grabbed her pant legs and yanked off her pants, then her Victoria Secret panties. As Rose reached back to undo her bra, she looked at him, this wild man who not two minutes before said he wanted to fire her. His deep blue eyes, eyes that had made women want to swoon, gazed down at her with an intensity that was unnerving.

"God damn, I don't know how I resisted this long." Then he took off his T-shirt the irresistible way men do—by reaching back behind his neck and pulling it off in one fluid motion. He fell on top of her, crushing her against him.

She wasn't long and leggy. She wasn't big-chested. She wasn't perfect. But Declan knew when he looked at her lying beneath him that he'd never seen a woman as beautiful as Rose. She had curves and the smoothest skin he'd ever felt. Her breasts her nice, round, with small areoles and hard little nipples that begged for his tongue. *Sweet.*

He sucked one nipple, and she arched against him, her hand searching and immediately finding his penis. More than two years since a woman had touched him, and Lord above, this woman could touch. She wrapped her hand around him, squeezing, then stroking.

"Nice, McDonald. I don't want to give you a big head or anything." She started laughing, tucking her head against his neck. "No pun intended." She lifted her face and smiled up at him. "You've got a nice package there."

"You're always joking," he said, feeling something hard and awful grow in his throat. He was about two seconds away from telling her he loved her, but he stopped himself.

"It's what I do. Makes life better."

"No," he said, taking one nipple in his mouth, licking her, listening for her gasp. "This makes life better."

Rose couldn't argue, especially not when he moved his hand between her legs and let out such a nice sound when he found out just how hot she was for him. It might have been embarrassing if she hadn't wanted so very much for him to come inside her.

Come inside her. Shit.

"Declan. Do you have protection?"

He lifted his head and stopped his hand. "You don't?"

Rose might have laughed if this hadn't been so very, very awful. She shook her head. "What, do you think I'm some sort of floozy?" she joked.

"I was hoping so. God, I was hoping so."

"I *am* on the pill." In her mind, she saw the parade of women he must have slept with—disease-ridden groupies looking to put a notch on their bedposts.

Declan looked up. "Thank God." He started kissing her again, moving his hand between her legs. *Oh, not fair.*

"But . . ."

"But what?"

"It's just that I'm sure you've been with a lot of women. I'm pretty sure I can vouch for myself."

"Rose, I haven't been with anyone in more than two years." He looked down at her, and Rose must have shown her reticence because he said, "But we shouldn't take the chance. Right?"

Rose let out a mock sob. "Right."

Declan rolled onto his back, then onto his stomach. "I'm just not the kind of person who carries condoms around with her. You're sure you don't have any?"

"Not close by," he said, his voice muffled by his pillow.

Rose lay flat out, naked, her body still buzzing from their almost lovemaking. "Well, this is a bummer."

He chuckled and turned his head toward her. "I still think I should fire you."

"Is this sexual harassment?" she said, raising one eyebrow.

"If I remember correctly, you jumped me."

She pretended to contemplate his argument. "Yes. But I could claim I felt pressured to. Or I could claim you intended to seduce me. Just look at the way you were dressed. No court would find against me. I could claim no woman would have been able to resist you—something you were calculatingly aware of."

"Still, I don't know how you could file suit against someone who's supposed to be dead." He smiled a victory.

"I could expose you."

"You already have," he said, looking back at his very naked body.

She laughed, her eyes traveling over his gorgeous posterior. She was about to lean down to kiss his very nice backside, when the phone rang. Reaching past her, but pausing to give her a quick kiss, he grabbed for the phone.

"Probably my mother," he mumbled before bringing the receiver to his ear.

"Hello?" He looked confused for a minute, then brought the receiver down and handed the phone to her.

"It's *your* mother."

Chapter 9

Providence Medical Center, like all hospitals, had that peculiar and awful smell: polish, urine, disinfectant. The minute it hit Rose, she wanted to run back out. It was impossible that she was here, impossible that not thirty minutes earlier she'd been naked and in Declan's arms. While her grandmother was suffering a heart attack.

It was impossible because Rose, like most mornings, had stopped in to see her grandmother to bring her a coffee from Dunkin' Donuts. She'd been fine. Maybe a little off; she'd even said she was tired. But she'd been fine. Rose didn't belong in this hospital walking up to the blue-haired volunteers to ask what room her grandmother was in.

"I'm looking for Angelica Fortino."

The woman tap-tapped onto her keyboard. "She's still in Emergency. Just follow the blue tiles until you get to the elevator. Go up to the main level, then follow the yellow tiles until you get to Emergency."

"I thought this was the main level."

The woman smiled blandly and looked behind Rose to the next person.

Rose looked down at her feet, seeing blue, red, and green tiles against a white floor and dutifully began following the blue tiles around a corner and to a bank of elevators.

Massive. Her mother had said it had been a massive heart attack. That they were still working on her. Working on her? What did that mean? Rose closed her eyes as the elevator door slid shut. *Okay, God, just get her through this. Just let me have a little more time with her. Please.*

The door opened, and Rose found herself in a large lobby area that looked more like a hotel than a hospital. But it still smelled. She stepped out and stopped. Her mother sat in one of the chairs directly across from the elevator. She looked up, and when she saw Rose, her face crumpled.

"She's gone." She stood and threw herself into her daughter's arms, sobbing and shaking and clinging.

No. It wasn't true. She'd just seen her grandmother. She was *fine*. She hadn't driven here like a maniac, hadn't begged God the whole way only to be too late. Nonna would wait for her. She couldn't be dead. Impossible.

And who the hell was this woman crying in her arms? Rose had never in her life seen her mother cry. What right did she have? She hadn't even liked Angelica. Rose was the one who should be crying, sobbing out gut-wrenching tears, not her mother, her cold mother who cared more about her career than her family.

As Rose held her grief-stricken mother it occurred to her that she had just lost her own mother. She must have loved her. Through all the disapproval, all the embarrassment, she'd loved her more than Rose could ever know. It tilted her world to think something she'd thought true all her life—that Rose's mother felt about her mother the same way Rose felt about hers— was not at all true.

"Oh, Rose, what am I going to do without her?" she

asked, squeezing her daughter tightly. "What am I going to do?"

Her mother was a mess, leaving Rose to handle everything. Rose, who had lost the only person in the world she'd loved unconditionally, had to pick out a coffin, make funeral arrangements at St. Anthony's, fill out a form the funeral home would use for Angelica's obituary. Rose cleaned her grandmother's already-spotless house to make it ready for the visitors who were certain to come. She picked out the dress she would be buried in, the flowers that would adorn the casket. She took the wedding ring Angelica had never taken off when her husband died and placed it in her grandmother's jewelry box. All this she handled, her throat thick and hurting from unshed tears, while her mother locked herself in her East Side brownstone and lay in bed. Ms. Heart of Stone had crumbled at the perfect time, Rose thought with little sympathy.

She was exhausted as she kicked off her Ecco boots and lay back on her well-worn brown plaid couch. She'd just closed her eyes when the phone rang.

"Hello."

"It's me."

Declan. The emotion that swept through Rose was frightening. At that moment, the need to see him, to hold him, nearly overwhelmed her. Rose clenched her jaw against the grief that welled up like a hot surging wave.

"Hey," she said, her voice soft and thin.

"I didn't hear from you, so I wanted to know if everything's okay."

Rose concentrated on breathing. She didn't want to break down now, not on the phone, not with him so far away. "She died," she choked out, then swallowed, gaining control. "It was a heart attack."

"Oh, God, I'm so sorry."

"Me, too." It was all she could manage because this being strong stuff was just getting too damned difficult. "The wake is tomorrow, and the funeral is Wednesday." She didn't ask him to be there; she knew he couldn't. But just the same, she wanted him there, needed him. She wanted him to be a hero, not a guy who was scared and hiding.

"That's going to be hard for you."

Especially alone. "Yeah. Listen, I can't make it into work until maybe Friday." She was disappointed, angry, even though she knew he couldn't come. Wouldn't come.

"Take the whole week off."

"I'll see you Monday, then." Rose hung up, not waiting for him to say good-bye, knowing she was asking too much of him and not caring. She was in a place she'd never been before, suffocating from sadness and a heart so hollow she didn't think anything could ever fill it. And the one other person she gave a damn about didn't give a damn about her. Rose knew she was being unfair but was too sad, too tired, to care.

"Why is she wearing that dress?"

Rose had a vivid fantasy of putting her hands around her mother's throat and squeezing. Her mother, who looked decidedly put-together, wore a black Chanel dress, a Gucci handbag on one arm and a boyfriend on the other, a state senator, no less. House Majority Whip. How nice for her.

"It was her favorite dress, Mother."

"I'm sure it was, but it's not appropriate for a casket."

Rose stared at her mother and blinked. "What?"

"She should be buried in a suit."

"She didn't have a suit."

"Well, good God, Rose, you should have known enough to get her one." Lucia darted a look at her boyfriend, then softened. "Honey, I know it was difficult, but even you must know that a faded old black dress is not appropriate."

Tears welled up in Rose's eyes as she pictured her grandmother in that dress her mother claimed was so inappropriate. She'd loved it, worn it often over the years to christenings and weddings, and to church on Sundays. Like all Nonna's dresses, it was black, but it had the prettiest cream-colored lace collar. Sure it was old and a little faded, but Rose couldn't imagine her grandmother wearing anything else. Certainly not a new suit.

"It was her favorite," she repeated, feeling twelve and stupid. And right. Even when she was a kid she always knew in her heart she'd been right about everything her mother said was improper or inappropriate.

"Well, it's too late now."

As soon as the first mourners arrived, her mother, clinging to the boyfriend, wept softly. Rose didn't want to think the tears were insincere; she'd seen real sorrow that day at the hospital. But it appeared her mother's lapse into human emotion had been brief. She was doing what she thought she ought, and doing it well. Rose stood slightly apart from the pair and stared at her grandmother, wishing she were alive so she could say something to make her laugh. *Will you look at her, Nonna? I can't believe she's letting salty tears get on that new dress.*

When Jenn arrived, her big belly leading the way, Rose broke down. The two friends cried together and clung while Jenn's husband stood back looking—and probably feeling—like this was the last place on earth he wanted to be.

"I can't believe it, Rose. I can't believe we're never going to sit in her kitchen and watch her cook. She was like a grandmother to me, too."

"It's still not real," Rose said, wiping her face with a soggy tissue.

"Your mother mourns well," Jenn said under her breath, and Rose had to bite her lip not to laugh. Good ol' Jenn.

"She actually told me I should have gone out and gotten my grandmother a new suit for the casket."

Jenn looked at Angelica. "But that's her favorite dress," she said, bewildered.

"That's what I said. I knew I was right," she said low and fierce.

Jenn gave her another hug. "I'm going to say a prayer. I'll stop by again before we leave. And I'll see you tomorrow, okay?"

Rose nodded and watched Jenn and her husband make their way to the casket, feeling more alone than ever. Hating herself, she looked toward the entrance thinking that maybe Declan would come. She knew he wouldn't, and he didn't. After two hours of steady visitors, the funeral director came in and quietly ushered the last mourners out of the room so he could give some last-minute instructions to the family.

Rose left the funeral parlor trailing after her mother and boyfriend and watched in near disbelief as the two went directly to their car, got in, and drove away without even saying good night. She was left standing there in the chilly night berating herself for wanting her mother to just once act as though she'd ever wanted her. Dead leaves swirled around her legs, scratching against the pavement. Dark. Still.

She shoved her hands deep into her coat pockets realizing with self-disgust that she'd been waiting for Declan to come out of hiding. *Hey, I came after all. I knew you'd need me.*

"Rose Pisano, you are pathetic," she said aloud, and made her way to her car.

*   *   *

At night in the early spring, the beach is a lonely place. No footprints mar the sand, no debris floats by on a breeze. No couples stroll by or huddle beneath a blanket. It's as if humankind has disappeared, leaving the ocean without witness to its endless motion.

Declan's cheeks stung from the wind, but he didn't care. Maybe he'd stay out on the beach all night, let the wind batter him, let the tide come in and rush around his legs. What the hell was he doing with this life of his? The woman he might possibly someday maybe fall in love with was going through hell right now, and he was here on this beach. He knew what it was like to lose someone you loved more than life itself. He'd seen for himself that the bond Rose had shared with her grandmother went beyond a normal granddaughter-grandmother relationship. She'd never know how close he came to calling a taxi and going to the wake. He'd even dialed the number before hanging up. What a guy— they ought to hand him a relationship medal for that one.

In the end, he'd talked himself out of it. If he'd shown up, someone would certainly have recognized him, and the wake would have turned into a fiasco. His own brother's funeral had been a nightmare because of his fame. One helicopter had come so close flower arrangements started falling off the casket. That was when his mother had lost it, and that was when whatever hadn't died with his brother went numb.

In the past two years he'd come to accept some of the blame for the public's fascination with him. In the beginning, when he hadn't a clue as to what his life would become, he gave his publicist free rein. He couldn't blame the guy; he was just doing his job and doing it well. Declan was on the cover of every major teen magazine, then on *People,* then *Time.* It was ridiculous. He got dates with super models, mega stars. He went to the hippest clubs in New York and L.A., photographers happily trailing after him. He didn't drink or do drugs, so even grandmothers loved him. He slept with more women than he cared to remember—even if he could. At first, he had a hell of a time—what red-blooded American man wouldn't want beautiful women at his feet? By the time he wanted it to stop, it was too late. He was a young Elvis, a male Princess Di. He was bigger than the biggest star. And he was miserable.

A fucking cliché, is what he was.

And now he was dead and nearly in love with a normal woman who made him laugh when he didn't want to. Who needed him now. The past two days he couldn't get her out of his head, couldn't stop seeing her standing in front of him and ripping off that smock with such abandon. The taste of her. The sounds she made. He put his hands on either side of his head and tried to squeeze the images out.

Tomorrow was the funeral, and of course he wouldn't go. Maybe he should call. Maybe he should just pretend he'd never seen her naked, never taken her nipples into his mouth, never felt how hot and wet she was between her legs. Declan picked up a rock and threw it as hard as he could into the roaring surf. It disappeared beneath the black surging water.

This not falling in love stuff was easy, he'd told his mother, just like shutting off a faucet. Just like plugging a fire hose with a grain of sand. Easy.

" 'Leah's Song' is at number four."

"Hello to you, too, Mom."

"I think we've got to start thinking about what's going to happen when this all busts open." Declan could imagine his mother's pensive expression as he listened to the hissing sound of empty air on the phone. Then: "I guess I should have called you last night—but it was late and I think I didn't want to alarm you—but some private detective called me."

Declan felt his stomach drop about ten inches. "What did he say?"

"*She* wanted to know if I knew anything about Angel's Songs, and I panicked and lied."

Declan swore beneath his breath. "I knew this was a bad idea."

"I'm sorry, honey, but I didn't know what else to do."

"I'm not blaming you." He let out a humorless laugh. "How the hell did things get so crazy? How did I let all this happen? I'm not stupid. And I'm not a coward. But here I am hiding out in the middle of nowhere with a private detective tracking me down like I'm some sort of criminal. How did this happen?"

It was a rhetorical question, but his mother answered anyway. "You are not a coward," she said forcefully, making Declan smile. "You saved my sanity. Do you realize that for the first time in a decade I can go to the store without someone trailing after me with a camera? And your brother . . ."

Declan heard her voice catch and felt the rage that threatened to choke him build. It was enough the photographers trailed him, but that they followed his mother and brother around had been maddening. They'd claimed his celebrity made them fair game. His brother had dabbled in acting, and so the tabloid press used that to justify their tactics. But it was all because of him. The headline that sealed his brother's fate hadn't read: MICHAEL MCDONALD DRUNK AGAIN. It was DECLAN MCDONALD KIN IN DETOX.

Poor Michael. He liked to drink but always made certain he didn't drive. But that one time he'd used poor judgment and drove and got arrested for DUI. Declan had paid for a jaunt in the Betty Ford Center, and Michael had been on the wagon for months. The medical examiner had determined alcohol was not a factor in the single car accident that had ended his life. Michael had simply been driving too fast on a road he was not familiar with, and Declan was convinced his brother had been trying to avoid the photographers who had dogged him ever since his arrest.

Dogged him because he had a famous brother.

"Mom, what am I going to do?"

He heard her long breath and closed his eyes, knowing his mother was more frightened than he about what would happen.

When she finally spoke, her voice was surprisingly strong. "When you're ready, you're going to call your publicist and organize a press conference. You're going to tell them the truth, that you never meant to pretend to be dead until everyone assumed you were. That it was the paparazzi that drove you underground, that you're sorry for any trouble you might have caused anyone. I'm pretty sure no laws were broken, no fraud committed, because no insurance was involved and I paid all your taxes. You simply wanted to be left alone."

Declan felt the bile rise in his throat. "This is going to suck."

His mother let out a low chuckle. "Honey, it's going to be worse than that. You have to decide what comes next, whether you disappear again or whether you do the talk show circuit and restart your career."

Disappear. Forever this time. He could move to a foreign country—something he'd contemplated before. But he'd always rejected the idea that he could be forced to leave the country he loved by a bunch of newshounds. He wouldn't go that route. No matter what he did, where he went, he couldn't hope to have a normal life now. He couldn't live in a simple little bungalow on a quiet city street and spend the rest of his life raising kids with . . .

He'd have to say good-bye to Rose. Thank God they

never made love, for saying good-bye would have been all the more difficult.

"Two weeks. No, a month. I'll call Judy and arrange a press conference in a month." A month with Rose, thirty days. "When the time comes, you should go off somewhere. I don't want you getting involved."

"Oh, Declan, of course I'm involved."

"I mean it. I want you gone. I can't stand thinking that this is going to hurt you. Please go somewhere."

"All right. Just give me a little bit of a warning."

Declan gripped the phone hard at the way his mother sounded—frightened and worried. "Okay. Call me if anything else happens. And, Mom? I'm so damned sorry about all this."

" 'Leah's Song' is number four. I want to know what's going on with the investigation."

Jill Brighton leaned back in her black leather chair, steepled her fingers beneath her chin, and smiled at Ellen Lang. She'd been a cop for twenty years and a private investigator for five, and she knew when a person was teetering on the edge—and this women, she was just about hanging on by her well-polished fingernails. When she'd marched into her office two weeks ago, Jill had thought she'd be calling Lang the next day. But the mysterious songwriter was a bit more elusive than she'd thought thanks to the secretive staff at Angel's Songs. It took her nearly two weeks to find an employee who was desperate enough for cash to sell her information. She hadn't gotten a lot, just the name of a company out of Delaware to which Angel's Songs had been sending its checks. That led her to Arizona, to a quiet street outside of Tempe where she found the surprise of a lifetime.

"Angel's Songs has been sending its checks to a

company called Clarke Enterprises. Its only officer is Carol Clarke."

Ellen shook her head, her soft, well-cut, and expertly dyed brown hair moving slightly. She looked irritated and impatient. "That name doesn't mean anything to me."

"How about the name Declan McDonald."

Ellen laughed. "He's dead."

"Is he now? They never did find his body. And Miss Clarke happens to be Declan McDonald's grieving mother." She smiled. "Ding, ding, ding, we have a winner."

Ellen frowned at her sound effect, and Jill decided then and there the woman didn't have a sense of humor. Not about Angel's Songs anyway.

"Maybe she wrote the song but because of her son's notoriety wanted to remain anonymous. He had to get his talent somewhere."

Jill's smile deflated. "Yeah, I thought of that. But when I visited Ms. Clarke, she denied knowing anything about Angel's Songs."

"You think she's lying?"

"Like a rug." And she smiled again. Declan McDonald was alive and writing songs, and she wanted to be the one to expose him. Talk about a coup. It wasn't easy being one of only a few women in the private investigator business, and news like this would bring in big-time business. She knew the *Star* and *Enquirer* had their so-called investigative reporters on the case, but they'd get nowhere. The employees at Angel's Songs were surprisingly ethical. The only reason the one woman helped her was because she represented Ellen Lang, whom she admired. The cash was only part of the incentive.

"Did you tell her why you are looking for her? That I simply want to thank her?"

"She didn't buy it. And frankly, Mrs. Lang, I don't either. You're spending a lot of cash on a thank-you card, if you ask me."

"I'm not asking you. However, it's the truth. 'Leah's Song' has had a profound affect on myself and my husband, not to mention a boon to fund-raising for childhood leukemia research. Call it curiosity or obsession, but I need to find the song's author."

Lang was telling the truth. Jill's gut told her that, and her gut was almost never wrong. "I need another five thousand."

The woman didn't even try to hide her irritation. "But you haven't found anything yet. At least nothing concrete."

"I don't get paid by my success rate, Mrs. Lang. I get paid for the hours I put in, and I get paid up front. Flying around the country is expensive. Unless you're done?"

Lang pressed her lips together. "All right, I'll give you the five thousand. But I would like to know what you plan."

Jill smiled. "I plan to prove Declan McDonald is alive and that he wrote 'Leah's Song.' "

Ellen lay next to Matthew, wide awake in their darkened bedroom. "Do you think we should give up trying to find who wrote the song?"

"For one thing, I really don't care who wrote the song. For another, since when has my opinion on any of this mattered?"

Ellen tried to not let his hostility get to her. "I really want to know what you think?"

Matthew let out a sigh and got up on one elbow to let her know he was listening. "Why is it so important to you, Ellen? We've spent God knows how much money on private investigators and for what purpose. To find someone who obviously doesn't want to be found."

"What if the person who wrote it could triple sales of 'Leah's Song.' What if that money led to a cure?"

"Sounds like an ethical dilemma that I'm not up for solving right now. Besides, you know I've never been an advocate of the ends justifying the means."

Ellen fiddled with the comforter, not liking that Matthew was probably right. "What if the person who wrote 'Leah's Song' is Declan McDonald," she said in a small voice. She didn't believe it, but what if Jill Brighton was right? If Declan McDonald wrote that song, it would be an incredible boon.

"Isn't he dead?"

Ellen rolled her eyes. "Yes, he's supposed to be dead. But Jill thinks he might be alive and wrote 'Leah's Song.' If that's true, just think what it could mean."

"Does she have any proof?"

"Actually, she does. Angel's Songs sends checks to a company called Clarke Enterprises, whose principal officer is Carol Clarke. Declan McDonald's mother."

"Well, then, she wrote the song. Isn't that more likely than claiming someone who's been dead for years wrote it?"

"That's what I thought, too. But Clarke insisted she didn't know anything about the song. If she did write it, why would she do that when all I want to do is thank the woman?"

"I don't know, babe," Matthew said, clearly tired of this conversation. He turned over, and Ellen stared at his back for a long time, feeling depressed as hell. He'd just ended the longest conversation they'd had in weeks, and Ellen couldn't remember the last time they'd made love. It had been months ago, a decision made by mutual but silent agreement. If things didn't change soon, they weren't going to make it. After everything they'd gone through together, Ellen wasn't ready to say goodbye. Not yet.

"Matthew?"

"What." From his tone, she was obviously trying his patience.

"Are you having an affair?"

"What?"

"Because, well . . ."

"Oh, for God's sakes, Ellen."

"But it's not natural for a man and a woman, for us, to go without sex for so long."

He reached over and turned on the light so he could look her in the eye. "I am not having an affair. I've just been busy and, well, not particularly interested if you want the truth."

"Oh." Neither had she, but having him say such a thing out loud was surprisingly crushing.

"Well, have *you* been interested?"

"Not really."

He turned off the light.

"Matthew?"

A grunt.

"I think we should make love."

"All right."

Ellen grimaced. "Not tonight. But soon, okay?"

"Fine."

She lay there, wide awake, staring at the ceiling, and wondering if they could ever be normal again. It seemed a lifetime ago when they'd needed and loved each other so much it was intoxicating. Leah's illness and death had sucked them dry of any emotion but anger. What the hell were they so angry about? So many couples divorced after losing a child, and she didn't want to be one of them. Matthew was a stranger, and she was pretty damn certain that she was a stranger to him. He didn't understand her involvement with fund-raising, her obsession with "Leah's Song," her nearly physical need to find out who wrote it. She could hardly understand it herself.

Before Leah had become sick, they'd talked about more kids, two or three. Everything had been put on hold, their very lives. And it was still like that, suspended animation; breathing, eating, sleeping, but not truly living. For the longest time, Ellen had liked her numb half-life. But it was time, she realized, to start living again.

Chapter 10

*Roasted whole tautog for two with sauce puttanesca,
atop wilted spinach served with couscous, $38.00*

Rose sat in her car for a long time before garnering
the energy to get out and walk toward Declan's home.
She didn't know what she was going to say to him, how
she was going to act, and right now her emotions were
so raw, she was afraid she might say something she'd
regret. Maybe she should take another day off. Maybe
she should just quit this job and go on her merry way.
Her heart, so battered now, couldn't take a conversation
with Declan that left her feeling like some lovesick idiot.
He hadn't sounded like a boyfriend on the phone when
she'd told him her grandmother died; he'd sounded like
a concerned employer. A concerned employer she'd almost been dumb enough to sleep with. Thank God that
didn't happen.

She gripped the steering wheel hard before shoving
the door open. It was bone-chilling cold, the wind off
the water damp and hard, blowing in a fog so thick she
could feel it against her face like a mist. Declan's house
stood out stark white against the dark sky, looking par-

ticularly uninviting. Huddling in her coat, she ducked her head and jogged to the door. Before she could press the buzzer, the door clicked, and she knew he'd been watching for her.

Inside, it was dark and cold and damp. "You could put the heat on," she mumbled, shoving her hands deeper into her pockets.

"There's something wrong with the furnace."

Rose nearly jumped out of her coat to see him there, sitting on the bottom step of the stairs that led to his lair. "You scared the hell out of me."

"Sorry." He stood, looking pensive and unsure, the way people look when they don't know what to say to someone who's just lost someone they love. "If you're not up to working today . . ."

"I'm fine," she said, and walked toward the kitchen. "I don't know what's in the pantry, but I'll figure something out."

"Bert's made their delivery this morning," he said, following behind her.

"I'll come up with something, then. I'll send it up at lunch." Okay, she did know how she felt. She was angry with him, majorly mad and feeling surly.

She heard his footsteps stop, and she kept walking because there was nothing more scary than her mouth when she was feeling surly. She was definitely going to say something she'd regret if he was stupid enough to follow her into the kitchen.

"I couldn't go, Rose."

She stopped dead, closing her eyes and pressing her lips together. *Don't talk, don't say a word. Don't do it, Rose.*

"It would have turned your grandmother's funeral into a circus."

She turned slowly, with careful precision. In control. "I know," she said pleasantly.

"Then why are you acting so pissy?"

She raised her eyebrows as if truly surprised by his observation. "I'm not."

"Okay. You're not mad because I couldn't be there for you when the most important person in the world to you died. You're not upset at all. I can tell."

That did it. Rose was only human, and with him baiting her, how could she not respond. No normal person could expect her to stand there and not launch into a tirade. Rose clenched her teeth together, stalwartly keeping that tirade she so desperately wanted to launch inside her gut. It was making her sick, this awful fight with sanity, but in the end it would be worth it, she told herself.

"I was, I'll admit that. But"—*And here comes the biggest lie*—"I'm not now. I understand." *You big jerk.*

He stared at her for a long time, his blue eyes searching her face, which she kept carefully bland. "I almost called a cab." And then he smiled one of his lopsided smiles meant to make a woman forgive him for just about anything.

"Wow. I think I'll nominate you for hero of the year."

He ducked his head then, but kept his eyes on her, a gesture that told Rose he was getting angry with her. "It would have been a fiasco, Rose."

It bubbled up out of deep in her gut before she even knew it was coming. "You big, egotistical idiot. Do you think that's all I cared about, was you standing next to me holding my hand? You didn't have to come to the wake or the funeral. You didn't have to announce your presence. But you could have been there for me. You could have called or come to my house and been there. I almost slept with you. I know that doesn't mean squat to you, but it meant something to me. Thank God for small favors that I didn't. I'm sorry that I thought there was more to us than sex. When you care about someone, you don't hide away in a cave." She stopped, putting her fists against her forehead. "God, I hate that I'm doing this. I hate that I'm turning into some needy woman. Because I'm not, but my Nonna just died and, damn it, it would have been nice if you'd at least called. Shit! Never mind. Just never mind." She was talking in circles, mad at him, mad at herself.

His expression had turned to stone. "Are you finished?"

Rose swallowed and shook her head. "I guess I just realized that even if we were friends and nothing more that you'll still never be there for me. Ever. Not as long as you're living like this."

He closed his eyes briefly, and an odd little smile touched his lips. "You're right. But if you think I could have been there for you if I wasn't hiding, you're wrong."

"What do you mean?"

"I mean someday this is going to end. I can't live the rest of my life like this. And when I do decide to come out of hiding I can't carry any baggage with me."

Rose raised one eyebrow. "Are you calling me baggage?"

"Not in the negative sense, in the metaphorical sense."

"You're telling me that there's absolutely no future for us."

"That's right."

Rose started to laugh. "No kidding. And here I was planning our wedding." She hooted even louder, and he was beginning to look even more annoyed.

"I wanted to be honest with you."

She waved a hand at him and doubled over. "Stop it, you're killing me."

"Hey, don't take it so badly," he said dryly, a little irritated.

"I'm sorry," she said, wiping her eyes. And suddenly her face crumpled, and she wasn't laughing-crying. She was crying-crying, because it wasn't funny. It was horrible, because she'd been laughing at herself as much as at him. Deep down inside, where she hadn't wanted to look, a fantasy had been brewing that put them together forever, that had him growing old with her. "My emotions are a little raw right now," she said, getting herself under control.

"I can see that."

"I'm going to get lunch together. I think working will help. Forget everything I said, everything. I mean, sex is just sex, right? We both know there's nothing else going on here."

Declan watched her go, fighting the urge to follow her and hold her and tell her he was full of shit. He wanted to tell her everything would be all right; they could live happily ever after, even after he called the press conference that he inevitably would have to call. He couldn't do that because if he did, it would all be lies. He couldn't protect his brother; he wouldn't be able to protect her.

At lunchtime, she brought up a tray looking a bit sheepish. She didn't look directly at him, keeping her gaze on the food in front of her as she placed the tray on his cluttered table. "Chicken salad with thyme on foccacia. Sprouts and tomato. I've got a cold pasta salad on the side."

"Would you like to take a walk on the beach with me tonight?"

She didn't look up. "The lettuce is a little wilty, so I put in sprouts. I'm going to have to call Bert's and complain."

Okay, she doesn't want to do this. But he did. He wanted to be able to talk to her, to hold her. He wanted her lying next to him in his bed and to hell with the future. "It's supposed to be pretty warm out. Only in the fifties. I'll bring a blanket."

"The bread's still a little warm, but I think it's—"

"Rose. Stop it."

She glared at him, taking his water off the tray and placing it a bit too roughly on the table. "And this is spring water. Not from the tap, even though the water here is some of the best quality in the country."

"I'm sorry."

"Okay. Great. You're all set."

"Jesus, Rose, what do you want from me?"

"Nothing. Listen, I understand that you're lonely, that you don't have anyone to talk to, but I can't do this. I can't be your friend and I can't be your lover. I can't. You're used to this, I'm not."

"What the hell is that supposed to mean?"

"Only that you can walk away without looking back and I can't. I feel bad about breaking up with guys I can't stand, never mind someone I like."

He grinned at her. "So, you like me, huh?"

She narrowed her eyes at him. "When I don't want to kill you, sure."

"That's something."

She looked up at the ceiling and let out a puff of air. She was giving in. *Please let her give in,* Declan prayed. "Rose. Walk on the beach with me tonight. That's all. Just a walk. Let's not think about tomorrow."

"Not thinking about it doesn't mean it's not going to happen."

He gave her a boyishly endearing shrug.

"Okay. I'll walk on the beach with you." Rose knew she sounded like a woman giving in to torture, and it didn't help that all he could do was smile. "But before we do, I want to get something straight."

"Yes, I want to sleep with you."

Rose gave him a look. "No strings attached, right?" Why did that sound so damned awful? And like such a lie?

"Right," he answered with depressing speed.

She could do this. She could sleep with him and make certain she didn't fall in love—okay, fall more in love with him. At least she'd have wonderful memories, and maybe one day when all this was over and he was back to his old life, he might send her front row tickets to one of his concerts. And she'd be one of about a thousand idiots gazing up on stage in love with him.

"I don't know, Declan, it all seems kind of sleazy to plan it all out. To announce it. Why don't we just see what happens. You know, we might start kissing and find out all that chemistry stuff is all gone."

He gave her a lopsided grin. "I don't think so."

She looked up at the ceiling. "I don't really find you all that attractive anymore."

"Liar."

"No, really," she said innocently. "I'm over that oh-my-God-it's-Declan-McDonald thing. Now you're just a guy. A weird guy, actually, who has this strange fascination with walking on the beach at night."

"Actually, I have a strange fascination with you."

She gave him a look of disbelief. "You've got to get it through your head that lines like that don't work on me."

"It's the truth." He seemed a bit put out that she wasn't going to fall at his feet and beg for his kisses.

"Yeah, yeah." She turned to leave and waved a hand. "See you when the sun goes down."

"Come on, let's go." He threw a small bundle at her and began walking toward the back of the house.

"I think I've changed my mind."

"I can beg," he said, clearly not thinking he'd have to.

"That would be interesting to watch."

He kept walking, and she gave in—again. She caught up to him and walked beside him, not touching but feeling strange and jittery. If she wanted to, they would make love tonight. The thing was, she wasn't certain if she wanted to. She was disappointed in him, hurt by him, and she knew he didn't come close to feeling about her the way she felt about him. He liked her and was horny, and that was probably enough for him. Rose knew herself enough to realize that if they made love, she'd be a goner. She could feel it happening, a pull that was both frightening and exciting.

The moon was remarkably bright, casting everything in a light silvery glow. When they reached the end of a short path, the Atlantic Ocean opened up before them, a low roar that rose and fell with each wave that came ashore. Declan spread out one blanket and dropped the other in the middle, then stood staring at the waves, pensive and silent.

"Okay. We're at the beach. What now?"

"Tell me about your childhood."

Rose smiled. "You're kidding."

"No. Go ahead." He sat down at the edge of the blanket, picked up some sand and let it drift through his fingers.

"Aren't we going to walk on the beach?"

"We just did. Come on, sit."

Rose was, she could admit it, disappointed. She had expected him to hold her hand as they had a romantic walk, then draw her into his arms, the waves crashing near their feet, right before they fell together and made passionate love on the beach. *Rose, Rose, you're beautiful. My God, I love you. How could I have thought otherwise?*

"Okay," she said, sitting next to him. "My mother and father got divorced when I was two. He remarried a year later and moved to Florida. He calls on my birthday and sends a gift for Christmas. My mother is an attorney. Corporate law. She divorced my father because he wanted her to be a good Italian wife and my mother didn't. I spent most of my childhood with my grandparents while my mother went to school. That's about it."

"Who was your best friend?"

"My grandmother," she answered without hesitation. She lay down, resting her head on her folded hands, and gazed up at the few stars bright enough to fight the moon for the sky. "My mother never wanted me. I know that, and it really doesn't bother me. I always had Nonna. I've learned that just because someone gives birth to you doesn't mean you automatically have to love them. I love my mother, but it's this cold, unloving, realistic love. Does that make sense?"

She saw Declan shrug. "I was always close to my mother, so it's hard to imagine that kind of relationship."

"What about your father?"

Declan lay back on the blanket, turning on his side and resting his head on one hand. "He died in a plane crash when I was eight."

"Oh. I think I remember reading that. Do you remember him?"

"Sometimes it's hard to know what are memories and what comes from my mother's stories. She never remarried and never dated. When I was a kid, I never even thought about how unusual that was. But now I wonder why she never remarried. I think that was it for her. She had found a man to love, and when he died, she couldn't imagine loving anyone else."

Rose, already an emotional wreck, felt tears burning her eyes. "That's so sad."

"My father is just a shadowy figure in my head. But I have this memory that's so damn sharp. Right before he left, he came into our room. We had bunk beds and I was on the top bunk. It must have been early morning because it was so dark. He came in to say good-bye. And he told me I was a big boy and to take care of my mother and brother."

Rose turned her head to look at him. "Oh, Dec."

"Yeah. I was just a kid, but I took those words to heart, especially when he died. If he'd have known he was going to die, I know he never would have said something like that."

"I never read that story anywhere."

"I never told anyone." He let out a soft, sad laugh. "Not even my mother."

Rose's heart broke for that little boy who'd been shouldered with the burden of "taking care" of his mother and brother. She let out a long sigh. "I suppose I'm going to have to give you pity sex now."

He laughed and shook his head. "You have to, huh?"

"Yes." And suddenly, Rose wasn't joking. It was so strange how just minutes ago they were merely friends talking about their childhoods, and with one look, she was flooded with lust. He saw it, too, because that smile slowly disappeared, then bloomed again.

"Let's go back to the house."

Chapter 11

Spinach "nudies" under a blanket of homemade pasta sheets with browned butter and parmigiano, $16.00

Rose knew what she was doing. She wasn't a virgin, but her heart was, and so she wasn't truly prepared for what making love to Declan would do to her. Perhaps had she known, she would have run to her car rather than hold hands and snuggle together all the way back to the house. Rose was about to find out what making love was, not in the physical sense—she had a pretty good handle on that part—but in the emotional, heart, I-can't-live-without-you sense. All the lectures she'd given herself, every word pleading with herself not to fall too hard, were as futile as dusting.

They were in his bedroom, he rummaging in a closet that looked as disorganized as the rest of the room, and she sitting on his sofa barefoot, arms crossed, fingers digging hard into her skin. "What are you looking for?"

"Condoms," he said, throwing a sneaker out of the way. "Aha." He held up the box and read: "Ribbed for her pleasure. Extra large."

"Oh, no," moaned Rose.

"What? Don't tell me you're allergic to latex."

"No, it's that extra large part. Won't it just slip right off?" She giggle evilly.

"Come here and I'll show you," he said, waggling his eyebrows.

"Oh, don't frighten me so," she said. "You know I've never seen a man so big. I'm sooo scared." With that, she pulled off her shirt, unsnapped her bra, and started unbuttoning her pants.

"Don't be shy."

"It's just that I'm so very, very afraid." She pulled off her pants and went to him wearing only her panties, her hand going immediately to the nicely sized penile shape beneath his pants.

"Oh, God," he said, letting out a shaking breath. "Don't hurt me."

Rose laughed, throwing back her head, her eyes sparkling and alive with what she knew was love. She just hoped he'd mistake that look for lust, because she was feeling plenty of that, too. "Let's just take a look at you." She unbuttoned and unzipped and knelt down in front of him, smiling when she heard his breath come in, sharp and harsh. "I'd say above average," she said, watching his penis spring out of his boxers. "But certainly not extra large." She grinned up at him right before laying her lips softly on the very tip. She darted out her tongue. And he pushed her head away.

"Rose. Jesus."

"What's wrong?" she asked, all innocence.

"You do realize I haven't had sex for more than two years."

"Mmmm-hmmm."

"And you do know that I've sort of had this in mind— only in fantasy mode—since the day I saw you."

"So?" She kissed him again. "Mmmm."

"If you do that again, we're not going to need that condom. Get it?"

Rose couldn't stop the roaring thrill that sloshed through her. No one had ever wanted her so much. Granted, the poor guy hadn't gotten any in years, but it was still heady, powerful stuff. Just to torture him, she gave him one, long French kiss before standing up and grinning at him.

"You are something, you know that, Rose?"

"I know."

He pulled her to him, his mouth open and wonderfully intoxicating. His tongue moving slowly against hers, their teeth crashing together before they found the perfect position. He was such a good kisser, Rose thought, feeling more frenzied with each sweep of his tongue. Sex had always been pleasant, but it had never been the stuff she'd read about in novels, that overwhelming strip-off-your-clothes-and-let-me-fuck-you stuff. He let out a low rumbling moan that was like a stroke between her legs.

He stepped back only long enough to pull off his shirt, kick off his shoes, and step out of his jeans. Then he dragged her to his bed, and they fell together, a laughing tangle of arms and legs.

"If I start to cry, ignore me," he said, nuzzling her neck.

"I like the neck thing."

"Oh?" And so he stayed there awhile, kissing and sucking gently while his hands on her breasts drove her absolutely insane.

"I like the breast thing, too," she said, hearing herself sounding breathy, like an Italian Marilyn Monroe.

"What about the between the legs thing?" he asked, and before she could answer, he was there, pulling down her panties, kissing her and moving his tongue against her and generally driving her insane.

"I like," was all she could get out before she screamed. Rose was not a screamer. But apparently now she was.

While she was still loving the feeling of coming harder

than she had her entire life, he was slipping the condom on and slipping inside her. He kissed her nipples, all the while making these deep sounds of masculine pleasure that were nearly as erotic as everything else he was doing to her.

"Oh, Dec." *I love you. Oh, damn, I love you so much.*

He began moving faster, and Rose could feel herself again climbing toward orgasm, something that had never happened before. She came, sudden and hot, and he moved fast and hard and groaned out her name when he came. She could feel his heart pumping madly against her breast, so fast it seemed impossible that he wasn't in some sort of cardiac distress.

Declan pressed his lips against her neck and heard her sigh his name and knew—if he didn't love her before—that he sure as hell loved her now. The panic that hit him then was enough to make a weaker man die on the spot. His heart, which had begun to slow down a notch, sped up again, but this time it was a painful, scary feeling. This was no good. How in hell was he going to be able to say good-bye to her when at this moment all he could think of was how right she felt lying next to him. She moved a little, luxuriating in the feel of their bodies, and he barely stopped himself from groaning in agony.

Okay, stop it, you idiot. She's just a woman. Nothing special. She's just the sexiest, funniest, warmest, most understanding, toughest, most honest woman you've ever met. You can get over her. Just don't let it go too far.

He lifted his head and looked down at her. She smiled at him, her brown eyes lit with humor, her hair mussy from being tousled by their lovemaking, her lips red and puffy and sexy as hell from their kisses. And his heart nearly exploded again.

Crap.

"You were worth the wait," he said, trying with all his being to sound nonchalant, to sound as if he didn't want to run out and buy the biggest diamond ring at Tiffany's and slap it on her finger. All that time trying not to hurt her, all his noble efforts came down to this: he was the one who was going to get hurt. He hurt already knowing in less than a month he'd have to walk away. He'd have to be an ass, thank her for being a great "friend," and never call her again. He'd done it at least a dozen times in the past without a second thought. He was slightly ashamed of that fact, but he couldn't hide from the truth. He'd been a one-man heart-wrecking crew and hadn't really cared until this moment. Because until this moment he hadn't understood the devastation that love could bring.

He drew her closer, burying his head in her hair, breathing deeply—damn, she smelled good, a funny little mix of shampoo and good cooking—telling himself to remember this moment and all the moments they'd share in the next few weeks. Then, maybe, they could work something out. Maybe he'd be able to protect her from the cameras and the media. Maybe when he called that press conference no one would care. And maybe he'd sprout wings and start to fly around and around and . . .

"You know, Declan, if I didn't know any better, I'd say this was more than just sex. You like me."

He lifted his head again, unable to come up with some smart-aleck reply. Jesus, if he'd have known falling in love hurt this much, he would have done a better job keeping her away. "I like you too damn much," he said, then kissed her cheek right at the corner of her mouth, feeling her smile against his lips.

She sighed. "This is so tragic. The famous star falls for the simple country girl but must leave her and his broken heart behind."

Her joking made him mad, really mad, for the first time. This wasn't funny. And the only way she could think it was funny was because she didn't love him. He sat up, bringing his legs over the side of the bed and drawing the sheet with him so it covered his lap. "Everything isn't a joke," he said. He felt a warm hand on his back, and he closed his eyes.

"Hey, I'm sorry. I know I joke too much. Wouldn't you rather have me cracking jokes than crying?"

Joking again. This girl was a laugh a minute. He stood up, dragging the sheet with him, unwilling to let her see him naked, even though they'd just made love. He dropped the sheet but quickly pulled on his sweats before turning back to her. And catching his breath. She was still lying there naked on her stomach, but she'd twisted around a bit so she could look at him. His eyes rested on her perfectly round bum, then drifted up to her face. She was smiling.

"Declan, I'm trying real hard here to be nonchalant about having sex with a guy I like more than any other guy I've ever liked in my life. You've got to work with me or I'm going to turn into a basket case and get all clingy and girlfriendy, and you and I both know that would drive you crazy."

Declan knew Rose was making sense, but he couldn't bring himself to admit it.

"I should go."

No. "No."

She got up, walked to her clothes, and began getting dressed. "It's late and I've got a long drive."

"Stay." That single word came out much too intense, so he smiled. "Stay tonight. You said yourself you've got a long drive. Just stay. Tonight."

She drew in a long breath, and he held his.

"I knew this was a bad idea," she said, her tone accusing, but when he opened his arms, she stepped right in.

She'd known all along he was gorgeous, that he could sing pretty good and, obviously, write music. She hadn't been kidding when she'd told him she wasn't a big fan and believed his music was sentimental crap. All along, Rose believed he was a good-looking guy with just enough talent and sex appeal to make it big in a business that chewed up people and spit them out. So on the second night of her stay, Rose was floored, completely blown away, when he took out a bunch of old sheet music and began playing like a friggin' virtuoso. He played Chopin, Beethoven, Schumann, Bach, and he played so well it brought tears to her eyes.

It all started when she'd begun kidding him about his lack of talent. "All good looks, McDonald, and a smidgeon of talent. I'm not saying you weren't a genius for exploiting that bit of talent, but you're no Bruce Springsteen."

He smiled. "That's your type of music, huh?"

Rose gave him a small shrug. "Am I hurting your feelings?"

"Not at all. Because you're wrong."

"Can you even play that thing?" she asked, knowing full well he could but unwilling to admit she'd been spying on him. "Or do you just write music with it. I know your hands felt like you could play, but . . ."

"I play okay."

Rose plunked herself down on his couch, pulled up her knees, and wrapped her arms around her legs. "Play for me. I command it." She looked him over. He was dressed in a faded old T-shirt and sweats he'd cut into shorts, his feet bare and his hair a mess from being Rose-tousled. He was a jock who needed a shower, not a pianist.

He started with something simple, a piece even Rose, who by no means was a classical music fan, recognized. "Fur Elise." She remembered her neighbor playing that very same song during the first year of her piano lessons. Even the song she'd heard him play earlier, while hauntingly beautiful, had not sounded particularly difficult to play.

"Not impressed, McDonald," she said when he finished.

He just smiled and flipped through his music. "Just wanted to limber up," he said, then placed a book on the baby grand's music stand and flattened the pages. And then he started to play, and after just a few moments, her body felt a tingling rush of emotion.

"Man oh man," she whispered. "He's a friggin' concert pianist."

Rose had been to a few concerts at the Providence Performing Arts Center, and she knew enough to know that Declan was good—damn good. She sat there mesmerized, watching his fingers fly over the keys, pounding, pounding, then soft as a butterfly, sweeping over the keys, looking as if he wasn't touching them, but producing a sound so beautiful her eyes burned with tears.

When he was done, he turned, an I-told-you-so look on his face.

"Play another," was all she could say. And he did. For hours he gave her a free concert, until he worked up a sweat, his blond hair turning dark and spiky at the base of his neck from the moisture. Finally, he rested his fingers lightly on the keys, still stroking them but not making a sound.

"Why aren't you a concert pianist? You're incredible."

He turned, giving her a half-smile, and shook his head. "I'm not good enough."

"But you are. You're unbelievably good."

"If you heard a real virtuoso playing those same pieces, you'd know what I mean. I'm okay. I can entertain at a party, but not with a symphony orchestra and not alone. I figured that out when I was sixteen and I started taking jazz lessons." He turned and played a few bars of "Don't Get Around Much Anymore."

"I started writing songs and got a bunch of kids together. Formed a band. The Desert Sons. S-O-N."

"Cute."

"We were from Arizona." He shrugged. "The rest is history."

"What happened to the band."

"You really don't read you *People* magazine, do you? I was the singer, the songwriter, the best musician. A guy named Bart Bunker spotted us at a Chinese restaurant one Saturday night and signed me, and not the rest of the band. Said they stunk and I guess they did. Bunker was my first manager. My mom didn't trust him, so I fired him and hired Melissa Sturn."

"Even I've heard of Melissa Sturn."

"Yeah. She promised to do great things for me, but I really didn't care. I was so into the music, the sounds, the music in my head that I had to write down. I was just a stupid, idealistic kid. My lyrics needed help, but the music made them sound better than they really were. The first time I heard one of my songs on the radio, it was surreal. Some guy had headphones on, and the volume was up high, and I could hear my song. His eyes were closed, and he was groovin' to it. It was bizarre. And great. I thought I could write these songs, give them to people, and go on with my life. That's all I ever really wanted. Then everything snowballed. Melissa got my career into high gear, and I was flying above the clouds. My biggest mistake was believing everything the press said about me. That and hiring a publicist." Declan shook his head. "It was good for a long time. And then it wasn't. The photographers started hounding my family. I still don't get why. My brother acted a little bit, local theater, and the press was all over him. My mother couldn't go grocery shopping without seeing a photographer. It was crazy."

Rose walked to him and climbed on his lap, wrapping her legs around his body and throwing her arms around his neck. "Let's talk about something else," she said, kissing him. He smelled so good, warm and slightly sweaty, but in a good way. His arms came around her instantly, his fingers interlocking behind her back.

"Do you really want to talk?"

Rose pressed herself against his erection. "No. I hate talking during sex."

Declan smiled against her mouth. "I noticed you were the strong and silent type."

"And I can only thank the gods you're not one of those men who like to have a play-by-play thing going on." She lowered her voice. "Oh, baby, I'm going to touch your breast now. You like that, don't you. Oh, yeah. You're so wet for me, baby. I'm gonna come, baby. I'm coming, I'm coming." Rose laughed at herself.

"Some women like that," Declan said.

"Maybe. I had a neighbor once who screamed so loud I almost called 911. I thought she was getting killed." When Declan laughed, she said, "I'm not kidding. She'd scream, then stop. Then she'd start all over again. It was hysterical. I called her the screamer."

"You scream."

He had her there. Rose put on a sly smile. "You make me scream, baby. Make me scream now."

And he did.

Rose opened her eyes, amazed she was looking into the baby blues of the man she loved. When she was a dried-up old woman living alone in her very nice but very lonely town house in Newport, she would close her eyes and relive every moment of the past week she'd shared with Declan. Because she had a feeling this was it. You didn't fall this hard and get back up for a long time. She figured by the time she got over Declan, she'd be too busy making her restaurant a success to have time for men. And that was just fine. She'd had her man; she'd have her wonderful memories. Rose would feel just fine if this all didn't remind her of an old movie she'd watched one rainy Saturday about a woman who'd had one great love in her life. She spent her entire life pining for this man she'd spent a fantastic month with, only to find out years later that it had meant nothing to him. He couldn't even remember her, never mind what she'd thought was a magical month. She'd rejected man after man, unable to shake the grips of this one true love, and the whole time it was a fantasy conjured up in a dried-up old spinster's mind.

Rose blinked away those awful thoughts and gave Declan a soft smile. "Hey."

"Hey, beautiful." He did that, he called her beautiful in a way that made it seem easy to accept. He did all kinds of wonderful things, and every day that went by her heart broke a little bit more. Neither had said anything more about a future. They had agreed, hadn't they? They'd agreed they could enjoy each other, have fun— this was fun, wasn't it?—and then go their separate ways in the end. A handshake, a kiss on the cheek. All very sophisticated and modern. Except Rose had never been a modern woman, and this purely sucked. Plain and simple.

"You know, Dec, a person could get used to this life. Staying in bed all day, getting everything delivered to your door, endless physical pleasure. I think Paul is getting suspicious, though. My car hasn't moved an inch for six days. They all probably think you've got me tied up somewhere."

Declan grinned sleepily. "Now that's an idea. We haven't tried that."

Rose smiled back. No, they hadn't tied each other up yet, but they'd had some pretty wonderful and inventive sex. Rose would never be able to work in the kitchen again without getting all hot and bothered. Heck, she'd never be able to cook up a good tomato sauce without remembering how wonderful it was to lick it off of every part of Declan's beautiful body, slowly, savoring every nuance, every hard curve, every velvety inch of him.

"I was thinking of making spaghetti with a nice marinara tonight."

"How about al fredo?"

Rose wrinkled her nose. "Too fattening."

"I'll eat it all," he said, lifting his eyebrows and sending a sharp knife of desire through her. She'd never been like this: insatiable. Declan drove her crazy with it, making her want to do things she'd never wanted to before. Sex standing up, sex on the table, sex, sex, sex. Except it was more than that. Rose had never had this kind of connection with another human being. She'd never wanted more of anyone; she'd never enjoyed anyone's company, other than Nonna's, for more than a couple of hours. Even Jenn got on her nerves after a while. But Declan, he was different. He was funny and sexy and unexpectedly charming and nice even when they weren't naked and kissing each other crazy. Making love had never been more than something that happened to make a relationship progress. It wasn't this madness, this weird and very scary *need*.

"You know, I should go home tonight. I need to do laundry, and my plants are dying." *And I've got to pull back because if I don't do it now, I'm not sure I'll be able to.*

Besides, she hadn't spent more than fifteen minutes at home for the past week, running into her apartment just long enough to grab some clean clothes. "I've got strange things growing in my refrigerator," she said, watching as her finger dipped into that sexy place where his throat touched his clavicle.

"Okay. I've got some work to do here anyway." He sat up and walked straight to the bathroom. Rose stared at the bathroom door awhile, looking a bit dumbfounded when she heard the shower turn on. He was taking a shower without her. He was waking up and not making love.

He's pulling away, too.

Rose let out a puff of air, then tucked her lips in and bit down. *Be tough. Don't go in there. Don't give in. It's for the best.*

"Hey, you coming in or what?" Declan called from the shower.

Rose grinned and bounded out of bed like a puppy, all thoughts of pulling away going right down the shower drain.

Chapter 12

Spaghetti bolognese with parmigiano-reggiano and fresh herbs, $16.00

It had been only a week, but it felt strange to be home. And good. Rose had lived alone for ten years and liked her solitude, as long as she knew someone she loved was only a phone call away. Smiling, she reached for the phone, and for a tiny, horrible moment, she thought of calling her grandmother.

"Oh." It came out soft, a sound of despair when she remembered her Nonna was gone. She sat on her old couch and picked up her favorite picture of her grandmother, tears welling in her eyes. In the picture, her grandmother was in full laughter, standing at the stove and holding a spoon that dripped with her rich tomato sauce. Rose never knew what was so funny that her grandmother laughed so, probably something her grandfather said right before snapping the picture. "What did he say?" she whispered through a tear-clogged throat. She had other pictures scattered about her apartment, of her grandmother and grandfather working side-by-side in their barbershop, of her as a little kid on her grandmother's lap. But this was one that could almost guarantee to make her smile. Except today, when she'd thought for a fleeting moment that Nonna was still alive, that she could call her up and tell her she was in love.

Rose broke down and had a long and satisfying bout of crying, real body-wracking, sloppy sobbing. The kind that left you tired and puffy and feeling imminently better. Rose placed the picture back on her end table, then rested her head on the soft, cushy arm of her comfortable old couch and fell asleep.

It was dark when the phone rang, wrenching her out of the dream whose subject became elusive as soon as she opened her eyes.

"Hello?"

"So. You're not dead."

"Jenn?" she asked, befuddled and groggy from her nap.

"Don't you dare Jenn me. Where the hell have you been? I was about twenty-four hours away from calling in a missing persons report. I did call your mother, but she's off in Florida, according her office."

"You tried to call my mother?" Rose asked, shaking her head hard to wake up.

"Have you even checked your answering machine?"

"Uhhh." Rose leaned over and grimaced when she saw it flashing four messages. "Oh yeah. Sorry."

"Where have you been?"

"At Dec—at work. With my boss, Mac. I, um, we . . ."

"Spare me the details and do me a favor. Give me his number so if there's an emergency, I can get ahold of you."

Jenn sounded truly upset, and suddenly Rose felt like the worst of friends. "My God, Jenn, are you okay? The baby?"

"Oh. Fine. I didn't mean there was an emergency this time. But there could have been. And when I couldn't reach you and you didn't return your messages . . ." Her voice drifted off, and Rose could tell she felt a bit sheepish for panicking. "The last time I saw you was at your grandmother's funeral, and then all of a sudden I can't reach you. Well, I was worried is all."

"Oh, Jenn, I'm so sorry." Rose began rummaging through her pocketbook. "I'll give you his number. You ready?"

"Ready. It'll be good to have because I want you there when I do go into labor. I know I've got a while to go, but I would like you there."

Rose creased her eyes in worry. Jenn sounded as if she was ready to cry, and Jenn rarely cried.

"They ought to warn women that getting pregnant turns them into basket cases. My hormones are turning me into an insane woman. Poor Brian doesn't even recognize me anymore. Physically or emotionally."

"I've heard that being pregnant does that. So, what were you trying to call me about?"

"I can't even remember now. You spent the entire week with him?"

"Yup."

"And, of course, you're in love."

"Yup again."

"And he's madly in love with you."

The silence was painful.

"Rose, what are you doing?"

Rose hated that you're-an-idiot-when-it-comes-to-men tone Jenn was using with her. Even if it was justified. Rose didn't want to admit it to Jenn, but she was being an idiot this time, too. She might as well get an "I am an idiot" stamp and decorate her body with it, because if there was one thing she knew, Declan McDonald was never, ever going to commit to her and she was definitely going to end up with a broken heart. Knowing that, telling herself that a hundred times, wasn't about to stop her, though.

"He likes me," she said.

"Obviously you know this guy's whole story now, and you're not going to tell me, your best friend."

"Obviously."

She must have sounded mad, because Jenn immediately got defensive. "I'm just looking out for you, you know that."

"I know."

A pause. "Is he worth it?"

"Oh yeah."

"Let's get together for lunch Saturday." Jenn put on a German accent: "I haf vays of making you talk."

"Lunch sounds good, but you're not getting a word out of me. Not one."

"You do know this is driving me crazy. I just might figure out who he is."

Rose laughed, but inside she felt a stab of nervousness. "Never."

"We'll see," Jenn said, and hung up.

Rose pressed the off button thoughtfully. What would Declan do if he was revealed? Would that be it between them? Or would he try to make it work? Or would she just be another footnote in his biography? She could just hear the *E! Entertainment* narrator now: "Declan McDonald had a brief affair with his personal chef, Rose Pisano, during his seclusion." *E!* probably wouldn't even bother with her name.

She stared at his phone number trying to come up with an excuse to call.

"Oh, you are so pathetic!" she yelled, and stashed the piece of paper back into her handbag.

With renewed energy, she cleaned up her apartment and decided to check into her former normal life. Thursday night at Anthony's Ristorante was a busy night. She hadn't been back to the restaurant in weeks and hadn't seen Tony since her grandmother's wake. She threw on a pair of jeans and a pale yellow sweater and headed out.

Rose walked the five blocks to the restaurant, glad to be home in her gritty little neighborhood where she knew nearly every face and they knew her. It was eight o'clock, and the sky still glowed from the setting sun, making everything seem soft and safe, the way it had seemed when she was sixteen and walking to work on a Friday night when everyone else her age was heading to the malls. As she turned the corner of Earl Street, she was immediately hit by the warm and homey smell of good Italian cooking, and she was transported instantly back in time to when she worked here seventy hours a week for a pittance but loved every minute of it. Rose had known she missed the restaurant, but it wasn't until she walked up the ramp and into the main dining room, felt the old deep red floral carpet beneath her feet, breathed in deeply of Anthony's famous marinara, heard the chatter of waitresses talking to customers, that she realized just how much she missed this place. It had been a second home to her, and everyone in it a second family—including the customers. It was as busy as usual, something that Tony would be quick to point out.

"Rosalie, you coming back to work here?"

Rose walked over to the Schmidts, a couple who had been coming to Anthony's every Thursday night since she could remember. They were one of those couples who never seemed to age because they'd been old for as long as Rose had known them. They always ordered the same thing—stuffed shells for her, chicken marsala for him—and insisted that they be allowed to tell the waitress, who knew their order by heart, exactly what they wanted and how they wanted it.

"No, I'm just here to visit."

"How have you been, Rose? We were so sorry to hear about your grandmother," Mrs. Schmidt said.

"Thank you."

"Since you're not working, why not sit with us awhile?" Mr. Schmidt asked. "Tell us all about your new job."

"New job," came a decidedly gruff voice. "That's not a job. That's a vacation Rosalie is on."

Rose shot Tony a withering look. "Hello, Tony. I see business is slowing a bit, hmmm?" Rose knew which buttons to press, and Tony always accommodated her. It was the meat of their relationship, each pressing buttons, each enjoying the other's offended reaction.

"Slowing down?" he said, putting on a show of pure dismay. "It has never been busier. I've had customers come in that haven't come here in years. They tell me they've heard the food is finally good again."

She leaned down conspiratorially to the Schmidts, who enjoyed watching the two spar. "There are always those who prefer Chef Boyardee to real Italian cooking."

Tony narrowed his eyes, then threw back his head and laughed. "She spends a few weeks cooking for some hoity-toity California-type, and now she's a chef. She forgets who taught her everything she knows."

Rose smiled. "I'll never forget Nonna, Tony, you know that."

He waved a dismissive hand at her. "I got to get back to the business of cooking for my customers. Don't you come back there and get in my way, Rose."

Which she took, properly, as an invitation to follow Tony into his kitchen.

"I'll see you two later," she said to the Schmidts, and followed Tony into the kitchen.

When they were alone, Tony became more serious. "You still like that new job of yours?"

"Yeah, Tony, it's nice. And the money . . ." She let her voice trail off, flushing deeply. She was having an affair with her boss, and he was paying her an outrageous amount of money. To cook, of course. Good sex was just an added benefit. Rose hated the dirty little thought that popped into her head at the moment, but she couldn't help herself. She'd honestly never thought of the ethics of what she was doing, not until confronted by Tony, who wrote the book on high morals.

Tony turned away, misunderstanding the reason for her blush. "You know if I could afford to pay you a better salary, I would."

"I would never expect that of you," Rose said, feeling worse by the moment.

He moved his hands over the gleaming stainless steel surface of the workstation, still not looking at her. "I plan to retire in fifteen years. I have no one, no family. I planned to give you Anthony's, you know."

Rose let out an audible gasp. "Oh, I could never accept that. Besides, you know I want my own restaurant."

His hands stopped their motion, and he gripped the edge of the table. "Or you could marry me."

Ohmigod. Knock me down with a feather.

He finally looked up at her, too quickly for Rose to school her features. He pushed away and grinned, then laughed and pointed a finger at her. "Gotcha!" he said, then put on a real good show of laughing at his joke. Except Rose knew it wasn't a joke.

Oh, Tony.

And so she laughed, too. "You almost had me going, Tone." *Ha ha.*

He grabbed down an order. "Yeah. I'm a funny guy."

Rose bit her lips, hating that she'd hurt him, hating that she'd never noticed he'd thought of her as anything more than a daughter or maybe a little sister. Just then, Gloria walked in with another order. Gloria had been working at Anthony's nearly as long as Rose. She looked from one to the other, then flung the order in front of Tony. "Just soup," she said. "I think old Mr. Rimaldi is dying. He used to scarf down a pound of pasta not too long ago."

"Or maybe he just doesn't like the food here anymore," Rose said in an attempt to get her and Tony back on track.

"The food is better than ever," Tony said, his words sharp and lacking even the smallest amount of teasing.

"I've got to get going, Tone."

He kept busy spooning the soup into a large bowl. "Yeah. We'll see you, Rose."

Rose walked out of the swinging door that led from the kitchen to a short hallway leading to the dining area. Gloria was there waiting for her, and she grabbed Rose's arm and pulled her into the ladies' room.

"What was going on in there? You two have a fight?"

"No. Nothing like that. I think Tony's still upset that I left. That's all." *Oh, and he's in love with me and asked me to marry him.*

Gloria peered directly into Rose's eyes, and Rose made a good show of staring right back. "That's all?" the older woman demanded. "Tony didn't say anything, um, stupid, did he?"

Cautiously, Rose said, "Stupid like what?"

Gloria glanced at the door as if half expecting Tony to barge in at any moment. "You know how he is. Since you've been gone he's been a real joy to work for. I never know what's going to set him off. I'm actually thinking of quitting. Glenn's sick of me working weekends, and I'm sick of Tony."

Rose grimaced. "It's been that bad? He does look awfully tired. Why doesn't Tony hire another cook? He's just strung out trying to do everything again. He's not thirty anymore."

"I told him he should, but he's so stubborn. I think he thinks you're coming back. Rose, maybe there's something I should tell you."

Panic flooded Rose. She did not want to discuss this right now. She was still in shock, and the last thing she needed was Gloria telling her that Tony was in love with her. She grabbed Gloria's wrist and looked at her watch.

"Wow. It's that late? I've got to get going. We'll talk another time, Glo." Rose flung open the door and hurried away.

"Got a hot date tonight?" she heard Gloria call, but Rose kept on going, pretending she didn't hear her.

When Rose got to the street she stopped and took a deep breath. And then another. It couldn't be true. Tony couldn't think of her like that. It was like realizing you loved your first cousin or something. She wrinkled her nose at the thought. She just wanted Tony to be himself and her to visit and insult him, and he'd insult her and they'd laugh. But now, how could she go back and look at him and know what he was thinking? It all made her feel sad, for him and for their friendship, which would probably never be the same. How long had he been keeping his feelings to himself? Since she was sixteen and she'd thought of him as this old guy who owned the restaurant? He'd been only thirty-two, not old at all, and probably not too happy he was attracted to a teenager. And then, she'd dated and he'd dated and he'd fallen in love with her but never told her because he was too old and she was too young. Was that how it had been? Or had he realized he loved her only after she was gone.

Rose walked home, her thoughts driving her a little crazy. If Tony had said something years ago, what would she have done? She probably would have quit, and that was why he'd never told her because he'd known what she'd do.

Why did everything have to be so complicated? Why couldn't she fall in love with a guy who wasn't supposed to be dead, a guy who was normal, had a normal job and a normal life? Just her luck that a normal guy did love her, but she didn't love him.

Rose reached her house, questions buzzing in her head. Tomorrow she was going back to work, back to the man she loved. Her boss. The guy paying her eighty thousand dollars a year to cook for him. He was not paying her to sleep with him.

A job with nice bennies.

A job she'd have to quit.

Damn.

Chapter 13

Cheese fondue for two with garlic crostini, $12.00

"I have to quit."

Declan knew by the crossed arms, the wide-legged stance, that she meant every word and was braced for battle. So he knew he was being a bit mean when he said, "Okay. But can you stay for the two weeks promised in the contract?"

She sort of dissolved and ended up standing in his room looking more like an unstrung marrionette than the she-warrior she impersonated when she walked in. "Fine. It's just that I really don't think I should be sleeping with my boss."

Declan suppressed a smile and turned back to his music sheet. "I agree."

"I'm making good money—ridiculous money to be honest—and I'm starting to feel . . ."

"Like some sort of call girl?" he asked blandly, looking up for her reaction. He got it all right, fire shooting straight from her eyes to his.

"You bastard!" And then she must have seen his smile,

because she suddenly got what he was doing and started to laugh. Declan hurried over to her and picked her up into a bear hug, pressing his nose against the curve of her neck. God, he'd missed her. Gone only one night and he felt like a tiger pacing a too-small cage. It had taken him forever to fall asleep without her warm body next to him. He'd never been a guy who liked to cuddle, who liked to have someone in his space. But a few days with Rose and he caught himself reaching for her to pull her near.

She hit him on his shoulder with her hard fist.

"Ow."

"That was mean," she said, but she was smiling.

"It was. What do you expect, you come in here without even saying hello and announce you're quitting. You deserved a little bit of mean."

"Didn't."

"Did." And he kissed her to shut her up.

"I missed you," he said against her mouth, feeling her lips turn up in a grin. She wrapped her legs around his waist and crossed her ankles, anchoring herself to his body. He liked the way she used her whole body, threw herself into everything with such abandon. He walked over to the bed and flopped down on top of her, kissing her all the while, listening to the sounds she made, feeling her breasts press against his chest, her hair drift over his arms. He'd more than missed her, he admitted. It had physically hurt, which scared the hell out of him.

Declan lifted his head. "You're not quitting." He watched as a crease formed between her eyebrows.

"Yes, I am." She shoved him off her, and he let her because he knew she was serious and he wanted to get all this talking business over with and make love.

"You can't quit. I'd starve."

"You did just fine for the first two years before you

hired me, Declan, and I'm sure you'll survive. I could still come over and cook you a couple of meals." She pointed a finger at him. "But without being paid."

"Ah," he said, "the barter method."

She narrowed her eyes, and he laughed.

"I'm serious, Declan."

He got all solemn. "I can tell." He went to kiss her, but she placed her palm against his forehead and pushed. Hard. "What the hell?" He was beginning to get the tiniest bit angry.

She'd gotten off the bed and was standing there, hands on hips, with an expression he'd never seen on her face before. "Why did you hire me?"

Uh oh.

"Because you were the only one I interviewed who actually stayed for the entire interview." It was the truth. She didn't need to know he'd hired her because she'd seemed the most desperate. And because he'd immediately been attracted to her. "Okay. The truth is I thought you were nice looking, but I never intended to meet you." He could tell she was struggling to believe him. "Rose, I swear. Don't you remember how mad I was when you came up here? Or the lengths I'd gone to to make certain you'd never see me?"

She thrust out her jaw stubbornly. "I remember you kissing me in the dark before we even knew each other. I remember that."

Declan got off the bed and walked angrily to his piano. "I don't know what the hell brought all this on, but if you're going to stand there and accuse me of lying to you, or worse, hiring you for sex, you can leave right now."

Rose stood there staring at his angry profile, feeling as if her stomach might flip. Why had she said that? She'd never even thought it, and there it was, popping out of her mouth. Did she really think he'd hired her knowing they'd end up in bed together?

Ladies and gentlemen, I'm pleased to announce the Idiot of the Year Award. And it goes to . . . Drum roll please . . . Rosalie Pisano.

"Declan?" she asked uncertainly. The only response she got was a bulging of that sexy muscle in his jaw. "I really don't know what made me accuse you of that." He turned to her, and she thought she detected the slightest gentling of his expression. "I don't really think that. I don't. But it does bother me that I'm working for you and sleeping with you. That has to stop."

He turned fully toward her, still looking a little mad. Then he smiled, a jerky turning up of his lips, as if smiling was difficult at the moment. Declan walked over to her, his expression taught, his eyes hard and so intense, Rose felt all weak-kneed. She'd hurt him, she realized, and now she felt like crying. "Are you saying you want to end this relationship?"

"No. I'm not saying that at all. I'm saying I don't want to work for you anymore. Is that okay?"

He let out a long breath. "That's okay."

Declan, I love you. Say it say it say it. Oh, God, don't be stupid, don't you dare tell him you love him. Don't you dare don't you . . .

"I love you," she gushed out, breathy and through lips that barely moved. She bit her lips, all panicky now. "Did I really say that?"

His beautiful eyes moved over her face. "You really said it." He put his hands on either side of her face and kissed her hard and long, letting out this long, groaning sound that for some odd reason, made Rose's eyes burn.

They made love and it was wonderful. It was slow and intense, and when he put himself inside her he looked down at her and kept watching her until she came.

It wasn't until later, when she was driving home, that Rose let herself think about why Declan hadn't said he loved her, too. Because she had a feeling she did know why. He was so much smarter than she was. They both knew they had no real future, and yet she'd succumbed; she'd allowed her heart to be completely captured by a man who probably, deep inside, didn't want it. Rose pulled over at the Narragansett Beach boardwalk and stared out at the Atlantic Ocean. It was nearly midnight, but there were people—mostly couples she noted wryly—walking along the wall, huddled close against the cool night breeze. She should never go back. She should stop this before it got too hard to pull away.

"It's already too late," she whispered brokenly as she lay her head against the steering wheel and tried not to cry. She had to tell him she loved him, didn't she? She couldn't just feel the love and keep her big mouth shut. "I knew this was going to happen. I knew it." She banged her head lightly against the steering wheel, angry with herself, angry with Declan for being so much better at protecting his heart.

Rose awoke the next morning, her eyes gritty and slightly swollen from a small bout of self-pity she'd succumbed to right before bed. It was Saturday, and she had no legitimate reason to go to Kingstown and Declan. When she'd said good-bye the night before, Declan had been half asleep and given her a drowsy protest that she stay. Rose left anyway, knowing she needed to be alone. If he called and asked her to come over, she would. Otherwise, she'd just go on about her life, unresolved as it was. She was officially unemployed but had absolutely no desire to go out and look for another job.

She forced herself out of bed and into the shower, emerging feeling much better. She checked her answering machine, but got only a dial tone from someone who had called, listened to her greeting, but hung up before leaving a message. She hated that.

She was just pulling on an oversized sweatshirt and a faded, too-big pair of jeans when someone knocked on her door. Rose frowned. She could probably count on one hand the number of times someone had come to her door. As she walked to the door, she mentally listed the people it could be: her mother, Jenn, her landlord. Certainly not Declan.

It was a stranger, a woman in her forties wearing an ugly tan pantsuit, dressed way too dowdy to be a Jehovah's Witness. Keeping the chain on the door, Rose peered through the crack. "Yes?"

"Are you Rosalie Pisano?" she asked with an accent so Southern Rose barely recognized her own name.

Rose looked down the hall to see if the woman had any companions. "I'm sorry, who are you?"

"Miss Pisano, my name is Jill Brighton. I'm a private detective." She showed her an I.D. "I was wondering if I could come in and talk with you about Declan McDonald."

Uh oh.

Rose felt her entire body heat, and she tried with all her being not to react. She pretended to study the I.D., all the while her brain telling her to calm down. *"Who* are you looking for?" she asked, being purposefully dense.

The woman smiled tightly, her eyes never leaving Rose's face. "Declan McDonald. Your boss."

"My boss's name is Mac."

"Miss Pisano, I'm a busy woman." She pasted on a smile, but Rose could tell she was getting impatient. "This will only take a few moments of your time. If you'd let me in . . ."

Rose shrugged. *Shit shit.* "Sure." *Okay, nonchalant. Nothing big here, just a woman looking for a guy everyone knows is dead except her and Declan's mother. And now, apparently, this woman.* She closed the door to get the chain off, then opened it wide and welcoming. *Nothing to hide here, lady.*

"Nice place," she said, and that made Rose laugh.

"No, really, I love these old places." She pointed to the bull's-eye molding. "Some parts of the country people pay top dollar to get this old look."

"Yeah? I only pay four hundred a month. Where are you from?" Rose was pretty proud of herself, acting as if it were an everyday occurrence that she invited a private detective into her home. Maybe she shouldn't be quite so calm. Maybe someone with nothing to hide would be more nervous.

"Tennessee."

"Ahh. That explains it, then. Are you looking for Elvis, too?"

The woman didn't even crack a smile. "They had Elvis's body. No one ever found McDonald's."

Rose stifled a laugh. "And you think Mac is Declan McDonald?" She shook her head, pretending to find the concept too funny for words. "I don't think so."

"What does he look like?" Brighton persisted.

"Actually, I don't know. I've never seen him." The detective raised her eyebrows in disbelief. "Listen, Mac is a recluse. Maybe he's disfigured or something and doesn't want anyone to see him."

"Or maybe he's Declan McDonald."

"Is he from Australia? Because Mac's got this gruff Aussie accent. When I first started working there I could hardly understand a word out of the guy's mouth."

Brighton pursed her lips together, thoroughly frustrated by Rose's answers.

Too bad, sister, you're not getting squat from me.

"I guess I'm wrong," she said, a bit too easily. Rose knew she wasn't going to give up yet.

"Yup. I guess so." Rose grinned and began to lead the woman to the door.

"One more thing." *Uh oh, here comes the Columbo question.* Rose wondered when the woman was going to scratch her head and squint her eyes. "I wonder if you could tell me this Mac's address. I'd like to talk to him myself."

Relief flooded Rose. This woman was clearly on a fishing trip and wasn't about to get even the hint of a bite from her. "I'm sorry, I don't think I should. Mac's so private, he just might fire me if I start giving out his address to strangers. I'm sure you wouldn't want me to lose my job."

"Of course not. Thank you, Miss Pisano. You've been very helpful." With that last remark, she closed the door.

What did she mean, "You've been very helpful." Had she somehow blown it? Rose went to the window and peeked carefully through the curtains to see if the woman had left. She watched her climb into a Ford Escort, then write something in a notebook, before pulling away from the front of her apartment.

Rose ran to her purse, dumped out its contents, and found Declan's number. She jabbed the numbers in, her breath coming fast, her heart beating hard in her chest. "Ugh!" Busy. She waited three seconds, then hit redial. Busy again. She paced. Dialed again.

"Shit, Declan, get off the friggin' phone."

How had the detective found her? How did she even suspect Declan was alive? She had to warn him. If this Jill Brighton could find her, certainly she could find out where he lived.

One more time she dialed his number only to hear the busy signal. What if he had taken his phone off the hook to work? He'd done that before, gotten so wrapped up in writing that he refused to have any interruptions. Rose grabbed her keys and headed out the door. Let her try to follow; no one knew Providence better than she did. By the time she reached the highway, Miss Tennessee would be very lost and very pissed.

* * *

Jill couldn't have been happier. She waited two blocks down from Rose's house munching on a bagel, knowing that eventually she would lead her right to Declan McDonald. Rose Pisano was pretty good at hiding her thoughts, but not nearly good enough. It was that first moment when she'd said his name that she'd given everything away. She'd seen surprise and fear, not just curiosity, in those big brown eyes. Rose had recovered well; she had to give her credit for that. And she didn't hold it against her for hiding what she knew; she knew Rose was trying to protect her boss.

Finding Rose had been easy enough. The woman at the payroll company that issued the checks for Clarke Enterprises hated her boss, and there was nothing better than dealing with an underling who felt unappreciated. Checks went to the Best Security Company and Rose Pisano. No one at the security company would talk, but she figured Rose Pisano would be the best bet in any case. Even if she didn't give up anything, Jill knew she could follow her to work and get to McDonald that way. If it was McDonald. It didn't matter who the hell it was, just as long as she found out who was behind that stupid song. Finding the long-dead Declan McDonald alive, well, that would be icing on the cake. She'd even thought about writing a book about the whole thing, going on *Oprah*. Why not cash in?

She saw the flash of a small woman, hair flying behind her, running to a beat-up Honda. In that moment she knew: Declan McDonald was alive and well and living in—of all places—Rhode Island. *That didn't take long,* she thought, chuckling as she watched Rose. "Bingo." The girl was smart enough to stop at her car and look around before hopping in, and Jill shook her head. Payoff time was here, she thought.

She let Rose pull out and go to the end of the block and take a left before pulling out to follow her. Gunning it, she made it to the intersection just in time to see her take another turn, this time a right. The girl was driving fast, another clue she was on the right track. "Slow down, Rose, you don't want to get yourself killed," Jill murmured. Pulling out, she pressed on the accelerator again, slowing only to take the turn.

"Aw, shit."

At the next intersection was an accident—a bad one—involving a big ol' garbage truck, and a battered Honda.

Chapter 14

Sugar tart with fresh lemon curd "fool," raspberries and vanilla custard sauce, $9.99

Declan sat slouched in a chair staring out the window wondering why the hell Rose hadn't stayed for the weekend, wondering why she hadn't called and why she wasn't home, when the phone rang.

"Hello. Is this Mac?"

He sat up straight at the use of that name. "Yes."

"Hi. My name's Jenn, I'm Rose's friend. Rose got into a car accident, and she got pretty banged up." The woman's voice was shaking, and Declan's entire body began to shake. "So she won't be into work for a while."

"How hurt is she? Where is she?"

"She broke some ribs, punctured a lung, and damaged her spleen. They had to operate, and she's still pretty out of it."

"She's okay, though? She's not . . ." He had to stop, get a grip. God, if anything happened to Rose . . .

"She could have died, but she's all right now. She's in serious condition. She even called me before they operated, and she sounded pretty good. I think she's going to be okay." Jenn didn't sound at all convincing; what she sounded was scared.

For a moment, Declan couldn't talk past the roaring sound in his ears. "What hospital is she in?"

"She's still sedated. I can call you when—"

"Jenn, just tell me what hospital."

"Rhode Island. Room 465."

"Thanks. And thanks for calling." Declan hung up, then immediately picked up again to dial the guard-house. "Paul?"

"Yes sir."

"Rose was in a car accident, and I need you to drive me to the hospital. I'll be down in five minutes." He hung up again, threw on some clothes, and began walking out of his room before stopping dead-cold.

"Shit," he yelled, knowing what he was about to do. Knowing and not caring. He grabbed a baseball hat, jammed it on his head, and put on sunglasses, even though it was a cloudy day. Then he headed out of his house for what could be one of the last times. All it would take would be for one person to recognize him. One person and it was all over. He hoped Paul was too nervous to really take a hard look at him. As disguises went, sunglasses and a baseball hat wasn't very good.

He walked out of the house, a vampire testing fate by leaving his lair in the daytime. Paul stood by his car staring at him, trying to see what was wrong with him, making Declan so nervous he dropped his head and walked directly to the passenger side of a Jeep that was covered with mud on the outside but surprisingly clean on the inside.

"Should I call the security office and get a replacement here while we're gone?"

"No. Let's go." Declan sat in the Jeep, his heart racing, his breath shallow, hating himself and his fear. He ought to rip off the sunglasses and hat and introduce himself to Paul like a man. Instead, he stared out the passenger side window and waited for Paul to get into the car and drive. He heard the door open and close.

"Is she badly hurt?"

"Yes."

Paul beat a hand against the steering wheel hard, startling Declan. He glanced over at Declan, embarrassed by his show of emotion, as if he had sat there and sobbed instead of banging something. "She's a real cool girl," he said as explanation, then backed up, dirt flying, and threw the car into forward. Declan smiled. He'd picked the right person to drive him to the hospital: they broke every speed limit and nearly every traffic law in the state on the way to Providence.

In twenty minutes, Paul was pulling into the visitor's parking lot behind the hospital. He threw his security I.D. on the dash board and parked in an empty handicapped spot. "I want you to wait here for me. When I come back, you can go to see her. Is that okay?"

It wasn't, Declan could tell by the way Paul shifted restlessly in his seat, but he nodded.

Declan got out of the car and pulled the baseball cap even lower on his head. He jammed his hands into his pants pockets and walked straight to the entrance without looking left or right. When he entered the hospital, he walked directly to the bank of elevators, then jabbed at the button that would bring him to the fourth floor. The doors were sliding closed when a family of five piled into the car with him. He pressed into the back of the elevator keeping his eyes on the floor. At the fourth floor, he pushed himself through the family and heard the woman say behind him, "Ever hear of the words excuse me?" Declan didn't care. He only wanted to reach Rose, to make certain she was alive. God, he felt like throwing up at the familiar smell of the hospital. Michael had lived on life support for three days, brain dead, before his mother gave the hospital permission to turn off the machines. He'd died almost immediately. Declan had watched his chest rise and fall, then stop. He'd wanted to shake him, to bring him to life, to tell him he was sorry, to hold him and laugh with him. But he was dead and that was forever.

Declan blinked hard. Rose wouldn't die. Jenn had said she'd suffered a punctured lung, a ruptured spleen. Serious, but not deadly. He stopped outside the room, took a deep breath, then entered, a spark of panic gripping him when he saw the empty bed. Almost immediately he realized Rose was in the far bed near the window overlooking a brick wall and a bank of miniblinded windows. He could see the smallest little hill beneath the white blanket made by her feet. He turned the corner more afraid than he'd ever been, only to be greeted by a sleepy smile that quickly turned into fear.

"Declan, what are you doing here?" She darted a look past him, almost as if she expected to see an entourage of reporters following him.

"I wore a disguise," he said, taking off his sunglasses and hat. He hovered by the foot of the bed, looking her over, making certain she was alive. One side of her face near her temple was bruised, and her dark hair was tousled and messy. Other than that, she looked so normal he nearly sagged with relief.

"I would have called you, but I couldn't remember your stupid number."

"I had to come," he said. "How could I stay away?" And yet he was, still standing at the end of her bed, afraid for some reason to touch her.

"Oh, Dec. Thanks."

"How are you doing? I'm running out of food, you know."

"Ha, ha. You'll live." And then she reached for his hand, and he placed his in hers, gripping hard—a man holding on for dear life. "Oh, Dec, you've got to leave. A woman came to see me, a private investigator. She knows I work for you, at least she suspects so. I said I only knew you as Mac and you had an Australian accent. I think I blew it, though. I don't think she believed me. I'm sorry."

"*You're* sorry. Rose, I'm sorry. I never should have put you in a position that you'd have to lie for me." That was when a horrible thought came to him. "Where were you driving when you had the accident?"

Rose bit her lip and looked away. "In Providence."

"Where were you going?"

He could see her debating whether or not to lie to him.

"Were you coming to warn me about the P.I.?"

Her eyes fluttered shut. "So tired," she muttered, and he laughed aloud.

"Rose."

"Oh, okay. I was driving to your house."

"Why didn't you call?" And then he answered that question himself. "Because the phone was off the hook." He felt sick again.

Rose grabbed his sleeve and forced him down for a kiss. "Don't be an idiot and start blaming yourself. Don't."

"You could have died."

Panic filled Rose's eyes when his voice closed up. "Don't you dare cry. Oh my God. *Declan.*"

He laughed instead, then got serious. "Are you all right? Are you? No bullshit answer."

"Honestly? I feel like crap. But I feel a lot better now than I did when they brought me in here. The doctor said I'll be able to go home in two days, depending on whether anything gets infected or not." She pulled a face.

"Hey, Rose, I brought you some of those cooking maga—Oh my God." Jenn walked over to Rose's bed, her eyes never leaving Declan's face, like a fan from zombie land. "It's . . . it's . . ."

"Hello. Declan McDonald. You must be Jenn." His extended hand was ignored by Rose's drooling friend.

"Declan," Rose said, horrified that he'd been outed.

"Dec . . . Dec . . ."

"De-clan Mc-Don-ald," Rose said, annunciating every syllable. Jenn had been a huge fan; she had all his CDs and had kept the *People* magazine special edition that came out after Declan was declared dead. She'd even gone into a bit of a funk when he supposedly died, so Rose would allow Jenn some leeway in her gaping.

"You mean he's, this is, Declan McDonald is your boss?"

Rose winced, knowing what was coming next.

"You mean Declan McDonald is your boss and you didn't tell me? And you've been, the two of you—" She looked at Rose awestruck. "And you never said one word."

Declan gave Jenn his classic charming smile. It was a look that bothered Rose, because now she recognized the pain behind it. "I swore her to secrecy."

Jenn squinted her eyes and pointed an accusing finger at Declan. "I knew you weren't dead. Didn't I say that, Rose? Didn't I? And here he is in flesh and blood. Fuck me," she said in wonder.

"That trash mouth sounds real lousy on a pregnant woman, Jenn," Rose said dryly.

"Sorry. But geez."

"By the way, I'm feeling much better."

"Yeah." Jenn kept staring at Declan, and Rose was starting to get bothered by it. Big time.

"You can't tell anyone, Jenn," Rose warned.

Finally, Jenn looked her way. "Aw."

"I mean it, Jenn."

Rose glanced at Declan and hated what she saw. He was all closed down, gone. He smiled, but something was missing in his eyes, something vital, something familiar. He was a stranger, she realized.

"Can I have your autograph?"

Declan smiled. "Dead men don't give autographs."

Rose had this overwhelming desire to protect him, to hold him or hold back the hordes, to do something to make him look at her as if he was still alive.

"Jenn, would you mind waiting outside for a minute so I can talk to Declan alone?"

With one lingering glance Declan's way, Jenn left the room.

"I'm so sorry. Jenn won't say anything, not if I swear her to secrecy. Are you okay?"

Like that he was back, looking at her as if he was human again. "Would you stop worrying about me? It was inevitable that someday I'd have to come out of hiding. It happened a little sooner than I would have liked, that's all."

"Nothing's changed. I told you, Jenn won't say a word." Rose tried to sit up, but that hurt like hell, and she couldn't help wincing. The next thing she knew, Declan was holding her, rubbing her back, kissing her hair.

He pulled away, his eyes filled with some horrible emotion, pain or sadness or even worse, regret. Rose hated that look almost as much as she hated that fake smile of his, that worthless easy grin. "Nothing's changed," she repeated, willing it to be so. She wanted him a bit longer. Heck, who was she kidding? She wanted him forever, she didn't want her own stupidity to be the thing that drove them apart.

His face softened, and he smiled for real. "Okay. Nothing's changed."

Rose wanted to believe that more than anything in the world.

Declan kissed her good-bye, promising to return the next day. He'd meant it with all his heart when he'd said nothing had changed. But he was smart enough to know that saying something wouldn't necessarily make it so.

"Jenn, you can go in now."

She stared a little too long, and he gave her a mock warning look, then turned down the hall.

"Mr. McDonald, I'm so pleased to meet you."

Two years ago, he would have been more attuned to such an introduction. He either would have said hello to the person, or completely ignored them, leaving the person to wonder if they'd made a mistake about his identity. He'd gotten so good at ignoring someone yelling his name, he'd found himself snubbing close friends by mistake. But that was two years ago, and his senses had dulled in those years. So when the middle-aged woman came up behind him calling his name, he automatically turned.

The smile on the woman's face was one of triumph. "My name is Jill Brighton, I'm a private investigator working for Ellen Lang. She—"

"I know who she is," he said tightly. "If you'll excuse me."

She lay a restraining hand on his arm. "Mrs. Lang would like to meet with you, to thank you in person. I'd like to arrange the meeting."

"Sorry." He pulled away, his heart ready to beat out of his chest. He wanted to punch something. Himself, actually, for bringing this hell to his doorstep. He pushed the elevator button and looked down the hall to make certain the P.I. wasn't following him. She was.

"I've got nothing more to say right now."

"How can Mrs. Lang reach you?"

"She can't." The doors opened, and he stepped in. The private detective made to follow, but he looked at her with murder in his eyes, and she stepped hastily back. Once in the lobby, he went directly to the pay phones and dialed a number he hadn't dialed in more than two years. Somewhere in California, Rick Metzger, one of the most powerful publicists in the entertainment industry, was sitting in his posh office, probably with his feet up. He was about to get a phone call from a dead man.

"Yeah."

"It's Declan McDonald, Rick. I need for you to set up a press conference in Providence, Rhode Island, for tomorrow at noon. Got that?"

"Who the hell is this?"

"It's Declan, the man whose life you ruined. By the way, were those tears at my funeral for me or for the money you wouldn't be making off me."

"Fuck you, McDonald."

"Now. About that press conference."

"How do I know it's really you?"

"Call the damn press conference, Rick. If you don't, I'll find someone who will."

"What's my wife's name?"

"You're not married. You're gay, and no one knows it but me because you tried to hit on me when you started to believe the rumors that you probably started that I was gay."

"Jesus Christ, Dec, where the hell have you been?"

"Just call the press conference. Noon tomorrow in Providence. You pick the place, just call me and let me know. Here's my number." He left the hospital and headed out the door, fear eating at his gut. Not for himself, but for Rose.

When he reached Paul's Jeep, he took off his hat and sunglasses. "Paul, I'm Declan McDonald. How'd you like to be my personal bodyguard?"

Declan never truly blamed Rick Metzger for his mercurial climb to stardom; the guy in the mirror could shoulder that offense. Despite his ill feelings over the mess his life was in, he liked Rick; he was one of the few honest people he'd dealt with in Hollywood, with the possible exception of his sexuality. Rick was firmly in the closet, suffering from a tragic combination of homosexuality and political conservatism. He was constantly at war with himself, and with the gay "community" that he understood and yet disagreed with. And he was the best publicist in Hollywood, the liberal Mecca of the world.

He arrived at Declan's house at midnight, looking as fresh and put-together as a man could after a six-hour flight.

"So, this is where you've been hiding for the past two years. Nice."

He was being sarcastic, Declan knew. At midnight, the place looked as antiseptic and cold as the inside of a brand-new walk-in freezer.

"C'mon upstairs. I've actually got some furniture up there. I'll get you up-to-date; then we can talk about how we're going to handle this."

Rick stopped and stared at him, and then, to both men's horror, Rick's eyes filled with tears. "Thought you were dead, man," he managed, wiping his face.

Declan threw his arm around Rick's shoulder and gave him a quick, hard squeeze. "Sorry to do this to you, Rick. I screwed up, and now I've got to try to straighten everything up." They walked up the stairs, Declan's arm still around Rick's shoulders—the poor guy was so shaken, he hardly could manage the stairs. By the time they reached his room, though, Rick had complete control of himself and was all business.

"Tell me the true story. Then I'll come up with something to tell the media."

Declan smiled. "No. I've got to come clean with this one." Declan told him the whole story, how he never intended to "play dead," how his mother out of love and fear for him urged him to remain dead, why he had continued with the ruse even though he knew it was crazy.

"The longer I waited, the harder it became to let people know I wasn't really dead. At first, it was great. I

was with my mom, and we were both so relieved that it
was all over. The only thing I want to change about my
story is my mother's involvement. I don't want her hound-
ed by the press. I don't know whether or not what I've
done has criminal implications. But I want to state up
front that I fully intend to pay restitution to those indi-
viduals and agencies who searched for me after I disappeared."

Rick sat back after Declan finished, a stunned look
on his face. For a man who'd heard just about everything in his career, it was a difficult look to generate.

Rick took a short breath and shook his head. "Okay.
You disappear. People will understand that part. The
authorities suspect you're dead. You hear that and you
think, hey, maybe that's not such a bad idea. You can
take a breather, a vacation. Except things go on longer
than you thought, and you find yourself between a rock
and a hard place. No way out without looking like a
fool or an insensitive jerk. So you stay hidden. You decide to live like a recluse. Until . . . Until what. What
happened to bring you out?"

"Oh. I forgot to tell you part of it. You've heard of
'Leah's Song'?"

"Who hasn't." Rick shrugged, then froze. "You're
kidding me. You wrote that song?"

"I've been working for Angel's Songs for nearly the
entire time I've been in hiding."

Rick barked out a laugh. "You, my friend, have just
redeemed yourself. Who the hell is going to crucify the
guy who wrote 'Leah's Song'? A guy who's been writing
songs for terminally ill kids. I couldn't have come up with
a better story myself. You're a genius, McDonald."

"And you are a cynical bastard."

Rick looked surprised. "No. I just have a gift for
seeing the cynical side of things. This is going to be insane. Do you realize the press this is going to gener-

ate?" Rick did everything but rub his hands together greedily.

"I know this is going to be a boon for you, Rick. Frankly, I'm not looking forward to this."

Rick stood and began pacing. "Maybe we should have the press conference here. This is so huge. Hey. You never told me why all this is happening now."

"It has to do with 'Leah's Song.' The girl's mother is the wife of some politician in Tennessee. She's been all over the media looking for whoever wrote the song and trying to raise money for leukemia research."

"Yeah, yeah. She was on *Oprah.*"

"She hired a private investigator to track down the author. Today, the P.I. found me." *Through Rose.* Until that moment, Declan had no intention to tell Rick anything about Rose. He'd thought if he played things right, her name would never be mentioned, and she wouldn't come under scrutiny from the press. But someone already knew about Rose, at least knew she worked for him.

He let out another curse, stirring Rick from his publicist's dream come true.

"There's more? A secret hidden baby perhaps?"

Declan gave him a withering look. "I hired a chef about six months ago. We're friends, and I don't want her name mentioned."

"A woman, hmm?"

"Yes. Some chefs are women, Rick. No matter what, Rose is my employee only. Period. I want you to be clear on that point. Understood?"

"You were laying your chef?" Rick started laughing. "Man," he said, wiping his eyes, "Leno could have a field day with that one. I could write his monologue myself."

"Can it," Declan said, looking mad and slightly amused by Rick's antics. "Rose is strictly off limits."

"Okay, okay. I get the message. Do you think it will come up?"

"I hope not, but I can almost bet it will. She got hurt in a car accident, and I was in the hospital visiting her when the private detective spotted me."

Rick stared at him levelly. "You care about her."

Declan looked to the floor. "Yeah," he said, glancing up. "I do."

"All right, Dec. She's off limits."

Suddenly, Declan didn't want to talk anymore. He didn't want to think about anything, because every thought led back to the most depressing aspect about this whole debacle. He would have to say good-bye to Rose. His life was about to turn into a nightmare, and he'd be damned if he dragged her along for the ride. Not that he didn't want her there, not that the thought of saying good-bye to her wasn't enough to make his gut feel as if someone had just punched him. Hard.

He'd called his mother, told her to take the first plane to Italy and go to a small resort off Sardinia. She'd be safe there until the worst of this blew over. But he couldn't very well tell Rose to take off. It was better he kept her a secret, or at least kept their relationship a secret. The private investigator had no reason to ever mention Rose's involvement, but that didn't mean she wouldn't.

"You take the couch. Sorry I don't have the guest room set up. The bathroom's down the hall. Third door. If you don't mind, I'm going to crash."

"Tomorrow's going to be a long day, my friend. Try to get some sleep. Good night. Oh, and for the record, I never started the rumors that you were gay. You're not, right?"

Declan laughed at Rick's mock-hopeful tone. "Good night, Rick. And thanks."

Long after Rick fell asleep—Declan could tell by the soft snores—Declan lay awake staring at the ceiling and rehearsing in his head what he'd say to Rose.

He didn't know how to handle this break. In the past, he hadn't honestly considered the woman's feelings; he just wanted out and managed to convey those thoughts in a way that left the woman still liking him. He knew one thing: He couldn't leave the door open. He couldn't let her think that he'd come back, that they could ever have what they'd had. It was better to break it clean; clean breaks didn't hurt as much or for as long.

Ellen stared at the pregnancy test in shock. "Matt? Come here please."

"I'm in a real rush here. We're voting on the final budget amendment, and Chronley's mad as shit that his own party is trying to sabotage his plan."

She was breathing fast and shallow, staring at the little pink plus sign. "It's kind of important."

"What?" he snapped, standing in the bathroom looking completely put out. And then he froze, his eyes on that little stick in Ellen's hand.

"I'm pregnant." *I'm terrified and happy and horrified and sick.*

Matt slumped against the doorjamb. "Wow."

"Wow? Wow good or wow bad."

"Good, I guess."

"Oh God."

"How did it happen?"

Ellen gave him a look. "The usual way, you idiot," she said with a smile. And she realized, then and there, that she was happy about this baby. "I'm happy. I think I'm happy, Matt."

"Jesus. A baby." He stared at her flat stomach. "Do you think we can do this? Shit."

Ellen's eyes teared up. "We don't have much choice, do we? We have to be ready."

Matthew swallowed convulsively. "I love you. You know that, right?"

"I know." She pressed her lips together, determination in every line in her face. "We'll be okay. We can do this." She ran into his arms and whispered that she loved him, and for the first time in a very long time, she really did. It came back like a flood. That thing that had lodged in her heart all these months popped free and let her feel real for the first time since Leah's death.

The phone rang, and he kissed her forehead. "I've got to go. I'll call you."

"Okay. I'm going to call Sally and get a blood test authorized." She watched Matt run down the stairs and smiled as she picked up the hallway phone. "Hello?"

"Ellen, it's Jill Brighton. I've got your songwriter. Are you sitting down? It's Declan McDonald."

"You're kidding."

"I spoke to the man. He admitted who he was then disappeared. I told him you wanted to talk to him, and he wasn't agreeable at this point, but I think he'll come around."

"Where did you find him?" Ellen asked, her heart beating hard, her brain hearing the *ka-ching* of money in her head.

"A friend of his got in a car accident, and he was visiting her in the hospital."

"That's fantastic news, Jill. Great work."

"Thanks."

Ellen listened to a moment of dead air. "Is there anything else?"

"I thought it would be more appropriate for you to go to the media."

She heard Matthew's voice in her head lecturing her on the ends justifying the means. "I'm not certain either of us should. He didn't want to be found, and I don't know if it's right exposing him this way. I have to think about it."

"Think quickly, then. Because if you don't, I'm going to. I don't intend to suffer from a bout of conscientiousness. I have to be practical. This story is going to double my business, and I intend to milk every little drop."

"I don't want my name mentioned if you do. I've made my decision," Ellen said, feeling proud and right-minded. "I won't expose him, and I want nothing to do with it. I never intended to do anything but thank whoever wrote 'Leah's Song,' and that's all I intend to do now."

"Fair enough. I'll keep my client confidential. And I'll be back in Tennessee in two days to collect the rest of my retainer."

"I wish you would reconsider, Jill."

"No chance. See you Thursday."

Ellen hung up the phone carefully. Somehow, seeing that little plus sign helped to put everything in perspective. Finding who wrote "Leah's Song" had diminished to almost something insignificant, and now Ellen found herself battling a terrible bout of guilt. She realized she'd have to find Declan McDonald and talk to him face-to-face, if only to apologize. Ellen was savvy enough to realize finding Declan McDonald alive was a huge story—one the media would have a field day with. She only hoped Jill kept her word and kept her mouth shut about who had hired her.

Chapter 15

Roasted chicken wrapped in bacon with gnocchi and roasted endive, $22.00

Rose awoke the next day feeling groggy from a fitful sleep. It seemed as if every time she drifted off, some smiling nurse was flicking on the light to check her blood pressure or her I.V.

"Good morning, Rose. Time to remove that nasty catheter."

"Oh. Yippee."

Nurse Amy pulled back her blanket and sheet. "Did you hear all about the excitement? Scooch down, please."

Rose scooched. "What excitement?"

"Declan McDonald, you know, the singer who's supposed to be dead? He's alive, and his girlfriend is in *this* hospital."

Rose winced and let out a groan, the wince for the catheter, the groan for the nurse's news.

"Oh, sorry," Chirpy the Nurse said.

"There's about ten news crews outside the hospital, and you should see the administrator. She doesn't know what to do with them all because no one knows who she is."

"Wow," Rose said, sounding sick.

"And," Amy said with emphasis, "Declan McDonald was in this hospital. Can you believe it? He must have been disguised or something. We all think his girlfriend must be this gorgeous woman on the fifth floor. She just got breast enhancement surgery. I can't imagine who else it could be. Do you have to pee?"

Rose had to think about it for a couple of seconds. "Yes. I think I do." She didn't, but she had to get away from Amy so she could digest the latest debacle. The nurse helped ease her out of bed and walked her to the bathroom.

"Do you want me to wait here for you? How do you feel. Any dizziness? Nausea?"

Oh, there was nausea all right, but not because of any physical ailment. Even though she knew rationally it wasn't her fault, she couldn't help but feel guilty that the reason Declan had been discovered was because of her. The proverbial shit was hitting the fan. This was exactly what Declan had wanted to avoid. She knew it was big news, but she'd become so used to Declan being alive, she'd forgotten the impact it had had on her. The world would be in shock. And feeling angry and betrayed. Declan, one of the best-loved entertainers, was about to become a pariah.

And she was about to become the center of one of the biggest stories of the year. Rose planted her palms on either side of the sink, leaned over, and started breathing heavily, trying to catch her breath, trying not to vomit.

"Okay. You're okay. No one knows who you are. Yet. And when they do find out, who cares? We'll get through this. It'll pass," she whispered to herself in an attempt to stop her hyperventilating. Rose splashed water on her face. With a sense of dread, she walked back into the room half expecting a news crew led by Lois Lane to barge in at any minute.

"Are you sleeping with Declan McDonald?" Lois thrusts the microphone into her face. "Er, none of your business?" "So, you are, you slut." Lois turns back to the camera. "This is Lois Lane for News Channel Ten with an exclusive interview with Rose Pisano, who actually thinks we'll believe Declan McDonald is her boyfriend." The news crew begins to leave. "I never said that! He's my . . . He's my boss. And sure, we slept together, but that was it. I'm not his girlfriend. Sheesh. I'm his . . . employee. I'm nothing." But the news crew is gone, leaving Rose alone, clutching a wound that has just reopened. "Nurse. Nurse. I think I'm dying here."

"Nurse." Rose snapped out of her horrible fantasy when her new roommate called out to a nurse passing by.

"Oh, hell," said a woman in her late forties. "I can't get this thing to work." She kept jabbing the hospital remote control at the television. "Do you know how to work it?"

"Sure." Rose pressed a button on the woman's bed, then handed her the remote. "You have to turn it on and off with the bed for some reason."

The small television flickered on to Carrie Denise, one of Declan's former girlfriends. "Until I see him, touch him, I won't believe it's true," she said, her eyes tearing up as Rose rolled her own. "I just don't think Declan would have disappeared and then not contacted me."

"Good riddance to bad rubbish, I say. Never did like him, like him even less now that he's alive," muttered the hag from the bed.

Trying to keep her temper in check, Rose said evenly, "I always read he was well liked."

"By the women. *Supposedly*, that is." Ah, a *National Enquirer* reader.

"I take it you're not the mystery woman who's been dating him, then?" Rose asked, pasting a smile on her face.

The woman let out a snort, blowing the gray nose hairs from her nostrils. "About as much chance of that as you being the mystery woman."

Rose picks up the pillow, places it over the woman's head, and presses, ignoring the screams, the flaying, flapping arms . . .

"No offense," the woman said, letting out a witchy cackle. "Those Hollywood types never go after the ordinary girls. All flash and no substance."

And when she finally stops moving, Rose lifts the pillow, an ethereal smile on her lips.

"You're probably right. Have a nice day." She slipped behind her curtain and gingerly lay down. Was that how everyone was going to react? If so, Declan was a goner.

And she was a joke.

"Aw, crap," Declan said, flicking off the kitchen television.

"Sorry, Dec. I guess that P.I. had a bigger mouth than you thought."

"Why would she do that? Why? What purpose does it serve? I'll never be able to get into that hospital today. Did you see that mob scene?" Declan clutched the back of his neck and squeezed. "I am done screwing up other people's lives."

Rick gave Declan a concerned look. "Hey, don't get maudlin on me here. Today will be the worst. You're a villain right now, but once we put your baby blues in front of the camera, you'll be golden again. We'll play up the charity work, the way you agonized about your decision, which we'll make sure people know was about protecting your family, not yourself."

Declan looked, and felt, sick. "That's not entirely true. Everything was so crazy back then, I wasn't even thinking straight. My brother had died, my mother had just gotten out of a freaking mental hospital, and I . . ." Declan stopped and squeezed his head between his palms. "There is no excuse. What I did was wrong. Cowardly and wrong. You can't paint it any other way. And stop looking at me like that."

Rick threw his hands to his sides. "Like what?"

"Like you feel sorry for me. Don't. I did this to myself." He pressed his lips together, livid with anger. "And I did it to Rose, too. Her life's going to be turned upside down by this. By me. And I can't to a damned thing about it."

"Will you stop the woe-is-me act and get yourself together? How many times have I told you, this is a game. A money game. You get them to believe what you want. Keep yourself together, Dec, or I'm out the door. I mean it."

Declan swallowed down the bile gathering in his throat. "If it was just me . . ." He stopped and squeezed his eyes shut until he felt a firm grip on his shoulder.

"I'll do my best to keep her out of it. Fair enough? Before you know it, any interest in her will be gone. The focus will be on you. She's just a sidebar to a huge story, right?"

Declan let out a shaking breath. "You're right. I've got to get to her, to warn her, to talk to her. Do you think we can get past those reporters?"

Rick smiled. "Does the Pope wear a funny hat?"

Paul came through in a big way by supplying Declan with a security uniform. Once he'd put it on, he and Paul had walked right through the crowd of cameras and reporters. Heck, they'd even parted like the Red Sea to let them through. Getting to Rose's room was just as easy with Paul leading the way, loving life and his new job as bodyguard for one of the most famous faces in the world.

"That worked great," Declan said outside Rose's room.

"No problem, sir," Paul said, sounding official until he sheepishly added, "but I need to get that uniform back by tonight."

"You can have it back as soon as we're out of here. After this, no more hiding out. No more disguises."

Declan walked into the room, gave an official nod to Rose's new roommate, then peered around the curtain, cautious and uncertain how she would react to seeing him. He whipped off his hat and glasses and pressed his index finger to his lips. She was sitting up in bed, her hair pulled back into a loose ponytail, some kind of cooking magazine on her lap. When she saw him, Rose gave him a dazzling smile, and he wished he could bottle it and take it out in about a day. It hit him then that in about ten minutes, after he was done giving her the brush-off, he'd never see her smile at him like that again. Better to hurt her a little now than ruin her life later. He kept telling himself that, kept reminding himself that his brother's only crime had been being his brother, but at this moment, looking at Rose and wanting to hold her hard against him, he simply wanted her with him. Forever.

Rose smiled, even though her eyes scanned his face worriedly for signs of stress and meltdown. "Hey, famous man," she said softly, as aware as he was how precarious their position was.

His expression changed then, went from endearingly worried to almost normal, and Rose narrowed her eyes. "Hey, beautiful. How are you feeling?"

"Physically or emotionally. I'll answer both. Pretty crappy. How about you?"

He grinned. "I'll get through it."

"We'll get through it." And that was when he looked away to stare out the window so she could see only his hard profile. "Okay, Declan, give it to me straight. What's the plan?"

Rose watched the muscle in his jaw bulge a few times, noticed how his entire face tightened.

And then he said it; he actually put into words what that expression had already told her. He put on a big show of looking all concerned, of softening that sexy voice of his. "These past weeks have been terrific. But we both knew up front it wasn't going anywhere. I never meant to hurt you, Rose. I never meant for any of this to happen."

Rose pointed an angry finger to her eye. "Do you see any tears here?"

"I don't want you mad at me, Rose. I don't want any of this. My life is going to turn into a circus, and I don't want you part of that."

Rose let out a humorless laugh. "What makes you so sure I want to be part of your life?" He looked so taken aback, Rose almost laughed—and she would have if she wasn't about a millisecond away from crying and begging him to love her the way she loved him.

"This is one of the most difficult decisions I've ever made in my life and you're going to make a joke of it?"

Rose stared at her hospital blanket, at the words stamped in blue, "R.I. Hospital," until her eyes burned and the words got all blurry. "You'd think," she started, but stopped because her voice croaked. "You'd think you'd know well enough by now that I joke when I don't want to cry." She wiped at her eyes with the corner of the blanket. "Is this what you want, me to cry and beg you to keep me with you? Well, I'm not going to do it. You're right, I knew up front that we were nothing. But it doesn't mean I have to like it. I can't shut down my emotions as easily as you can. I knew I would like you too much, and I knew I'd be the one act-ing like an idiot when you said good-bye."

"Rose," he choked out, then pressed his forehead against hers. They stayed that way for a long moment before Rose subtly pushed him back.

She bit her lip, debating whether to have it spelled out completely. "So this is it, right? No phone calls, no me flying out to California to see you. This is good-bye."

"Yes."

Even though she knew he was going to say that word, it still felt like another nail pounded into her, this time directly into her heart. "Okay. Good-bye."

He had the gall to look as though she'd just crushed him. He pressed a kiss against her lips and whispered, "Good-bye."

And then, Declan McDonald walked out of her life.

Chapter 16

Steamed mussels in an aromatic broth with crème fraiche, Pernod and fresh herbs, $9.00

"Is he a good lover?"

That one stopped Rose in her tracks as she tried to make her way from her beat-up Honda to her apartment building. She'd been home from the hospital for two days, and ever since reporters had been camped out outside her home waiting for her appearance. Rose wasn't certain how her identity had gotten out, but her hospital roommate and that detective were prime suspects. Jenn swore up and down that she hadn't said a word to anyone "even though it's killing me" and that left only Declan, the P.I., and the hag as the likely culprits. She might be angry at Declan for leaving her cold, but she knew he'd never voluntarily give up her name. Unfortunately, confronted with the question, Declan had to tell the truth, that she'd been his personal chef. That was when the reporters started showing up outside her door. She hadn't a clue what they thought they were going to find out—that was until the reporter called out whether or not Declan was good in bed.

Rose's eyes scanned the crowd of reporters and photographers for the insensitive slob who'd shouted that question. "Who asked that?" she demanded.

"Well, is he?" another reporter asked, to the great amusement of the others present. Rose just stared at them, hoping beyond hope to shame them. It got all quiet until the only sounds she could hear were the rattle of equipment and the whir of cameras advancing film.

Rose gave the crowd a blazing smile. "I'll tell you what he really likes," she said, a spark of humor in her eyes as she watched them lean forward to hear, microphones pushed toward her in anticipation. "He loves veal medallions seared on the grill, then smothered with a white wine and garlic sauce. Oh, and linguini tossed with seafood." The microphones moved back, the reporters giving her a look of disgust. "I'd be more than happy to share some of my recipes. In fact, I plan to open a restaurant in the next year or so, and you're all invited to the grand opening." She continued talking about her plans until only one reporter remained, diligently writing down everything she said. Finally, curiosity got the best of her.

"Who are you with?" she asked.

"Good Eats magazine," the woman said.

Rose raised her eyebrows in surprise. "Really?" Then her surprise turned into suspicion. "Do you have any identification? A press card or something?"

The woman dug into a canvas bag with the words *Good Eats* silk-screened on it. Rose could see copies of the magazine, one of her favorite cooking publications, amidst the reporter's notebooks and a cell phone. "Here it is."

Sure enough the woman, Francine Talbot, was the magazine's East Coast contributor. "You want an exclusive interview?" Rose asked. "You know, a tell-all about Declan McDonald's palate?"

Francine's blue eyes lit up. "That sounds great."

Rose looked at the other reporters as they huddled on the sidewalk muttering to themselves and probably debating whether hanging out outside her apartment was worth the time. They were collectively startled to see Francine troop up the stairs behind her, the muttering taking on tones of panic. Francine turned and waggled her fingers at them before disappearing into the dim foyer of Rose's apartment. When the door closed, she leaned against it and laughed aloud. "Oh, God, did you see the looks on those vultures' faces? What a bunch of jerks. You should have heard some of the stuff they were saying."

"I can imagine," Rose said, deciding immediately that she liked Francine. She was warm and open and loved to talk about food as much as Rose did. Francine looked too thin to enjoy food as much as she let on, but Rose suspected she expended so much energy she was likely one of those women who could eat heartily without gaining an ounce. She had thick red hair, parted in the middle and brushed under at her jaw. Francine was one of those mile-a-minute talkers and acted as if everything Rose said was intensely interesting. She *ooh*ed over her use of cinnamon in her marinara, and *aahh*ed over her description of her artichoke and mushroom raviolis. The article would be a fun piece about Declan's favorite foods and would include two recipes, as well as a small head-and-shoulders shot of Rose. A food tell-all, so to speak. Francine even promised to include a paragraph about the restaurant Rose was planning. Rose didn't feel even an inkling of concern about the article, which Francine promised would be about food, not about Declan or her personal life. She couldn't imagine Declan seeing any harm in this type of article. If a little publicity made her restaurant a success, what harm could it do?

"Do you mind if I call my editor and tell him the good news?"

Rose shook her head.

"Martin, it's Francine. Guess where I am right now?" she asked her boss, giving Rose a happy wink. "I got an exclusive with Declan McDonald's chef." She made the appropriate responses to her boss's questions before saying good-bye and snapping her phone closed. "He's ecstatic. We're going to try to get this into next month's issue, and I've got a good chance at a cover story. Deadline is Thursday, so that gives me one day to write the article and get your picture taken. Are you available tomorrow? I'll call you and give you the details on where to go for the picture as soon as I make arrangements. Wear your chef's uniform. Better yet, wear just a white lacy bra and your chef's pants."

At Rose's shocked look, Francine laughed. "Only kidding."

"Oh." And Rose did laugh, at the joke and her own gullibility.

Francine gathered up all her things. "Bring a couple of recipes with you. A main course and an appetizer would be great. Can't wait to see those reporters when I waltz out of here. I think I'll have a little bit of fun with them. Think I should?"

"Just don't say anything that will get me into trouble. They might print whatever you say."

Francine waved a hand at her. "Don't worry. I'll keep 'em guessing. They all think I work for *Time*. I don't know where they got that idea," she said facetiously.

Rose closed the door behind her with a smile on her face. She glanced at the telephone and wondered who she could call to tell about the article. Only two people would truly care, and one was dead and the other dead to her. How excited Nonna would have been to see Rose's picture on the cover of *Good Eats* magazine. Declan would have gotten a kick out it, too. Or maybe not. Maybe he would have pretended to be excited for her; maybe the entire time they were together he was just biding his time. After all, she was the only woman around, not half bad looking, why not have a little fun with her? Rose tried, she really, really did try, not to think that way. It demeaned her more than she thought she deserved. She couldn't be that stupid.

But maybe she had been. Maybe she'd been blinded by his celebrity and let herself believe in things she had no right to believe in. Had she actually fantasized about them spending their lives together? It was so pathetic. And it hurt like hell.

The thrill of the interview vanished, and depression washed over her. Instead of picking up the phone, she sat on the couch and stared at the blank television screen, too sapped to even bother pushing the remote keys. Anyway, every time she turned on the television she saw him, looking a combination of repentant and confident. It was purely sickening to watch the display. He'd flash his smile, wave to the crowd, then be all concerned and sad when someone asked him why he'd pretended to be dead.

The worst had been when a reporter at the press conference had asked, "Who's Rose Pisano?" Without missing a beat, he'd informed the crowd that she was a chef who worked for him. And then he'd looked to the reporters for another question.

What had she expected? That he'd break down and confess his undying love for her on national television? That he'd look right into that camera and talk just to her and tell her how sorry he was that he'd ripped her heart from her chest?

In her saner moments, Rose was much better at rationalizing what had happened. She'd had great sex with a really hot guy. The end.

Except she hadn't been able to keep her heart out of

the equation, and he had. He wasn't to blame for being honest. He'd never lied to her, never hinted for even a moment that they might share something more. If she felt betrayed, it was because she was manufacturing a relationship that hadn't existed except in her own demented head. Still, she couldn't help but think back on how he'd looked at her when they'd made love. She could have sworn he'd felt *something* for her. He was one heck of an actor.

Rose pushed her head back against the couch and squeezed her eyes closed. It didn't matter how or what happened. It hurt now, and it hurt bad.

Someone knocked on her door, and Rose's heart raced, even as she told herself it wouldn't be him, even as she thought maybe it was him. She peeked through the peephole and stifled a groan. It was her mother.

Rose opened the door, and her mother darted inside as if she were being chased. "Do you know there's a horde of reporters out there?"

"They'll go away eventually," Rose said, sitting back down on her couch as her mother glanced around her apartment, a look of distaste on her face. She wore one of her power lawyer suits, a gray flannel with a severe cut and subtle pinstripes. She moved over to Rose's only other place to sit, a battered old wingback that used to be in her grandmother's basement, looking at the chair to be sure it was clean before sitting down.

"What did you do, Rosalie? Do you have any idea how embarrassing this is?"

"To you or to me?"

"To me."

Rose could only smile at her mother's reply. "Sorry, but I wasn't really thinking about you at the time. Besides, how many people even know I'm your daughter?"

"Mark knows," she said, referring to her boyfriend. "That's enough. He's got an extremely tenuous position on that shipping port legislation, and he doesn't need anything to disrupt him."

"Does anyone know that you're the attorney for the company that wants to build the port? To me, that would be a lot more embarrassing than your daughter being Declan McDonald's chef."

Her mother pursed her lips, her lemon-sour face that told Rose she was extremely displeased. "No one has ever raised it as an issue. And I don't appreciate you questioning my professional integrity."

"You mean the way you're questioning mine?" Rose would have said it with much more force if she hadn't been sleeping with her boss. She hadn't a leg to stand on in the morality fight with her mother.

Her mother sighed and relaxed. "How are you holding up?"

"Fine. I'm actually going to be on the cover of *Good Eats*."

Lucia shook her head. "I've never heard of it."

"It's not nearly as big as *Bon Appetite,* but it's a well-read magazine. I have to go to a photo studio tomorrow to get my picture taken."

"Don't wear green."

"I'm wearing a lacy bra on top and my chef pants. They want something a little risqué, given the rumors and everything."

Her mother got another sour lemon ball in her mouth. "That's not funny, Rosalie."

"I'm wearing my chefs uniform."

"I suppose that's appropriate. I actually stopped by because of this." Lucia dug into her briefcase and held up a copy of the *National News*. The first thing Rose saw was a gorgeous picture of Declan, and the second thing she saw was a picture of herself taken outside her apartment house and the headline: SOMETHING COOKIN' IN DECLAN'S KITCHEN?

Rose's initial horror quickly turned to hilarity, and she burst out laughing. "Oh, God, that's so funny."

"It is not funny. Is it true?"

Rose couldn't stop the blush from burning her cheeks, and she debated whether to pretend her redness was from anger or chagrined. "We had a brief, torrid affair."

"Thank God. At least you didn't sleep with him."

Rose was slightly dumbfounded that her mother believed she'd been lying and was about to insist she'd had an affair with Declan before coming to her senses. The fewer people who knew the truth, the better.

"One more thing. Your grandmother left her house to you, which is just as well because I certainly don't have any use for it."

Rose was stunned. "When did this come about?"

"When you were in the hospital." Her mother pulled out a folder. "The deed is in here. I took the liberty to have a realtor do a market evaluation on the house in case you want to sell. She said it's worth about one hundred eighty thousand, though I can't imagine that little house selling for that."

Rose looked blindly at the lease her mother had just handed her, her throat so clogged with unshed tears, it hurt. A tear splashed directly on top of the word "deed." She was unaware her mother had moved until she saw her well-manicured hand on her own.

"She knew how much having a restaurant of your own meant to you. This was her way of making sure you got your dream, Rosalie."

Rose looked up at her mother, shocked that the two of them had talked about her dreams, and stunned that her mother actually seemed to care.

"You were her whole world, you know."

More tears spilled over as Rose tried a shaky smile. "I really miss her."

"So do I. It's strange, but I miss her disapproving of

me. I'd visit her once a week, and nearly the entire time we'd fight. I miss those visits more than I could have imagined." Her mother laughed and shook her head, puzzled by her own admission. Then she pushed up, shaking off expertly any bit of sentimentality she'd displayed. "I'm off. I have to be in court," she flicked her wrist and looked at her watch, "in twenty minutes." When she got to the door, she turned. "Call me if you need a lawyer settling the sale. I'll give you a family discount."

After she was gone, Rose sagged down even lower on the couch and wished her mother would be less schizophrenic. The deed to her grandmother's house sat next to her, her ticket to the life she'd always wanted. Rose picked it up, refolded it carefully, then put it in her sock drawer. She sat back down on the couch feeling as if she needed a good long bout of tears. Instead, with the greatest effort, she turned her head toward the picture of her grandmother laughing in the kitchen, and she smiled.

Rose knew she was going a little crazy when she decided that Francine's joke about wearing nothing but a bra for the cover picture was actually a good idea.

She woke up feeling renewed and almost happy, and with a brain filled with so many great ideas she had to write some of them down. "Look sexy for picture." It was the first thing she wrote. Then: "Shamelessly ride Declan's coattails." It all made wonderful perfect sense. Opening a restaurant was perhaps one of the scariest things a chef could do. The easy way out was to get a job at an already-established restaurant, then slowly and methodically put your own stamp on the food there. Even that was a difficult proposition because the owner didn't like messing with success.

Every time Rose saw a new restaurant open downcity, she got a nervous twist in her gut—fear for the poor schmuck who was putting their neck on the line. Half the restaurants failed. Half. And it wasn't always because the food was bad or the location stunk. Sometimes you couldn't put your finger on why a restaurant stuck out in the middle of the woods thrived while another on a busy four-lane road located across from a multiplex cinema failed. You had to get the customers through the door, and you had to keep them coming back for more.

If she sold Nonna's house, she could be up and running within a month or two after that. Between her own savings, which got a healthy injection during the six months she'd worked for Declan, and her Nonna's money, Rose would have cash to spare for advertising and an interior decorator. She was going first class, all the way.

And Declan, whether he knew it or not, was going to help her.

All that morning she set up a strategy for fame. She wasn't going to settle for fifteen minutes in the limelight; she was going to milk this until the cow was dry. She had fifteen messages on her answering machine, most of them from reporters requesting interviews. With pencil in hand, she started writing down the names and numbers. Several local television and radio stations had called, the private detective who had exposed Declan, her father, Jenn—twice—and her mother, telling her she was on her way over. Her first call was to a realtor to put her grandmother's house on the market and to get a list of restaurants for sale in the Providence area. After that, she spent about an hour making arrangements for interviews. She told each reporter she wanted to talk about her job as a personal chef and had nothing to say about Declan's personal life—other than what he ate. She was booked for two weeks. That was fourteen days of free advertising for her new restaurant that didn't exist yet. When she opened Rosalie's she wanted it to be an event. Politicians, food critics, the media, friends and family would all be invited to a private grand opening. She just might invite a famous songwriter.

Rose's last call before getting ready for the photo shoot was to Jenn. "*Good Eats* magazine wants to do a cover story about me, and I have to get my picture taken. I need to look sexy." Rose thought she heard Jenn snicker. "Are you laughing?"

"No. Of course not. How much time do we have?"

"Ha, ha. I've got about an hour before I have to leave." Rose told her about her plans for a media blitz. "Do you think it's a good idea? Or should I just look like myself?"

"Let's go for it. I'll bring my makeup, 'cause I assume the one tube of lipstick you own might not be enough. The worst that could happen is that you'll look completely foolish and you'll spend your life dodging food-loving perverts. Besides, how sexy can you look?"

Apparently, pretty sexy. With her hair down and wearing makeup, Rose was a knockout. She wore a chef's top that zippered up to her chin. But Rose decided to upzip it a bit, just enough to show the cleavage revealed by her one and only push-up bra. Jenn let out a whistle. "Rose, I didn't know you had it in you."

"I look like a prostitute," she said, gazing at her just-from-the-bed, tousled look. Then she smiled. "It's perfect."

"You don't look like a prostitute, you look gorgeous. Any guy who sees this magazine is going to want to go to Rosalie's restaurant in a minute just to get a glimpse of you."

Rose let out a groan. "I can't cook with all this crap on my face. I'll melt!"

"By the time they're sitting down and taste your food they won't care what you look like," Jenn said.

Rose went to the kitchen, grabbed one of her wooden

spoons, and held it to her bottom lip making it pout slightly. "How's that?" she asked.

Jenn was laughing too hard to answer.

"What about this?" And she stuck out her tongue to lap at the spoon.

"Stop it," Jenn gasped, holding her stomach. "You're going to make me pee."

"Okay. Let's go."

Richard Metzger was picking up groceries and waiting in the checkout line when he spied the October issue of *Good Eats*. "Holy moly."

Richard loved all things beautiful, and the woman on the cover was drop-dead gorgeous. She was looking directly at the camera, a wooden spoon held to her lower lip in a come-hither pout, wearing what he supposed was a chef's uniform. He'd never seen a chef quite like that one, though, and dollar signs floated in front of him. A chef like that could use a publicist. That was when he read the headline: DECLAN MCDONALD'S CHEF TELLS ALL.

"Holy shit."

He ignored the dirty looks he got from the woman standing behind him with a passel of kids, then pulled out his cell phone and called Declan. "Dec. Meet me at my house in ten. Okay, twenty. It's important."

Declan drove his vintage sky blue VW bug that his mother had kept in storage for him to Santa Monica, one town over from where he'd found a secluded rental. He wasn't in the mood to talk to Richard, or anyone else for that matter. It was Sunday, the one day he could almost count on for a little peace and quiet. Two days ago, he'd given Barbara Walters an interview, and the entire experience had been nerve-wracking because her staff had done their research exceptionally well. The interview was the most in-depth he'd given thus far. In the four weeks he'd left Rhode Island, he'd mostly been on late night talk shows and a couple of daytime fluff shows. Easy to handle. He was still recovering from Barbara, though.

Richard lived in a gated community where every house looked just about like its neighbor. Because of that, people had put overlarge numbers on their houses in an effort to individualize their cookie-cutter existence. Richard liked the normalcy of the place, though. The kids running around, riding bikes, the homeowners out mowing lawns.

Declan's VW buzzed down the street attracting little attention. He pulled into Richard's tiny driveway, surprised to see his friend tinkering in the garage with a gorgeous 1955 Thunderbird, cherry red with brilliant chrome detailing.

"Um, James Dean, I presume?"

"I took this darn thing in for a tune-up, but I think the spark plugs weren't changed," he grumbled before standing up. Weekends Richard was hardly recognizable. He wore an old faded T-shirt, khaki cargo shorts, and a pair of Chuck Taylors that were probably older than some of the kids playing in the street. "I hate to bother you on a Sunday, but I didn't think this could wait. Come on inside."

Curiosity eating at him, Declan followed Richard into his house. Richard motioned for him to take a seat at the kitchen's center island, then slapped a magazine in front of him. It took Declan three heartbeats before he realized what he was looking at. Then his eyes scanned the headline, and confusion took over.

"Is this some sort of joke?" he said, half to himself.

"Afraid not."

"What the hell was she thinking?"

"Apparently your old girlfriend is one smart customer. She's promoting her new restaurant. The article inside is pretty lame. Just her talking about what foods you ate, how she prepared them, blah, blah, blah. Then there's a sidebar about the restaurant she plans to open by Christmas."

"She looks . . . she looks . . ."

"Sexy?"

Declan couldn't take his eyes off the magazine. He'd known Rose was pretty, in a cute, perky, wholesome way. She wasn't this pouting woman that screamed sex. He didn't like the woman in the photograph, but he sure as hell wanted her. "She looks like a *Playboy* centerfold."

"There's more."

Declan was beginning to feel slightly ill. She didn't know, she couldn't know, what she was doing, what she was inviting. All because of him. "I don't want to know."

"I made a phone call before you got here so I could have the whole story, and she's been all over the media from Boston to New York. The Food Network is talking with her about her own show."

"Where'd you get all this information?"

Richard shrugged. "Mostly from the *Providence Journal* food editor. Oh, and I also spoke with the photographer who took that shot of her. Apparently she was just goofing around with some friend of hers, he kept snapping, and the editor thought it would sell a few extra copies."

Poor Rose. She was finding out firsthand how it felt to be manipulated and used. She was probably mortified. "If I were her, I'd sue."

Richard coughed into his hand. "Actually, the editor isn't a complete jerk. He consulted her first. It was her decision to go with that shot."

Declan shook his head. "He's got to be lying. Rose would never pose for a picture like that. She likes to clown around, sure, but to allow her photo to be plastered all over the country looking like . . . like . . ." Declan was too disturbed to continue.

"I think you ought to give her more credit. According to the *Journal* guy, she's been incredibly savvy about the entire thing. She uses your name to get an interview, then spends nearly the entire time talking about her restaurant and how her Italian grandmother taught her the secrets of the old country. She's funny, smart, and, as you can see, good in front of a camera. By the time she actually opens that restaurant of hers, her ticket's going to be made."

Declan stared at the magazine again, at the woman he thought he knew.

"Guess she hasn't spent a lot of time getting over you, Dec. You must be losing your touch."

Richard was right. He'd spent the last month in hell missing her, making himself not call her about a hundred times, while Rose had been living it up, using his name and his fame to her advantage.

"Why don't you call her?"

Declan shook his head. "And say what?"

"Say you have a publicist who thinks she'd be a great client."

"Don't even think about it. If you get ahold of her, she won't be able to use a public bathroom without a crowd of reporters following her."

Richard rolled his eyes dramatically. "That again? None of those shots was ever published. Except on the Internet. After you were dead."

Declan swore. "Rose is off limits. We agreed."

"Okay. The thought to represent her was fleeting at best," Richard said, holding up his hands as if to ward off an attack.

Declan stayed for another hour, discussing appearances scheduled for the next week, one of which included a much-dreaded meeting with Ellen Lang. He might spend a week with his mother, still in Sardinia, before heading into the studio to work on a twenty-song CD. A year-long concert tour would follow its release. The public had been remarkably forgiving of him, considering what he'd done to betray just about everyone he knew. Richard had been right: writing songs for dying children had redeemed him in the eyes of the public, and the ever-cynical media.

His initial meeting with Mrs. Lang would be public and well covered, and it promised to be exceedingly uncomfortable. He still harbored anger toward her for going to such lengths to find the author of "Leah's Song." Still, he was curious as to why she'd done what she'd done.

Declan walked into his new house feeling about as low as he'd felt in a long time. The home's décor did nothing to lift his spirits. He'd been living there for more than a month and hadn't bought a stick of furniture except for a chair that sat in front of a flat-panel television and a bed. He didn't even watch television.

He really ought to hire a decorator and do the place up right, make it comfortable. He really ought to stop thinking about Rose. She'd obviously gotten over him. He glanced at the phone that sat on the floor next to his chair and debated whether to call her. He should warn her to take things more slowly, that fame wasn't what it was cracked up to be, a phone call from a friend.

Who was he kidding? He just wanted to hear her voice, her laugh. He wanted to hold her again, bury his face against her hair, his body into hers. He reminded himself that he was the one who had set the rules. The thing was, he'd thought it would be much easier to follow them. Cut it off clean. Leave no doubt that there was ever a chance for them. Obviously, Rose was getting on with her life, bouncing back like a super ball, apparently.

He lay down on his bed and picked up the magazine to stare at her face. God, she was gorgeous. On the way home, he'd had to stop at two newsstands before he found a copy of the October *Good Eats*. It had sold out at the first one. He flipped open to the article and read it for the first time, dreading that she'd said something that might be misconstrued and hurt her. Richard had been right. She'd talked about food and her restaurant. Hell, the article for all its hype about him, hardly even mentioned his name. Inside was a picture of a seafood appetizer she'd never made for him and a picture of her with her uniform zipped and a cute smile on her face. He shut the magazine feeling slightly depressed.

Sure, they'd agreed not to mention their real relationship, but she could have at least said something more than, "He doesn't eat red meat except for veal." That was as personal as the article got. All those animal rights fanatics would probably line up outside his recording studio and protest his next CD. He ought to name it *Declan ReVealed*. Ha ha.

He tossed the magazine off his bed, tucked his hands beneath his head, stared at the ceiling, and tried real hard to resist the terrible temptation to call her.

Chapter 17

Cool asparagus and carrot "slaw" with English peas and robust vinaigrette, $9.00

"Wow. How much bigger can you get?"

Jenn gave her a look of pure misery. "I don't know."

"Aw, come here and give me a hug, you silly." Rose tried a frontal hug, then immediately shifted to the side. "There. All better?"

"Other than the fact I haven't had sex in two months, I'm just dandy."

"Brian's not putting out, huh?"

Jenn waddled to her well-worn couch and sat down in that pregnant-woman way and laughed. "Would *you* make love to me?"

"Sorry," Rose said, purposefully misunderstanding. "I'm not in the mood."

"Very funny. I'm serious. I'm freakishly big. Have you ever in your life seen a stomach that sticks out this far. And I still have two months to go," she moaned.

"I thought men were supposed to think pregnant women were sexy. Brian's not still mad about that almost kiss, is he?"

"Not as far as I know," Jenn said, looking away. "Now that we all know how I'm doing, how are you doing?"

Rose sat down cross-legged beside Jenn. "I'm okay. I guess. Pretty good for a woman who got dumped by *People*'s Sexiest Man of the Year."

"I still can't believe it. It's like I don't even know you. And I'm still mad that you didn't tell me."

Rose hugged a pillow to her. "I couldn't."

"Has he called?"

She tucked the pillow under her chin. "No."

"Jerk." Jenn tilted her head so she could better see Rose's expression. "Isn't he a jerk?"

Rose managed a shrug.

"You're still in love with the jerk," Jenn pronounced.

"Of course I am," she said quietly.

"Then why are you subjecting yourself to watching him interviewed by Barbara Walters?"

Because I miss him. "Because I want to see if they talk about me." That was partly true. So far Rose had been telling the myriad reporters dogging her that she had been his chef and nothing else. Most of them took one look at her and believed her; she wasn't Declan McDonald's type. Since *Good Eats* hit the newsstands, though, she'd seen a lot more speculation in their eyes. Rose was the girl-next-door type, the perky one with the ready smile and cheerful hello. She wasn't worldly or beautiful or leggy or blond or big-breasted. She was just a girl from Federal Hill who cooked real well and had learned very quickly how to market herself. "I appreciate you coming over to watch with me."

Jenn picked up the remote and turned on the television. They sat through two other interviews waiting for Declan—he was the main attraction, the one all the promotions featured. His first in-depth interview since coming out of hiding.

"Here it is," Jenn said, giving Rose's arm a little squeeze. "You okay?"

Rose just stared at the television, at Declan's face, a promotional picture that was a few years old. The past weeks had been incredibly hard. Everywhere she looked, she saw his picture, heard his name, his voice as she passed by a television. It still got to her, that deep timber sliding through her, reminding her how wonderful it had been to make love, to feel his body over hers, to run her hands over his taut stomach. Her chest hurt, her throat ached, and her eyes burned, but she was determined to listen to every word that came out of his mouth. His beautiful, sexy, cold-as-ice mouth.

Ms. Walters went through a brief biography, talking about his childhood, his close relationships with his mother and kid brother, his whirlwind career that seemed to tragically end two years ago. It was an incredible story about an incredible man.

"I'm going to ask you the one question that everyone wants answered. Why? Why did you disappear and allow everyone to believe you died."

The camera shot went to Declan, and Rose stopped breathing. He looked wonderful, but tired. And thin. "Doesn't he look thin?" Rose whispered.

Declan described that day on the mountain, the rage he'd felt standing there and looking down at the photographers. "I never intended to let everyone think I'd died. That's the one thing I'm sorry about, letting those men and women spend days searching for me. At the time, I didn't realize all that was happening. I called my mother, and she told me that everyone thought I was dead."

"It was her suggestion, wasn't it, that you just let people assume what they would. Why did you go along with it?"

He gave her a faint smile. "Because being dead sounded pretty good at the time."

Barbara leaned forward, got that concerned look in her eyes, and said, "Did you ever think about killing yourself?"

"No. Never. Not in any real sense. I wanted to be gone, to disappear, yes, but I never contemplated killing myself."

"But your mother worried, didn't she?"

Declan shifted in his chair. "I didn't know that at the time. I never gave her any indication that I would do something like that."

"You spent two years in seclusion. Not a soul saw you until you hired a personal chef, Rose Pisano."

Rose leaned forward, staring hard to see if Declan's face changed, if the mention of her name evoked any emotion.

"That's right." He gave her his patented winning smile. "Best Italian food I've ever had."

"Some people have speculated there was more to your relationship than employee/employer. After all, she was the reason you were discovered. She was in a car accident, and you visited her in the hospital."

Jenn grabbed Rose's hand and held on tight as they waited for the answer.

"I had already contacted my publicist prior to her accident and arranged a press conference."

Jenn turned to Rose. "Is that true?"

"I don't know."

Ms. Walters pressed. "What was your relationship with Miss Pisano."

That smile again. Rose wished he was in the room so she could slap him. "We had no relationship," he said, putting quote marks around the word "relationship."

Rose's eyes filled, even though she'd known he would say that, even though she'd done the same thing herself. She didn't care that she was being a hypocrite, it hurt. "I'd like to know what his definition of a relationship is," she said shakily.

"Bastard." Good ol' loyal Jenn.

The interview shifted to his career plans, and Rose sat there wondering if he truly thought what they'd had wasn't a relationship. It was possible she'd been a fun diversion for him, while he'd been everything to her. She'd actually believed in her heart he'd loved her just because she so desperately loved him. She thought back to the last time she'd seen him, how businesslike he'd been, how pitying. God, it was so humiliating.

"Eight years ago I interviewed you and asked whether you'd ever been in love. Here's what you said":

A younger, brasher looking Declan appeared on the television. "I never found a woman I could spend more than a few hours with before I wanted to leave. I like women, but not in long doses. I honestly don't think I'll ever fall in love. The thought of spending my life with someone just doesn't enthrall me. I think I'd die of boredom." And he grinned.

An older, harder-looking man looked up from the tape, an unfathomable look in his eyes, an ironic smile on his mouth.

"I'll ask you the same question. Have you ever been in love?"

He was silent a long moment, and Rose held her breath. He could say it now without naming names. He could let her know. He studied the floor in the way Rose used to think was endearing. "No," he said finally.

Tears spilled from Rose's eyes.

"This interview is done." He got up and left, leaving a bewildered Barbara Walters behind.

Jenn pressed the remote, shutting the TV off, and stared at Rose uncertainly. "You okay?"

Rose stood abruptly, hugging her arms about her waist. "I keep telling myself it was nothing. Just some affair. But the thing is, it was everything. But only to me. If he loved me, he could have said it right then. But he didn't love me. He didn't." Rose noisily blew her nose.

"He must have felt something."

"I can't believe I let this happen," Rose said brokenly. "I'm such an idiot. I kept telling myself the whole time that maybe it wasn't real, that I was being stupid for falling for him. He's such a good liar."

"Did he tell you he loved you?" Jenn asked, caution in every syllable.

Rose fought to keep from dissolving to the floor in complete misery. "No," she whispered. "I think because he knew, he always knew this would happen."

"I'm sorry, honey."

"He hasn't even called," she said, completely dejected.

The phone rang, and they stared at each other.

"It's him," Jenn said dramatically.

"No it's not." Rose stared at the phone. "I wish I had caller I.D." It rang again.

"Answer it, or I will."

Rose picked up the phone, cleared her throat of clogged tears, and said as perky as she could, "Hello."

"It's me." She felt the blood drain from her head. "It's Declan."

"I knew who 'me' was. Hey, I was just watching you on television." Good. She sounded natural, happy even, just talking to an old friend. She felt Jenn hovering near the earpiece, then motioned for her to leave. Jenn pulled a face, then grabbed her coat and purse and left, but not before giving her a frantic "call me" motion with an invisible phone.

"Yeah? What did you think?"

"I thought your hair looked like it needed combing." She heard him chuckle, and her stomach wrenched. Maybe she couldn't do this after all. "Did you want anything in particular?"

He was silent so long, Rose thought he might have hung up. Then: "I'm sorry, Rose. Things were so crazy and I handled it badly."

"Yes. You did."

"That's why I called. I saw your picture on that magazine. It was a little . . ."

"Surprising? I thought it was a hilarious."

"Wasn't it a bit, um, out of character?" he asked, sounding slightly put off by her response.

"You really wouldn't know that," Rose said, feeling anger build.

"I guess not. I . . ." He stopped again, but this time she could hear him breathing. "During that interview, I lied."

"No kidding."

"This isn't easy for me." He sounded impatient, even a little mad, and that got Rose mad. Who the hell was he to get mad at her?

"Thanks for calling," she said curtly and was ready to slam down the phone, but stopped when she heard him say her name. "What?" Impatient.

"I want you to be careful, to go slowly. I'm glad good things are happening for you, but . . ."

"Thanks for the advice." Rose figured Declan's ear must be getting a bit frostbitten.

"I miss you."

Oh, shit. Rose's heart melted; she literally felt it sort of collapse in her chest. "I miss you, too."

"I've got to go. I have this thing . . ."

"Oh. Sure."

"Rose, I . . . Good-bye."

She furrowed her brow. "Bye." She listened until she heard him disconnect, then placed the phone down. This time, his good-bye had a definite ring of finality to it. She stared at the phone for a long moment before giving in to the tears she'd been fighting all night.

Chapter 18

Rosalie's bouillabaisse featuring cod, scallops, shrimp, clams and calamari in a spicy aromatic saffron broth with roasted red pepper rouille and garlic crostini, $32.00

Chelsea Sampson, a television producer who played musical beds better than Itzhak Perlman played the violin, lived in one of those Los Angeles homes that Rose had seen only on TV. It sat high on a hill surrounded by tall hedges that were fortified by a brick wall. Even though the Spanish-style villa had far more character, it reminded her of Declan's hideaway in Kingstown and that reminded her of Declan and that made her sick to her stomach.

Rose pulled up in her rented Escort and was about to get out to ring the bell for the gate, when it opened automatically. She knew all about Ms. Sampson, that she was rich, extremely powerful in a town that was all about power, and had undergone several surgeries to remove what she didn't want and add what she did. She also was Declan's former lover. She'd read all about her in last year's September issue of *Variety*. The magazine even had a picture of her standing next to Declan at some celebrity telethon charity thing. Rose had stared at Declan's face in that photograph and decided he looked like a jerk. *Good photography.*

It gave her no small satisfaction to know she was charging Ms. Sampson a small fortune to cook dinner for her party that would have cost less than two hundred dollars at Anthony's—including tip.

Her telephone call from Chelsea had been surrealistic. "I'm putting on a dinner party for ten of my closest friends, and I want to hire you as my personal chef. I want you to cook Declan's favorite dish—what did you say it was?"

"Linguini pescatore. I'm sorry, who did you say you were?"

"Chelsea Sampson. I produce *All About You* for NBC. Declan has gone on and on about your cooking. Everyone is mad to get you for their party, but no one knew how to reach you." She'd managed to impart a great deal of information in those few sentences. She was rich Hollywood, she knew Declan well, and she fancied herself clever. Maybe she was, but Rose never did like it when someone tried to schmooze her.

"You don't have directory assistance in California?"

Chelsea laughed, but Rose sensed she wasn't amused by her smart mouth. "I'll pay you five thousand. Is that fair?"

Rose almost dropped the phone. That kind of money would go a long way toward buying her restaurant— and the publicity wouldn't hurt either. If she got a few more gigs for some high-profile customers, her restaurant would be famous before it even opened its doors. "Five thousand is fine. I do have a question, though. Since I'll be making his favorite dish, will Declan be attending your party?"

"He's not on the list," she said, and then gave her times and dates.

And here she was in California ready to launch her celebrity chef career. Someday she'd have to thank Declan. Right after she spooned out his heart and served it over linguini.

Chelsea Sampson, wearing tight white capris and a pale yellow blouse that matched her salon-made hair, walked out of the house to greet her, a stick with hair and boobs. Rose tried not to picture it, but a sharp image slammed into her of Declan sweating and thrusting over her, her bony legs wrapped around his thick torso. It was decidedly repulsive.

"Look at you, you're just a little peanut," she said, holding out her hand in greeting.

"I'm the tall one in my family," Rose said, not knowing how else to respond to such a greeting. She gripped her hand, slightly shocked by how fragile it felt, and she experienced the tiniest bit of pity for this powerhouse of a woman who, as successful as she was, still felt the need to starve herself.

"When will the rest of your staff arrive?" she asked, looking behind Rose as if she expected to see a busload of assistant chefs piling out.

Rose didn't miss a beat. "For a party this small, I like to handle everything myself."

"I see. Let me show you to the kitchen. I think you'll find everything you need."

"I'm sure I will, Miss Sampson."

"Call me Chelsea. I won't answer to anything but."

Rose tried not to be impressed by the house, by the fact she was in California getting ready to cook a meal for Hollywood's heavy hitters. But she couldn't act completely blasé about walking into a house that probably cost more than some of the town budgets back home. Rose was greeted by a blast of cold air as they entered the foyer. Beneath her sneakers was a mosaic of the sun, tiny tiles of bright yellow, orange, and red on a brilliant blue background. Above her was a large round skylight and huge cast-iron chandelier that held at least twenty thick, red candles that must have looked incredible when lit. The circular foyer was filled with greenery, well-tended ferns, and even a climbing vine that had brilliant red flowers blooming all over it.

"This is my favorite part of the whole house," Chelsea said, taking in Rose's look of awe.

"I can see why," she said, turning in a small circle.

"As for the kitchen, I think I've been in it half a dozen times. Once this morning to make certain everything was ready for you." She let out a laugh, that lovely sort of laugh that some women have. Rose did not. She snorted and guffawed.

"I think everything works," Chelsea said when they passed through the restaurant-style swinging doors. "The wait staff should arrive about an hour before the guests so you can get them ready and give them any special instructions. The dining room is through those doors." Rose looked across the vast, brilliantly clean kitchen to the doors at the far end and couldn't help wondering why people who never cooked would bother investing in the kind of equipment that graced this room. Everything in it was professional grade, from the eight-burner Viking stove to the All-Clad pans hanging above a huge stainless steel work island.

"If you need anything, pick up the phone and ask for Cleo. She'll send someone out. Dinner is at eight."

Declan had a nice little one-beer buzz. After not drinking at all for two years, it didn't take much for him to feel the alcohol sluicing warmly through his veins. He rarely drank, but decided a beer before going over to Chelsea's might not be such a bad idea. She was trying to get him back into her bed, and he wasn't interested. Strangely uninterested. Because he couldn't remember a time in his life when he would have turned down a beautiful woman. He might not be all hot and bothered over every woman he'd slept with, but he sure as hell didn't push them away. The thing was, he didn't find Chelsea remotely beautiful or sexy, though he knew at one time he had. In fact, the two of them had enjoyed some pretty athletic sex. It had been a lot of fun until she'd started getting serious on him and wanting to talk about their relationship and where was this all going and will you marry me someday because I'm in love with you. What a load of crap. It had taken Chelsea, who claimed to have a broken heart, about a week before she was screwing someone else.

Now she was hinting that she missed the sex, not him. She knew just how to get to him. He had to respect that much about her. Declan knew better. Women were always claiming that it was sex when it was really about trying to snare him into something he didn't want—whether it be a public outing or some kind of commitment.

And then there was Rose, the one woman who didn't want anything. The one woman he wanted to give everything. Declan tipped back the rest of his now-warm beer, hating that he was letting her invade his thoughts again. He just couldn't shake her, couldn't stop thinking about her, dreaming about her. It didn't help that during those first few hellish weeks, her face started showing up in the tabloids. Like some love-sick fan, he'd even clipped a couple out and stuck them to his refrigerator door. But he'd known when he saw her picture with the headline SOMETHIN' COOKIN' IN DECLAN'S KITCHEN? that he'd made the right decision. It had killed him to see that, to see her exposed, stripped raw by people who didn't even know her. He'd fallen hard for her, and it was reduced to a cheesy headline: SOMETHIN' COOKIN'. He'd expected that after those first few appearances in the tabloid, she'd disappear, that the press would quickly lose interest in her. But they hadn't. He'd even seen a piece on her locally, a quick mention that Declan McDonald's former chef planned to open an East Coast restaurant and was considering one on the West Coast as well. He figure that was pretty much bullshit, just Rose's way of grabbing more headlines. After he'd seen the piece, he'd called Richard to make certain he hadn't signed Rose as a client. He swore he hadn't, but Declan was still suspicious.

He missed her. He'd never missed anyone, other than his brother, quite this much. And the thing was, it wasn't going away. It was getting worse. Now that he was surrounded by people again all he could think of was Rose, and how glad he was that she wasn't with him, that she was safe in her own world. Even though it was slowly killing him, making him crazy. Making him lonely as hell. These people who flocked around him, who fawned over him, who pulled him aside at parties, they all wanted a piece of him, ripped from his soul. What would these kinds of people do to Rose?

All he wanted was to be left alone. Well, not quite alone. He wanted to live on a mountaintop in a log cabin with Rose curled up beside him while a pot of tomato sauce gurgled on the stove. Declan smiled at the thought, then crushed the beer can viciously. He'd made his choice, and now he had to be a big boy and live with it.

Before he left for Chelsea's, Declan gave himself a quick look in the mirror. He looked like hell. That was what little sleep and lots of soul-searching did to a guy. Plus, he hadn't shaved in two days and had lost about ten pounds since leaving Rhode Island. Since leaving Rose.

Christ, what the hell was wrong with him? He wished his brother were alive so he could tell Michael to bash his head in. That was what he needed, a sharp jab to the side of his jaw.

The ride to Chelsea's took an hour, so by the time he got there he was feeling foul. He didn't want to be here, but Chelsea said she'd invited John Bohnner, a young director who said publicly he wanted Declan to star in his next movie about a cop gone bad, though he hadn't bothered calling his agent. The gate to Chelsea's was open, so he drove his Mercedes sports coupe right in, parking behind a red Escort with an Enterprise rental sticker on it.

"Declan."

He looked up and smiled. "Chelsea, what do you do, hover at the window?"

"Only for you," she said, giving him a dazzling smile. She was braless and practically topless, wearing a blouse that didn't sport any buttons until it reached her navel and a skirt so short and tight it left very little to the imagination.

"That's some outfit," he said.

"You like?" She beamed. Then she leaned forward, just in case he missed the fact she was practically naked, and said, "I'm not wearing anything underneath, you know."

"Neither am I," he lied, then began walking toward the door, ignoring her pout.

He didn't bother waiting for his host and went on inside. And stopped dead. Because in that instant, he was transported back to Kingstown, back to his house. Back to Rose. "What's on the menu tonight," he asked Chelsea as she came up behind him.

She placed one finely manicured hand on his shoulder and slowly moved in front of him, trying her best for her trademark feline-seductive look. "Only your favorite dish. I saw you on *Entertainment Tonight*. Linguini pesto."

"Linguini pescatore," he said, automatically correcting her. "Very thoughtful, Chels." He was mad as hell. The last thing he needed tonight was a reminder of the only time in his life when he'd been truly happy.

She put on an uncertain smile at his abrupt tone. "I

thought so. Come on. I'll introduce you to John Bohnner. Would you like something to drink?"

He shook his head, too distracted by the intoxicating smells in this normally antiseptically clean house to talk. When John Bohnner started talking about his next project, Declan told him to call his agent.

"I never talk business," he said to Bohnner, who had to be all of twenty-three. Still, even he'd heard good things about him, that he was the next Scorcese. "But for the record, I'd like to hear more after you do talk to Carl." And then he grinned, and if he'd insulted the man a minute ago, all was forgotten. The rest was just small talk with the handful of guests, most of whom he knew in at least a perfunctory way. Every once in a while a member of the wait staff would walk by with a tray filled with hors d'oeuvres, bits of herbed chicken, focaccia bread topped with cheese and prosciutto, and tiny slices of pizza. Chelsea had gone all out, it seemed, to make this meal special for him. In an effort to lead the media away from speculating about a relationship between him and Rose, he'd gushed about the Italian cooking. And so now he was being tortured by reminder after reminder of her. Everywhere he went someone was forcing Italian food at him.

Chelsea, the ever-present white wine in hand, announced dinner, then walked over and tucked her hand in Declan's elbow. "You've been ignoring me," she teased, then pushed one of her large breasts against his arm. She directed him to a chair, then sat at the head of the table, taking rather obvious care to expose her entire bosom to his view.

"Watch it, Chelsea," said Roger Herbert, who was very loud and very gay. "Not all of us appreciate a room with a view." Everyone laughed, Chelsea the loudest. She absolutely adored being the center of attention. Declan cracked a smile and wished he were home reading. Alone.

The wait staff entered with a flourish, bringing in first small bowls of steaming soup.

"How homey," Roger said, looking down at his bowl. "And scrumptious," after taking a taste.

Declan took a spoonful and frowned.

"Don't you like it?" Chelsea asked.

It flashed in his brain, hot and white: Rose, naked and beautiful, stretched out on that cold, cold island in his kitchen, her nipples tight from excitement and the chill, her legs spread wide, her mouth open slightly.

"What?"

"I said, don't you like the soup?"

He blinked to clear his head. "Yeah. It's fine."

Next came an antipasto, most of which went uneaten by the skinny, non-meat-eating people at the table. He ate every bite and stole a piece of salami from Chelsea's plate. Then two baskets of still-steaming crusty Italian bread were placed on the table, just before the wait staff walked in carrying huge plates filled with linguini pescatore.

"I know shellfish isn't everyone's cup of tea, but this party is for Declan, after all," Chelsea said, looking down at her food with a slight frown of distaste.

In front of Declan was a plate of linguini tossed with mussels and clams still in their shells, shrimp, and squid, all swimming in a light white wine sauce that he'd dreamed about since leaving his haven by the beach. It smelled exactly the same as Rose's. It looked exactly the same. He knew it was almost impossible to duplicate because he'd tried. He'd been to some of the best Italian restaurants on the West Coast and never gotten a dish quite like the one Rose made.

Slowly, he pushed his fork into a tender clam, pulling it from the shell, then twirled it around to capture some linguini. And then he carefully put it in his mouth. And chewed. And closed his eyes.

Beside him Chelsea let out a pleased little gasp. "You like it?"

He opened his eyes, and smiled, truly smiled at his former lover. "This is fantastic," he said.

"It's heaven," Roger said. "I haven't had this since I left New York. Who is your chef, Chelsea. I have to have him for my next dinner party."

"Only the best for Declan," Chelsea said, her eyes sparkling with her victory as she looked at each of her guests, save Declan. "Shall I bring the chef out?"

And Declan knew in that moment who would walk through the double doors leading to the kitchen. All he could do was sit there and wait for her to appear and try like hell not to do anything crazy like drag her to him for a kiss. He put his fork down with care, aware his hand was shaking slightly.

"Here she is," Chelsea announced.

Rose walked into the room, a huge smile on her face after being complimented by her employer. She was a huge hit, Chelsea had said, and everyone wanted to meet her. Sure, she could do that. Take a little bow, then discreetly put some business cards on the side table near the wine. She could almost smell the new paint and carpeting in her restaurant, almost hear the intoxicating sounds of a full dining room.

As she entered, the people at the dinner table gave her a polite round of applause. She couldn't help it; she smiled so much her face hurt. She gave a little bow and looked up.

Right into Declan's baby blues. She stopped halfway between the bow and standing straight. She wanted to scream at Chelsea for lying to her, for telling her Declan was not on the damned guest list, for making her already-broken heart shatter to bits.

Finally she straightened, her smile tight. "Hello, Mr. McDonald."

"Rose."

That one word, that low-timbered tone, affected her as it always had, and she hated him all the more.

"What do you think about my surprise?" Chelsea asked, still beaming and looking from her chef to her guest. "Isn't it wonderful that I got Declan to come?" Rose could swear devil's horns sprang from her head and her eyes began to glow. "I mean to the dinner party, of course." She paused, making sure Rose and the other guests got the double meaning. Then she gave Rose the once-over and apparently dismissed rumors that she and Declan had ever been lovers. "I hope you're not too angry?"

Her horns grow pointier, her eyes more evil, but Rose throws a pot of chicken stock on her, and the beast dissolves. "Not at all."

"This is *the* Rose Pisano?" Roger asked. "Why, Chelsea, what a fantastic idea."

Rose smiled at the man who called her a *the*. She'd never been anything but Tony's cook, even now after she'd established some minor celebrity since Declan came out of hiding.

"How would you like to be on the *L.A. Today* show with Declan? I can arrange it."

Chelsea chimed in, "This is Martha Toulet. She's one of the producers over there. Wouldn't that be marvelous. You could cook something for Declan."

Rose dragged her eyes away from Declan to look at Martha Toulet, a pretty redhead with the palest skin she'd ever seen. "I suppose that would be okay."

"No. It wouldn't."

Rose turned back to Declan, startled by the hard look in his eyes, at the anger directed at her. "I think I can make my own decisions, Mr. McDonald."

"Good heavens, Rose, did Declan actually make you call him mister?" asked Martha.

"I really do have to get back in the kitchen," she said,

ignoring Martha's question. "I'll leave my cards here." She placed a small stack of cards on the side table.

"Rose, where are you staying while you're in California?" Chelsea called.

With supreme effort, she looked directly at Chelsea, even though she could see Declan peripherally. "At the Best Western on West Seventh." She could tell Declan was staring at his plate, so she chanced a quick look and saw his jaw clench slightly. Then she turned and entered the kitchen, her haven. At the far end, the wait staff stood just outside the door having a smoke. They wouldn't be needed until dessert was served in about an hour.

Her legs trembling, Rose leaned against the wall and squeezed her eyes shut. She felt as if an elephant was pushing against her chest—the residual pain of that battered heart of hers. Why, why did he have to be here? Why did her heart still hurt so much? Why did he look so lost and angry?

Without thinking, she started cleaning up. It was something she did when she was upset, and man-oh-man, she was upset. Rose swallowed down a lump that was forming in her throat. *I will not cry, I will not cry.* But God, how she wanted to. She shook her head, flexing her neck much like a prize fighter did right before a bout. *Toughen up, girl. Don't you dare let anyone see what a complete wimp you are.*

"What are you doing here?"

Rose spun around to find Declan staring at her without a hint of pleasantness on his gorgeous face.

"Cooking. I'm a chef, remember?" And she went about cleaning up the already-gleaming stainless steel workstation, bending over and scrubbing with particular vigor at an imaginary fingerprint.

"I don't want you to be part of my life."

Whoa. That hurt. Okay, keep cleaning. Get mad. Or smile. Or anything but don't you dare cry.

"I didn't know you were going to be here. If I had known, I wouldn't have accepted the job. You're not first on the list of people I want to see." She paused in her wiping to look at him, feeling safe now that she'd spoken and her voice hadn't cracked and she hadn't dissolved into tears. "And for the record, if I want to work in this town, I can. I'm opening a restaurant, if you've forgotten, and having the support of some of the people out here could really help."

His nostrils flared. "How much do you need?"

That one floored her. She stumbled back as if pushed by his words; the rag lay limp in her hand. "You'd *pay* me to leave town?"

Something flickered in his eyes, but was gone almost as quickly. "How much?"

"You're being a real ass, you know that?"

He looked away with a jerk of his head and pressed his lips together. "I know."

"You look like hell."

"Thank you. I know that, too."

"You forget how to shave?"

She could tell he was fighting a smile, and for the life of her she didn't know why she was trying to make a man she hated smile; but she was glad to see it there, tugging at those lips that had haunted her dreams for weeks.

Just then, Chelsea walked in and draped an arm around Declan's waist. Staking a claim.

"I hope you'll forgive me, you two. But I wanted this to be a surprise for Declan."

Rose tried not to care about that finely manicured hand resting so possessively around Declan's waist, but she couldn't help but wonder if they were not just *former* lovers anymore.

"It certainly was a surprise," Rose said lightly, as if she didn't want to rip Chelsea's claws off of Declan.

Jealousy, hot and painful, almost made her dizzy, and she found she couldn't be perky little Rose after all. "I'll have dessert for everyone in about an hour. If you'll excuse me . . ."

"Of course." Chelsea turned, languid and graceful, so that she was pressing the entire length of her body against Declan. "Why don't we go have an after-dinner drink in the library. Everyone else is in the media room."

Rose swallowed hard, feeling suddenly sick. Her back was to them, but she clearly heard a kiss, a moist sucking sound. *Okay, go away now.*

"You go take care of your guests. I just want to catch up a little with Rose—and explain to her why going on *L.A. Today* is a bad idea. It might get ugly, and I don't want any witnesses," he said, laughter in his voice.

"All right. I'll see you in a few minutes."

Rose turned her head slightly and waited until the swinging doors were still before facing him. They stood staring at each other, Rose's face impassive, his hard and angry.

"I'm not sleeping with her."

"I don't care one way or the other. And why should you care whether I care or not?"

"I don't."

"Then why did you bring it up? You obviously are worried that I think you're bopping Barbie."

He laughed and shook his head. "You haven't changed," he said, grinning at her.

But Rose wasn't smiling. She couldn't, because she hurt too damned much. "I have changed. I'm old and bitter." And then she did laugh, because she found herself funny.

"How have you been?" he asked, suddenly serious.

"Don't. I don't want you being nice. I don't want laughing at my smart mouth. I don't want to see you, Declan."

He looked down at the floor, that familiar and endearing gesture, and something sharp tugged at her heart.

"I thought . . . I hoped, that is, that we could be friends."

She willed the tears that burned in her eyes to disappear. "I can't be friends with someone I've seen naked," she said, letting out a humorless laugh. "And that includes Chelsea."

"Smart mouth."

She shrugged. "I really do have work to do."

He rubbed a hand through his too-long hair. He truly did look like hell, and Rose tried not to let that bother her. "How long are you going to be in town?"

"I thought a week unless I get some more jobs. Are you okay?" Rose grimaced, hating that she'd gone soft on him already, and when he looked down at the damned floor, she wanted to hug him, to run her hand through his hair and tell him everything was going to be all right. When he finally looked up at her, another piece of her anger died. He opened his mouth as if he was going to say something. Then he pressed his lips together and shook his head, a nearly imperceptible motion.

"I'm fine," he said, finally. But his hands had turned to fists, and he looked like a man who was anything but fine.

"Listen. I know you don't want anything to do with me, and I don't want you to take this the wrong way, but if you ever need to escape for just a little while, you know where I live. I promise I'll let you be. I won't attack you or anything. I don't even have to be there."

He looked at her, and for just a second she thought she saw the old Declan, the one who kissed her forehead after making love, the one she could have sworn loved her as much as she loved him. "I appreciate the offer, but I think it would be a bad idea."

And then he twists the knife he so expertly placed in my back two months ago.

She nodded as if there was a spring in her neck. "Sure. No problem. Just trying to help."

"Rose."

"I've got to get back to work," she said, sounding and feeling bitchy.

And then he was there, standing in front of her, looking mad. Not angry mad, crazy mad. "Do you think this is easy, that I can just walk away and feel nothing? Do you think this is even close to the way I want it? Do you?"

Rose blinked rapidly during his verbal onslaught. "I guess I think I do."

He looked down at her, breathing heavily through his mouth, his arms straight by his sides but straining as if his hands were chained there. "Christ, I'm going to regret this."

"What?"

And he pulled her to him roughly, a football player maneuver that almost knocked the wind from her lungs. She didn't have time to let out a squeak of protest or even drag a breath into her lungs before he was kissing her. He was making the strangest sounds, as if someone were torturing him as he kissed her. Rose didn't resist. She let it happen, and then she helped it happen. She flung her arms around his neck, she pressed her body against his, she moved against his erection, she thrust her tongue into his mouth. His hands moved from her back to her hair to her buttocks and stayed there, pulling her close, moving her against him.

"The pantry," she gasped, fumbling for the door that was just out of reach. He opened it, dragging her with him, slamming it shut, never letting his mouth leave hers. His hands moved to her breasts, slowed, stayed. Delicious.

"Unsnap it," she said, and he did, revealing her lacy bra.

He let out a strangled sound before pushing her bra aside and kissing her nipple. When he took her in his mouth Rose dropped her head back and sighed. Finally, finally.

"Declan? Rose?"

"Déjà vu all over again," Rose whispered, looking down to see Declan still mouthing her nipple.

"She'll go away," he said, exposing her other breast.

"Declan."

"Don't tell me to stop."

"Stop."

"I told you not to tell me that."

Rose forcefully pulled him from her chest and immediately fixed her clothes. She heard the double door swing closed, then peeked out of the pantry. Declan stood behind her looking disgruntled and frustrated.

"I can't believe I did that," Rose said.

"I'm sorry."

"You are not sorry. You're smiling."

He shrugged. "C'mon, Rose. You've got to admit this is funny."

She gave him a look of disgust before entering the kitchen, only to see the four-member wait staff staring at her, all wearing knowing grins. Rose gave them a good-natured shrug and a sheepish grin, but Declan swore.

"Do any of you speak English?" he demanded. Two nodded. Declan reached into his back pocket for his wallet. "Here's three hundred each for you to forget what you just saw. *Comprendez?*"

"Declan, that is so horrible."

"It's necessary, believe me," he said, counting out the cash. When he was done, he turned to her and pulled her aside. "I never should have let that happen."

"It's okay."

"No. It's not. We've got a fifty-fifty chance of not seeing a story about this in the tabloids. It was stupid of me," he said viciously. "Do you understand now? Do you get it now?"

"You don't have to be mad at me, Declan."

"I do, because you don't understand. You can't be part of my life."

"Hey," she said, finally getting mad herself. "I'm not the one who started this. Next time you get horny, go play with Chelsea or one of your other girlfriends and leave me alone."

"You got it." He stormed out the doors.

"Jerk," she said, and threw a dirty rag at the still-swinging doors. She fumed for a good ten minutes and managed to clean the entire kitchen while the wait staff went out to have another smoke and celebrate their good fortune. He'd just shelled out twelve hundred big ones to keep their affair out of the tabloids. She knew he was trying to protect her, but she also figured his bigger motivation was his own privacy.

Just because she understood his motivation for pushing her away didn't mean she forgave him for making a fool of her. He'd proven that all he had to do was kiss her silly and she was ready to hop back into bed with him. The worst thing was knowing she might just do the same thing again.

Feeling glum, she went about drizzling dark raspberry-chocolate syrup over her tiny little cheesecakes. Not an Italian delicacy, but a sure crowd pleaser. She decided to bring the dessert tray out herself so she could try to talk to Declan, to tell him they could never be friends; they could never be anything. But when she brought it out, Chelsea looked majorly upset, and Declan was gone.

Chapter 19

Fresh strawberry cream shortcake with whipped cream and chocolate sauce, $9.00

The "green" room for the *L.A. Today* show was about as comfortable as a nice doctor's office, a doctors office with a table laden with Danish and fruit. One wall was decorated with a collage of guests that the show had spotlighted over the years, including an old shot of Declan. Rose wondered if she'd ever get used to seeing his face pop up unexpectedly and if she'd ever be able to see him without her heart hurting.

Martha Toulet had already stopped in to make certain Rose had everything she needed. Rose had arrived an hour ago to set up the kitchen for the five-minute cooking demonstration and now had another twenty-minute wait in the green room before she went on.

"Have fun with Burt," Martha had said. "He likes to joke around, so go with it. You don't strike me as being overly serious, so I'm sure you'll do just fine. Is there anything else you need? Do you have any questions?"

Rose was as nervous as a cat in the dog pound, but she didn't say so. It had hit her as she drove through the security gates outside the studio that this was the big time. *L.A. Today* wasn't quite national, but it had a huge audience. What the heck was she thinking? She was Rosalie Pisano, Tony's cook, who hadn't even been to culinary school. She wasn't a chef, she was a cook, and she was going on big-time television as a fraud. All this was going through her head, but she just smiled at Martha.

"I think I'm all set. I do have one question. You mentioned that Declan McDonald is also scheduled for today. We're not going to be on at the same time, are we?"

Martha manufactured a worried look. "I'm sure I told you. He goes on in front of you, you come on, talk to Burt, then go cook, and Declan and Burt eat. That is if your friend Declan ever gets here."

Rose got a heap more nervous. "You didn't tell me."

"Is that a problem?" Martha asked, clearly expecting Rose to say no.

"Yes, it is. But I suppose it's too late now to change."

Martha pursed her lips. "I'm certain I told you."

She left Rose alone wondering whether she should just leave. She didn't want to see Declan, not after Chelsea's disastrous dinner and his inexcusable behavior. Okay, she'd acted inexcusable, too. She was the one who dragged him into the pantry, and she'd been the one who suggested he unsnap her top. But she was in love, and he was . . . taking advantage of a lovesick, pathetic groupie. Maybe it wouldn't be so bad if they were in front of a camera, being broadcast live to four million people. She could pretend he hadn't shredded her heart with his cold, callous, thoughtless good-bye. She could pretend that she didn't get all soft and melty inside when she heard his voice. She could pretend anything for the five minutes she was supposed to be on.

The door opened so suddenly Rose let out a frightened squeak. Declan stood there, his hair carefully messy, his hard jaw sprinkled with that ever-present two-days' growth, wearing jeans, a charcoal jacket, and black crew-neck underneath. As much as Rose told herself not to react to his masculine beauty, her heart sped up, and her stomach twisted.

"This is just unbelievable," Declan said, staring at her with incredulity.

"I'm not happy about this either," Rose shot back. "By the way, do you ever shave? Or comb your hair?"

He jabbed a finger at her, ignoring her remark. "Martha told me you'd agreed to do the show, but I didn't believe it. Do you know what you're doing? Oh, I know you *think* you know. Grabbing a little fame, promoting your restaurant. It's fun, isn't it? People come up to you and tell you how wonderful you are. You get your first bit of fan mail; you get a little thrill. And then someone writes something nasty to you and it's not fun anymore, so you hire someone to open your mail. An agent calls and convinces you it would be much better to have someone else handle the business side of things, and then you're so busy, you hire a publicist to book all your appearances, and before you know it you don't have a life anymore." Declan started his tirade calm enough, but by the time he was finished he was nearly shouting.

"Clearly, we are talking about you. Again. You are so boring, Declan."

Declan rubbed his hands harshly over his face. "I'm just trying to save you some grief, Rose. By the way, that skirt is a bit high, isn't it?"

Rose looked down at her black skirt that was about an inch above her knee, then shook her head, refusing to be deflected by Declan's erroneous observation. "No, it's not too short, and, no, you are not trying to save me grief. You're giving me your life story. Hey, I'm sorry you're so unhappy. I'm sorry your life turned out so crappy. But a thousand people out there would trade places with you in a second. Stop feeling so sorry for yourself."

"You think this is about me?"

"Of course it is," she said.

"It's never been about me," he shouted, making her blink and feel just the tiniest twinge of fear. He pressed his lips together so hard, they lost all color. "I won't let you do this. I—"

Someone knocked on the door. "Mr. McDonald, five minutes."

"Okay," he said, sounding almost normal.

He turned back to her, looking tortured and confusing Rose all the more. "Rose. Please."

"Declan," she said, keeping her voice even. "I know what I'm doing. I'm not trying to get famous. I'm trying to drum up business for my pathetic little restaurant in Providence. That's all. No one's even tried to take my picture going pee."

"This isn't a joke."

"Yes. It is. It's all a joke, Dec. Your problem is that you take everything so seriously. Who cares if someone takes your picture. Who cares if they write that you're gay or you sleep with animals?"

He stared at her so long and with so much anger Rose wanted to shrivel up. And then, letting out a big breath of air, he changed instantly. "Maybe you're right."

Rose narrowed her eyes suspiciously. "About what?"

"About everything, particularly about me taking the paparazzi too seriously. I apologize." He even gave her an old-fashioned bow, a slight downward tilt of his head. He looked and sounded sincere, but Rose sensed something wasn't quite right with that admission. It came too easily.

"Let me take you out to dinner tonight. To apologize."

"Really?" Her eyebrows snapped together as she searched his face for an ulterior motive.

"Really. Anywhere you want to go."

"On one condition. No, um, you know. No kissing.

Nothing physical." She pointed a finger at him as if he were the only one to blame for their attraction. "I mean it, Declan."

He grinned. "Two old pals going out to eat. Sure."

The assistant knocked on the door again, and this time it opened. "You're on next, Mr. McDonald."

"Right there," he said, then walked over to Rose and kissed her until her legs got all rubbery. It wasn't even a long kiss, and Rose was about to drag him to that soft leather couch. "I figured I better get that in before dinner." And then he left.

"Creep," she muttered, even as she tried to suppress a smile.

Burt Barden was a real pro. He'd been the host of *L.A. Today* for eight years and had a knack for putting people at ease. During the short segment while he interviewed Rose, she felt herself relax, even though Declan sat six inches away from her. Burt asked her about growing up in an Italian family, her relationship with her grandmother, the plans for her restaurant. He stuck to the pre-interview questions and didn't throw out any surprises, including stooping to the tabloid are-you-sleeping-with-Declan question. Declan, on the other hand, did nothing but try to rattle her. He'd propped a foot on his knee, and he jangled it there in beat with her responses during the entire interview.

"I learned nearly everything I know from my Nonna." Foot foot foot-foot foot-foot-foot foot. . . . It required all her willpower not to smack that foot off his knee. During the commercial break, she turned to him and said pleasantly, "Real cute, McDonald."

He didn't bother trying to deny what he'd been doing anything, giving her a smile that spoke volumes. He leaned over and whispered, "You're the one who wanted to do this show, sweetheart."

He wanted to get tough? Well, she could play his game.

They moved to the small kitchen set with Burt standing to the side and in front of the kitchen island and Rose and Declan behind it. The red camera light went on, some guy counted down with his fingers, and Burt flashed a smile. "Hi, we're back with Declan McDonald and Chef Rosalie Pisano." He turned to Rose. "Okay. I understand we're making ravioli stuffed with mushrooms and artichoke hearts."

Declan watched as Rose granted Burt a smile he'd seen only after some incredible sex, and his gut clenched hard. She was too damned beautiful to be on television. He could see it happening; he'd heard the buzz about the sexiest chef on television already, and she'd been in town only a few days. He glanced at the monitor and felt sick—somehow Rose looked even better on that small television. The lighting, the makeup, and excitement of being in the spotlight were all combining to create an intoxicating mix of innocence and sex appeal that both men and women liked. He watched her, he listened to her talk, as relaxed and put-together as someone who'd been in front of the camera for twenty years, and felt his heart expand with pride—and fear. He'd always known Rose was witty and charming, but he never guessed that this self-assured, business-savvy woman lay beneath her smart-mouthed, joke-a-minute exterior.

"Declan," she said, bringing him away from his miserable thoughts. "Why don't you roll out the dough for the ravioli."

Declan stared at her until he felt her cool hand grab his and slap a rolling pin in his palm.

"Here, I'll help."

She nestled up beside him and placed a hand on each of his, then pushed the rolling pin smoothly over the creamy dough. Back and forth, back and forth, brushing her body against his, breathing softly near his ear. Lust hit him like a blast of heat on a hot summer's day, nearly bowling him over. He almost lost his grip on the damned rolling thingy.

"There you go," she said lightly, blessedly letting go of his hands. She moved slightly behind him, and he breathed easy. Then jerked when he felt her hand alight softly on his backside.

"That's perfect. A little faster. That's right."

Declan was so hard now he wanted to wrap his hands around Rose's throat. Or throw her down and make love. Or kill her. Or kiss her until she felt the way he did at this instant.

"That's great. I think I'll hire you as my assistant," Rose said lightly and with a wink to Burt. "See how I can pick up the dough? It's soft but firm and pliable."

"Very firm," Declan said, making Rose laugh.

"We don't want it too firm."

"Why not?"

"Because it just might break apart. And we wouldn't want that," Rose said, perky and seemingly oblivious to what she'd done to him. He knew better.

"What's next?" Burt asked, giving the two of them a searching look.

"Now we fill them. I think Declan and you can handle that on your own."

Rose left Declan alone for the rest of the segment, but as soon as the camera was off and Declan had shaken Burt's hand, he grabbed her floury hand and pulled her down the hall and into an empty green room. "That was a dirty trick," Declan said, trying to look menacing.

Rose grinned at him, completely unapologetic. "I figured I'd get that in before dinner tonight. Because after that, we're just friends, remember?"

"You're the one who wanted that rule, Rose."

"And you're the one," she said, jabbing a finger at him, "who came up with the no-call rule. You broke that one."

"I was worried about you."

Rose let out a snort and crossed her arms under her breasts. Her sweet breasts. Declan's dick seemed to have a mind of its own, and he shoved his hands in his pockets in an attempt to hide his physical reaction to her. He blamed his high state of arousal on the fact that he hadn't had sex since the last time he'd been with Rose. Not because he hadn't had the opportunity. God knew the women of the world instantly forgave him for any transgressions he'd committed. The one woman he wanted to make love to was standing in front of him, mad as heck, when he was the one who should be angry. He'd been mauled in front of a live audience.

"There's only one thing to do," Declan said, feeling inspired.

"And what's that?"

"We need to make love one more time. Before dinner." He didn't really mean it. Well, he hoped she might jump up and down and declare that a fine idea, but deep down he knew she wouldn't.

"Do you see how casual you are about sex? You're depraved."

Declan shrugged, admitting his depravity. "I'm not the one who was rubbing herself all over me in front of millions of people. You," he said, chucking a finger under her chin, "shouldn't be such a hypocrite."

"I wanted to get back at you for kissing me that way in the green room. In a few days, I'm going back to Providence and you're staying here. And you won't call me and I sure as heck won't call you. I'm not your girlfriend, Declan. I'm not your lover anymore, either. And I'm not some girl you screw just because she's in town."

"I know that. I'm . . ." And it came out, wrenched from his throat. "I'm sorry. I was only joking. Half joking."

"You ought to be sorry. Boy, a few weeks out here and you lose all sense of morality. Personally, I'd rather not be the latest notch on your piano."

Anger hit him, swift and searing. "For your information, I haven't been with anyone since you." Then he swore, angry with himself for letting that little bit of information slip. It was none of her business.

"Oh."

"You know, I think dinner is a bad idea after all."

"Oh, don't be a baby. I'm sorry." And then in a soft voice, "You really haven't been with anyone?"

"I'm getting too old for bed hopping," he said moodily. She didn't understand him, and it was his own fault. He'd never given even a hint of his feelings for her. He tried, he really did try, to understand her point of view. All he knew was that he loved her and he wanted to make love to her. But then it would start all over again, the loneliness, the longing, the wishing his life were different. Rose was right. She was going back to Providence, to open her restaurant, and he was staying here.

But first, he had to teach her a little lesson.

Chapter 20

Crab chowder with avocada puree, $10.00

Rose suspected something wasn't quite right when a police officer signaled for her to stop her car. She rolled down the windows to explain she needed to get to Casa Pedro, which she could see about fifty yards up the street. Hoards of people lined the street, and she could see a few camera crews hanging around in front of the restaurant amidst a crowd of photographers and onlookers.

"I'm meeting someone," she told the officer. "What's going on, anyway? Who are all those people?"

"Are you Rosalie Pisano?"

Rose was so startled to hear her name come out of the officer's mouth she just stared at him for a few seconds before slowly answering, "Yes."

He asked her for some I.D., which Rose produced. Then he waved her through.

"Officer, what's going on?"

"You really don't know?"

She shook her head.

"Your boyfriend, that's what's going on. Someone

leaked that he was eating dinner here tonight with his personal chef. That's you, right."

Rose narrowed her eyes. "That rat."

"Yeah. So we have to baby-sit this crowd while you eat your dinner."

Rose shook her head. She simply could not believe the lengths to which he was going to get rid of her. She ought to teach him a lesson. She ought to do something completely outrageous like announce she was carrying Declan's love child. As she pulled carefully up to the restaurant, a hundred eyes tried to peer into her rented Escort to see if they recognized her. The poor valet pushed his way through the crowd and opened her door. Rose schooled her features, trying not to show how very angry she was at Declan's little joke.

"Sorry about all this," she said.

"Ningun problema." No problem for him, maybe.

"Hello, everyone," Rose said, smiling widely at the photographers and trying not to blink at all the flashing cameras. "Here to watch me and my former boss eat dinner? How exciting."

Cameras whirred; flashes lit up the early evening air.

"Is Mr. McDonald here yet?"

Someone shouted that he was. Then: "Why didn't you come together?"

Good question. It had been Declan's idea to come separately, and at the time, Rose had thought it was his way of cementing the ruse that they were "just friends."

"This is a business meeting. As you all know, I'm planning to open a restaurant, Rosalie's, in Providence sometime before Christmas. I'm going to ask Declan if he'd like to invest in my restaurant. By the way, if you all could leave your business cards with the maître d', I can make certain you're invited to the grand opening."

She gave a little wave and started going into the entrance of the restaurant and had almost made it in when she heard, "Are you and Declan dating?"

She turned, a self-deprecating smile on her face. "You're kidding, right. Me? And Declan McDonald? We are not dating. We have never dated. And we will never date. But, thanks for thinking it was possible."

"I'll date you," someone yelled.

She smiled again, and listened to the chuckles as her heart twisted painfully. She'd told the complete truth. She and Declan had never dated. They'd just slept together.

"Is there anything else? Did you get everything you need?" The reporters seemed a bit taken aback to be talked to so cordially.

"How 'bout a shot of you and Declan together?"

Rose put on a puzzled face. "Why? I'll tell you what. Declan will be invited to my grand opening, and I can guarantee you pictures of us together. Especially if he decides to invest in Rosalie's. Deal?"

She heard a bit of grumbling, then someone say, "Let's get out of here. I hear Bruce Willis is over at The Club."

Rose watched the crowd disperse, a feeling of triumph growing inside her. Declan had meant to teach her a lesson: See how horrible it is to be famous? Boo hoo. She waved to the last of the photographers, then went into the restaurant, seething with anger and trying not to show it.

"Oh, Miss Pisano," said a man, rushing to her side. "I'm so honored that you've chosen my restaurant to dine in. My name is Gregory Pinto."

"Not Pedro?"

"Who would eat at Casa Gregory's?" he asked with a laugh. "I would like it if you could autograph this." He brought out the cover of the *Good Eats* magazine and a black permanent marker.

"Sure." Rose signed it simply, "Best Wishes, Rosalie Pisano."

"Thank you. I'll hang it up, and next time you come in, you can see it," he said, indicating a wall behind her.

Rose looked and saw an entire stucco wall covered with signed pictures of celebrities. Rosalie Pisano was going on a Hollywood wall of fame. What a world.

"I'm honored, Gregory. And I'm also terribly sorry, but I can't stay to eat. An emergency has come up, and I just have enough time to tell Mr. McDonald I won't be able to join him. Next time I'm on the West Coast, I'll be sure to come in. I've heard you have the best Mexican food in California."

Gregory looked slightly distressed at her news, then beamed at her compliment. "You will always be welcome, Miss Pisano."

"Gracias. If you could show me where Mr. McDonald is, I can tell him my bad news."

"Certainly. This way."

Rose followed him into a lush, tropical garden. Tucked behind ferns and palm trees and other exotic flowering plants, diners sat in near privacy beneath a towering atrium. The air was humid and laced with the intoxicating combination of spices, herbs, flowers, and a musty fecund scent that was exhilarating. Rose was amazed at the dramatic change from the street to the interior of this renowned restaurant. The tables were brightly tiled, the tableware multicolored and robust. A parrot flew over Rose's head letting out a squawk. If there was such a thing as tacky elegance, this was it. Diners seemed relaxed, the way people got when they were on vacation.

"You've done a fantastic job, Gregory," Rose said.

"Gracias."

Rose was disappointed to not taste Casa Pedro's renowned Mexican food. She'd really been looking forward to it; Rhode Island's Mexican fare was mostly limited to Taco Bell. She was slightly more disappointed when she saw how Declan looked. He'd shaved, combed his hair like a real person, and wore a navy blazer over a white shirt with a red, white, and blue tie. He looked as if he was running for office or had stepped out of a

Ralph Lauren ad. He took her breath away, and Rose had to remind herself that she had never been more angry with another person in her entire life.

Gregory bowed, and moved discreetly away as Declan flashed her his most irritatingly brilliant smile. "Get through the crowd okay?"

"I just came in to tell you to go to hell. Good-bye, Declan. And really, don't bother calling me." Then Rose, who would have laughed at Declan's shocked face if she hadn't felt so close to tears, walked calmly away. She was pretty sure he wouldn't follow her, because if there was one thing Declan avoided at all costs, it was a public scene.

She was nearly to the wall of fame when she felt his iron grip on her upper arm. "Where are you going?"

The foyer of the restaurant was crowded with people waiting to be seated, but he seemed oblivious to their stares. "I didn't like your little setup. Let me go, I'm leaving."

His eyes flickered downward, and she thought he might be feeling a bit of guilt. He pulled her slightly aside, gently but firmly. "Are you okay? I'm sorry I had to do that, but you wouldn't listen. I told Richard to let out a rumor, but he went overboard. As usual. I'm glad he did, though. You think this is a big joke. I had to show you what you're in for." He looked past her toward the door as if he expected to see a crowd of photographers there clicking away.

"You need to get a real life, Declan." Rose pulled her arm away and walked out the door. This time, he didn't follow.

"Maid service."

Rose rolled her eyes at the sound of Declan's familiar voice coming through her hotel door. "No thank you," she called, slamming a crumpled pair of nylons into her suitcase. Silence followed, and Rose fought a feeling of disappointment that he'd left. Then: "Room service."

She fought a traitorous grin as she opened the door and, without looking at him, immediately turned and went back to the king-sized bed and continued packing, refusing to entertain the thought of how much fun she and Declan could have had on that bed if things were different. "Just put it on the desk, please."

"I'm sorry."

"That's nice, Declan. You can go now."

He heaved a much-beleaguered sigh, and Rose clenched her teeth together to stop her Italian temper from flaring out of control again.

"I don't want you to leave angry. Okay?"

"I'm not angry." She looked up and flashed him a smile. "I'm just sick of this woe-is-me crap."

He pressed his lips together, clearly irritated with her stubbornness. "I didn't come here for this."

Rose stopped shoving her clothes into her suitcase and pressed her fists into the mattress. "Why did you come, then?"

"Not for this."

Rose gave him a look. "You want me to run into your arms? You want me to tell you I learned my lesson and tell you we'll be friends forever?"

He looked slightly put out by her hostility, as if he hadn't a clue where it was coming from. "Something like that."

"You want to fuck?"

His face got all tight, and he stared at her as if he didn't know her at all. Maybe he didn't. He didn't know this woman, the one who hurt, the one who was so damned confused by her feelings for a man who clearly felt *concerned* for her, but didn't love her. He lusted after her. Then he grinned. "Sure."

Despite her real anger, Rose let out a laugh. "No, Dec. I think this time I'll just say good-bye."

"I'm getting sick of saying good-bye to you." Rose's heart stopped beating, and she couldn't help it, she thought: *Oh my God, he's going to ask me to stay. And I will.*

And then, that knife he'd buried in her heart, so long ago the pain of it had dulled to a steady throb, was thrust even deeper. "But I just don't see any other way. I wish you'd never come to L.A."

Later, Rose might look back at this moment and see some glimmer of regret and sadness, but at that moment, she saw only the man who had once again ripped her heart out. Then stepped on it. With cleats.

She'd been a heartbeat away from throwing herself into his arms and telling him she'd stay with him forever, she'd leave everything behind just to be with him. It was a demeaning thought, but there it was. Man oh man did she hate unrequited love. It wasn't romantic, it sucked, and it hurt like hell and reduced her to the kind of woman she'd always felt sorry for, a woman who'd do anything for the man she loved. Well, screw that. If she ever had such a thought again, she'd have to poke herself with a pin.

"I wish I'd never come here, either. But it was real nice seeing you, Dec. Bye." Bitter sarcasm ejected from a tightly false smile.

Again, that stupidly confused look on his gorgeous face. "I didn't mean it like that. I was glad to see you, Rose. Hell, I *needed* to see you."

Rose held her hand up to stop his mouth. "Okay. You can go now. Because, frankly, it doesn't matter how you meant it; the gist is the same. Jesus, Declan, go. Go!"

Rose turned and slammed her suitcase shut, not wanting him to see the tears streaming down her face.

"Rose."

"I said, go," she whispered, begged really. And this time, finally, he listened.

"I screwed up, Richard."

Richard, wearing a headset, waved a finger in the air. "Okay. Got it. Talk to you tomorrow." He disconnected, tore off his headset, and smiled widely at Declan. "You've got one hell of a girlfriend there."

"She's not my girlfriend and what are you talking about."

"You didn't see it, did you."

Declan closed his eyes and let out a groan. "See what?" He didn't want to know; he really didn't want to hear what Rose had done now.

"You're in luck. I taped it." He put on the television, pressed play on the VCR, and sat back, his eyes not on the TV, but on Declan's face as he watched Rose play the press like a pro.

At first, Declan couldn't hear past the roaring in his ears as he watched Rose beset by the paparazzi. What the hell had he been thinking of? She was completely unprepared for that kind of onslaught, those cameras, those piranha shouting out questions. She looked so little against that mob. He could have done something else to teach her a lesson. He could have shown her tapes or something. Anything but submit her to the pack. No wonder she'd been so angry.

Then he heard her voice, calm and normal. "I'm going to ask Declan if he'd like to invest in my restaurant. By the way, if you all could leave your business cards with the maître d', I can make certain you're invited to the grand opening."

"Are you and Declan dating?"

Declan braced himself, his eyes on Rose, his heart breaking for her. "You're kidding, right. Me? And Declan McDonald? We are not dating. We have never dated.

And we will never date. But, thanks for thinking it was possible."

And then: "I'll date you."

Richard reached up and shut off the monitor. "Apparently, she started talking about her restaurant and how if they wanted a picture of the two of you together, they should attend the grand opening. She's one hot ticket."

Declan sat down in a slump.

"She's incredible, isn't she? I mean, she could take this town and . . . Are you sure she doesn't need a publicist?"

Declan held up his hand wearily. "Enough."

"So, what brings you to my den? I thought I heard you say something about you screwing up?"

Declan let out a bitter laugh. "I thought she was angry with me for putting her through the hell of the press. Now I don't know what the hell she's mad about. I guess that we pulled such a stunt. But she still doesn't get it. She still thinks this is a big joke." Declan had never felt so helpless. It was like flushing the toilet the moment you spied a priceless jewel in the water. She was spiraling down, oblivious to the consequences, enjoying the ride. Just like he had. Just before it all turned to shit.

Richard sat down behind his desk and steepled his fingers. "Declan, do you mind if I ask you a personal question?"

"Why not?"

"What the hell are you doing here?"

Declan stared at Richard a full beat before responding. "Here in L.A. or here in your office."

Richard let out a long-beleaguered sigh. "Here in L.A. Why don't you quit this business."

"I tried that, remember?"

His friend gave him a withering look. "I don't expect you to play dead again, I mean just leave. Stop going on talk shows. Stop performing. Just stop. Other stars have done it, they've faded away. Sure, they pop up once in a while for those where-are-they-now pieces, but for the most part they have a normal life."

"What about my music?"

Richard leapt up and pointed an accusing finger at him. "Ah ha!"

"Ah ha, what?" Declan asked, thoroughly irritated.

"For all your lamenting and whining, the truth is, you like this business. You need it."

He shook his head sharply. "No, that's not true. Why do you think I did what I did?"

"Because you love your mother and you think you killed your brother."

Declan flushed deeply. That was it in a nutshell, wasn't it? If he was honest with himself, and God knew that meant he'd really have to think about his life and not just react, he loved writing and performing his music. He just hated what it had done to his family. If he could write and perform in a vacuum, he'd be happy. But that was impossible.

"I don't know what I want."

"I think you should get married. To Rose, maybe. To someone grounded who can handle the press. Or maybe someone in the business who's used to all this craziness. Half the time the press are following you around just to see who you're dating. Get married and half the intrigue is gone."

Declan stood and started pacing. "I've thought of that, of what our life would be like."

"And what would it be like?"

He stared out over the city sprawl for a long moment, following a car on the freeway until it went out of sight. "I can't do it to her."

"I think she could handle it," Richard said.

"She's got her own life, a real one, in Providence."

"Declan. Look at me. I've decided that for the most part, I'm going to spend my life alone. There aren't a lot of guys like me, and if there are, I haven't found them. But if I did find someone who makes me as happy as Rose makes you, I wouldn't let him go."

"Even if keeping her means destroying her?" Declan swallowed heavily. "I have a responsibility to those I love. Sure, I'd like to be an ordinary guy, but it's too late for that, isn't it?"

"Your brother died—"

"I don't want to talk about my brother," Declan bit out.

"Your brother died," Richard persisted, "because he was driving too fast and had too much to drink. You didn't kill your brother, Declan. The kid's own stupidity killed him. Why can't you admit that?"

Declan shook his head. "The bottom line is that he wouldn't have gone down that road, he wouldn't have been driving that fast, if photographers hadn't been behind him."

"You don't know that."

"I do," he shouted, then swore beneath his breath. "I've got to go."

As he was walking through the door, Richard shouted, "Does she even know you love her?"

But Declan had already left the room.

Chapter 21

Griddled sirloin steak with chimichurri sauce, home-made guacamole and Rosalie's French fries, $27.00

Rose looked at the pile of paper in front of her—a five hundred thousand dollar small business loan, liquor license, food and beverage permit, five thousand dollar a month lease, contractor's bills, job applicants—and felt a little sick. Okay, a lot sick. She had more money than most start-up restaurants, but looking at all those zeros was a scary thing. In her brain, she knew people did this all the time, that in the world of business, a half million dollars was chicken change. But in Rose's mind she saw an endless mountain of cash, an empty restaurant, bad reviews, angry employees, impatient vendors.

"Oh, God, what am I getting myself into?" Maybe she should save more money. Maybe she should be smart and save enough cash for the whole thing. Maybe when she was eighty she'd have enough money to open up her restaurant. The loan officer acted as if this was a no-brainer, pointing out that she had a ton of equity through her name alone, not to mention a boatload of cash from her own savings and the sale of her grandmother's house. He'd even joked—ha ha ha—that she should call her restaurant McDonald's. Rose got a big chuckle over that one. Now all she had to do was file a bunch of stuff in City Hall and hire wait staff and chefs. Interviews were in a week. She'd been back from California for a month, and in that time she'd found a terrific location, gotten the loan, and started renovations and hiring staff.

The restaurant, which most recently had served Indian cuisine, was near the theater district and had closed two months ago. The kitchen was perfect with fairly new equipment, a large prep line, huge walk-in refrigerator. She did a walk through with Jenn, who, it turned out, had a remarkable talent for decorating. It was Jenn who suggested she tear down the awful dark paneling, leading to the wonderful discovery of shabby-chic brick. Jenn directed the demolition crew to tear down the thick, dark red velvet drapes, then scrape the painted-over glass, letting light in through the multipaned windows. Rose simply nodded as Jenn waddled through the space throwing out idea after idea. She covered up the deep-red-painted ceiling with white bead board and tore up the dark red carpeting revealing gorgeous wide-plank floors, which she told Rose to refinish and bleach. By that time, Jenn was no longer making suggestions, but giving orders. She was in heaven, her artistic eye getting a good workout.

After it was done, Rose had walked through with her mother, holding her breath, waiting for her mother's classic well-meaning criticism. Instead, schizo mom started crying. "It's beautiful, Rose." You could have knocked Rose over with a wet noodle.

Damn, this was scary. Because if Rosalie's failed, if she went down the tubes and crashed and burned, she had nothing to fall back on, no one to blame but herself. Restaurants failed all the time—good ones that for one reason or another never caught on with the public. Heck, she was moving into a building that had housed not one, but two failed ventures. Everything about the building pointed to success—great downtown location, close to the theaters, off-street parking. Why had the other restaurants failed? They were probably under-capitalized, which led to no advertising, which led to no customers. Indian cuisine might have been too exotic for Rhode Islanders, and the first restaurant had banked on a gimmick: an Italian restaurant with an Irish pub flavor, O'Malley's Pasta House. It had been a fatal combination, though perhaps on paper it had seemed like a good idea.

Rose took a deep breath, picked up her pen, and began filling out the endless paperwork. When the phone rang, she jumped up and grabbed it, overly thankful for the interruption.

"Rose Pisano?"

"Speaking."

"This is Declan McDonald's mother. I'm sorry to bother you, but I was wondering if you've heard from him."

Just hearing his name again took another scoop out of her heart. She thought she was over it, over him, but obviously not. It had been one month since she'd left L.A., since she'd seen Declan. One month without a call, thirty-two days of trying to keep out of sight of any television in fear she'd see him and start bawling. Even in the supermarket checkout, she avoided looking at the tabloids because more often than not, his picture was plastered on at least one of them—and usually with some glamorous actress on his arm. The worst had been a headline that said, DECLAN FINALLY IN LOVE? And there he was, looking down at some gorgeous girl who was looking up at him as if he were the sole reason for taking a breath. He sure didn't seem to mind getting his picture taken with her on his arm. Bastard.

And now, his mother was calling her, of all people, to see if she'd heard from him.

"Mrs. Clarke, I haven't seen or heard from Declan in more than a month."

"Oh." She sounded surprised. "If you do hear from him, would you tell him to call his mother."

Something in the woman's voice made Rose's flash of anger fizzle. "Has something happened?"

A long shaky breath. "I don't know. He's disappeared. I haven't heard from him in more than a week, and his agent and publicist both called me wondering why he hasn't been to any of his appearances. He didn't even call to cancel, he just didn't show up, and that's not like him."

Rose rolled her eyes. "With all due respect, didn't he pull something like this already?"

"He called me that time. He would call me if something was wrong. I'm on the verge of contacting the police, but I don't want to embarrass him. I don't know what to do," she said brokenly.

Hearing the woman fighting tears got to Rose. "I'm sure he's all right. Maybe he just wanted to get away for a little while. I'm sure he'll call you. When was the last time you saw him."

"A little over a week ago when he was here for a visit. He needed his old passport because he wanted to go overseas, part of some group going to entertain the troops around Christmastime. I'm not sure. I had to go to the store to get some onions—I was planning to make onion soup—and when I got back he was gone. He didn't leave a note. Nothing. He never even met with that lady, the one who was looking for him. Leah's mother."

Rose wrinkled her brow. That *did* sound strange. "I don't know what to tell you, but maybe you should call the police," she said hesitantly. People didn't just disappear. But this one did, he had a history of it, and that

was what kept both women from sounding any alarm,
Rose realized. If the police were called, the fact that
Declan McDonald was missing—again—would be the
lead story in every newscast in the country. Rose still
cared enough about him to avoid that scenario. But what
if something horrible had happened? What if some deranged fan had kidnapped him? "Maybe you should
give him two more days. If he doesn't turn up, you've
got to do something. And he'll only have himself to
blame."

"You're right. I just don't want to hurt him anymore.
He's been through hell, but you know that."

Rose had mostly been dwelling on the hell she'd been
through, so she didn't respond to his mother's statement.
"How many people have you told this to?" Rose asked,
realizing that if Declan's mother was calling everyone
he knew, she had no hopes of keeping it from the press.

"No one. Only you. When I spoke with his agent
and publicist I pretended I wasn't alarmed. Maybe I
should talk to Richard again. He seems to be the closest to Declan."

"Why call me?"

"Because you're the only person, besides me, Declan
ever trusted, and as far as I know, the only girl he's ever
loved."

A wave hit her, pain and hope and denial. Rose's grip
on the phone became painful. *Don't ask her how she
knows, don't do it. If he did love you, you don't want to
know. Do you? Because it will make things worse,
worse, worse, knowing that he loved you and could still
leave you, could still drive a knife through your heart.*
"What makes you think he loved me?" Rose winced
and slapped her forehead.

"I could tell."

Hope and pain and denial turned into a hard jab of
disappointment. Mother's intuition wasn't worth squat.
"I'll call you if I hear anything. Good-bye, Mrs. Clarke."

After Rose hung up she paced around her little apartment, disturbed by that phone call. Declan would never leave his mother to worry like that. She was the first person he'd called when he'd climbed down from that mountain. And why would he leave without saying good-bye or leaving a note? What a jerk to let his mom worry like that. If she ever did see him, she'd give him a piece of her mind.

Unless he was dead or kidnapped or in a ravine somewhere waiting to be rescued.

"Declan," she whispered, liking the way his name felt in her mouth, her tongue clicking up against the back of her teeth. "Where the hell are you?"

Rose didn't like unexpected knocks at her door. No one visited her unannounced, not even her mother. So when someone banged on her door at ten o'clock that night, she figured whoever it was had the wrong apartment. Then her heart slammed hard against her chest. *It could be Declan.*

Wearing a T-shirt and short sweats, she cautiously moved to her door.

"Who is it?"

"It's Richard Metzger."

Rose wrinkled her brow. Why was that name so familiar?

"Declan's publicist."

Rose opened the door immediately. "What's wrong?"

"Is he here?"

"Declan? No, he's not. What the heck is going on? First his mother calls; then you show up at my door. You could have called, you know."

Richard looked painfully disappointed. "I thought sure he'd be here. Where else would he be?" He looked beyond her shoulder as if expecting to see Declan appear behind her.

Rose was getting a bit irritated. "Why does everyone think Declan would be here? I haven't heard from him since I left California. If Declan's disappeared, I imagine there are a hundred women he could be with."

"No. He's on his way here. He'd come here."

Rose rolled her eyes dramatically. "Why don't you come on in and tell me why you're so certain a man who dumped me—twice—would show up at my door." Rose closed the door and waved Richard to her old worn-out couch.

He sat down at the edge, his elbows on his knees without looking around, so distracted he didn't even bother with the polite nice-place bullshit, for which Rose was grateful. Richard was a good-looking guy, very put-together for someone who was apparently on the verge of some kind of emotional breakdown. He ran a manicured hand through his well-groomed, highlighted hair, letting out a long sigh. "I'm worried about him," he said, and the anguish in his eyes scared Rose.

"Why? Tell me what's happening."

"You haven't heard from him at all?"

"No," Rose said, feeling fear clog her throat.

"It's about his brother. He didn't die in a car accident. At least it wasn't an accident. The stupid kid killed himself, and Declan found out last week. He found Mike's suicide note at his mother's."

"Oh no. Declan." Rose's eyes burned with tears. His disappearance took on a whole new horror. Over a week and no one, not his mother, not his only trusted friend, knew where he was.

"You don't think he'd . . . Declan wouldn't. Would he? He'd get mad. He'd blame himself. But he wouldn't . . . Would he?"

Richard's eyes welled up with tears. "I thought he'd be here," he repeated brokenly, as if this had been his last hope. "I figured if I called first, he might take off. I was so sure . . ." His voice trailed off.

"He wouldn't hurt himself," Rose said firmly. "And I'll tell you why. Because he wouldn't want to cause his mother or anyone else any more pain, that's why. Right?"

"But where is he?" Richard said, half sobbing. "The last time he disappeared, he called his mother at least. I'm still mad at him for not letting me in on his plans. But, hey, I'm just his publicist, right? Just an employee."

"Like me," Rose said in a small voice.

"No," Richard said, letting out a bitter laugh, "not quite like you. I think his feelings for you are a bit different than his feelings for me."

Rose squeezed her eyes shut. "Okay, what do we know. We know he's disappeared. We know he must be terribly upset. Maybe despondent. Probably angry at his mother for hiding the note from him all this time. He's blamed himself for years for his brother's death, and now he probably feels even more guilty. He might have visited his brother's grave. And then what? What would he do? Did he have his car?"

"Yes."

"If he abandoned his car somewhere, someone would have found it by now and reported it. It wouldn't take long for that sort of thing to hit the news. So we have to assume he's still with his car, driving somewhere. Maybe just thinking things through."

"Maybe driving here."

Rose gave him a look. "Will you stop it already? I mean nothing to Declan."

"I know about you two, if that's what you're hiding."

Rose was stunned. "He told you?"

"He told me a lot of things."

Rose furrowed her brows, irritated that Declan had apparently kissed and told. "Okay. Declan and I had a meaningless fling. So what?"

"So you love him, right?"

Rose snapped her mouth shut, closed down her expression. "Who doesn't love Declan McDonald?"

Richard stared at her a long time. "Declan is one of my few friends. I . . . I love him, like a brother. And so do you." He grinned. "But not quite like a brother, right?"

"It doesn't matter who I love."

"Does Declan know that you love him?"

Rose turned away from his searching gaze. "He knows. And it didn't matter."

It was perfect.

The house was nestled into a forested hill, four stories jumbled together in a charmingly odd combination of craftsman and Victorian styles. Clean lines meshed with ornate gingerbread-house adornments giving it a storybook quality. It had five bedrooms, three full and two half baths, and was as different from their huge and painfully formal brick colonial-style house as existed. Ellen loved it at first sight.

It needed updating. The fourth floor would have to be gutted thanks to a leaking roof that had been allowed to leak too long before being repaired. The kitchen would have to be completely redone, two of the bathrooms . . .

Ellen sighed. What a house like this really needed was a big family. And that was the single thing that made this perfect house not so perfect, because it forced her to think seriously about something she'd been avoiding for a long time. At thirty-two, she was still young enough to have two or three more children. Replacements.

She squeezed her eyes shut, telling herself she wasn't being fair to anyone thinking such a horrible thought. She and Matthew had talked for hours about starting over completely, taking this pregnancy as a sign that their life wasn't over just because Leah's life was. Having another child was so scary. Because what if something happened to one of them, what if they got sick. What if another child died. Ellen knew she could not face that again. Everyone had assured her this child would live to a ripe old age, but no one would promise. No one could make any guarantees. And that was what she needed, for someone to say, "You will never face this loss again."

The doorbell chimes sounded, pulling her away from the documents the realtor had given her. When she opened her door, she felt her jaw drop.

"Mrs. Lang, I'm . . ."

"I know who you are, Mr. McDonald."

"I should have called." He shuffled his feet nervously, America's heartthrob feeling awkward and nervous. Ellen had never been a celebrity watcher, but even she couldn't stop her pulse from picking up a beat at the sight of Declan McDonald standing on her front steps. His uncertainty was endearing—and revealing.

"No, not at all. Come in. Your publicist called four days ago to postpone our meeting. Is that why you're here?" she asked, leading him into their formal parlor.

"I decided I didn't want our meeting to be in such a public venue. I understand you want to raise awareness and money for cancer research, but I . . ."

He stopped talking, and Ellen turned to him, her eyes sweeping over his face. "This is all very difficult, isn't it?" She indicated a chair for him to sit. The man who always seemed so at ease was acting terribly uncomfortable at the moment. He sat down, looking too big for the delicate Queen Anne reproduction she'd chosen for him. He wore a forest green golf shirt and khakis, and a pair of beat-up running shoes. His hair was neat, his jaw clean-shaven, his expression so taught, Ellen almost thought he appeared angry. Even during his press conference at what must have been an incredibly stressful time, he'd come across as confident and charming, with a lazy smile and casual air. The man sitting across from her seemed uncertain and tense, and she blamed herself. "If I had known what my obsession with 'Leah's Song' would mean to you, I wouldn't have pursued it quite so militantly."

He shrugged, but even that seemed like a forced gesture, as if his joints were too stiff to move in a casual manner. "It was bound to happen. I should be grateful."

"But you're not." Pain. That was what she saw in his eyes. Not anger, not discomfort, but pain. She watched as he forced a smile, and she felt even more guilty.

"I'm getting there, Mrs. Lang. Let's just say it was everything I expected and more. But please don't think it's your fault. I only blame myself."

Ellen found she believed him. He looked to be a man tortured by his deeds, and a part of her felt he deserved it, no matter that he'd written "Leah's Song." Like her, he'd run away from life and hurt people along the way. He might have chosen a different path, but the result had been the same—isolation and despair. And, like her, he was clawing his way back to a reality that wasn't pretty and didn't always have happy endings.

"Still, I am sorry if I've caused you difficulties. It was never my intention. I want you to know that I asked the private detective to not go public about your identity, but she, obviously, refused. As I said, it was your song, not you, I wanted to understand. The first time I listened to the song, Leah was dying. We were waiting by her bedside, taking turns sitting by her, and the Angel's Songs package arrived. I don't know what I expected, but that wasn't it. The words you wrote touched me inside, helped me get through the worst of those days. You don't have children, do you?"

Declan shook his head.

"I know you've had feelings of loss with your brother, but losing a child goes deeper." She pressed her fists into her stomach. "It's this place inside you that you don't know is there until your child dies. Your song for Leah, it touched that place. Do you understand? That bottomless place, so deep inside it can never be touched; your song touched that place. I just wanted—needed—to thank you."

He leaned forward and smiled. "I don't know how many songs I wrote for Angel's Songs over those two years. I was writing music, the thing I love most, but I never really thought about the families that would some-day listen to them. On a certain level, of course I knew. But I didn't let myself think about the kids dying. I'd watch the videos and look at their pictures and write a song that I thought they'd like. 'Leah's Song' was dif-ferent. For some reason, she reminded me of my brother. I think I was writing it for him."

"Your brother died in a car accident, didn't he?" It was one of the things she'd learned in the past few months—most people liked to talk about their loved ones, how they lived and how they'd died. Apparently, though, Declan McDonald was not one of them. He stood abruptly, startling her slightly.

"I have to go now. Good luck with your fund-raising." Declan stood, feeling a wave of anger, of sadness, come over him so fiercely, he knew he had to leave. Had to get out or do something embarrassing like cry or scream or . . .

"My brother killed himself." It came out, like a sliver long buried beneath the skin, poking through painfully.

"Oh."

"He killed himself over a girl. I didn't even know he was in love with her."

"I'm so sorry," Ellen said, heartfelt and sincere.

He saw a flicker of panic in her eyes and knew he should keep his mouth shut, but when he'd blurted it out it felt so damn good. This woman didn't know the half of why she should be sorry. She didn't know that everything he'd done in the past three years had been based on the misguided belief that he'd been responsi-ble for his brother's death. And it had been over a girl.

Michael hadn't been fleeing the paparazzi; he'd been driving away from her house where he'd found his girlfriend in bed with her ex-husband. Declan knew all this because the first thing he'd done after leaving his mother's house was pay a visit to Allison Kurtzkoff, Michael's very pretty and very high former girlfriend.

"Yeah. I was really bummed about that. But he should have called, you know?"

"Sorry to bother you, ma'am, now you have a nice day."

Michael had written the suicide note on the back of a liquor store bag, one of those long ones for wine or a big bottle of vodka. He hadn't written to him or to his mother. He'd written the damn note to his girlfriend. Short and not so sweet.

"Allison, I'm going to kill myself. Fuck you."

If Michael had lived, that note might have been amusing because it was so like his brother. He was coarse and rude and funny as hell. Declan didn't know how that note ended up in his mother's safe, but he assumed she pulled some strings to get it from the police or the hospital. Why would she keep something like that? Then again, his mother kept everything, from his first grade workbooks to a copy of the first recording contract he'd gotten when he was twenty. After finding that note, he couldn't face his mother. He was too angry, and he knew he'd say something he'd regret. Like, you ruined my life, you manipulative bitch. Already, having told a stranger his family's deep, dark secret, he felt better.

"I just found out." Declan shook his head, trying to find some sanity in his brain. "My mom hid the note and never told me."

"She was trying to protect you, I suppose."

"I think I could have handled the truth," he said with anger.

Ellen laughed. "She apparently didn't think so. Don't forget, you were her last remaining child, her last baby. I know it's a cliché, but it's true. In your mother's eyes, you never really grow up. When I looked at my daughter those last days, I didn't see her. I saw her as a baby. My baby. And I think that had she lived, on some level I never would have been able to let that go."

"With all due respect, you don't know how far my mother was willing to go to protect me. She lied to me." *She let me believe I was responsible for his death.*

"She'd just lost a son," Ellen said softly and with such kindness Declan wanted to scream. "It makes you a little crazy when you lose a child. She was probably scared to death she was going to lose you, too. It's likely the reason she wanted you to go into hiding. You'd be safe. No one could hurt you."

Declan let out a humorless laugh. "I see you've been talking to my mother."

"Not at all. But I was a mother. And I know what I would do to protect my child."

If he had to be honest, his mother had never made the leap that he had, that the paparazzi helped to kill his brother, therefore Declan was to blame. She'd allowed him to blame the press. *He* was the one who blamed himself. But hadn't she complained almost nonstop about her lack of privacy, about how her life and Michael's were so difficult because of the press? She'd never blamed him, never directly, but she'd made her message loud and clear, and as a man who loved his mother he'd done what it took to protect her. He'd killed himself. Except his death was far less permanent than Michael's. Whatever she'd done, he realized, she'd done because she loved him. Through his haze of anger, he knew her complaints had been more insensitive than manipulative. Declan pinched the bridge of his nose.

"Thank you," he said finally.

"You can thank me by appearing at a benefit next month in Chicago. Maybe you could sing 'Leah's Song'?"

Declan's immediate inclination was to decline. Then he stopped himself. He could do one more appearance, one more before calling it quits. "Sure. Call my manager and set it up."

"Thank you, I will."

He gave her one last handshake and smile and moved to the door. "By the way," he said, just as he was about to leave. "If I ever need a new publicist, I'll call you. You've done a remarkable job with 'Leah's Song.' "

Her face lit up from the compliment. "I was a madwoman," she said with a laugh. "Don't ever get in the way of a driven madwoman from Tennessee."

"I'll remember that."

Declan drove a mile from the house before pulling his car over and grabbing his cell phone. "Mom."

"Oh, my God, Declan. Where are you?"

"I'm in Tennessee."

"Tennessee?" He could hear the panicked confusion in her voice and knew she was on the verge of hysterical tears. His mother did hysteria better than anyone he knew.

"I'm fine, Mom."

A shaky breath. "Okay. Really?"

Declan's grip on the phone became almost painful. "I want to know why you didn't tell me."

"Oh, God."

"Mom. Breathe. Don't lose it."

He could hear her taking long, deep breaths. "You felt so responsible for your brother. Every time he got arrested, every time he started drinking, you'd blame yourself. You always took things so hard, honey. It broke my heart. I knew you'd blame yourself for his suicide, and I just couldn't stand the thought of that. But then you got so sad after he died. You changed, honey, and I didn't know how to make things better for you. I could tell things were spiraling out of control. You hated everyone. You vented all your frustration, your anger, on the press. And for a while I thought that was a good thing, that at least you weren't blaming yourself for his death. Don't you understand, hon? If you knew he'd been drinking, if you'd known he'd gone off that edge on purpose, it would have destroyed you."

"It would have made me do something foolish," he said, his tone listless. "It would have made me crazy enough to listen to you when you told me to pretend I was dead."

"What are you talking about?"

Declan let out a long sigh. "Mom. All this time, I blamed myself for Michael's death. When I came to the conclusion that the press was partially responsible for what I thought was an accident, I also concluded they wouldn't have been following Michael if it weren't for his famous brother."

"Oh, no," she whispered in horror. "Oh, honey, no."

"I lost two years of my life because I was so fucking self-centered."

"I'm so sorry, Declan. You should have told me. I thought you might take on that extra guilt; I prayed you wouldn't, but I couldn't talk about him, about how he died. I couldn't. And I'm sorry."

"Mom, none of this is your fault. I've learned something in the past few months, though. Lousy things happen whether I'm around or not. The world goes on. I can't stop it. I can't even control my own life, never mind everyone else's."

"It's about time you learned that. It'll sure make life easier. But, honey, you weren't self-centered. You were selfless. You didn't care about yourself nearly as much as you cared about me and Michael, and I should have seen that."

"I could have quit anytime. I saw what my career was

doing to you and Michael. I could have quit a long time ago."

"But that would have been ridiculous. You have a gift, Declan, a rare, wonderful gift. Your music makes people happy. Just look what you did for that woman whose daughter died. Sure, I complained about the photographers, and I'm sorry if that made you think I was miserable. The truth is, when they were gone, I, just a tiny bit, missed them being around."

"You're kidding."

"You made me special. When you were gone, I was just Carol Clarke again. It was boring." A pause. "You want to strangle me, don't you?"

"A little."

His mother laughed, sounding normal again. "I don't blame you. Listen, if things get too crazy again, I'll head off to Sardinia again. But don't stop writing, Declan. Please."

"I'll think about it. I don't know what I'm going to do." He thought of Rose, and an ache hit him, bone-deep and untouchable.

"Just try to be happy. That's all I ever wanted. You do know that, don't you, honey?"

"I know, Mom. I'll call you in a couple of days."

Chapter 22

Baby artichokes with gorgonzola, $7.00

Rose woke up to the sounds of rain hitting her window and of someone in her kitchen opening and shutting cabinets. Richard. She climbed out of bed, stuffed her feet into a pair of ratty old slippers Nonna had knitted for her two years ago, and shuffled out into the world wearing an oversized Mickey Mouse T-shirt and baggy sweat shorts from Victoria's Secret.

"What are you looking for?"

"Your cappuccino maker."

"Mr. Coffee's right there and you just hurt his feelings."

Richard gave her a look of horror. "I thought you were a chef."

"This is the East Coast, Richard. We just never really got into that coffee thing here. Some of us pretend, but we're all still a bit baffled by it all. And, as an Italian chef, I should at least have an espresso maker, but honestly I just don't like the stuff, though I used to pretend in front of my grandfather. Too strong." She opened the fridge and pulled out a can of Mrs. Folgers. "Will this do? I think there's a Starbucks in the mall, but it doesn't open until nine."

He sighed. "It will do."

Once the coffee was made, they'd had time to watch the news and learn that no one had reported Declan missing or found a body resembling a Greek god. Rose tucked her feet underneath her and sipped her Coffee-mate-laced coffee, bemused by Richard's true horror at putting something so pedestrian in her java. Richard was steaming his suit, the hissing and gurgling sound nearly drowning out the news.

"You know, I suggested Declan get married."

Rose lowered her coffee slowly. "And?"

Richard shrugged and studied his suit. "I thought it would help him become less a target for the paparazzi. But he didn't want to subject his new bride to that kind of scrutiny."

"Does he have someone in mind? Or are you handling that?"

Richard gave her a penetrating look. "I suggested you."

Laughter rose up and bubbled out. "I can imagine what his response was to that one."

"Can you."

"Oh, for God's sakes will you just get to the point, Richard?"

He shrugged, and made a great show of examining his left suit coat sleeve. "I think he cares about you too much to even think of hurting you by subjecting you to that kind of life."

"Oh, really." Rose refused to participate in such a ridiculous conversation. The I-dumped-you-because-I-love-you line was something even she wasn't gullible enough to fall for. You either loved someone and wanted to spend the rest of your life with them or you didn't. Maybe Rose was a romantic, but she believed in her heart that a couple could get through just about anything as long as they loved each other enough.

"What are your plans today?" Rose said, purposefully changing the subject. "You're welcome to hang out here and wait for him if you want, but I have a feeling it's going to be a waste of time."

Richard sagged visibly and lowered the steamer. "I don't know what to do. Maybe we should call Declan's mother and ask if she's heard from him."

Rose grimaced at the thought. "She seemed so emotional the last time I spoke with her. I'm afraid to upset her all over again. You call."

Richard gave his suit an assessing once-over before yanking out the cord. "I suppose I could call. We're three hours ahead of her, though." He flicked his wrist and glanced at his watch. "We have to wait at least until ten."

"What if she hasn't heard anything. What then?"

"Then I go home and wait for him to call. Or you or his mother."

Rose sat up straight. "He has a cell phone, doesn't he?"

Richard looked sick. "He didn't answer it. I only got his voice mail, and I left a message. Three messages, actually. I checked my voice mail this morning, and he hasn't called." Richard swallowed, again overcome by emotion. "He's dead."

"He's not dead. And he's not pretending to be dead. He's just . . . regrouping. He's insensitive and self-centered by not returning your calls, but he's not dead."

"We don't know that. We don't know anything. I swear to God if he is alive—" Richard stopped. "I just hope he's alive."

The phone rang, and they looked at each other like deer caught in the headlights. Rose picked up, then shook her head to Richard. "Hi, Jenn."

"I'm getting some twinges."

Rose furrowed her brow. "What kind of twinges?"

"You know, having baby twinges. I think I'm in prelabor. I think. Either that or I have really bad gas."

"Wow. Jenn. Wow. Are you going to the hospital? Is Brian there? Has your water broke? Does it hurt?"

Jenn laughed. "I may just have to have a BM."

"Oh. Okay, I don't want to know anything else."

"But I haven't talked to you in a while and thought I'd see how the restaurant is going?"

"I've been working out a business plan, putting ads in the paper for managers and decorators, and I'm looking for a PR firm to handle the restaurant's opening. Oh, did I tell you I'm going to have a website? You remember Tim McMahon from high school? He develops websites for small businesses. He's building me a site."

"Wow. You've been busy."

"But the big part is done. Even my mother thought the place was beautiful. You did an amazing job."

"Oh, stop," Jenn said, and even though she was joking, Rose knew she was also probably blushing. "What else is a bored housewife supposed to do?"

Taking pity on her friend, Rose decided to let her in on the big drama happening.

"Declan's missing."

"What?"

"His mother called looking for him, and his publicist is here because he thought Declan might be here. Of course, he's not."

"The jerk."

"Jenn, he's *missing*. Everyone's really worried."

"Even you?"

Rose turned away from Richard, who was pretending badly to not listen. "Well, I don't want him to be dead."

"I suppose not."

Rose laughed. "So, am I going to be there for the birth of your baby?"

"You better be. I'm due in a week, so this is all probably nothing. I'll call if it's something. Okay?"

"Call anyway." Rose hung up. "My friend Jenn's expecting a baby any day and thinks she might be going into labor."

"I take it she's not a big fan of Declan's," Richard said, unapologetic for eavesdropping on her conversation.

"She's very protective of me. She didn't like seeing her best friend's heart trampled on by an egotistical loser who thinks the world and all the planets exist to screw him over." Rose gave him a smile, then went to get dressed.

"You don't mean that," he yelled to her. "You're madly in love, and if he walked through that door right now, you'd be in his arms in a minute."

"Oh, Richard, you're such a girly-man."

Richard smiled, outed by Declan's ex. When she came back in, Rose looked all apologetic. "I'm sorry, you're not a girly-man. I don't even know you, and here I've gone and insulted you."

He narrowed his eyes at Rose, and she could feel herself shrink down to about the size of a crumb. "I've never been outed in less than twenty-four hours."

"You're gay?" Rose gave him a grin. "I should have known when I saw that steamer."

"Straight men steam their clothes," he said dryly.

"But not when they're emotionally distraught."

"I'll have to remember that."

Rose gave him an assessing look. "Is it a big secret? Does Declan know?"

"Declan's one of about five people who do know."

"You know, it's no big deal anymore. They even have a sitcom or two featuring gay characters," she said, as if she were letting him in on a big secret.

"I'm just not the rainbow-flag-waving type. What happens in my private life is private. I'm a guy, right? I like guy things."

"Obviously," Rose said with levity.

He gave her a smirk. "I'm not ashamed of what I am. I just don't want to advertise it."

"As long as you're happy, right?"

He took his suit down and headed to the bathroom to change. "Happy as a clam," he said.

"I don't think clams are that happy. I mean, they live in the muck all there life, sticking that disgusting tube up to grab a trickle of fresh air, and the first time they see the sunlight, it's either from the shovel of a clammer or the beak of a seagull."

She could hear Richard chuckling on the other side of the bathroom door and smiled. Poor guy needed to laugh more. No wonder he and Declan were pals; the two of them couldn't be happy on Christmas Day. At least they got her sense of humor.

Richard emerged fifteen minutes later, showered, pressed, and shaved.

"You look like a high-priced lawyer," she said, and he gave her a beaming smile. "Where are you headed?"

"To the Westin. I'm going to hang out in Providence for a few days. I still think he's on his way here. Here's my card. It's got my cell phone on it if you can't reach me at the hotel."

Rose swallowed, feeling depressed. "Richard, you're a nice man, but Declan isn't coming here. And even if he did, it wouldn't mean anything, not to me. Okay? It's over. Whatever we had—and apparently it wasn't much—it's o-v-e-r," she spelled out.

"Just be nice, then. He's had a real shit life."

Rose barely stopped herself from rolling her eyes and launching into her own life story which was certainly far shittier than anything Declan had experienced. Abandoned by her father, ignored by her mother, trampled on by every man she'd ever loved, mourning a grandmother, childless and husbandless at thirty-two, and twice dumped by America's heartthrob.

Great, now I'm really depressed.

"Richard, if he shows up at my doorstep, you'll be the first person I'll call. Promise."

Rose closed the door behind him and leaned her forehead against the cool surface. The phone rang again, and she let out a groan. It was probably her mother calling to torture her. She just had to get caller I.D. or learn how to let herself allow the answering machine to pick up.

"Hello."

"My water broke. I'm going to have a baby."

Something was very wrong.

Rose had seen enough television shows to know that Brian wasn't acting quite right. Jenn's husband was a good-looking Scotch-Irish man, the kind some might describe as brawny or strapping. He wasn't tall enough to play football, but he had that kind of no-neck bigness to him. Rose liked Brian. He'd always seemed a genuinely nice guy, and he loved Jenn to distraction. Except, today he wasn't acting like a man who was about to become a parent with the love of his life. He was acting as cold and clinical as the nurses. Heck, even they exuded more warmth than he was.

Rose looked from Jenn to Brian about a hundred times, finally coming to the conclusion that he must be the type to hold grudges about almost kisses. Because nothing else could explain why he was standing there stoically while Jenn screamed, "Where's the fucking anesthesiologist. I can't take this fucking pain another minute."

Okay, he flinched a little bit, got even more stiff as he stared at the little blips representing the baby's heartbeat.

"Breathe, Jenn." And Rose did the little hee-hee-hee-hee-hhhooo thing with her. Okay, Rose did it alone while Jenn glared at her as if she were the devil.

After the contraction, Jenn said, her face contorted in pain, "Will you quit it with the breathing? It doesn't work, and I'd like to kill the person who came up with it and told women everywhere *breathing* would get you through this kind of hell." Rose felt so helpless witnessing her best friend in so much agony, her stomach grotesquely big, her normally sleek hair damp and limp. "It'll be over before you know it, kiddo."

"I want it over now," she said through gritted teeth. "You cannot believe how much this hurts. They don't tell you. They tell you it hurts, but fuck this! Oh God, here it comes. I can't do it I can't do it I can't do it." Jenn squeezed her hand so hard Rose thought she might have an inkling about pain. A doctor type walked in with a big grin on his face.

"I hear you were looking for me?"

"Are you the epidural guy? Please, God, tell me you're him."

"I'm him."

And then, even though the contractions were just as strong, they became more bearable because Jenn knew there was an end in sight. Within twenty minutes, she was Jenn again, chatting and smiling with Rose while completely ignoring Brian. When he finally left the room, muttering about getting something to eat, Rose said, "What's going on with you two?"

Jenn bit her lip and looked guilty as hell. "He thinks that maybe it's not his baby."

"What?"

"It is. I know that for a fact, but he thinks maybe it's not."

Rose closed her eyes briefly. "And why would he think such a thing?" Jenn looked away. "Jenn?"

"I told you. Because I almost—*almost*—had a quickie with our contractor. But I didn't!"

"Oh my God. You said it was just a kiss. Not even a kiss, and *almost* kiss."

"Okay, it was one kiss, but when he wanted another, I stopped. I came to my senses. I was still in single mode. Flirt-and-sex mode. You know."

Rose lifted an eyebrow. "No, I don't know. So, Brian obviously believes it was some sort of affair."

"Yes," she said in a tiny voice.

"Oh, Jenn."

"Brian walked in just as I was pushing him away after a very brief kiss." She ignored Rose's eye-rolling. "I mean, the minute my lips touched his I came to my senses and thought, 'What the hell are you doing?' And that's when he walked in. Two weeks later I found out I was pregnant and it's been hell ever since."

"Oh, Jenn."

Jenn got all teary. "He won't believe me, and at first I didn't blame him but, come on! It's been nine months of him being so cold, and I don't deserve it. I never cheated on him." Rose handed Jenn a tissue, and she sloppily blew her nose. "He's going to order a paternity test the minute the baby's born. Do you know how humiliating that is?"

Rose hugged her friend, rocking back and forth while she sobbed into her shoulder. "Why didn't you tell me?"

"Because I knew I'd gone over the line and even you wouldn't understand. It was just so hard when we first got married. I didn't take it seriously enough, I didn't appreciate what we had, and I was stupid. And now I might lose him even after all this, even when he knows the baby is his." She lost it again, crying copiously while Rose held her helplessly. A nurse came in, and Jenn straightened.

"Are you all right?"

Jenn managed a weak smile. "Just overwhelmed with joy," she said, tragically unconvincing.

Rose looked away while the nurse examined her. "Nine centimeters. We'll be pushing within twenty minutes. Are you ready?"

"As I'll ever be."

Jenn began pushing forty minutes later, with Rose by her head encouraging her and Brian staring at the place where the baby would come out. It seemed impossible, but he was even more tense than before, barely sparing Jenn a glance. And then it happened.

"Looks like we've got a little redhead here," the doctor said from behind her mask. "Just like Daddy."

Rose had seen men cry before, but the body-wracking sobs that consumed Brian were heartbreaking to witness. He stood there, shaking, letting out these funny grunt sounds, tears streaming down his face, as he stared at the curling red hair of his child.

"Oh, baby, I'm sorry," he said, then threw himself at Jenn, who, over and over, said she was sorry, too. They were so wrapped up in their own forgiveness fest, they forgot about the little redheaded baby waiting to make an appearance, until the doctor let out a loud *ahem*.

"Do you think we can have this baby now?"

A half-hour later, Brian and Jenn's son was brought into the world. Everyone in the room was crying, including Rose, who stood back and let the parents have their moment. She went to the window and looked out through the rain-covered panes at Providence, lit up and pretty at night. The baby squalled, his parents told each other a hundred times how much they loved each other, and Rose stood there, feeling incredibly alone and sad. It was such an unexpected emotion, it made her mad. Her best friend had just had a healthy baby boy. She should be happy. And she was. But she was also fiercely jealous. Not of the baby, but of the moment they were sharing, that pure joy and happiness that she'd never experienced and might never have. Rose squeezed her eyes shut, willing such a self-centered thought from her brain. After Declan dumped her again in L.A., she'd secretly sworn off men. She either was ambiguous about them or so much in love she'd made a complete fool of herself.

"Rose. Come meet James Sean. Isn't he beautiful?"

Rose gazed down at the red-faced, swollen little guy who was trying to open his eyes, and teared up all over again. Ugly little sucker. "He's the most beautiful baby boy I've ever seen," she said, her voice watery.

The nurse came and gently took James away to weigh him and give him a nice cleaning. Jenn followed the nurse's progress, looking back only when her son was out of sight. "Thanks for being here for me."

"I'm glad you wanted me here. It was an incredible experience." Rose flexed her right hand. "I don't think my fingers will ever be the same." Jenn laughed, but Rose could tell she was tired. "I've got to go now. I'll see you when you get home. But call me if you need anything." Rose walked over to Brian and gave him a kiss and a hug. "Congratulations."

He said a gruff thanks, and Rose guessed he was embarrassed about his emotional display.

When Rose left the room, she looked back at them through the small wire-meshed window, their heads together, their hands entwined, their lives forever changed.

Chapter 23

*Ice cream duet featuring chocolate and fresh raspberry,
$8.00*

It was still raining when Rose pulled up in front of
her apartment, a soft, cold drizzle that only made her
feel more depressed. She sat in her car lacking the energy to get out. Having a baby was exhausting even if it
wasn't you having it, she thought, making herself
chuckle. Rose always liked coming home; it gave her a
warm, cozy feeling to know that wherever she'd been,
her shabby apartment would still be there exactly as
she'd left it. Not tonight. She was in a major funk about
life and where hers was, even though she ought to be
excited about opening her restaurant. Instead she felt
gloomy and mildly depressed and knew it was because
Jenn, despite her problems, had what she secretly wanted.
A home and a family. And a successful restaurant. Was
that so much to ask for?

Rose shook her head to rid herself of her gloomy
mood, wishing she'd taken after her mother. She loved
being alone, which was why it was so shocking that after

nearly thirty years of living single, her mother was dating a man. Her mother was dating and she wasn't. Rose had been alone for years and years, but had never truly felt alone until recently. Until her grandmother died.

Let's be completely honest, Rose. You started feeling this way after Declan. Because you really hoped you weren't being an idiot and that the most-famous and most-fucked man on the planet had fallen in love with you.

Somewhere behind her a car door shut and that stirred her into action and out of her funk. She got out of her car, locked the door, and slammed it shut with the vigor of a woman on a mission. She would not allow herself to get all maudlin and depressed just because she thought that maybe she someday wanted what her best friend had. Heck, all this time she'd thought Jenn was living the perfect life, and she'd been living in a frigid hell with a man who suspected the baby she was carrying wasn't his. No one's life was perfect, but hers was pretty close. She was independent, smart, and about to embark on the adventure of a lifetime. She started humming that old Helen Reddy song, "I am woman."

"Rose."

A melting, deeply, foolishly in love woman.

Rose slowly turned, not quite believing Declan would be standing there behind her. But there he was, looking beautiful and tired, and staring at her in a way she'd never seen before and couldn't even begin to understand. "I was expecting you," she said, and sighed. "Come on up."

She felt him behind her, willed herself not to turn around and throw herself in his arms and betray the emotions warring inside her. It had already been one hell of a day, between worrying about Declan with Richard and worrying about Brian with Jenn. "Have you called your mother?"

"Yes."

She turned when she got to the top of her stoop. "What about Richard. He's worried sick."

"No. I haven't called him."

"You should. He showed up here convinced you were here. Either that or dead. Nice work, by the way, scaring the hell out of everyone." Rose hadn't even known she was angry until that moment when she felt it surge, a hot, prickly sensation on the back of her neck.

"I'm sorry."

"You ought to be." But he'd taken the air out of her anger by apologizing so readily. She hadn't expected him to. She'd thought he'd have been all defensive. Rose went up the dimly lit stairs to the second floor and opened her door, leaving it ajar so he could follow and so she could gather her thoughts and figure out exactly what she was feeling at this moment. It was extremely disheartening to realize she still loved him, and just as disturbing that she could feel herself ready to fold so easily. He'd dumped her. Twice.

Rose tossed her keys near her phone and noticed her answering machine had a message. She pressed play, guessing it would be Richard. It was. "It's Richard. I called Declan's mother. The asshole's fine, and I'm heading back to L.A. If you do see him, tell him to find another publicist."

Rose looked up at Declan with a grimace. "Guess he's a little upset."

Declan rubbed a weary hand through his hair. He was a mess of wrinkled clothes and mussy hair. His jaw was sprinkled lightly with his beard, and he appeared almost gaunt, his eyes slightly hollow. He looked pathetic, and Rose tried to harden her heart.

"I don't blame him for wanting to quit me."

"Okay, who are you and what have you done with Declan?" She tried a smile, but it came out all shaky because she couldn't stand to see him this way.

He shrugged and shook his head. "I don't know."

What was left of her heart melted into a little puddle and settled down by her toes. "Oh, Dec," she said, and he went into her arms, a boy who was lost and needed someone—anyone—to hold him.

"God, Rose," he whispered against her ear, "I missed you so damned much." He pulled her against him fiercely, frantically, pressing her close, and she grabbed the wrist of one hand with the other around his back so she could squeeze just as tightly. She didn't use her smart mouth, even though she instantly thought, *Yeah, funny way of showing you missed me by not calling for a month.* She knew he needed her and in a way was using her, a warm body, a happy memory, to get him through whatever he was going through. In that moment, she didn't care, not enough to pull away. To be honest, she needed him too, a warm body, a happy memory. So when he moved his head down and pressed his lips over hers, she offered herself to him with an intensity that scared the hell out of her. Without another meaningful word, she moved them toward her bedroom and pulled him down on top of her. It didn't matter that this was probably the dumbest thing she'd ever knowingly done.

She was electrified, turned on by every moan, every touch, everything heightened because it had been so long and she wanted him so much. In her head she told him she loved him, and out loud she told him he felt good beneath her hands. He pulled her shirt off and she unhooked her bra, and he put his hands on her breasts and looked at them as if he'd never seen her before. He looked up at her and smiled, and for an instant, she saw him, that devilish, arrogant man she fell in love with.

"Rose, I—" She put a finger to his lips.

"No talking," she said against his mouth, slipping her tongue inside to suck away whatever he was going to say. She slipped her hand into his jeans, smiling when she heard his sucking breath. "Still there," she said, and he laughed. He kicked off his shoes, undid his jeans, lay down, and wiggled out of them, and she kissed the tip of his penis right before she reached into her bedside table drawer for a condom.

"Rose, I'm healthy as a horse, and I want to feel you this time."

He dragged her down to him for a kiss. She landed on top of him, his erection pressing between her legs, electric friction. "Declan," she said, breathless. "I want to, too, but—" She gasped as he inserted two fingers inside her, stroking slowly. "Oh God," she managed.

"There's been no one since you," he said, and she wasn't certain if she believed him. After all, they hadn't been together in months, and she knew for a fact Declan had been linked to at least four Hollywood-type women. "How could there be?"

And then, before Rose could even begin to think about those words, he slipped inside of her and started bringing her to heaven with his body and his hands. Slow, easy, and the most erotic sex she'd had in her life, because he seemed—maybe she was crazy and maybe it was just because she loved him so much—to be making *love* for the first time. When she came, arching her back, feeling that wonderful electricity travel from between her legs to her toes, he moved faster, gripping her head in his hands, kissing her mouth, and coming with a groan that sounded as if it were torn painfully from the depth of his soul.

He moved off her, kissing her slightly moist cheek. "Rose," he said, before falling asleep.

After a few minutes, Rose, in utter disbelief, sat up and looked down at his sleeping form. She wanted to shake him awake, but figured he was exhausted from his cross-country trek. They'd have plenty of time for talking in the morning.

Rose didn't want to be one of those women who made love and then regretted it an instant later. She never had been. But now, looking at him sleeping on her bed, contented and oblivious, she was beginning to regret dragging him to her room and making love. *Oops, I did it again.*

But, of course, it wasn't *his* heart that would be crushed. It never was. Nothing had changed. He was still Declan McDonald, superstar, and she was still Rose Pisano, small-time Italian cook. They were two needy people who found some solace in each other's arms. Rose wished it were that simple.

She sat in bed for a long time, getting herself good and mad at herself and at the man sleeping blissfully beside her. It was midnight when he stirred, stretched, and reached for her. He tugged her down and nestled beside her, a small smile on his sexy mouth. "Mmmmm," he said.

Rose pulled away. "I have to pee."

She didn't know how he tuned in on her anger through that innocuous little sentence, but he did.

"You're mad."

"No." Which, of course, came out sounding like "yes" from her tone.

Rose told herself Declan hadn't been privy to the long and involved debate she'd been having inside her head for the past two hours, but she couldn't help it. She was good and worked up, and, even though she knew she was about to say and do things she'd definitely regret later—even more than the fantastic sex she'd just had—she couldn't stop herself. All that resentment and anger that had built up in the past month was going to vomit out of her mouth, and there wasn't a thing she could do about it. She could feel it and almost warned Declan but was too mad to give him even that courtesy.

By the time she got back to her bed, she'd almost convinced herself to cut the poor guy a break. "Declan, I know about your brother and I'm sorry. I know I said you could come here and hang out for a while, but that was before." Rose meant to say all that in a gentle, soothing tone, but somehow it came out sounding slightly bitchy. Okay, very bitchy.

He looked at her as if he didn't have a clue what she was talking about. "Before what?"

"Before you dumped me. Again."

"I'm too tired for this conversation. I just need some sleep."

Rose turned away from him, because if she'd continued to look at him, she would have grabbed the first sharp object she could find and thrust it into his "too tired" body.

"You're mad. Don't be."

"It's my own fault. I know that. I let you in. I'm the one who dragged you to this bed. I've got only myself to blame." Here she was, on a wonderful tirade, and he was staring at her as if she were speaking a foreign language.

"Please, Rose. I had one hell of a week, and I don't need this right now. Can we go back to bed and have this conversation in the morning?"

She turned back to him. He looked tired and sincere, and she was a second away from lying down next to him and tucking her head in that little nook between his neck and his shoulder. "Why did you come here?"

His jaw clenched. "I love you."

She blinked rapidly. There it was, the words she'd never thought she'd hear thrown at her, a lofty, easy-to-catch lob, and she was going to miss it. On purpose and for the better good. For once, she was going to use her brain, think clearly. This man, this beautiful man lying next to her claiming he loved her, was someone she didn't know. She knew the man who had been hiding out, that fun, gentle, scared-as-shit guy who'd leaned on her and used her and, in the end, left her.

"I don't believe you." And she didn't. Maybe at this moment, Declan thought he loved her. He was lonely and sad, and she was the comfort food he needed. Chicken soup for the megastar's soul.

"Don't say that. You don't know how hard this is for me. You don't know."

Rose's eyes filled with tears, and she swallowed. "It shouldn't be hard, Dec. I'm not your go-to girl. The one who'll always be there for you when things get tough. I won't let you do this to me again. I can't."

He looked at her as if she were a curious object. It was a look of irony and puzzlement and sudden acceptance. "Okay," he said, as if she'd asked him for a glass of water.

She narrowed her eyes, suspicious. "Okay?"

He shrugged. "Okay. It's official now. You win."

Rose lowered her head and looked up at him. "Win what?"

"The prize for pigheadedness. I was close," he said, anger finally touching his voice. "But you got it, baby. You fucking win." He was really, really mad and trying to control it. Rose bit her lip.

"I drive across the country to come to see you to tell you I love you and ask you to marry me and you sit there and tell me, too late? Not enough? Well, fuck you."

Rose shook her head. "Whoa. Back up. Did I hear you right? Did you just say you came here to ask me to marry you?"

Wasn't this rich? Looked like he was taking his publicist's advice after all. She doesn't hear from him in a month, and he shows up at her door wanting to marry her. And the thing was, he didn't find that at all strange, which was strange in itself—and incredibly suspect.

"That's right," he said, still angry as hell.

"We haven't even dated yet," Rose said, so mad she could hardly speak. "We hardly know each other. Sure, the sex is great, but that won't last."

"I said I love you."

Poor guy, he looks so confused. "Why doesn't she

just throw herself at me and scream, 'Yes, yes, I'll marry you. I'm just the luckiest li'l ol' girl in the whole wide world.' "

"You know, Dec? I didn't think you had it in you. I really thought you were one of the good guys."

His expression was so baffled, he was acting so absolutely clueless, that for a second Rose thought that maybe he was being sincere. "What the hell are you talking about?"

"I'm saying no. I won't marry you."

His face got all tight, and his eyes turned hard. "I don't recall asking."

"Well, then, no one's hurt, right?"

He rubbed the top of his head, mussing up his hair into sexy spikes. "Are you the same woman who I just made love to? I don't know what I did or said that turned you into some kind of psycho bitch, but whatever it is I'd like to know."

"I guess it was all that love and marriage stuff. It's all a little out of the blue, don't you think?"

"You think I've come to this revelation suddenly?"

"Oh," Rose said, pressing her fingers against her temples like a psychic. "Yes, I'm getting it now, loud and clear. My mind-reading skills have been a bit rusty lately, and I didn't pick up on all that *love* you were throwing my way. 'I want you to go, Rose. I don't want you in my life, Rose.' Did you mean all *that* love? Because somehow I missed it, Declan. Of course now I'm supposed to believe you love me and want to get married. How stupid do you think I am? Feel free to leave anytime."

"That's just what I'll do."

"Fine."

He got out of bed and jerked on his clothes faster than he'd gotten out of them. And he was out the door before she could call him back the way her heart was shouting for her to do. It wasn't until about ten minutes later, when her temper was finally subsiding, that she let it sink in that maybe he had driven across the country to see her because he loved her and wanted to marry her. And she'd thrown him out of her house. What was *wrong* with her?

"It's for the best," she said to herself aloud. She'd been right. She wasn't a go-to girl, and he couldn't really love her. If he had, why would he have pushed her away so coldly? And if he loved her, he wouldn't have left so easily. A woman needed convincing, especially after being treated so rotten. Who did he think he was? If he thought he could just waltz back into her life after a month, make love to her, *claim* he loved her, and expect her to believe him, then he wasn't as brilliant as everyone thought he was.

She was too smart for him. Yes siree. She wouldn't fall for that bunch of hooey. Not in this lifetime.

She marched right over to her phone and called his cell phone.

"Hello."

"It's me. I'm sorry. I love you, too."

"Who is this? Rose?"

"Richard? Oh, God, I dialed the wrong number. I thought, oh, never mind what I thought."

"I take it he finally showed up at your place."

"Oh, yeah."

"And you fought."

"I fought. He left."

"Do you have his cell phone number?" Richard asked with utmost patience.

Rose started to cry and could barely speak. "Yes, but . . ."

"Rose, are you crying?"

"Yes," she croaked out.

"I'll be right over. I'm still at the airport."

"Oh, no, Richard, I'm all right." She sniffed, swallowed, and got herself together.

"Are you going to call him?"

"I'm not sure. Bye, Richard."

Before she could press the off button, she heard him say, "Call him."

But she didn't.

Chapter 24

The Queen Bee-Rosewater and honey mousse on a chocolate honeycomb with barenjager chocolate sauce, sprinkle of Lancaster County bee pollen, lemon zest shortbread and a drizzle of honey, $9.00

Richard looked at his old friend and frowned. He looked like shit, like a man who'd been on a month-long bender, except Declan didn't drink. He just shut down.

He'd called sounding real rough for a guy who was able to fake his way through just about anything. "I need to talk," he'd said, and Richard's heart had hurt. And then he'd shown up looking about as worn-out as a man could look and still be functioning. He'd sat down in a chair, thrown his head back and stared at the ceiling for a good five minutes before he said a word.

"What the hell am I doing back here?" He'd brought his head down then, and the look on his face was scary. Declan McDonald looked like a man who was about a hairsbreadth away from losing his grip on sanity.

"Tell me what happened."

"No big deal. I told her I loved her. I asked her to marry me. Sort of. And she said no. The end."

Richard sat up straight. "You asked her to marry you?"

"Yep."

"How did she react?"

Declan shook his head, apparently reliving in disbelief what had happened. "She got pissed. She threw me out. Told me she didn't believe me. I don't get it."

Unfortunately, Richard did get it, but he wasn't about to fess up to Declan. He'd just fix things, that was all. It was one of the things he did best: fixing other people's lives.

Rosalie's was a madhouse. Her 104-seat restaurant was filled to capacity, and if she let in another person, she was afraid the fire marshal, who was at this moment enjoying some stuffed artichokes, would issue her a citation.

Twelve waiters and waitresses were walking around offering appetizers: fried calamari, tiny bits of spicy artichoke pizza, scallops and shrimp, and roasted asparagus. In the kitchen, her entire staff of line cooks was putting the final touches on the three main courses she was offering: baccala with creamy polenta, friend eggplants with mozzarella rotalo, and roasted quail stuffed with caramelized pears and liver pate. Rose had just forced herself to come out of the kitchen after being assured by her staff that everything was under control. For this evening only she'd spend more time on the floor than preparing and supervising the food. A flash of red hair caught her eye, and she smiled when she recognized Francine from *Good Eats*.

"Hi, Francine. Thanks for making it," Rose said after making her way through the throng.

"Hell of a turnout. By the way, the pizza is out of this world."

"This is insanity. And I realize one thing: I've got to do something about the noise level in this place." Rose looked up at the ceiling to see if she could determine just what was making the room so loud.

"It's really not so bad considering how many people are here. But I suppose I expected it."

Rose smiled at Francine's compliment. "I just hope the crowds stick around after tonight." Rose spotted her mother over Francine's head. "My mother just got here with her boyfriend. I'm going to say hi. Oh, and there's Jenn. You remember her from the photo shoot?"

"Go ahead. I'm too busy eating to talk." And to demonstrate, she shoved a shrimp dripping with marinara sauce into her mouth.

Rose spent the next ten minutes talking to her customers, enjoying for the moment what was turning out to be a triumphant debut.

"I have a complaint," a rough-voiced man said from behind her. Tony.

"What? You don't recognize good food when you taste it?"

"This isn't Italian food. This is *California* Italian food." He popped one of her pizza's in his mouth. "What is this stuff?"

"Don't you like it, Tone?"

"I didn't say that. I just said it wasn't Italian."

Rose smiled and gave Tony a big hug. She stepped back, slightly embarrassed when he didn't return her embrace. "Who's minding the store?"

"No one. I closed down for the night."

"Oh, Tony," Rose said, moved nearly to tears.

"Don't 'oh, Tony' me. My place has been so crowded I can afford to take a night off once in a while." He looked around the room. "Be nice if you can keep this up."

"I really don't know how this happened. I didn't even know we sent out this many invitations." Now that she thought about it, it was a little strange. She'd known her self-promotion was smart, but even she was shocked by the number of people to turn out. She even recognized a couple of reporters from L.A. It was crazy.

"I'll catch up to you later, Tony. Enjoy your night off," Rose said after spotting the woman she'd hired to organize her opening and waved her over. "Who the hell are all these people," she whispered to her publicist, a twenty-four-year-old whose skills in public relations were much sharper than Rose would have imagined. Melanie Pratt had come across as perky and bright, but seeing her in action was more like watching a piranha in a river of soft flesh. She'd handled the press like a pro, handing out press kits, directing them to the bar area where a spread of appetizers was laid out.

"Mostly the press." Melanie tilted her chin. "There's the mayor. I'm expecting the governor in"—she checked her watch—"twenty minutes or so. We've got *People,* a couple of tabloids, all the local TV and radio stations, newspapers. You know, the works. Some people from Trinity and a couple from Brown."

"How did you pull this off? I talked to you a week ago, and you told me you were afraid it would be a bust."

"I'd better get to the door. I think I see someone from *Bon Appetite.*" A guilty flush stained her cheeks.

Rose grabbed Melanie's arm. "You didn't invite him. Tell me you didn't. I told you specifically not to."

Melanie didn't even bother to look guilty. "Look, Rose, you wanted to generate some buzz. Look around. This is the biggest fucking event this town has seen in months. I'm not going to apologize for creating publicity for you."

A FedEx guy walked up to them. "Are you Melanie Pratt? Sign here."

With a quick, efficient stroke of her pen, Melanie signed for the package.

"That's from Richard Metzger."

"He's incredible. He's a legend. I wanted to thank you for giving me the opportunity to work with him."

"I didn't," Rose said with abject frustration. Then she sighed and grimaced. "When is he supposed to arrive?"

There was a loud commotion at the door. Rose looked up and saw Paul towering over the crowd, looking official and gorgeous as ever, apparently reveling in his new position as Declan's bodyguard.

"There he is now." For an instant, Melanie slipped out of her professional demeanor. "Oh, my God, I can't believe I pulled this off." She clutched Rose's arm. "Do you realize how awesome this is? My boss is going to shit."

"Great," Rose said between gritted teeth. "I'll be in the kitchen." Rose left the room, and no one noticed. She had to admit Melanie had gotten her restaurant filled, but she wished she hadn't used Declan to do it. Frankly, she was a bit shocked that Declan had shown up. Shocked and scared out of her mind. She nodded to her line cooks and waitresses hanging around waiting for the service to begin and went straight to the walk-in refrigerator, opened the door, and slammed it shut.

She pressed her fingertips against her eyelids, letting out a shaking breath. What was she supposed to say to him?

Time stands still as she walks out into the dining room. She enters and all grows quiet. The crowd parts before her, and there he is, Declan McDonald. He sinks to one knee, a small box extended in one hand, a red rose in the other. She walks as if on clouds to where he waits. And when she gets there, he shoves her aside. "Not you.

You had your chance." Over the roar in her head she hears Melanie squeal, "Omigod. Yes."

Rose banged her head against the refer door. "Shit." She couldn't stay in the cold forever. She'd have to go out and face him. She'd smile graciously, pose for some photos, then go about the business of running her restaurant, trying to ignore the fact that her heart was about to jump ship and dive into Declan's arms.

Someone banged on the refer door.

"I was looking for . . ." She stopped. "Declan."

"What the hell is this?" he said, shoving a piece of paper in front of her.

Furrowing her brow, she took the piece of paper and began to read about her engagement to Declan McDonald, set to be announced formally at the opening of her restaurant.

"I've been used before, Rose, but never in my life has anyone sunk this low trying to profit off my name."

"You think I'm responsible for this?" One look at his livid face told her that he did, indeed, think she was responsible.

"The only reason I showed up here today was because you asked and I figured I might owe you that much. I was being a nice guy. I can't believe you'd put out crap like this."

"Declan. Shut. Up," she said, clamping her hand over his mouth. "Listen to me. I did not put this out. And I did not invite you here."

"Then who did?"

Rose shook her head slowly, feeling as confused and betrayed as Declan. "My PR firm invited you, but I know Melanie wouldn't have put out something like this." Rose looked past Declan to see six of her line cooks pretending not to be listening to their conversation. "Hey, Arlene. Could you go find Melanie Pratt for me. She's in red."

"You want me to bring her into the refer?"

Rose gave her a stare.

"Okay, okay."

Rose crossed her arms and stared at the bin of tomatoes in front of her, and apparently Declan found something interesting to stare at because he didn't say a word either.

"What are you doing in the refrigerator?" Melanie asked, sounding harassed.

Rose held out the press release. "Do you know where this came from?"

Melanie gave the paper a quick look and grinned. "Is it true?"

"Of course not."

"No." Declan's voice rumbled through her body.

"It came in that FedEx package."

"Oh, no. Okay, Melanie, go back out and make everyone happy." She looked back at the release and said one word: "Richard."

"Richard put this out? No way."

"I'm afraid so, though I don't know what the hell he was thinking. Do you realize that when we go back out there everyone is going to assume we have a big announcement to make? What a disaster."

Declan's expression instantly became as cold as the side of beef hanging behind him. And nearly as red.

It hit her then, an emotional Mack truck slamming into her heart, that Declan's almost proposal three weeks before had been real. And it hit her just as hard that she, the Wicked Witch of the East, had broken his heart.

And he'd still come to her grand opening.

"Oh, boy," she said under her breath.

"I gotta get out of here. I made my appearance. You tell everyone whatever you want, but I'm leaving."

Rose heard his angry tone through the roaring in her ears, but it took her a second to digest his words. "Declan, don't go." He continued to head for the exit leading to a back alley, so Rose ran after him.

"Wait. Don't leave."

He turned, his face contorted with anger and pain. "Listen. I showed up. You got your crowd here. You'll get your restaurant on the news."

"I love you."

He swore and jerked his head away from her.

"I do. I just didn't know that you loved me until this moment. It was the beef."

"What?" he bit out, distracted and still mad.

"Your face. It was all red and hard, and I thought, 'Wow, Declan's really upset.' And then I knew that you must love me because if you didn't, you would have been really pissed about the press release but you weren't." She tilted his head to see his face. "You were hurt by it, weren't you?"

He didn't answer, just flexed his jaw a couple of times.

Rose swallowed down the growing lump in her throat. He had to forgive her, he had to. Because she'd forgiven him. Just like that. "Dec, I don't know what to say. I really screwed up. And you're partially to blame, too. I mean, you dumped me."

"Twice," he said, and she could see the barest hint of a smile on his lips.

"You hurt me. You put me through hell, and I think part of me wanted you to know what it was like."

Declan turned fully toward her and put his hands on her shoulders near her neck, moving his thumbs on her smooth skin. "I put myself through hell. I was being noble. At least I thought I was. You have to understand, Rose, that I was trying to protect you. I was scared to hell that your life would be ruined if you were with me. I thought having you with me was the most selfish thing I could do, and for once in my life I wanted to make sure I didn't hurt someone I loved."

"I can handle it, you know."

He smiled and drew her close. "I know," he said over her head. "And if you can't, too bad."

Rose laughed. "How bad can hell be if you're there? It's the hell without you that sounds so, well, hellish." She pulled back and looked up at him. "I accept, if the offer is still good."

"I can't back out now," he said, pulling the press release from her hand. "It says right here in black and white that we're engaged."

"Does it say anything about a date?"

Declan pretended to scan the copy. "Nah. But I was thinking something very private."

"But just think how much fun it would be to have helicopters buzzing over our heads at an outdoor event."

He kissed her, long and hard, stopping only when they heard the sound of applause behind them. Declan flashed her line cooks his classic grin, and Rose gave them a look of exasperation. "Get to work, you guys. We've got a big night ahead of us. You," she said, pressing an index finger into his chest. "Go out there and act famous. And confirm that press release. It ought to do wonders for business."

When they walked out of the kitchen, a crowd had gathered around the bar, apparently waiting for Declan to make another appearance.

"Are you two getting married?" one reporter asked, shaking the press release in his hand.

And Declan, right in front of a crowd of reporters and politicians, educators and minor celebrities, gave Rose a very classy but extremely possessive kiss. Cameras whirred; flashes went off.

"It's all in the press release," he said. Then he turned to Rose. "This is your night. Do you want me to leave?"

"Not on your life. In fact, it looks like I'm a bit short-handed behind he bar. Do you mind?"

"You're kidding."

She gave him a quick kiss. "You know I never kid."

Epilogue

After the grand opening, Rosalie's was the hottest restaurant north of New York. People came from all over New England to dine there, and Rose didn't care if it was because they wanted a quick look at the woman who'd captured Declan McDonald's heart. They returned because the food was terrific.

Declan went off to L.A. to thank Richard and work in the studio for a month to cut a twenty-song CD, which the music world was already buzzing about. Though his fans were clamoring for a concert tour, Declan declined, singing in public once: at the benefit concert in Chicago. He sang "Leah's Song," and if he hadn't already won back the hearts of his fans, he did that night. Rose watched it all on the television in her bar, not caring that about a hundred patrons watched her fall in love all over again.

Declan announced his semiretirement the next day. "Semi" because he knew in his heart he wouldn't be able to stop writing and performing his songs forever. "I'm going to try to have a normal life for a while, and I'd appreciate it if you all would let me," he told the press. He'd looked out over the crowd of reporters, blinking against the flashes, and smiled. He knew they wouldn't honor his request, but for some reason the deep anger and raging fear was gone. "See you guys later," he said, and they all laughed.

And when he was done, he came back to Providence, back to Rose. Because if there was one thing he'd discovered, it was that he needed Rose to be complete. The cherry on top, so to speak. And Declan, well, he was Rose's secret ingredient, the bit of spice, the extra splash of flavor, that made life damn good.